Homegrown

Land of the Evergreens – Book I

Johnny Sundstrom

Prelude

"This Land is Whose Land?
This Land was Their Land,
It's not Your land,
It can be Our Land
From the Cascade Mountains
To the Shining Sea,
This Land belongs to Those
Who Care.

Homage to Woody Guthrie

By the same Author and available from Xlibris, the Author, & Amazon, etc.

Dawn's Early Light *(2011)*

Land of Promise Trilogy
For Spacious Skies *(Book I – 2014)*
Mine Eyes Have Seen *(Book II – 2016)*
Looked Over Jordan *(Book III – 2017)*

Library of Congress Control Number:		*2019907262*
ISBN:	*Hardcover*	*978-1-7960-3671-8*
	Softcover	*978-1-7960-3670-1*
	eBook	*978-1-7960-3669-5*

Print information available on the last page.

Rev. date: 06/21/2019

To order additional copies of this book, contact:
Xlibris
1-888-795-4274
www.Xlibris.com
Orders@Xlibris.com
781024

The events of this book are set mostly in Western Oregon, occurring in the mid-1980s, during the so-called "Pot War of '84"

Dedicated to the Homegrown Heroes

of the Pacific Northwest
who risked losing their property,
their children, and years of their lives
behind bars, for the 'crime' of growing a
fugitive plant and seeking the good life.

Acknowledgements

I give thanks every day for the
privilege and opportunity to live
in the Community of Deadwood, Oregon
located in the Siuslaw River Watershed.
For nearly 50 years this place has
sustained and supported my family,
my neighbors, and myself.

I am also very grateful for the assistance of
Felisa Rogers, a wonderful writer herself,
and my helper in correcting and shaping
the content and language of this book.

(All remaining errors are the responsibility of the author).

Cover Photo: ***"MORNING MIST"***
and Author Photo
donated for this use by **KATE HARNEDY**
www.katehphoto.com

Forward

This novel was originally written, but unpublished, during the 1980s when this country's government was led by those whose slogan was simply, "Just Say No," to which one of the answers was often "Why?"

At some point not long after that, the marketing wizards at Nike advanced a different and wildly successful slogan, "Just Do It." Our American society fluctuates between and incorporates each of these definitions of culture and behavior. Today, the legalization of marijuana in its multiple forms, both medical and recreational, is spreading across the country. Today, some of the very activities depicted in this novel, if done on a large-enough scale, could get a person featured on the cover of Business Week magazine as "Entrepreneur of the Month."

The story has been minimally revised for this edition and its subject matter is like so many things: if you live long enough you can often see them turn into their opposites.

– Johnny Sundstrom
siwash@peak.org

TABLE of CONTENTS

CHAPTER ONE

March

A seed knows. A seed can tell when the springtime sun first climbs into the winter sky. A seed can tell the difference between the time for rest and the time to grow. When the time is right, the sun tells the grower and the grower retrieves the seed from the stash where it has spent the winter in protected dryness, safe from rodents, waiting to be the next generation of a unique set of characteristics adapted from its beginnings until this moment, this awakening to the identity that is each individual's birth...So the grower spreads the seeds on a wooden tray, rolling them with fingertips and touching them with intention, feeling their readiness to respond to care and caring. Some are larger, some darker, their stripes subtle and their shape full. The grower selects with tweezers and the chosen ones are lifted up from among the others and dropped into a half-full cup of water. A new season begins. A season of digging, packing, planting, hiding, watering, hoping, waiting, and finally, maybe, harvesting. A new season of steady background fear and its contrasting continuum of needs and hopes that may or may not be fulfilled. The growing season begins even as winter drags on in impossible slowness. Finally, when there can be no more delay, the seed demands to grow, and the growers and the cops begin to think more about each other. March, with its lions and lambs, renews the struggle of the earth and its living creatures to produce and to consume...

Sonya Lehman dialed the Bay Area number of her ex-husband with some force. These days, it was never pleasant to talk to him. All that was left to say concerned the mess of separating the material remnants of an exhausted and failed ideal. She waited as the ring repeated and thought how difficult it was to ask his advice. Wait two more rings and then hang up. If he was out, the machine would answer. So maybe he's in the shower.

She'd arrived at her office early to make this call on the business number. It was, after all, business. She set the phone down, glanced for the thousandth time at the naked third finger of her left hand, and got up to start coffee in the old percolator. Maybe someday she would be able to justify spending the money for a Mr. Coffee, a Mr. Anybody. She laughed and spoke out loud, "Feeling sorry for ourselves this morning, aren't we?"

He had always taken long showers, using hot water like it was free. Now she tried to picture him toweling off, briskly rubbing the hair on his chest, his legs, and between his legs. She couldn't help going there. He had always attracted her physically. Although she tried to convince herself it wasn't true, maybe it was the main thing that kept her hanging on as long as she had. She would wait for the coffee to finish perking before trying the call again, but better not wait too long or he would be out for the day, lost in the whirl of courtrooms, executive lunch, appointments and so on and so forth.

She dialed again and he answered.

"Hello?"

"Mike, hello. Sonya."

She could feel his tension, and hers. Old habit.

"Don't worry. No problems. The tax return is finished. You should get it by the weekend. I just wanted to run something by you, something that's come up suddenly. Kind of weird." She hesitated.

"Well?"

"I wanted to ask your advice about this thing…Are you sitting down?"

"Sitting at the kitchen table, trying to read the newspaper. What is it?"

"Sorry to interrupt, but last week a couple of people from the party's nominating committee approached me. Promise you won't make fun?"

"Sure. What? They want you to run for governor, right?"

"Wrong. DA."

"Wait? Are you kidding? Is this for real?"

"Yes, it's for real. They have a couple of other people they're considering, but they think I have as good a chance against Reynolds as anyone."

"Meaning, no chance. They know they can't beat him so they want to experiment with a new face, get a name out there. Gonna lose anyway. And it's a good strategy, a pretty new face."

"Thanks, but I didn't call for your compliments. It could affect you. I'm still using your last name, the newspapers could get into personal stuff, whatever. I thought you should know. And I actually do want to know what you think."

"I don't know what to think. You need to know right now? I can think of lots of sarcastic things to say, but somehow I can't make sense of it right now," he said. After a pause, he went on, "I think it would be a terrible drain on you, the campaign. I think there's no way you could win. I think you ought to get out of that town anyway, and I think..."

"Mike, stop. You sure have a lot to say for not knowing what to think. I know it sounds absurd. It sounded absurd to me, but you know how things have been going here, the court scene and everything. If I could help change it in any way, I'd do it for that reason alone."

"So, you've made up your mind?"

She didn't answer for a moment, a long moment..."Mike, if I'd made up my mind I wouldn't be asking your opinion. I don't like asking for anything from you anymore, and you know that. But this is important, so call me back as soon as you've had time to think about it. They say they need to know by this weekend. The filing deadline is next Wednesday."

"All right, I'll give it some thought, but you think it over too. Being a big fish in that little pond probably won't be enough for you, even if you do get lucky."

"It wasn't enough for you, but you've never known what's best for me."

"Then why'd you ask?"

"Mike, don't start it. Just let me know what you really think. Okay?"

"Okay, thanks for thinking of me. Bye."

She hung up, relieved, refilled her cup of coffee, stirred in too much honey, sat back down at her desk, and tried to focus on the day ahead. So she'd told him and his reaction was totally predictable...Her first appointment of the day was that welfare appeal. She still didn't know what she felt about it. About what? The welfare case, the nomination, Mike, about anything anymore.

It had been easier six months ago, when he first moved out. The anger and hurt were sharp then, the good memories obscured. Now it was almost the other way around. "Big fish, little pond," huh? He was the one with all the big ideas, the grand schemes. The main question left in her mind: Why was it so good in the beginning if it wasn't supposed to work out? How could they have been so blind to their differences and tolerated them that long?

The phone rang, and her day began again. Outside, the March rain continued to soak into the mud of February with only an occasional break of brilliant sunshine to remind everyone that all rainy seasons must eventually come to an end: The clouds will move faster and the rain will be warmer on the face as the daylight hours begin to equal the dark ones. But it's still rain and still clouds and the mood among the land's people takes on a tone of resigned resentment.

Peter eased the old pickup alongside the pumps, shut it down, and climbed out. The attendant sloshed over to him and smiled, sort of.

"Fill it?"

"Yeah. Hey, you got wiper blades for this? Thought I could get through this year on one set, but no way."

"Not this year."

"Guess not. Odd size, it's so old. Got any?"

"Probably, not much call for this kind anymore. But we sure sold a lot of the newer ones. Only took eight gallons. Cash?"

"Yeah."

"Eight fifty-five. Can you get one of those old ones off?"

The rain seemed heavier as he pulled out from under the covering, but now it didn't matter so much. The new wiper blades did their job and he didn't have to crouch forward to see through one stripe of clear glass. Most things are like that. You let them go until they're useless before you break down and get them replaced. The kid at the gas station seemed like he had an idea of what Peter was up to. Not hard to guess this time of year. Lots of guys out driving back roads looking for patch sites. Easy to get stuck up there, too. Wished he'd done more looking last fall, but he hadn't known about the new logging operation up near last year's best spot.

He turned off the highway and onto one of the paved forest roads. The best strategy was to only use a truck close to a site a couple of times a season, once with fertilizer and a water system, again with the seedlings, and the final time for the harvest. You could cover yourself by getting a permit for firewood on the public lands. Watering and tending was the big challenge because they were out looking for repeat vehicles all summer long. Sometimes you could work a deal with someone to drop you off, or get a small, quiet dirt bike that could be hidden. It was getting harder and riskier every year, and every year he planned to make his last. Oh, sure.

He slowed and stopped where the pavement forked with a gravel side road, #3468. He unfolded the map, last year's forest service fire map, and found where he was on it. He was heading for an area close by. What he needed now was a good, mostly unused spur road to hide the truck, and a nice break in the rain. His finger traced the roads that fanned out from the paved one until he found what he thought he was looking for. As he turned off and headed up the ridge, some of the clouds were now below him, scraping through the steep-sided canyons. As the road went downhill again, he felt lost in the mist. He remembered reading about someone walking in the dense fog and colliding with a crow who was also lost, a total shock to both.

He almost drove right past the side road he was looking for, not noticing it in his concentration on wipers, mist, and the miscellaneous thoughts that rattled around in the cupboards of his mind. He liked being alone up here, how growing pot provided an excuse for getting away from everything. He backed up and turned onto the road, two tracks that were more mud than gravel. He'd have to risk showing his tire tracks, but with this rain they'd probably wash out overnight. Slapping the truck into granny-low, he charged the muddy surface around the first curve to a wide spot, where he shut off the engine and pulled out his pouch to roll a joint. He'd have to smoke in the truck, no way out there in this rain. Where was that break in the downpour he'd asked for?

He saved half the joint for later and cussed his way into his rain gear, thinking, as he always did, when it's raining, it's too warm to wear it and you get almost as wet from your own sweat as you would from the rain. Besides, at some point you're probably going to rip it on the brush as evidenced from the duct tape designs on these old rubber leggings. Well, everything has its advantages and disadvantages.

It was about half a mile to the top of the clear-cut. From there he could barely make out the creek at the bottom. This slope faced south and the trees looked like they'd been planted about three years ago, long enough that there wouldn't be a forest service crew coming through to cut the brush so it wouldn't shade them out. He scoped out what looked like a good route and jumped off the roadside, heading down. Planting these trees was the best experience for what he was now doing. Good motivation too, since most tree planters would be glad to do almost anything else than keep on planting trees for a living.

He stopped to rest against a huge old growth stump. The landing above was already lost in the mist, although the rain was letting up some. He sure as hell wasn't an economist, but sometimes he couldn't help thinking about the price, the cost of production, plus the risk of losing it all to predators, thieves, cops, the risk of getting caught and doing time. Then there was the ordeal of the rain in the early season and the battle with mold at harvest, the salmonberry bushes trying to scratch your eyes out, the biting bugs in the heat of summer, and all the back-breaking carrying: carrying shit, carrying hose, carrying water from the hose to the plants, then carrying the crop out. Always sneaking around, worrying all the time, just so some architect or computer programmer could reach into his inlaid Indian stash box, pull out a beautiful red-haired bud and show it off to his guests as if he'd grown it himself. But that's where the price comes from. If you want to show it off then you've got to pay for it, pay me for the mud, sweat, and paranoia. He laughed at himself for thinking like this and jumped down, sliding and nearly falling until he reached the small but roaring creek at the bottom.

The brush was thickest near the creek and he had to climb back out of it to make his way upstream where he thought there might be a small bench. He was looking for was a semi-level spot with a small feeder creek above it so he could get the water from gravity instead of hauling buckets. Nice that it had stopped raining altogether, but he hardly noticed as he fought through the tangled slash and vegetation, not thinking now—just moving, grabbing, and thrashing forward. Finally he could feel some flatness to the ground that he couldn't see through the mess of head-high bushes. The main creek was somewhere below, and by standing as tall as he could, he saw a small gully above him that twisted away up the slope. If that was a spring and its creek, he was in business. If it dried up before the end of the growing season, carrying water up from the larger creek was just part of the job.

This could be a good place. Must be room for about twenty plants spread around. The mist had lifted enough for him to make out the contours of the ridge above and he couldn't see any way for someone to look down in here. Of course, you can beat everything else and then have some deer hunter park up there in the fall, flip his beer can over the side, then scan the clear-cut with his scope and, bingo, there goes your crop. The guy goes back, pays a couple of high school kids to scramble down and drag it out, and you're belly up with no breakfast. Or if the guy's straight, he'll tell the cops where it is.

Peter knew he'd still have to come back and check this spot for visibility from every angle, as well as the path the sun would follow. But this place really did feel okay. It felt like he'd like coming here. He hassled the pants of his rain gear until he could get to the buttons of his jeans, and pissed around himself in a circle, marking his turf, pissing in the rain that had started in again. He only had one question right now: where was the easiest way back to the top? He adjusted himself for the climb and fought back to the smaller creek. He knelt and drank deeply, thinking, changing my water, leaving some, taking some. Fill'er up.

William J. "Big Bill" Reynolds leaned back in his desk chair and tucked his striped dress shirt into the waist of suit pants three sizes larger than he'd worn when he was first elected to be Chinook County District Attorney. He looked up across the desk at the man with the badge.

"Glad you came by, Marty. What's on your mind? I mean, besides illegal sex, drugs, crime in the streets…What's up?"

Martin "Marty" Johnson, long-time county sheriff, smiled and replied, "Bet you can guess. Same old, same old."

"Overcrowding at the facility, right?"

"Yep, we're up to here." He waved his hand above his uniform hat. "If you can't get them moving out any faster, that gal at the ACLU is gonna be breathing fire down my neck again."

"Yeah, I know, but I can't do much about it at my end. You guys keep busting folks, the judges keep sending stuff back to me so they can protect their asses, and I'm pretty much stuck in the middle. Unless you've got a batch of nice innocent types we can let out on furlough."

"Nope. Bill, you know I'm not holding anybody I don't have to. But if there's any more state investigations of our conditions, or a suit against me and the county, then I'm the one the press is gonna hang for it."

"I'm sorry, Marty, really sorry, but it seems to go with the territory. Just be glad you run non-partisan. Goddam party's telling me I have to campaign this year, raise my own money, the whole f-ing bit. All that shit. Even though I'll get reelected anyway, they want me out there for the party's image. And the way they put it, I owe it. Now, you know, do I have time for that?"

"Sounds like a hassle."

"I don't have time for anything these days. My kids are starting to introduce themselves to me when I come home. Like I say, it all goes with the territory. And Marty, about the overcrowding...You're not running again this year, lucky bastard. Maybe it's a good time to put the new jail idea to the voters." He leaned forward, confidentially. "You know what a big project like that would do? Be good for everybody, know what I mean? And it sure would help you hang on to your job, and at the same time make it easier. Tell me, who's going to change horses in the middle of a project like that?"

"It has crossed my mind." He paused and gave a half-smile. "Every time you mention it."

Reynolds reached over and pressed the button on the intercom. "Sally, two coffees, please, both with cream. Right, Marty."

"Yeah."

"So back to this jail thing. What do you really think?"

"Bill, I can't say. It might fly, might not. But me, I'm like you. I'm not sure I want to give up any more of myself, and it could take everything I've got. It'd be the same as that campaigning you're bitching about. It's politics and more politics, and I hate politics. I completely missed hunting season last fall, goddam election. Almost missed steelhead too."

"Didn't completely miss hunting season, did you? That fugitive thing must have been pretty exciting. Better than hunting elk, I bet."

"Yeah, but we couldn't eat him." Marty chuckled. Sally appeared with the coffee and set it down in front of them.

"Hello, Sheriff."

"Hi, Sally."

"Mr. Reynolds, your Mr. Harrison called and said it's important."

"Okay, okay. If he calls again, tell him I'm in court, and I'll call back soon as I can."

She nodded and left. The coffee was still too hot to drink.

"Mr. Republican calling for Mr. DA. Shit." Reynolds blew on his coffee. "Tell you what, Marty. Think about it some more. Deal like this could set you up for a long time, lot of contracts in this kind of thing. Help out your future once you're done man-hunting, give you something to look forward to. Might be worth giving up a little fishing this year so you can start fishing year- round a lot sooner."

"Yeah, I'll think about it. Who's the lead on this thing, from the commissioners?"

"Not sure, it's early yet. I'll check on it," he said, taking a sip of coffee. "One more thing. How's it coming with the DEA?"

"Too soon to tell there, too. Preliminary estimates give you around seventy-five thousand and us about two hundred grand. But still could change."

"What do they expect me to do with seventy-five? Can't do anything with that, can't even pay for two assistants. Hell, I don't even want to get involved with the damn feds for any less than one fifty. When do you talk to them again?"

"Don't know. Wait and see, I guess. I don't think they're interested in much prosecution this year. Like it was last year down south of here: just cut it down, get rid of it, and keep moving. Destroy the crop and it doesn't leave any loose ends for appeals and screw-ups on the paperwork. Makes sense in the long run."

"Makes sense to them, maybe to you, but what about the public? What're people going to say when nobody gets busted while you're out there playing Green Beret with their tax money? Shit, Marty, I need money for this, and I need convictions. I need this issue for the damn campaign."

"I don't know, Bill. Public doesn't seem to care so much anymore. Hell, half the public's getting something out of it somewhere along the line. Water systems, fertilizer, all that crap."

"Yeah, but the public still likes to use the woods and be safe out there. Hikers, sportsmen, no one likes being terrorized out of their rights."

"I know that, it sounds good in the media, but it's just not happening out there. Last year, we didn't have a single instance of growers harassing the public. They hassled some thieves, yes, but the innocent public, no."

"Then maybe we need to look harder for some incidents, find some boobytraps out there or whatever."

"Maybe so."

"I'll bet you could use more than that two hundred grand yourself."

"Probably could." The sheriff finished his coffee and stood up. "Got to get going. Good talking with you, Bill. Look on the bright side. Campaigning gets you out there, gets recognition. You're not going to be DA forever. The better you do in every election, the closer you get to that governor's job. Am I right?"

Reynolds stood and reached out his hand. They shook. "Yeah, Marty, you're right. Bright side." He slumped back in his chair as the office door closed behind his colleague, thinking, poor Marty. Might not have what it takes. He's sitting in the shotgun seat and he'd rather have a fishing pole. Two more years before he's up for his fifth term. Time enough to slowly phase him out, just as easy as helping him if he doesn't want it. No imagination. Didn't even bite at the jail thing. Probably best to wait for an off-year election anyway, economy might improve by then. Then there would still be three more years for him in the DA's office, time enough to consolidate his base for the future. Marty did pick up on that, didn't he? Well, everybody's got plans, just a question of how much ambition. The DEA thing is a little crazy. Can't get the exposure without the money for prosecutions, and just pulling up plants isn't going to stop it at all, no way. Wonder who Harrison knows in DC, with a connection to the Attorney-General? Wouldn't hurt to check that out. He pressed the call button.

"Yes, Mr. Reynolds."

"I'm ready to talk to Harrison now."

"I'll see if I can get him. One minute."

Reynolds leaned back, carefully cutting lines into the now empty Styrofoam cup with the longest of his two thumbnails, breaking off the little squares as he went around the top, and dropping them into the trash basket.

By March 15th, 12,000 seeds were soaking or sprouting in at least a hundred households across the county. This is the germination, the time in a seed's life when it can no longer turn back: it's either grow or die. And it's the fantasy time of year for the people who depend on this crop but continue to tell themselves every year that there's no security in it. If half those seeds were to survive, and the half of those seedlings that are female were planted and tended, that would be about 3,000 plants, in ideal conditions averaging a quarter of a pound of saleable bud each...At current prices, the fantasy income would total something like three million dollars. Some fantasy.

Aligned against this imagined reality are unpredictable weather conditions, mice in the greenhouse, mountain boomers in the hidden gardens, rabbits, deer, beaver, hunters, forest service and logging company employees, uncountable thieves, and at least a quarter of a million DEA dollars, plus state and county matching funds, not to mention law-abiding citizens who see it as their duty to turn in anyone they suspect of participating in the illegal production of a so-called controlled substance. In addition, at least one of the candidates for public office intends to make pot cultivation a major issue in his campaign.

All this energy was now poised in the downpours of mid-March, suspended on the brink of more than a season-long struggle in which a plant becomes the pivotal focus for an unknown number of people, simply because it has the remarkable attributes of being, at the same time, illegal, expensive, and illuminating to its users.

CHAPTER TWO

April

April can be the cruelest month, a poet once said, not because of its harshness and extremes, but because of its unkindness in teasing the whole northern world and its inhabitants. In the coastal mountains of Oregon, an April shower can last up to four days, and the only thing that makes it different from a winter rain is that it doesn't go on for eight days. A clear spell of brilliant blue skies and sparkling sunshine can persuade all the vegetation to risk everything on what seems to be the right time for growing, and then a single night of frost can kill just as easily as it does in November. The first fruit blossoms take that chance, getting knocked off by hailstones just as often as they succeed in being pollinated by insects, who themselves are gambling by hatching so early. The people continue to grease their boots and watch the calendar as if something will speed up this agonizing transition from wet to drier, from cold to warmer. It is a time for ordering seeds for the garden and repairing the greenhouse, a time for baby animals and fresh eggs. The push and the pull, the come-on and the refusal. April plays all the angles as expectations rise and fall, and the grass turns green in spite of everything.

Sonya hurried across the parking lot toward her car, dodging puddles and fumbling for the keys in one pocket or the other. It hadn't been raining when she'd arrived for work and walked bareheaded to the office. Now she was hoping this downpour wouldn't soak her hair beyond recognition. She was still a little upset from Mike's return call. He'd told her that her opponent, DA Reynolds, would likely enjoy running against her so he could make comments about how pretty she was and how he thought women lawyers were too soft to be prosecutors.

As she unlocked the car door, she heard her name called out from across the lot. A young woman was coming toward her, carrying a bundle like it was a small child. Sonya reached into the car and pulled out an umbrella, opened it and stood waiting.

The woman was out of breath, but smiling. "Ms. Lehman, I was just coming by to see you. I want to thank you so much."

"Why don't we get into the car and out of this rain?" She shook the umbrella, climbed into her seat and reached to unlock the door on the other side.

Corinne Nelson slid onto the seat and uncovered her two-year-old. He seemed to be sleeping. "Anyway," she said, "it all worked out like you said it would. They had to give me welfare even if Dave and I weren't married. I don't know what I could have done without it, so I wanted to let you know. So, thank you."

"I'm glad for your sakes." She reached across the seat and patted the bundled baby. "I was pretty sure they would have to do it this way, but you can never tell with all the cutbacks these days. Have you heard any news about Dave's case?"

"His lawyer said the way it looks now, he could be eligible for a parole hearing as soon as six months from now. Isn't that great?"

"It is. Now you realize your welfare will end as soon as he gets out, and if you ever try to get on again, they have a right to hold him responsible for child support. Married or not."

"I know, I remember you told me that. I hope we can get married as soon as he gets out. What a hassle. Anyway, I know I can't pay you, and I don't have to because of that ACLU thing, but I'd like to do something for you if I can. You helped me so much."

"Oh, it's all right. I'm just glad it worked out. And actually, there probably is something you can do. I don't know if you've heard, but I've been nominated to run for district attorney."

"Wow, that's super, Ms. Lehman. The one they have was so mean to Dave."

"You should call me Sonya. And yes, I know Mr. Reynolds. He does overdo things a bit, especially in this kind of case. If we can't beat him in this election, I hope to get him to be a little more responsive to people who get into trouble but aren't really bad people. Anyway, I'll have to put together a campaign organization, and we'll need all the help we can get. So, if it's all right, I'll let you know when we're having our first meeting."

"I'd love to help out, but I don't really know what I could do."

"I think everybody can do something."

"Well, I want to do what I can. I hope you can beat that guy, and Dave and I've got friends who would help too. I mean with leaflets and posters and stuff. It sounds exciting."

"I think it will be, win or lose," Sonya said quietly.

"I've got to run, get the baby to the clinic for his well-child checkup. I hope he's well. But let me know, for sure." She let herself out of the car and hurried off through the rain.

Sonya smiled at herself as she tried to rearrange her soggy hair in the rearview mirror. Well, there's my first vote, she thought, wondering just how well she really would do. It would certainly take more than welfare mothers and jail widows, but Corrine was a great girl and a fine start for her committee. This was all so strange. Here she was on her way to the Rotary Club luncheon to be introduced to a group of people, probably all men, who knew nothing about her and might not like her if they did. Here she was being presumptuous enough to get up in front of them as if she belonged there. She should have listened to Mike. She was wasting her time and energy. Yet, she mused as she started the car, if she could do any good at all by pointing out alternatives to Reynolds's way of handling things, it could be worth it. She checked the clock. At least she wasn't late.

The food at the luncheon wasn't worth remembering, and the level of conversation at the table wasn't very interesting to her, sports and national politics mostly. The five candidates for school superintendent were finding their way back to their seats as the MC began describing the duties of the office of district attorney, concluding with, "And we do hope that none of our Rotary brethren should ever have to encounter this office in anything other than a social situation. So, let's welcome a new candidate for public office here in Dixon City, a hard-working attorney and the ACLU representative hereabouts, Ms. Sonya Lehman."

Sony moved from her seat to stand beside the MC, who was beaming at her with an expression that seemed half-lecherous and half-conscious of the two photographers standing in front of them. He continued, "I know we didn't ask you to prepare any remarks, but I'm sure we'd all like to hear a word or two from you. After all, it isn't often that we have a representative of the fair sex at one of these luncheons."

Sonya smiled at him as sweetly as she could and then leaned toward the microphone, her mind racing from blank space to blank space. She looked out over the roomful of faces and suddenly felt naked. She cleared her throat, smiled out at their waiting looks, and said, "I'm afraid I'm overdressed for the occasion. I understand the last woman to appear at your front table came out a of giant birthday cake wearing just barely over the legal limit for a costume." There was some laughter, but it was restrained and died away quickly. "Really, I'm just following my opponent's example. His attitude toward the office seems to be to cover up as much as possible. So, thank you for having me here today."

As she turned to go back to her seat, the MC stopped her with a finger on her elbow and asked her to wait. As the subdued applause trickled to a stop, he motioned to Bill Reynolds to join them and addressed the group, saying, "The incumbent here needs no introduction to you, but perhaps he hasn't met his new opponent. So Bill, come on up and meet a feisty young lady who's going to give you a good run for your job."

Reynolds joined Sonya near the microphone and muttered under the cover of applause, "What the hell do you think you're doing anyway?"

She whispered back, "I think it's called politics, sir."

They smiled at each other and at the audience. The MC smiled at them and said, "You two have a good race now, and thanks for coming by today. Now I want all the candidates who have come here today to be assured of our gratitude, if not necessarily our votes. If you're not club members, you're free to go now. The rest of us have a little more business on the agenda."

Reynolds returned to his seat as several other candidates made their way out of the large banquet room. As they got their coats, the only other women at the luncheon, candidates for school board and utility commissioner, stopped to shake hands with Sonya and wish her luck. She felt drained and wondered if her smile muscles would get stronger as the campaign went along. If not, she was surely going to have a sore face for the next few months.

As she stepped outside the building, which was part of a large motel and dining complex, she noticed that the rain was letting up, not yet just a drizzle but certainly lighter than it had been. It rains like it's never going to stop, and then when it finally does it's like it never rained. What was it the commentator said on TV last night? This past March was the third wettest on record and April is already an inch ahead of normal in the first three days.

She looked up into the light gray sky and said softly, "Okay, you can stop now."

"Ms. Lehman, Ms. Lehman."

She turned toward a young man who was just coming out through the front doors. He caught up with her and she was surprised at his height, shorter than her. His face shone with the first really friendly smile she'd seen at the luncheon.

"I'm a reporter, radio reporter with the community college station, but I get my own press passes, just like the big guys, to just about anything, even here. I saw you in there. You all right?"

"Of course. What do you mean?"

"Sorry. Name's Lindsay, Terry Lindsay. I just thought maybe all that might have been a bit much for you. But if you're okay, how about an interview, just a couple of questions? You might be the only interesting news in this whole election."

"I don't think I know what you mean."

"Why don't we go have coffee or something somewhere? My treat."

"I do have some work to get back to. Maybe you could just ask me here."

"Here? Ms. Lehman, in a couple of minutes every one of those Rotors in there is going to come out those doors and walk right through this spot. Do you really want to be standing here for that?"

"No, I guess not. Let's go sit in my car."

"Take me to it."

She offered him a share of the umbrella as they crossed the half-full parking lot, but he declined, cheerfully bouncing alongside her, his curly red hair collecting droplets of the drizzly but still steady rain. She let herself into the car and unlocked the door for him. They sat quietly for a long moment, and then she turned to him.

"What did you mean by I might be the only news in this election?"

"Well, you saw most of what else there is. Not much excitement. A lot of unopposed stuff, low-profile bureaucrats, the usual. You, you've got some style, and you're a complete underdog. A total surprise as a candidate, both to the public and to your opponent. Whose idea was it anyway, you running?"

"On the record?"

"Both ways. On the record for the public, off for my own study of history."

"Actually, it doesn't make much difference. It's pretty much the same either way. The Democratic Party Nominating Committee approached me about three weeks ago. I said thanks, but no thanks. It seemed absurd, still does. And I don't know why I changed my mind and went along with it."

"I believe you, but who on the committee, any names, anyone you know who likes you, owes you a favor, or maybe doesn't like you and wants to see you lose?"

"I really don't know the answer to that. It's been suggested that since they know they're going to lose, it might be in their interest to lose with an unknown and a so-called pretty face. I'm the unknown part of it."

"As well as the pretty face." He smiled broadly and suddenly she knew who he reminded her of: Alfred E. Newman. She looked away to hide the silly feeling that gave her, and for a second time she thought about this smiling thing, wondering why it was always referred to like it was a disease, an infectious smile or a contagious smile. Whatever it was, he sure did have one.

"Say, while we're talking, do you think you could give me a lift, and drop me near the courthouse?"

"Of course. I'm actually going by there." She started up the car, relieved to be able to get going without being rude to him. As they drove slowly past the banquet hall, the crowd within began flowing out the doors.

"There they are," he said. "The cream of Dixon City's crap."

She laughed as she wiped fog from the windshield with her glove.

"Off the record," she said and smiled, "I have to agree with you."

The mid-day traffic seemed heavy and slow, although the rain had nearly stopped. Her thoughts recalled a scene, maybe from last year at this time, a scene of Mike rolling down his window to yell at some truck driver who'd stopped suddenly in the curb lane. Mike hated traffic, probably hated driving, but he'd never let her drive when they went anywhere together.

Terry was talking again, "Actually what I like doing, even more than being a reporter, what I really like doing is taking polls. You know, calling up complete strangers in the middle of the day or night, and trying to take them off guard with a question they never even thought of before, like, 'Do you think astronauts should be allowed to drink alcoholic beverages in space on Saturday nights?' I ran that one just for fun to twenty-eight randomly selected households. Can you guess the results?"

"I can't possibly."

"Fourteen had no opinion, six said yes, six said no, and two hung up without answering. What this shows is that we as a nation are equally divided between having an opinion and not having one." He paused and she waited for him to continue. "Anyway, I only brought it up because I don't know how far you've gotten on forming an organization, but I'd sure like to help you, especially if I could do polling for you, I mean serious stuff. It can really help you to know how and where to spend your money. I mean you certainly won't have as much as Reynolds, so you'll have to make every bit count, and that's where I can help. What do you say?"

"I think it sounds great. I don't have anyone for that yet, although the party probably does some of it for themselves."

"Sure, well, let me know. Here's my card, and you can get ahold of me afternoons at the radio station. Here's where I get out. Listen to our evening news tomorrow at six. Nice meeting you."

"Nice to meet you too, and I will get in touch when I know something."

She pulled alongside the curb. He jumped out and stood, staring after her as she drove away in the traffic. He crossed the street with the WALK light, thinking what a lucky break he'd just had. Have to be careful, though, about working with her, not for her. Have to stay independent so I can still keep this reporting thing going. Terry Lindsay, Pollster & Reporter. Right, and be careful not to fall in love. She might be almost twice my age and so pretty, and, no, whoa, Terry, get back to work and don't forget about independent journalistic objectivity. Speaking of which, can I get in to see Reynolds without an appointment for the rest of this breaking story?

It was one of those incredible mixed-up days when the sky was as blue as it ever gets, and huge dark clouds like aircraft carriers drifted through it bringing splatters of rain for no more than a few minutes at a time. Peter was still up on the hill behind his small mobile home when Jerry pulled into the yard in his green pickup with his dog barking in the back. Wondering what he wanted, Peter clambered down the slope and yelled.

Jerry was already at the door of the trailer. "Hey Peter, what's happening?"

"Sun, man, sun is what's happening. Great, huh?"

"Sure is. Got a minute?"

"Yeah, sure. Want some coffee? Have to boil the water, but it'll be quick."

"Sounds good. I'll take some."

Peter was tall enough that he had to duck going through the doorway into the trailer. "Grab a round of firewood there and have a seat. There's no room in here. Besides the sun's out there."

Jerry rolled two rounds out of the woodshed and set them upright, sitting on one. "You're almost out."

"Yeah, but I'm hoping I'm almost done needing a fire for the year. How's Carla?"

"Good, real good, considering."

"When's the baby due?"

"Two weeks, three, who knows?"

"Hey man, that's great. You're through the hard part, right?"

Jerry was quiet for a moment, and then said, "Hope so. Been hard enough. Mainly money. I haven't had hardly any work, and it's got Carla uptight. Me too, but I try to convince her that it's all okay, one of the mills has to be about ready to take on another shift once the weather gets good."

"That'd be good. You got anything else going?"

"That's what I wanted to talk to you about. I could trade you some wood. You'll probably need some more, more than you've got, and I've got extra."

"Yeah," Peter said, "but I don't have any extra money either. Not this time of year."

"I figured that, but I'll trade for something."

"Like what?"

"Seeds. See, I'm thinking there's a really good spot just off our property. Water, sun, nobody can get there except through our yard, and I've got the dog. Carla wouldn't even have to know, she'd freak out if she knew, but once I've got the money, she'll be happy. Besides, I'm not talking about a lot. How much do you get for seeds?"

"I don't very often sell them, but I could use a little help this spring. Maybe we could work something out." The whistle of the kettle boiling suddenly sounded urgent. He went inside quickly.

Jerry looked around at the little shed behind him. It was cluttered with gardening tools, hose, a bicycle, and the usual junk that builds up at the end of any country driveway. He picked up a chip of wood from near his feet, pulled off a long sliver, and picked at his teeth. He was thinking Peter didn't know him very well, maybe not well enough to trust him. And Jerry didn't know much about what this guy had done before he moved here five or six years ago. He knew Peter seemed to be alone most of the time, that he helped folks out, had helped him and Carla several times. He always said he had spare energy because he lived alone.

Peter called from inside, "Can't remember if you take anything in it?"

"No, thanks."

Jerry couldn't imagine living alone like that, for that long a time. Be nice some of the time, but not all that much. He did know that Peter was gone sometimes during the winters, and never talked much about himself, but that was okay, probably a good thing. Most people talked too much about themselves.

Peter ducked back out into the sunlight, carrying two steaming cups. "Couldn't be any fresher unless it was in Columbia," he said, handing one to Jerry.

"Thanks."

They sat there for a long silent moment, both blowing lightly on the dark brew, the warmth feeling good to their hands. It seemed like a good time for silence. Some times are like that, moments when the sky and the earth seem to stretch apart and everything in between needs to pause in what it's doing.

Peter looked up and caught Jerry kind of studying him. Jerry didn't look away and sipped from his cup, then said, "Good coffee. Hope you're not bummed at me. Bringing up the seeds, I mean. Maybe you don't want people knowing about that, but you're the one told me, told me you grow some yourself and I really don't know anyone else I could ask, at least I couldn't think of anyone."

"No, it's okay. I'm not all that paranoid. Anybody who looks close enough can tell when someone's growing. It's just being able to get enough on someone to prove it that makes the difference."

"Well, no one would ever get it out of me."

"Good. And don't worry about it. I trust you. Known you longer than anyone else out here, six years almost."

"Yeah, I suppose you do know me, I don't know. We don't hang out that much, but if you ever need anything, I'm there for it. You've helped us out a lot over the years. Hey, what about this? Could you use a better pick-up? My unemployment extension's almost up, and I could trade you mine for yours for the cash difference, pay it over time."

"No, thanks but no thanks. Me and that old truck are pretty tight. But you gave me an idea. Look, it's not easy to start these seeds and get them growing right, soil mix, timing, all that. Besides, it's getting a little late to start now. Be better for you if I just trade you some extras I've already started. I'll take care of them until they're ready to transplant into bigger pots. I'll show you how to do that. I've got more going than I can use anyway."

"That would be great. What would you want for maybe a dozen?"

"A dozen might only give you six or seven females. How many you think you have room for, not too close together?"

"Don't know. Berries and the brush are thick there. Maybe ten."

"All right, get it ready. But don't clear-cut the patch. They're looking for bare dirt when they do the springtime flyovers; that's all they can see, and they probably mark it on their maps so they can find it again when they come back, maybe in September, maybe August."

"Earlier every year, huh?"

"Yeah and they get better at it. So anyway, I'll set aside about twenty of them for you. We'll cull some males before you put them in, if they show themselves. The rest you just plant two to a hole and we'll see what happens. Maybe thin some out later."

"What do you want for them?"

"How about this? Your pickup looks a lot better than mine for cruising in the woods. I need to haul some stuff up to some spots in the forest and get dropped off with it. Maybe you let me use it, then if everything goes all right I could use it again in the fall for bringing my crop out. I'd look like any old hunter in that rig."

"Fine with me. Glad to do it. Just let me know the day before."

"More coffee?"

"Nope, thanks. Got to get moving. And thanks. Kind of scary, but it seems like the only way to make it these days. Just don't ever mention it to Carla. She's so jumpy these days anyway."

"I wouldn't. Take it easy. You two, I mean three, are going to be all right. Just need that baby to get here, and then everything's going to be easier, you'll see."

"You ever have any kids?"

Peter shook his head, "No."

"Okay, well, if you get lonesome, come by. We're usually home these days."

"I will. Take it easy."

Jerry handed Peter the empty cup and walked slowly back to his truck. He gave his dog's head a good scratching through the open window, climbed in, and yelled back, "Need bigger tires."

Peter laughed, watching the oversize treads turn as the truck backed around and pulled away. It was just the right truck for what he needed, redneck enough not to cause suspicion. This kind of solved his biggest problem, getting everything up to his patches without being noticed. Jerry was an all right guy, curious, but not pushy about it.

He turned to head up the trail behind his trailer. He still wanted to finish the new cold-frame he was working on. He had the materials, just a question of putting it all together. Big enough to hold all his start-ups, even with Jerry's added in.

As he got back to work, he was thinking about the package he'd picked up from the post office earlier in the day. From the record club, "Bruckner's Symphony No. 2" performed by the London Symphony. Something to look forward to, an evening with some of the craziest music of the 1860s. Back then they said it couldn't even be played. And it was loud if done right. Part of living alone out where he did was the sound he could get out of his audio setup, and no one around to complain. Almost like sitting in the brass section and playing the works himself.

The first French horn he'd ever played belonged to the grade school. It had a big elk head with branching antlers engraved on the bell, and the words, "Elkhart, Indiana." Wasn't until seventh grade that he could hold it up without resting his elbow on his knee. Now some nights he'd take out his horn and music he'd transcribed from one of the records, turn the volume up, sit out under the stars (if there were any) and pretend to be sitting in the middle of the brass section while he played along with the great works.

Stretching the translucent plastic over the frame, he thought about all the things you have to consider and make allowances for in this business. The plastic has to be at a good enough angle not to reflect the sun when they made their early season overflights. Funny how the sun was so impartial, helping the plant grow, feeding the plant and its grower, while at the same time showing the sky what might be going on down here, what might be worth checking out more closely.

Sheriff Johnson sat at his desk and picked through the pile of correspondence that never seemed to go away or get smaller. He was still puzzling over the interview he'd just had with some kid from the campus radio station. Questions like, "What effect, if any, do the opinions of the DA have on determining law enforcement policy and the priorities for your department?" and, "What can be done about overcrowding in your jail?" Good questions, or more likely, smart questions without good answers. He'd answered without directly answering as best he could, but the kid was insistent, and the sheriff didn't want it looking like he didn't know much when the story came out. He finally had to admit that he allocated his limited budget with some sort of criteria due to funding limitations. And yes, that was influenced by the type of cases the DA could move along through the courts with some speed. As far as overcrowding and how to deal with it, he'd shown the young reporter a catalogue with some of those bracelets that gave a warning, a trackable warning, when the person wearing it tries to move from a particular location or remove it. He said he planned to purchase some on a trial basis and make use of house arrest for some of the nonviolent offenders waiting for trial.

The question he hadn't answered and wouldn't, was whether there were some crimes on the books that just shouldn't be prosecuted in light of the financial difficulties facing law enforcement in these times. You don't answer that question because it makes too much sense and certainly the crimes you would let go of are the ones with no victims, like possession of small amounts of drugs. Problem was, prosecuting those cases was one of the main sources of income for both his department and the DA's office.

The desk buzzer rang sharply. He picked up the receiver. "Yeah, okay. Send him in." Just thinking about all this brings it to the door, he thought.

Detective Roy Stockton breezed in and sank into the empty chair opposite the desk.

"Hi Marty. What can you do for me?"

"Hello, Roy. How's it going?"

"Fine, fine. Got those figures you wanted. Got time now for a look?"

"Do you need to explain them, or can I get the gist myself?"

"Well, several times in here there's one or two options besides the way we've been doing things. I spent a lot of time talking with some of the fellas from south of here, fellas I met at that DEA conference last year. They've got good ideas, but of course they're way ahead of us in money and manpower."

"All right give me the main items. First, though, get this—I just got interviewed by some radio kid and he asked me pointblank about satellite photos, if we're using them."

"What'd you say?"

"I said it's classified information."

Stockton chuckled. "It sure is. Wish we could. Even without the satellites, we have enough to handle with the aircraft, and costs going up faster all the time. To start with, we need better weather projections. Long as we have to rent planes and reserve them ahead of time, rain and fog can cost us plenty in lost days."

"Do we even need spring flights anymore?" Johnson asked. "I mean how much do we get from them?"

"Hard to say. It's a lot easier to spot fresh-downed trees and bushes, and bare dirt now, than later on. Come on a flight with me sometime and I'll show you. I think it saves money in the long run. You mark a spot as suspicious in the spring and then later you just make one flyover. If it pays off, you're good to go. No circling and circling while you search from up there, no time for the grower to pull and run. Makes a difference."

"When's the latest you can get results?"

"You know those beautiful, lazy days in May when the trees are still leafing out and the sky is like blue glass? That's still time enough."

"What's lead time for reserving the plane this year?"

"Three days."

"All right. Put down two days for flying in late May or early June. Use our budget only on areas with private land and scattered population. I'll work on the forest service to pay for its own coverage and flights."

It took them most of the afternoon to run through and verify all the figures that would go with the final application for federal funds. As they were finishing up, the sheriff took the folder from Stockton and flipped through the forms once more, initialing their changes.

"You know Reynolds is going to ask for at least this much himself. He as much as told me that he couldn't do what's needed if he didn't get a lot more than last year."

"Pipe dream. The California guys told me they're hardly making any arrests anymore, just focusing on eradication. Only make unavoidable arrests, or on big operators. Slows down too much. Paperwork. I'd be surprised if he even gets as much."

"Going to piss him off."

"His problem. I'll finalize this by Friday. Needs your signature and then submitted by April 20th deadline. Looks good, though. No frills."

"Can't wait to get started, can you?"

"Hey, it's my job." He took the folder, smiling broadly, and turned to leave. "Marty, really, you've got to come up there with me one of these days."

"No thanks. I'm infantry all the way."

"You don't know what you're missing. Best part is watching our citizens run for cover when we go over. See ya."

Now Marty was going to have to face Reynolds with these figures. But should he tell him about the radio interview? Best not. Nobody listens to the campus station anyway. Still, the kid's questions made some sense. More like a survey than an interview. He reached into the lower drawer and pulled out a small bag of chips, popped it open and started crunching them down. The phone buzzer rang again, and again. He let it ring until it stopped. A moment later the door flew open. His dispatcher stood there, openmouthed.

"Sir, uh, you didn't answer."

"Maxwell, if you're not sure if I'm in here and I don't answer that buzzer, something might be wrong. Maybe somebody snuck in here and took me hostage. You need to be more careful."

"Yessir," Maxwell said, turning to go.

"Well, what did you want when you buzzed me?"

"Your wife's on line three, if she's still there."

"Thanks. Now be careful." Marty chuckled as the door closed and he picked up the phone and pushed number three. "Hi, Honey."

Sonya was tired, more like exhausted really, from spending the whole afternoon with Dan Neiman, the campaign manager she'd never met before that afternoon. He was so organized it was to the point of being unreal. She could see the advantage in being that way, especially if you're trying to get ahead in politics by managing a loser. She smiled and reprimanded herself. Shouldn't think like that, but just couldn't get that out of her head. This Dan said every campaign starts out with the same chances of succeeding or failing because of all the unknown possibilities. He went on to say that even with computers, statisticians, analysts and commentators, even with all that, no one ever knows for sure what button the individual voter is going to push when the moment finally comes. He really seemed to believe in that, and the only time he'd shown any emotion was when she mentioned that they'd most likely lose. His reply was, "Would I be doing this if I thought like that?" It was clear he needed to believe in what he was doing in order to do a good job. And it was good to have this input because she didn't want to feel cynical about her chances. Get over that. Who knew?

She let her clothing drop to the floor and stepped into the shower. God, it felt good. If she was this tired now, how was she going to have enough energy to get through this first time organizational meeting tonight? Had she remembered to call everyone? Stop worrying, she told herself. Right now, enjoy the shower. Celebrate. It's income tax day. We did it. Mike and I actually filed a joint return, on time. Even if it's the last thing we ever do together, at least we proved we can still function, if necessary. She listened to the sound of the spraying water, smelled the soap, and squinted to watch the foamy shampoo rinse down over her breasts and whirlpool into the drain. She needed this break, and she didn't need to be thinking about her ex. There'd never been room enough for both of them in this shower anyway.

She got out and toweled off. As she ran the blow dryer, she felt her energy returning. She had been thinking about taking up jogging or something. Now, looking herself over in the mirror, she convinced herself she still looked okay, but it was definitely time to start in on some preventative measures. That was something she could get to next weekend, go shopping for running shoes and warm-up stuff. She smiled at the thought of herself running through the streets, but other people made it look either fun or serious, and it was something else she could do alone.

She dressed in what she hoped was the right balance between a casual and business look, cleared the table and spread out the notes and forms she'd brought home. Dan had said he would run the meeting, but it was important to her that she at least looked like she knew what she was doing. Like he said, confidence is everything. You look confident and your campaign workers will act confident. He sounded like such an old pro but couldn't be over thirty. Not too young for her, really, and of course these days she couldn't be choosy, but she wasn't attracted to him anyway.

Funny how that part of her just didn't seem to exist right now. Too early for mid-life stuff, maybe separation trauma, whatever. It was kind of nice to just relax and accept being alone. Yes, it was lonely, but it wasn't intense; the ups and downs were gone. Like that sportscaster who Mike hated always said, the flights of ecstasy and the crush of despair...or something like that. Enough. She only had fifteen minutes till it was time to leave for the meeting. What was it Dan said about the fundraisers? They would either need to be bonded or provide some kind of letter of credit to cover themselves. She certainly hoped she wasn't going to attract potential embezzlers, but it was probably good to take precautions, maybe background checks. In any case, this whole fantasy was about to get very real in the next hour. She could only hope she was prepared for it.

She arrived early enough, and by 7:30 about ten people were already there and ready to get started. Dan was talking with a small group, obviously acquaintances, and she'd already said hello to the people she knew. Corinne, the welfare mom, showed up as promised, as well as another client of hers. She knew Florence because her husband's estate was tied up in his ex-partner's bankruptcy mess. The older woman was such a warm person that just seeing her there made Sonya feel better. Terry Lindsey, the reporter/pollster, had asked her what she thought of his news story on the DA race and she'd complimented him on being that thorough in so few minutes. What she really meant was that she'd been surprised hearing him quote both herself and Reynolds. He must've gone straight to her opponent after talking with her. It was well-done, and actually even a little favorable for her, but hearing her name and voice on the radio was almost enough to make her drop the whole thing. She had so many second thoughts and doubts these days, but now here were people willing to volunteer their time and energy to help her, even while she still hadn't fully convinced herself she was ready for the campaign. And especially not for the job, on the outside chance she ended up winning. But she kept telling herself: you just have to put one foot in front of the other. This meeting was the next step.

Dan was asking everyone to pull chairs into a circle so they could get started. She felt herself smiling, and she smiled even more at her own smiling. Here we go, she thought, might as well give it all we've got.

"Glad you could all make it tonight," Dan began. "We may still have a few others showing up, but this is already more of a turnout than I hoped for. I'm Dan Neiman, the campaign manager for this effort, and in case you haven't met her yet, this is Sonya Lehman, the next District Attorney of Chinook County."

Terry led a small round of applause and Sonya jokingly raised her hands over her head in a victory salute.

"Thank you for coming," she said quietly. "It's truly an honor to have you here."

Dan passed out paperwork while he was explaining, "We want you to fill this out. It mainly deals with your educational and political backgrounds. There's also a checklist of various types of campaign work we'll be doing and we'd like you to check off at least two of the categories you'd prefer to be involved in. Does anyone need a pen or pencil?"

Sonya glanced over the form. It was the first time she'd seen it and it looked very neat and well-organized. She was beginning to appreciate Dan's style of work. She had no idea what the two of them might talk about over dinner—besides politics and the campaign, of course. He did seem to know what he was doing, and he really seemed to like doing it.

An older woman raised her hand and Dan went over to her. Just then, a woman about Sonya's age appeared at the doorway, looking just a little lost. Sonya went to greet her.

"Can I help you?" she asked, thinking she recognized the woman from somewhere.

"Yes, I think so. Is this the campaign meeting for Sonya Lehman?"

"This is it. I'm Sonya. Are you here to sign up?"

"Well, maybe. I know a little about you, and I'm interested in finding out what there is to do, but I'm in a bit of an awkward position. My name is Janet, Janet Kraft. I work in the DA's office as a clerk in one of the deputy prosecutor's offices."

"Wow, and you're interested in helping us?"

"I can't say yet. See, I'm not a political appointee or anything. I mean I don't think it could be cause for getting me fired. It could just make it difficult if Mr. Reynolds or someone there found out. I'm a registered Democrat and supposedly I have a perfect right to do what I want to on my own time, but I think you know what I mean."

"I'll tell you what. Come on in and sit with us, fill out the little questionnaire, and after the meeting I'll be able to talk things over with you. We could even go out somewhere, if you want. I'll need to tell my campaign manager what's going on. That's him over there collecting the forms. But we won't make any big deal about it and it's all in confidence. Come on in, it's okay."

She led Janet to a seat by her own and they both sat down. Dan came over to show her the completed forms and she whispered a bit about Janet in his ear. He turned back to the group and announced, "We're going to take a minute to look through these. There's coffee and cookies on that table over there, so enjoy yourselves and spend a few minutes getting to know each other."

He sat and pulled his chair around so he was facing Sonya and Janet. "Hi, I'm Dan Neiman. Welcome aboard if you're interested. Welcome, in any case."

"Thank you."

"Dan, I think Janet is just checking us out first. She's probably in a tricky position, and until we can decide what we can do for each other, I think we should keep her situation just between ourselves."

"Of course, and I do hope we can work something else out. If you don't mind, would you just fill this out, answering only the questions you want to?"

"I don't want to give the wrong impression. I may not be any use at all. I've never been involved in politics. It's just that there's a lot going on at my job that I don't really like to see. I mean, I like the work, the research and everything, but there's this negative attitude that bothers me, that I'd like to help change. There, I've probably said too much."

"Okay," Dan said, "look, just fill in the parts of the form that don't deal with all that and then maybe later we can get some kind of understanding between ourselves." He smiled, and she began working on the form. He shifted his chair closer to Sonya and the two of them began skimming through the profile sheets he'd collected.

They looked good and it turned out there was at least one person for each of the work teams he'd outlined on the organizational chart. They were lucky to have a man who'd done printing work for the party before he retired. Besides Terry, there were three other people with some media experience and interest, and both Florence and Corinne signed up for the office work part of things. Florence had years of experience in a travel agency and seemed well-suited to be their office manager.

As Dan looked through the sheets, he announced that fundraising was the area where everyone would need to be involved in different ways. "We'll start out by calling it a committee of the whole, but I think we will ask you, Mr. Campbell, to consider taking on the official role of treasurer. It might even be a good addition to your job at the bank." The middle-aged man smiled, shrugged and looked like he was saying yes. Dan then gave a brief rundown to the folks and talked about their potential areas of focus for the campaign. "As you probably know, about 75% of Chinook County lives here in Dixon City. So, the bulk of our research and campaigning will be focused here, targeting our population of 140,000 people."

As the meeting was about to break up, after a summary of the beginning stages of the campaign, Dan asked Sonya if she cared to say a few words. She stayed in her seat, but leaned forward and began by saying, "I just want to thank you all for coming tonight. Maybe I didn't expect anyone to show up, but, in any case, this is just great. And I hope some of you will tell your friends about this. I'm sure we can use a few more volunteers. I want to be completely honest with all of you about this. Our opponent Mr. Reynolds is deeply entrenched in the Chinook County and Oregon state establishments. But he's no Goliath and I'm no David. We're just citizens with the opportunity to serve the people in the best ways we can. I have no illusions of winning, but nor am I planning to go through this campaign just to lose. I think we have a chance, and you can never tell what might happen. So, let's all work hard, have some fun, and see how much we can shake things up in this town and county."

As Dan called an end to the meeting, Sonya found herself the center of attention. It seemed everyone wanted to get in a personal word with her, and she was truly impressed with their friendliness and enthusiasm. She had never thought about the great personal level of people's involvement that must be behind every political campaign. She found herself feeling more like she was making new friends than hiring people, and the volunteer aspect made it so much easier to relate on an individual basis. She was really pleased and inspired by the meeting. As she said goodnight to the folks, she began to see the campaign as a kind of positive social process of its own. Winning or losing faded away in the brightness of this random new group of people who were saying how much they were looking forward to working together for her.

Later as she and Janet sat talking over a light supper and wine, they began finding common threads in their lives. Janet had given up on a law degree due to the financial crunch of a marriage that couldn't support two fulltime students. Their plan had been to get her husband settled into his career before she returned to school for her own degree. He had graduated and found work in the office of a large lumber mill, and that same year had brought them their first and only child. Janet became immersed in motherhood, really loving it, and her schooling dreams seemed to drift away during those next few years. Then when Kristi had finally reached school age, the mill relocated its corporate offices, and Janet's husband was suddenly forced to move or quit. She hadn't wanted to move away, to leave her mother and her hometown. Combined with the problems in their sometimes rocky relationship, the job relocation became the basis for a trial separation that was now in its third year. Janet had gone to work in the DA's office as soon as her mother moved in with her and could be there when the little girl came home from school each day.

"So where is he now?" Sonya asked as she poured them each another glass of wine.

"Working in Portland. He sees Kristi once a month, and that's when I see him. It's funny how there's no real intensity on either side. It's like we don't really need each other, but it seems like we're not holding anything against one another, either."

"Was it always kind of that way?"

"No, not at all. We started out very much in love. I've never felt like that with anyone else, but it just didn't last. Maybe there's something wrong with me."

"I wish I could talk about Mike without it being so intense, without it upsetting me. We had to split up for our own good, because every hassle seemed to go to the limit, well, nearly to the limit But, like you, it was mainly about his career. I didn't want to move to the Bay Area.

I'm happy here and this town is about as big as I can handle. I went to college in Seattle and that was way too much sometimes, even though they say it's a laidback city. I can't imagine New York or somewhere like that."

"I've never been further east than Colorado, and that was when I was little."

"It's strange how men, at least these two, can get so involved in their jobs. It's the competition, I suppose. Mike called it the daily give and take." She paused. "I like work, I like working, but I do love coming home when it's done for the day. Even though there's nobody else there these days."

"You'll have to come over, meet my mother and Kristi. But, hey, weren't we supposed to be talking about your campaign and me?"

"We are, aren't we? We're talking about you and me, and that's part of it, don't you think?"

"I do feel a lot better talking about it now that I know you a little. I just don't want to feel like I'm doing anything underhanded, you know, political espionage and that kind of stuff. But I want to do something about what goes on there."

"Don't worry," Sonya said. "We'll just start out getting to know each other. I'll let Dan know you're going to be helping me as an adviser about the job of DA, and what sorts of things I could talk about to improve that office's performance. You won't even have to be seen around the campaign or doing any of that with me. Unless you want, maybe later. For now, I'm just so glad you had the nerve to check it out."

"So am I. I think it's going to be fun, and even important. I'd love to see you beat Mr. Reynolds, just to be able to watch him pack up all his stuff and move out of the office." She gave a soft laugh, "He acts like it's all his own front room. He'll come by and sit on the corner of my desk and say something like, 'Hi Janet, how're your briefs today?' and laugh as he walks off."

They both giggled a little as Sonya emptied the last of the wine bottle into their glasses. "That's pretty bad," she said. "Maybe you should ask how long his shorts are?" They both giggled some more.

"But you know, none of them seem to know any better, it's just who they are," Janet said.

"You're probably right, the all-American male boss. Hey, it's getting late, maybe we should be going."

"You're right. That little girl of mine usually won't go to sleep until I get home. And, after all, we're both working girls. Sonya, I had a good time. Thank you."

"I know, it's great to have a new friend."

They got up and Sonya left the money for the bill, over Janet's protest, and they went out into the calm night air. They gave each other small hugs in the parking lot, promised to be in touch soon, and then separated to go to their own cars, Sonya thinking how unexpectedly nice it was to have this happen as part of her campaign.

Toward the end of April, the seedlings in Peter's greenhouse were better than a foot tall on average, and their color was as green as pool table felt. He was feeding them chicken shit tea and had transplanted over a hundred into individual pots. Almost all had survived and were thriving. The weather was warm and sunny and everyone he knew was hoping it would continue that way.

He was expecting Jerry to come by and let him know when they could make the first drop-off run into the hills. He'd collected all the fertilizer and hose needed for his main patch, but there still wasn't any hurry this early in the season. As he stood there almost meditating on each plant as he watered it, he could hear the distant droning of a faraway logging operation and the occasional whistle they used for signals. Once in a while he heard the low throbbing of a small airplane engine. The sun felt pleasantly warm through the shirt on his back and the whole world seemed to be content with itself.

He finished watering and pulled the plastic covering back over the frame. The sun would be down in less than an hour and there was still a chance of a surprise frost at night. He stopped beside his small tractor-rototiller and pulled the cover off. The machine was the key to one of his sidelines, helping people prepare their garden sites and small-scale landscaping. He would need to put ads up around soon, if spring was going to come early. Of course, it could just as easily all go back to winter again, but right now the ground was nearly dried out enough for him to till. He liked the work, which got him out and into contact with neighbors he might not otherwise get to know. Sometimes he worried about his image as a loner, and the suspicion that he might be a grower, or a hermit, or whatever people might imagine, but there wasn't much he could do about it. He sometimes wondered just how many guys there were like him, in the cities as well as in the country, guys who'd done Vietnam and come back loners. Probably a lot. It could give you a sense of belonging to some kind of a group if you thought about all those others alone in their own way of life for similar reasons.

His small tractor did need a cooling system flush, and fresh gas and oil. He'd have to get that all on his next trip to town, and also put up ads at a couple of small stores along the way. Just then he heard a rig coming down the road, slowing and turning into his driveway. As usual, the moment before he could identify the vehicle always had a bit of suspense, even though there shouldn't be much to worry about at this time of year.

Jerry pulled to a stop and jumped out of the high cab, striding across the space between them as if something were after him. "Peter!" he called. "She started, she's in labor. The midwife said it'll be quite a while yet, but I want to get back to her. Got any coffee?"

"Sure, let me heat it up. Slow down or you'll become the emergency." He went inside and turned on the burner.

"Listen, can you do us a favor? Can you get away to come to town with us? We're going in to that clinic where they have the birthing room, and it's going to be all ready for us. We just have to get there. Soon. But Carla wants me to help her on the way there, breathing and stuff. We took classes for this. I don't know if we have to start that stuff yet, but she wants to make sure I'm able to help her if she needs it on the way in. So, can you maybe come along and drive?"

"Somebody better drive," he said. "You probably don't even know how you got here." He was carrying out two lukewarm cups of coffee. "Carla's probably worried she's going to have to help you remember how to breathe."

"Can't help it. First time, you know."

"Yeah, well this is finally it. Almost over now."

"Almost over!" Jerry gave him a surprised look. "It's just starting."

"I meant the pregnancy is almost over. And yeah, I'll go with you. Got some stuff to pick up anyway. Should I come with you now, or are you coming back for me?"

"The midwife said when the contractions get regular, no matter how far apart, to come on in. They're still pretty irregular and far apart, but who knows?"

"Okay. Look, you go back and get everything ready. I'll be there soon. Meantime, take it easy. You'll probably be up all night."

"Thanks," he said and handed back the empty cup. "It might take a while, so you better bring something to do."

"Don't worry about me. Just get yourselves ready. Maybe you should take a little nap."

"No way he could sleep now." He drove off.

As Peter stood there watching the dust settle, he was surprised by the thought that moving from the womb to the world was the ultimate transplant.

CHAPTER THREE

May

May arrives just about halfway through the calendar's official spring. May Day, when people celebrate the beginning of the growing season with poles and banners, songs and dances, fertility ceremonies, and a communist and labor holiday throughout the world. A day carrying more than its share of importance for the cultures of the northern hemisphere, even as it brings the first real twinges of winter to the southern half of the world. May Day, with all its responsibilities, still skips lightly through the world as the blossoms open and waft their scents on gentle breezes, as children dance in circles in crisp clean clothing, as the ground warms enough to insulate the roots of grass and trees, and as the greening part of this world races toward maximum flourishing. May Day, throwing open the shutters of winter, opening up what is possibly the prettiest month of the year.

As the first light chased the darkness home for the day, Peter was walking the streets of Dixon City. He'd slept on and off through the night on a couch in the clinic waiting room. Carla's labor was in full swing now, but still moving along slowly. He'd remembered it was May Day when he looked up at the calendar in the office and had brushed thoughts of other May firsts from his mind. It was going to be another beautiful day. He turned into the park to watch the sun rise.

A few early joggers passed him by and he wondered how running on pavement could be good for anybody, wondering too what music or news was piping into their minds through the small headphones that made them look a little like insects in brightly colored sweat suits. Shouldn't put it down until I've tried it, though, he thought. He told himself for the thousandth time that he who judges will be judged. Then thinking about judges, about if he ever got picked up and went to court even for something small, how he'd probably blow it. Like with that staff sergeant who caught him and a buddy working a vodka still behind the firebase. It hadn't been a big thing, not even an official court-martial or anything serious, just a routine disciplinary hearing until the hearing officer pointed out how stupid they were to try to make it themselves when the stuff was virtually free over there anyway. It was Peter's instinctive reaction to being called stupid that turned what would have been only a reprimand into two weeks in the stockade and a transfer to a unit in a more dangerous location. May Day in Vietnam came close to being a holiday since the enemy played it pretty laidback. They didn't seem to have any other holidays besides New Year's.

He came to the edge of the park and saw the morning mist rising off to the east, with long high rays of the still-hidden sun piercing through to reach for the blue vagueness above. He climbed a small elevated area, stepping through the damp grass, feeling good in the stillness and coolness of the morning. He turned to face the coming sun and emptied his mind of its static, turning his whole consciousness into a calm waiting, open to the light, lost to the value of time, thinking only that God has so many names in so many places, and thinking that this new day is now here, and losing himself in its beginning for a while.

Soon the sun was gleaming through the branches of budding trees that lined the roadway beside the park, and suddenly he was aware of the sounds of traffic beyond the next row of trees. He stretched his arms skyward as far as possible, wiggling their fingers, and then shaking himself all over like a wet dog. He remembered the Indian line about it being a good day to die, changed it in his head and spoke out loud to the brand new morning: "Hoka-hey, it's a good day to be born." Then he turned and headed back down the slope toward the clinic to check in and see how this particular birth was coming along. Along the way he found an open market, bought donuts, some instant coffee he hoped he could find hot water for, and a morning newspaper. There would be time for a real breakfast later.

When he got back, Jerry was outside and waiting for him in the parking area, asking, "Where'd you go?"

"For a walk. Got some donuts and instant coffee here. Place to heat water in there?"

"I saw a hot plate. Man, she's getting tired. It's coming, but she's tired. The midwife, Doris, says she's in transition now. Whatever that means. If it goes as fast as it should from now on, she'll have enough energy to finish. Otherwise, they might have to help her with some drug. God, I hope she makes it okay, either way."

"Hey, I hope you make it. You're wiped out, too. You catch a nap?"

"No, not really. And I have to get back in there."

"Okay, find out about heating some water and I'll have an instant continental breakfast for you, instantly, good sir."

They went in and Jerry pointed the way to a small room with janitor equipment, a sink, and a hot plate. Peter started heating water in a pot he found. There was already an open jar of instant on the shelf, but he went ahead and opened the new one. It's a better brand, he thought, smiling at the idea that any one brand of instant coffee could be better than any other. He noticed a clock that said 7:15, another kind of instant. He wondered if a person's own instant of birth is any better than any other. When is it? When the face appears, breathing on your own starts, when the cord is cut, when is that second that means it's happened, that the little one's on its own for the first time? Who knows? Better to concentrate on the coffee water. First things first, let Carla and the baby work out their precise moment of separation, that unique moment when oneness becomes twoness, forever.

Arching her back and pressing her head against the pillows of the birthing bed, Carla's face shone with the sweat and glow of maximum effort. The contractions were coming harder and faster, closer together, with less time to rest between. The midwife smiled encouragement as she applied soothing oil to the straining passageway. Jerry was brushing a damp cloth back and forth across her forehead. She reached up, touching his face with her fingers, tapping his unshaven cheeks.

"You need a shave," she said, smiling weakly, and was then seized by a heavy shuddering. The groaning growl that escaped between her clenched teeth was nearly a bellowing sound, drowning out the sympathetic murmuring from Doris and the heavy breathing from Jerry as he lost himself in the strange combination of joy and fear that came from his feelings of helplessness. As the contraction passed through and subsided, all three of them seemed to exhale together in a kind of simultaneous relief. Doris's assistant, Rose, quietly pointed to the stopwatch in her hand, mumbling that it must be almost time to start pushing.

Carla squeezed Jerry's hand and pulled it to her lips. She spoke softly, hoarsely, "It's coming…Where's Peter?"

"Outside. Do you want him to come in?"

"If he wants." Her body shook again with the tremor of its ancient process, but this new baby's first and most total dance of life. Again, the tension, the crying out, the long wave of shudders, and then finally, the collapse and release.

Jerry motioned to the assistant and asked, "Could you get our friend and see if he wants to come in?"

Rose showed the watch to Doris again and then left quickly. The contractions were almost as long as the intervals between them. The midwife now massaging the opening, working it, gently stretching, able now to feel the harder surface of the baby's head still wedged by the soft tissue and the bones surrounding it, still being held back, still inside for just a little while longer.

Jerry was leaning onto the bed, his face above Carla's closed eyes. He blew softly on her forehead, reaching under her shoulders to massage the tightness there. She grabbed at him and tried to pull him around behind her. He kicked off his shoes and worked his way around until she seemed satisfied with how he was propping her up.

She leaned back against him, whispering, "Let me try this." He glanced at Doris and she nodded okay.

Rose and Peter came silently into the room just as another contraction wrenched its way through Carla, through the entire room, and then dissipated. Peter closed the door and leaned against it, awed by the power that had just met him and thinking, So now I'm going through this too, seeing, hearing, smelling, yes and feeling all of this that I never expected or planned on ever feeling. Here it is right in front of me. He didn't know if he was ready for it or if there was ever such a thing as being ready for this, thinking, but I'm just the driver.

Rose was working side by side with Doris now, each of them massaging one of Carla's thighs, which were shaking with weariness. The watch was no longer needed at this final stage, the end of pregnancy, the fruit of the conception. Carla opened her eyes wide, caught sight of Peter and smiled weakly. He smiled back and raised his first finger, wishing he could help. He had never before seen someone he knew look like that, so helpless and so powerful at the same time. It was unbelievable. Then suddenly he was fighting off the memories of the wounded he'd helped, memories of other smells and screams, other blood…But this was different, this was life not death, the opposite end of the tunnel, a time for celebration rather than grief. He clasped his hands together over his head in the universal sign of victory when she looked his way again. She moaned and then lifted her head again, flashing him a Victory "V" with her fingers as she sank back against Jerry's chest, readying for the next one, always one more coming, her thinking of the ocean and its endless waves, always another one crashing on the shore. Oh God, when will it ever end?

Again her body shuddered in the vise grip of its own full force, her breath holding itself inside, holding in, Doris talking, saying breathe, but don't push yet, and Carla not pushing, not breathing either, everything seeming to stop, and now screaming as the pain of this spasm shot out through her eyes, her legs thrashing on the bed as the two women tried to hold them. As it passed over and through her, her mind whispered that maybe it wasn't as bad as she thought it was because look, everyone's smiling, everyone's happy. Didn't they realize what was happening to her? Didn't they know she couldn't do this, couldn't do anymore? It stopped, and the baby stopped moving and it was all over and she couldn't do it anymore, but they were happy.

"I can't, I can't," she said when she could catch her breath enough to speak, and that moment she felt a slosh of heat flowing across her legs.

"Just more water, nothing to worry about. It will be easier now. If you feel the urge to push go right ahead. You're doing fine, the baby's fine, such a good strong heartbeat."

Jerry straightened her hair, wiping away sweat, whispering, "I love you, you're so strong, you're doing good. I love you."

She drew his hands over her throbbing belly, helping him to press down where the cramping was, him stroking her with his hands, breathing deeply, and her realizing that they were breathing together, unconsciously now, only it wasn't any effort at all, pant-pant-blow, pant-pant-blow. A rhythm for them both, a togetherness new and old, always there and never there before...

Suddenly she felt something totally different, the spasm now in a different place, deeper than ever before, blocking her breath, blocking everything. She tried to say something, to tell them. But she couldn't because something was wrong, she couldn't move, couldn't breathe. Then, "OH GOD, OH GOD!" She pushed at IT, but something was in the way. Pushing! "Oh GODDDD!"

"The head's here." Doris rapidly massaged the warm oil around the crown of the head, barely showing, but moving, now not in, not out, no longer in either place.

Doris urged, "Push again."

Carla pushed until darkness threatened to overwhelm her, until she had to gasp for air to fill her burning lungs, until she collapsed back hard against Jerry, with an almost complete feeling of having turned to liquid. She was totally helpless now, she would never be able to move again. They would have to do something, they didn't seem to know it, but she was done, done, done. Then it came again, shutting off her breathing, blocking all thoughts, stopping everything so she pushed again, pushing without stopping, all right then, this was all that was left of her, now, pushing, forever, never stopping...but then, leaning back against the wall of Jerry's chest she felt the blocking thing move and the deep cramps ease, and she could hear Doris far away saying something about the head.

And Carla felt the thrill go through her whole body, gently and painlessly…

Jerry stretched his neck to be able to see around her, looking and feeling more than hearing the soft low sound vibrating through Carla, knowing that this never had happened to either of them before, and knowing this was the goodness they'd been waiting for since before they even knew one another. It seemed like the world had suddenly paused and Jerry wondered what his own dad felt that moment he arrived, the moment of being pushed up the ladder another rung, making room for the next generation in his line. He had no idea where these thoughts were coming from and was surprised he was thinking at all, feeling a sudden rush of love for his own mother now that he knew what she'd gone through for him, her joining the multitudes of parents who have at one time or another recognized what their own parents had done for them that was beyond any repayment, beyond what anyone else could ever do for them.

Carla was trembling again, shivering all over, her eyes locked on Doris's head between her knees. Doris glanced up at her and nodded, saying, "Yes, now, yes."

And Carla, feeling it coming closer and closer from far away, a force, a strength that was no longer her own, coming at her and now through her, and her back arched, spasming, one leg jerked straight out sideways. For one long moment she and the baby were as effortless as gliding birds in the sky, floating freely, and now heaving high in one long thrust and falling, falling, falling.

The baby burst into the air, nearly slipping out of Doris's hands. Blood, water, and baby all spewing into the light. A snorting sound and a horse rasp as the first breath entered the newest lungs in the world, followed by a short coughing sound that became a whimper turning into a crying and ending in a gurgle. This little girl had arrived.

Doris held her up for her parents to see, then placed her gently across Carla's still trembling belly, saying, "She's a girl."

With one hand, Carla wiped at the sweat and tears of her face, drawing the little one to her breasts with the other arm, cradling this newness. The cord was still pumping, the baby making little sounds, Carla still panting, and Jerry motionless, truly stunned by it all.

Rose quietly announced, "9:08 time of birth. Date, May Day, 1984." Carla turned a little toward Jerry and said, "Jerry, it's May, and it's a girl. Say her name to her."

Jerry shook himself into awareness and eased around to where he could see this new little one. He bent forward as far as he could and whispered in her ear, and then looked into Carla's eyes and said, "We'll call her Maya, won't we, and we give thanks for her."

After a few minutes, Doris and Rosa began cleaning away the mess and the waste padding. Doris went over to a sink, washed her hands, then came back and turned the baby over to place a clamp on the cord, which had by now stopped pulsing. She put a second one farther up the cord near the baby's tummy and then offered a pair of scissors to Jerry.

"Would you like to cut the cord? Right there."

He took the scissors, holding them tightly as he tried to control the shaking of his hands. He looked at Doris and asked, "Now?"

"Don't worry, she won't feel a thing. Now is fine."

He made the cut as quickly as he could. Doris swabbed at a small gush of blood and pinched the end of the tube. He set the scissors out of the way and placed his arm around Carla and the new one. The three of them, who minutes before had been only two, locked in a hug for a long moment of timelessness which was finally broken by the little one's small cry coming again, and then again.

Jerry relaxed and leaned back against the wall, catching sight of Peter by the door, and remembering him for the first time in a long while. "Hey, how'd you like that, Uncle Peter?"

Peter gave a big smile and clapped his hands together silently. He was still too overwhelmed to use his voice and was at a loss for anything to say anyway. He was thinking that this was the strongest antidote for his broken spirit, and for his memory. Every time he experienced new life, every seed that sprouted for him, every young animal on his neighbors' farms, was a new starting place, and he needed each and every one as the only healing for a heart still numb from too much death and killing. Now came a real live human birth. His head still swirled with the feeling of it, with the realization of things going on and on, always ending, and always beginning, life coming as much as it was going. He suddenly wanted something to do, something to help with. Coffee? The water was still heating, or probably boiled away by now.

Rose gathered up an armload of sheets and towels that had been replaced, and said, "I turned off the water in the tea kettle," as he opened the door for her.

Doris continued cleaning and wiping any new discharge from Carla, saying quietly, "You've hardly torn at all, not enough to need any stitches, so I'm going to leave you three alone for a little while. Don't worry about any bleeding or anything. It's normal. I'll be right outside if you need me or start contracting again. There's still a placenta to come. And my congratulations. You all did so well." She placed more fresh pads under Carla and left the room.

"You did it," Jerry said as the door closed. "You're so beautiful, and you did it."

"I couldn't have done it without you, you know that?" They laughed together. "Just look at her, honey. She's ours, she's really ours."

"I know, it's so incredible."

They kissed, and a soft and complete silence settled over them, lasting until Carla felt another small tremor inside herself. "Look," she said, "she's already sleeping."

Doris came back into the room and said softly, "Anything happening?"

The campaign committee had begun meeting on Tuesday evenings. For the second week in a row, Sonya was having dinner with Janet and her mother Ellen and eleven-year-old Kristi. They'd promised each other not to discuss business or politics at dinner, and the four of them really enjoyed getting together and getting to know each other. Sonya was asked a lot of questions about her past and her family. Ellen was particularly interested in hearing about Sonya's father. He'd been travelling quite a bit since her mother's death a few years before. For

Sonya, these dinners at Janet's were the first real taste of family since she'd left her own home so many years before. There'd been holidays together when her mother was still alive, and there'd been the years with Mike, but family, the unexpected moods and constant interplay between generations...She could see that this had been missing from her life altogether. As a result, she found herself captivated by young Kristi's attempts to be a grown-up amid this adult situation.

They finished their pretty wedges of cheesecake and then Ellen spoke to Kristi, saying, "Come along, and bring the rest of the dishes. I need your help cleaning up."

"Grandma, can't that wait until Mom and Sonya have to go? I want to stay with them while they talk about their stuff."

"Go along," Janet said. "We have a lot of boring business to discuss before our meeting, and if you hurry we'll still be here when you finish. Now go help Grandma."

Kristi got up and cleared the table as slowly as she could without actually stopping. She was looking down and pouting, and Sonya was moved to try and cheer her up.

"You know, Kristi, there's going to be lots of things for you to do in this campaign if you're interested."

"How am I going to know if I'm interested if I can't even hear anything about it?" She tossed her ponytail over her shoulder and stalked out with a small pile of dishes and silver.

"Want her?" Janet said, watching her daughter with a look that was half pride and half exasperation.

"Sure, she's wonderful, really something. Maybe after we get to know each other better, she could come and stay over with me or we could go some places together. Give you a break."

"I'm sure we'd all love that. Now tell me about your meeting this afternoon." She stirred her coffee carefully, not letting the spoon touch the cup.

"Well, first of all, not one of them asked me for a date. Just as well because they're all old or married."

"So who was there?"

"The County Chairman, his assistant chair, the treasurer in charge of fundraising, the PR man for the Party, Dan and me." Sonya reached for the notebook in her shoulder bag. "Issues and money, that's what it's all about right now."

"And what did they have to say?"

"They were nice enough to ask me what I want to concentrate on, and then had some suggestions of their own. I listed overcrowding in the jail, and streamlining the whole process from arraignment to trial, priorities for plea-bargaining, and changes in the budget to focus more on violent crimes, and, finally, a more collective approach to the responsibilities of the office. They asked what I meant by that and I said allowing the deputy prosecutors to take a case all the way to trial more often, when they're qualified. Basically, I took what you and I had talked about and put it straight to them. Nicely, of course."

"More coffee?"

"No thanks."

"What did they say?"

"They thought it was fine as far as it went, but it didn't have all the hooks they said they needed. Hooks are to grab the attention of the public and the media. The chairman, you might know him, Berman is his name, he wants even more attention on violent versus non-violent crimes. He said Reynolds is doing almost nothing with the rape issue, and we can promise a task force, heavier sentences, etcetera. He also said that too much time and money is being wasted on the marijuana problem without really slowing it down in any way."

"Does he know that much of that money comes from the feds?"

"I don't know. I'll bring it up at the next meeting. We have another go-round with the same bunch next week. Would you want to come?"

Janet thought for a moment and said, "I don't think it's wise. At least not yet."

"You're probably right."

Kristi came back through the swinging door and sat down next to Sonya. "I'm done with the dishes. What're we talking about?"

Neither answered as they exchanged glances. Then Sonya said, "We're talking about the issues in my campaign. Do you know what that means?"

"Sure. It's what you're going to say bad about the other person, and what he's going to say bad about you."

"Well I hope it's about more than that. At least, I hope it starts out being more polite than that. First, we need to decide what the issues are, and that's what we're doing now. And issues are problems. One of them is that there isn't enough county money to pay for all of the cases that have to be tried in court. Do you understand that?"

Kristi nodded yes, and said, "Then you should make the bad people pay for their own."

Sonya looked over at Janet who smiled and said, "But many people commit crimes, like robbery, because they don't have enough money to live on."

Sonya went on, "So the people who nominated me want me to say that if we lose a case in court, one that's decided by a jury, you know what that is?"

"Yeah, it's those people that watch the court."

"Sort of." Sonya looked back over at Janet, who was enjoying the whole exchange. "Anyway, if the county loses a case, it can either go to trial again or stay the way the jury decided it. They want me to say that we leave those cases the way the jury decided, and we won't try to appeal and get them changed. They're calling that money saving and fairness. Understand?"

"Yeah, I think so. Except I thought the jury was always right."

Janet chimed in, "Honey, maybe that's the way it should be, but the way it is now, it turns into some sort of an ego trip. Anytime we lose, and I mean the DA's office loses, we automatically appeal and ask for a retrial in a different court, even if there's no good reason for it. I think this is a good idea, Sonya. Who thought it up?"

"I think it was the assistant chairman, Mr. Driscoll. He's an older man and a retired lawyer. He put it out as an issue that combined good old-line liberal traditions of trusting the people, at the same time as it's saving money. I think he's probably right."

"I'll tell you what," Janet said, "Reynolds hates to lose any case and he'd never go along with something like that. If you can make it an issue there will definitely be two sides to it."

"Good, that's what we need. Hey, I've got to get going. Kristi, your mom and I were talking about you spending some time with me if you want to. Like go on a short trip together, or you spend a night over with me, whatever, maybe after we get to know each other better, and if you want to."

"I think I'd like to, but can I go to the meeting with you now?"

Her mother answered. "No way. You said you have homework, and I won't be back until late. So, go get Sonya's coat for her and then get to work."

Kristi mimicked her mother, "All right, so go get Sonya's coat like a good girl." Again she stalked out of the room. The two women smiled, stood and prepared to go. Janet said, "My God, do you remember being like that?"

"Of course not," Sonya said, laughing.

"Was there much else? At the meeting, I mean."

"No more than we can cover in the car on the way."

Once a month the Chinook County Board of Commissioners held a day-long session in which the mayors or managers of the municipalities presented reports and requests and received updated consultations from the board. The May meeting was wrapping up later than usual due to snarls and appeals in the land-use planning process, and a heated discussion concerning the smaller school districts' share of timber tax revenue. The next meeting's agenda was finally being addressed when DA Reynolds approached Sheriff Johnson and invited him to step around the corner for a drink afterward.

Once they got to the bar the two men sat at a secluded table in the back, ordered drinks from a waiter who knew them, and loosened their ties, relaxing for the first time all day. Reynolds offered a cigarette. Johnson turned him down and said, "Kind of got by easy on the overcrowding thing, didn't we?"

"Oh yeah, postponed again," Reynold said, lighting his cigarette. "But it'll be back next month. Maybe we can set up some kind of exchange with our neighbor counties. How's their count, any idea?"

"Douglas has half the jail shut down for renovation and Lane County's ended up with the overflow from that. At least through June. No help there." Johnson paused and then said, "It's still up to your office, Bill. How about own recognizance for anyone with under $5,000 bail? That'd drop at least six to ten inmates."

"Can't do it. We'd never see them again—you know who they are."

"Solves the problem though, doesn't it? Good riddance."

"Yeah until one of them does something again, gets caught, and some reporter gets hold of it somewhere down the line."

They'd both finished their drinks and Reynolds signaled for another round. The sheriff asked, "You got any worries about this election?"

Their drinks arrived and the waiter asked if he could get them anything else. Reynolds nodded no and said, "Not yet, thanks," and went on. "Not worried, but you do have to consider everything these days."

Marty sipped slowly on his Bloody Mary, trying to remember the last time he got really drunk. Before this job, that was for sure. Now he couldn't risk it, but sometimes it almost seemed necessary. "You know, Bill, it's not our fault, not at all. We do what we have to do, and then get blamed for the consequences. That's what you need to tell the voters."

"Sure, I'd like to do nothing else, but the press would have a field day. Dereliction of duty or some such bullshit. They'd say, 'If you can't handle the job, step down.' Get what I mean?"

"Thing is, Bill, it makes sense. The more crowded it gets, the more trouble I have down there. I'm no crybaby liberal, and I don't give a damn how bad things get for the inmates, don't get me wrong. But the friggin' place could go up any night, fire, riot, hostage, whatever, it's that bad. And then who's going to get coverage, the blow-up, the front page? Not you, Bill, not you."

"I'm doing what I can, Marty. I'll have someone run a docket check in the morning, see if we can't squeeze something out somewhere, but no promises. If you really want to see things speed up, talk to the judges. They're so goddam hung up on procedure, my boys can't get a jay-walking case done in one day." He waved for a refill. "Another one Marty?"

"No thanks."

"Come on, it was a rough day."

Marty swallowed the rest of his drink, and said, "I'll just take a beer then. Did I tell you I ordered a couple of those new bracelets?"

"Send a signal or something? You didn't tell me, but I heard about them somewhere. You want to take that risk?"

"Yeah, but you'll have to recommend it at a presentencing hearing."

"Okay. I'll look for something where it makes sense. House arrest, huh? I'll make a note right now."

The new drinks arrived without Marty getting to order his beer. Bill started to tell the waiter, but Marty waved it off, "I'm good."

Reynolds took a swallow and looked at his watch. "Dammit, almost late, promised the wife I'd be home in time for dinner at least once this week. Haven't made it yet. Tell you what, I'll sign for this on the way out." He tossed back the rest of his drink. "Take your time Marty, and don't worry so much."

"Okay. But listen, we have to get together in the office real soon. On top of everything else I just got word from the Regional DEA that they want us to go ahead and map out and budget for our high-target areas. Use helicopters this summer."

"Helicopters?"

"Yeah, how do you like that?"

"I don't know. Have to think about it. Might be a good thing. Listen, give me a call in the morning. We'll set up a time. I'll be damned. Everybody knew it was coming someday, but it's a big change isn't it? Choppers. Look I really have to run. Call me first thing." He clapped the sheriff on the shoulder, gathered his coat and briefcase and left quickly.

Marty watched him striding out the door with a wave, thinking he'd forgotten to pay the check, also thinking it must be nice not to have to wear a uniform all the time you're working, just melt into the crowd on the street. Not that Marty minded the way people stepped around him or got out of his way when he was in a hurry, but it got to him sometimes, the constant awareness that he was the sheriff and everyone else knew it. He took another sip of his drink. Got to him a lot of the time. Made him remember how he preferred his days as a detective in Portland. Plainclothes was what they were called, that was the name of the game. Now he was all jingle-jangle, keys, cuffs, gun, more stuff than he could even use. Of course, these days some sheriffs wore suits. He'd met them, mostly from larger towns and cities, real bureaucrats. He didn't want any of that either.

He held off finishing the drink, thinking Reynolds hadn't really registered what the helicopter thing was going to mean. What it would mean for him was nowhere near so much paperwork. Can't do a search from a helicopter, then come all the way back, get warrants, and then go back out and expect to find anything or anyone there when you got back. Nope, this was pure search and destroy. Copters in the air, troops and trucks on the ground. Just like El Salvador or somewhere like that, only you hope the other side isn't shooting. Wouldn't be much prosecution unless you wanted to make an example of somebody who was still growing on private land. The higher-ups must be tired of all the botched warrants and sloppy paperwork that was bound to happen when you worked under such pressure and under-staffed like most departments. Marty was just as glad for this change in strategy but knew Reynolds wouldn't take it all laying down. He'd made half of his image out of the Pot War. Image? He wondered what Bill really thought about his sheriff's image. It was true he himself lacked ambition if ambition means always wanting to get ahead of where you're at. Hell, he'd be glad to retire from the public scene, get a good job running a private security set-up, regular hours, have some real time for steelhead and elk. He drained the last of the drink, sucked the last juice from the lemon, and stood to leave.

On his way out, he stopped to pay for the drinks, but the waiter came over to tell him it was taken care of.

"How? My friend just walked out several minutes ago."

"Mr. Reynolds signaled me as he left. He has an account."

"Okay, well, thanks."

As he stepped out into the darkening street he noticed fresh rain, computed its effect on the increase of possible car accidents during the night, hitched up his pants, smiled at the jingle of the keys, and unconsciously checked the strap securing his gun in its holster. The drinks felt good, warm inside, and he admitted to himself it had been a hard day. He decided to drop by the office for a quick check-in, then head home, knowing that if dinner was waiting for him it would have to be warmed up anyway. His wife never expected him at any particular time unless she'd invited guests, and he never knew when she'd be there anyway. It seemed to work out that way, though, now that the kids had moved on, seemed to be working out all right. He walked quickly through the rain to his office.

When he checked through the messages for the day, only one stood out. He was supposed to return the call of a Ms. Sonya Lehman. She'd called to request a tour of the jail sometime soon. She also wanted a listing of the present population with their charges, bails, etc. Goddam, he thought, here we go. Election crap already!

After the baby's birth, two weeks went by before Jerry and Peter got up into the hills for the trucking. All day they cruised the gravel roads, enjoying the beautiful day and dropping off four loads of fertilizer and watering equipment. Peter was hoping to use drip irrigation at two of the sites he'd tended the year before by hauling buckets. It would really make a difference if it worked, and he wouldn't have to check it as often, always taking the chance of exposing himself that way.

When they finished hiding the last stash off the road under a long rotting deadfall, they sank down onto the damp ground and rested, still breathing hard from the effort. None of the hiding places were more than a half-mile of their eventual patch destination, and Peter jokingly told Jerry to forget everything he'd seen and done that day. When they'd rested enough to sit up again, Peter began rolling a joint. In the canyon below them, a red-tailed hawk sailed effortlessly among the tall trees.

Jerry watched the bird closely, then tried to pick out its shape among the branches where it had disappeared. "Didn't see anyone all day," he said.

"That's good. I'm glad. Means we can use your truck again sometime. It's still fresh."

"What're you doing tonight?"

Peter finished rolling. Lit it, inhaled and passed it. "Don't know. Not much."

Jerry took a hit and passed it back. "Why don't you come with Carla and me to a little birthday party? You know Leslie Graham and her old man? It's for her, and there's a dessert potluck. You're invited if you want. I never got over to tell you before. Forgot until just now."

"Potluck? I don't have anything to bring."

"We'll stop at the store on the way. Get some ice cream."

The hawk leaped into the air from the top of a tree and spiraled up until it was above them. With one shrill whistle, it circled once and vanished over the ridge. They sat in silence for a while.

"Who else will be there?" The joint was almost finished, so he smoked it down to his fingertips.

"Don't know. Mostly people from around here. Probably those ones from over at Bobcat Creek. Al and Linda. A few others, who knows."

They stood, stretched, and Peter flapped his arms a couple of times. "Now, how did that hawk do it?"

When they reached the top by the road, Jerry grabbed his saw out of the back of the truck and cut some rounds off a slash pile at the edge of the landing. Peter threw the wood into the bed of the truck.

When they got back down and stopped to turn into Peter's driveway, he said he'd walk to the trailer. "Hey Jerry, thanks a lot. You really helped me out today. I thought it would take at least two days to get it all done."

"Well, I'm sorry it took so long to get around to it. Hope it didn't hold you up too much, but Carla's just getting back to some kind of normal."

"Sure. You didn't hold me up at all. The weather's just now getting right for this part. Dry enough we didn't hardly leave any tire tracks anywhere."

"Yeah, that's good with these big old monsters. Should we pick you up tonight?"

"What time?"

"Maybe around seven."

"I guess so. I might as well feel strange once in a while."

"Good, see ya then."

Jerry pulled away and Peter checked his mailbox before heading up the drive. Nothing in it, as usual.

It was still light out when they came for him. It was looking like the dry weather would hold for another day or two, at least. He climbed into the truck, sitting where he could just make out the baby's face in a bundle of blankets.

"Hey, how are you? Both of you."

Carla glanced at him and answered lightly, "Couldn't be better. This will be her first public appearance. She's doing great."

She had never been able to make up her mind about Peter. Part of her liked him, liked him a lot. He seemed more considerate than most of the men she and Jerry knew, and he'd done nice things for them. On the other hand, there was still something about him that bothered her. Sometimes she tried to figure out what it was, but there was basically nothing to back up the feeling. It was mostly a kind of alertness she felt when Jerry would say that he was going over to hang with Peter, almost a kind of fear on her part. It always passed, and she could usually forget about it because they really had no other close neighbors and he was so helpful when they needed it. Maybe it was just his aloneness and him seeming satisfied with it that made her nervous. Maybe any woman would feel threatened by a man who didn't seem to need anyone. Then there was the fact that he never talked to them about his past, and as near as she could tell he hadn't ever mentioned it to Jerry when they were off together, either. The strangest thing was that when the baby really started coming, it had seemed necessary to include him at the birth. Maybe she just felt she should invite someone because the midwife said she could, but she thought it might go deeper than that. They had other friends she could have asked, and her parents didn't live too far away, but she thought it went deeper than that. It was probably all just based on the sense that if they needed someone in an emergency, then he was that one.

They pulled out onto the main road and she was watching him watch the baby. She said, “I haven’t really got to talk to you since the birth. What did you think of it?”

“I’ve never been to anything like it. You were amazing.”

Jerry said, “Funny, but I really forgot you were even there until it was over.”

“And I didn’t notice anything any of the time,” Carla said. “I was so out of it.”

Jerry pulled the truck in next to the small store. “Still want to get some ice cream?”

“Sure.” Peter jumped out. “Anything else?”

“No thanks,” Carla answered. “We just stocked up.”

As they got closer to the party, Peter felt that rush of shyness he usually felt for social functions. It wasn’t that he didn’t like going out, or that he didn’t have a good time, it was just that you always had to be ready to deal with the unexpected when you put yourself in unknown situations. And that included meeting people you might or might not want to get to know. He was still thinking about what was coming as they got closer, what he might run into, nothing bad, but there were always the people who had a single woman guest or relative they wanted to introduce him to, or they’d watch you fumble around in a room full of semi-bored couples. Then there were the ones who always wanted to get him into something, like a petition changing the laws against pot, or an argument about preventing old growth timber from being cut, or stopping nuclear power, and all the other things he figured you couldn’t really do much about. It wasn’t that he didn’t believe in anything, it was just that he didn’t consider himself an activist and couldn’t take that kind of risk anyway. He always had himself ready for the vague possibility that someone from the past he was trying to leave buried would come along and upset his whole scene. On the other hand, there had to be times when the unexpected came along and turned out to be good.

They parked some way down the drive from the Grahams' house and got out to walk. Several other trucks and cars, mostly older models, were already parked. After he opened the door for her, Carla handed him the baby. He couldn't believe how light and tiny she was. The blankets might be heavier than the baby. Carla reached back into the cab and brought out a cake that had been riding on the divider in the front seat. And the diaper bag and ice cream.

"Would you like to carry her in?" she asked him.

"Uh, I don't know, sure, Okay."

They climbed the porch steps of the old farmhouse, two-story with a long closed-in porch. The sounds of Jackson Browne and laughing people came from inside. As they stepped through the door into the hallway, Carla found a place to set things down. She hung her coat and took the baby from him. When she entered the front room where folks were, there was an instant outburst of excitement as many of them crowded around her and the baby.

Jerry looked over at Peter and said, "Nobody's going to even know we're here."

"That's okay by me." He picked up the cake and ice cream. "Guess I better take these to the kitchen."

He eased his way through the main room, moving behind the group around Carla and the baby, nodding to those he knew and who noticed him. Once he reached the kitchen, he saw a table totally filled with cakes, puddings, pies and fruit dishes. One cake was five layers high with decorations. He looked for a place to set Carla's cake and ended up putting it on top of the cold stove next to a pie. He was able to just squeeze the ice cream into the freezer and was closing the door when a strong arm grabbed his shoulders from behind.

"Guess who?"

"Don't know." He turned. "Al, hey how are you?"

"Man, I am great. Where you been all winter?"

"Mostly here. You?"

"My friend, I have been to paradise and back. Look at this tan in the light. This is the winter version of Hawaii, land of volcanoes and much, much more. Here, sit down. Want you to try something? Here, smell it."

Al handed a bud, small but compact, frosty with resin and very strong smelling.

"Looks good."

"You bet it looks good. Wait till you smoke it. Here, let me roll it up. Wait till you hear how they grow it. Man, you won't believe it. See, I have this cousin over there. Went to visit him for the first time since he's been there. Had no idea of his scene. Last time I saw him he was straight, super straight, working computers for the phone company, but he split with his wife, quit his job, took off and ended up with a beautiful girl in Hawaii, a house, whatever he wants. Growing it, too. I couldn't believe it."

Just then Linda found them and interrupted, "Is he already trying to blow your mind with his 'report'? I think he wants everybody around here to pack up and move over there. How are you, Peter?"

"I'm fine. You look like you had a great time in the sun."

"I did. The people are kind of weird over there, the growers and all. It's so commercial compared to here, but the sun and the beaches are perfect. And the fruit…mmm..."

Al finished rolling and motioned for Peter to follow him out the back door. Outside he lit up and passed the joint. "Here, and this isn't pineapple or mangoes."

Peter took a hit. After choking a little on the fine, aromatic smoke he took another and passed it back. After a few more, they went back in. Linda was still in the kitchen, whipping cream with an egg beater.

"Are you still alone?" she asked Peter.

"Yeah."

"Too bad."

"Leave him alone," Al said. "He's probably better off. Look at us."

She swung a pot holder at him.

"Now, Peter, get ready for the clincher. This stuff grows with no watering, I mean, they plant it and they harvest it and that's it. They hardly have to look at it in between. Course they lose some to cops or thieves and some of it gets beat down by heavy rains once in a while. But they only have to grow it for a couple of months. It matures so fast, and rains almost every day, for maybe an hour." He held up the remains of the joint, which was still lit. "Like it?"

"It's good, but it sounds too easy."

"It is too easy, growing it is. The problem's getting it off the islands. Want any more?"

Peter shrugged a no and Al said, "I'll take it in the other room. Be right back."

Linda held out the beater, offering it to Peter, "Lick it off?"

"No thanks," he said, standing to follow Al into the other room. Linda blocked his way. "You know, you're a real mystery, not just to me, but probably to a lot of women around here. Can I ask you a personal question?"

"What if I say no?"

"How about I just ask it and then you don't have to answer it if you don't want to?"

Just then three more people came into the kitchen, including the birthday person and hostess, Leslie Graham.

"Well, hello, Peter. I saw you sneak by. How are you?"

"Fine. Happy Birthday, Les. Looks like there's enough dessert."

"I guess so! How about a birthday hug?"

"Sure." He hugged her lightly and stepped back, looking a little awkwardly at the two strangers who'd come in with her.

Leslie turned to them, saying, "This is our friend, Peter. He lives over near Carla and Jerry, who I just introduced you to. Peter, this is my brother and his wife, from Denver, Ron and Theresa Olsen. He's a lawyer."

Peter and Ron shook hands and Theresa gave him a bright smile. They both mumbled "Nice to meet you."

Leslie handed a pile of plates over to Theresa. "See if you can find a place for these somewhere. What were you smoking? Smells good."

"Some Hawaiian Al brought back."

"We'll have to catch up with him." She got out a batch of forks. "Ron's thinking of moving themselves out here, if there's enough work for him. You tell him, Ron."

"Well, I don't really know what we're doing. There're lots of things we don't like about Denver. The weather for one thing, in the winter.

And the pace is pretty heavy. I've worked some with the ACLU there and thought there might be a way to get started with them out here, and I've handled a few drug cases. Leslie tells me that stuff is getting heavier here all the time."

Someone else came in and Leslie handed her the bowl of whipped cream.

"Sounds good. I guess folks can always use friendly lawyers."

"So, I don't know…We really like this area and want to get out of the big city, try gardening, and more outdoor things."

Leslie offered them each a glass of wine. "Homemade blackberry. Peter, maybe you know somebody in the legal profession in Dixon."

"No, no I don't. So far I've been lucky. Not a speeding ticket since I moved here." He smiled. "Maybe the folks over on Bobcat Creek would know. You know them? Some guy named Dave got busted last year. He must have had a lawyer."

"Oh, that's right," Leslie said. "Dave and Corinne. I do know them. Matter of fact, I thought she might be coming tonight with Birdie and Sam. I'll ask them when I go back in."

"You make this wine?"

"Tom did. Like it?"

"It's great. Not too sweet."

Peter was the last one out of the kitchen, hoping to avoid Linda's question, whatever it was, and thinking he could just as easily have gone out the back door. Someone had turned off the tape player and someone else was warming up on the piano. A guitar was warming up as well. He could get into listening to some live music and maybe avoid any more questions. He did, however, wonder what Linda wanted to know.

The couple they'd been talking about, Birdie and Sam, turned out to be the musicians for the evening. They adjusted themselves in their seats and smiled at one another, then they hit the first three chords of "Happy Birthday' and stopped. Sam, on guitar, looked around at everyone, and said "Guess it's not time for that, yet."

Then they settled into an instrumental that was part rock, part jazz, an original that seemed to fit right in with the group that made up this party crowd. Peter found a seat at one end of the couch where Carla was changing baby Maya. Tom came by with a fresh bottle of wine and offered him a refill. Peter accepted, nodding, and complimented the wine. It was really very good and gave him a warm feeling around the solar plexus. The Hawaiian pot was giving him a good twist of the mind as well. He was wondering why that spot was called the "solar plexus." Was it because it was the center of the body with everything else orbiting around it, or what? Here came Linda again, but she went past him and sat on the couch arm near Carla, reaching out for the freshly-diapered infant.

Carla was beaming through the evening, her pride a kind of bubbling that had no ego in it, just sheer satisfaction with her baby and herself. Peter found himself really liking her, perhaps for the first time, not in any attraction way, but in a way that was made up of respect and the desire to show it to her. And to the baby. Just then Jerry came over and stood next to her. They made a super nice family and he was starting to feel glad they'd brought him along. The music was fading down and Linda came over and pulled on his arm.

"Come help put the candles on the cake."

He didn't particularly want to, but there wasn't much he could do about it. Once they got inside the kitchen, she leaned back against the door, closing it. and stared up at him. He looked back at her, not knowing what else to do. She reached out and took one of his hands. "Peter, I'm not trying to come on to you, although I would if I wasn't already pretty happy, but there's something I want to know."

He eased back a little, but didn't pull away his hand, "What's that?"

"Are you gay?"

He looked down at her upturned face. She was quite a bit shorter than him. He didn't answer for a long moment. Finally, he smiled the most lecherous smile he could manage, leaned toward, and, in clumsy Fred Astaire fashion, took her in his arms, leaned her over backwards and almost kissed her. As he held her there he looked deep into her eyes whispering, "No, me no gay." He stood her back up, released her and said, "Now where are those candles?"

She brushed her hair back into place, and said, "Over on that counter," as she tidied up the sink area.

"How many?"

"I don't really know. How many are there?"

"The box says thirty-six."

"How old do you think she is?"

"No idea. She probably wouldn't want to advertise it anyway. We can save some for her kids."

"Just put thirty on there. I know she's more than that." She dried her hands and turned to watch him. "You sure are weird."

"I know, but so are you and everybody else. Where are all the kids, anyway?"

"Upstairs. They rented a VCR and some films. The perfect babysitter. We'll have to call them down for the cake. I'll get someone to do that. Keep an eye on the cake," she said, leaving the kitchen.

That had been sort of fun, catching her off guard like that, paying her back for taking him off guard himself. Now he wondered how many other people had the same suspicion. It was either that from the women, or the men thinking he was some sort of deep-planted narc. Somehow people thought there was much more going on with him than there really was. He could see that not only did his life make him lonely, but being alone made him subject to so many guesses and opinions as to why he was like that. He didn't have any way of knowing if it would be different somewhere else, like in a city, worse or better because people didn't know so much about each other in there. Sometimes it felt like he should just have an affair just to shut down the speculation. He poured himself another glass of wine from the half-full bottle on the table. Wondering what folks would think about his hang-up on classical music if they knew about that. Now, that was really weird.

Linda came back and said, "They're all ready. I'll light the candles and you can carry it in, okay?"

As they came through the door, there was a burst of clapping and the man at the piano pounded out the birthday song. When they finished singing, the kids pushed Leslie toward Peter and the cake and crowded around them, crying out, "Make a wish, make a wish."

Peter could see Leslie mentally counting the candles and smiling up at him as she took in a big breath. She blew them all out and there was a sustained cheer and more piano. He carried the cake back into the kitchen when Linda motioned him that way, set it down, and this time did escape out the back door. He walked down the steps and around to the side of the house where he could look through a window at the confusion in the kitchen. There was probably four times as much sweets and food as was needed, but it seemed like everyone was trying to get in right away. The kids were being served first. Watching, Peter wasn't sure if he was even hungry anymore.

He heard the front door close on the other side of the wraparound porch and saw someone coming toward him in the shadows of dusk. The climbing moon shone briefly through the high clouds and slipped behind some mist. He always thought of that misty fog as a veil softening the features of the moon, but it also seemed to make her light brighter. He saw that it was Tom who had come outside, and he spoke up so as not to startle the man.

"Hey, it's me, Peter."

"Hi, how are you? Nice out here."

"Yeah. Beautiful. Not raining for a change."

"Yeah, I know. Might turn out to be one of our rainiest springs ever. Hope not."

"Me too. If you don't mind, how old is Leslie? I didn't know when Linda had me put the candles on the cake. Hope it didn't matter."

"No, looks like you were on the right side of 34. Incredible. When we met she was a very crazy twenty-year-old hippie girl. Neither one of us ever figured on settling down, for sure not together. But it's been good. How's it going for you?"

Peter could feel several questions in that one, but chose to play it lightly. "I'm doing pretty good. Yeah, I'm fine."

Tom took out a pack of cigarettes and offered it to Peter who waved it off. Tom lit one for himself and asked, "You still tilling gardens?"

"Yeah, if the mud ever dries out."

"No hurry," Tom said, peering in the window. "Things don't start up until late anyway. In California they have tomatoes ripening in July. Sure is different here. Anyway, I'd like you to do ours, soon as you can. We want to do a little more than last year. Some new ground, but it's not sod or anything. I guess you should call a day or two before you want to come on over so I can be sure to be here and show you what we want. How's the other crop?"

"Okay. They seem to like this weather, not cold at all. Be all right if they don't get leggy from lack of sun."

"Mine too. Did you get Al's rap on Hawaii?"

"Yeah, just the right amount of rain every day. Sounds great."

Tom licked his fingers and pinched out the cigarette, then put the filter in his jacket pocket and coughed lightly. "Got to quit smoking that stuff. Did he tell you about their cops?"

"No, mentioned thieves and cops, but nothing specific."

"It's all helicopters, all season long, crisscrossing the jungle. They get a lot. The more they get the more money to keep flying. But there's so much growing, no way to get it all, or even part of it."

Peter nodded and asked, "When you think they'll start using choppers out here? Planes didn't get much last year."

Tom thought for a moment. "Sure wish we had someone on the inside, but we don't so it's all guesswork. I figure they've got them in Hawaii, and now in some places in California and it's working for them. Haven't heard of any getting shot down, so I think it's coming soon."

"I think you're right, but shit, there goes the profit."

"Yeah, break even, just like any other job." Peter was finally starting to think about his ice cream and wondering if there'd be any left. Tom went on, "You hear this thing about the FBI?"

"That the National Forest is in their jurisdiction and they're going to start policing it?"

"Something like that. Going to get crowded out there. Come on, let's get some of that in there before it's gone. Enough paranoia. Doesn't do any good anyway."

Later that night, when Peter got home, he was surprised to find that he was somewhat drunk from all the wine he'd had, and more surprising, he'd had a pretty good time.

CHAPTER FOUR

June

In a rainy year, June can seem more like winter than the hoped-for beginning of summer. Day after day of a wet gray world, warming oh so slowly, interrupted only once in a while by a brilliant day or two of the sun transforming everything into the promise of a brighter future. As May ends and June begins, there are still bursts of hail on days when the sun and big dark clouds keep trading places in the sky. Fruit trees struggle along while the grass grows like crazy. Alders and maples fill up their branches with foliage and the valleys seem to become even smaller, the roads more like tunnels, the overwhelming color green almost blinding. The work of living continues and vegetable seedlings overflow their flats, waiting in greenhouses for the ground to dry enough to be tilled and turned. Other seedlings, hiding in their plastic-covered cold frames or lighted attics, grow too, and their growers face the weather with relatively good cheer as they dig the holes and transport fertilizer into position for the heavy and somewhat delicate work of transplanting. June is late for the main work of spring, but some years there's no sense in trying to fight the climate. The cycles must have their way. When June does finally whisk off her veil of mist and beams forth with bridal light, the whole world makes way for her. All the changes that have been slowly building to this climax are suddenly released, and the freedom to grow in the welcoming dirt is almost translated into the sound of the ground breathing.

It had been one of the rainiest springs on record, and now that it hadn't rained for over forty-eight hours, Peter was taking advantage and filling his truck and tractor with gas at the South Fork Store. The small tractor was chained down to its trailer and he rechecked the tie-downs as the tank filled. The clouds were gray but lacked the intensity of a rainfall sky—as least he was hoping so. If he had any luck and could get this tilling job done early enough, there would still be time to get to that one patch that he hadn't got ready for transplants yet. On the weekend he would be free to move over to Tom and Leslie's to till their land. By June he was usually wondering how he could keep up with being so busy, but this year was different and late, and everything was just starting now.

When he came out of the store he saw a state patrol car parked in front of the post office. As usual, he felt the quick, tight knot between his ribs and stomach. He'd been going into the post office himself. It wasn't really necessary, and he'd just as soon avoid even being seen by one of those guys. The officer was probably delivering more wanted posters or asking questions about someone in the area…or maybe just buying stamps. Peter knew he could just pull out and be gone, but the lights on the trailer weren't working and that might get him noticed. Better to wait, unless the cop was coming over to the store. This was the part he hated, being paranoid when he hadn't even done anything yet, just fearing the hassle of any encounter with the other side. Future recognition or whatever. Now thinking how cool it would feel to have a new rig with everything on it in working order, and nothing else to hide, to just be able to walk right past, smile and keep going with no bad vibes at all. But you'd probably be making the payments on that kind of rig for years and be heading off to work at some backbreaking dull job, and you might still be anxious because you left your wallet and license at home in another pair of jeans.

In any case, he had to get a move on, and the cop was still inside the post office. He got in the truck and drove onto the road back the way he came. As he went around the first big bend, he looked in the mirror and saw that the patrol car was still parked in the same place. So much for all his jitters.

When he pulled into the O'Hara place it was still before noon and he was doing well for time. Andy O'Hara lived with his wife and one son; his sister and her family had the place next to it. Their grandfolks originally homesteaded the place, and Peter really appreciated the sense of continuity this gave the land. Most folks he knew were relative newcomers like himself, and it was hard to find out much about the area's past without knowing someone like Andy. Peter remembered him saying they didn't even have electricity until the mid-fifties, and even then it was pretty unreliable.

The man said they wouldn't be home when he got there, but to go ahead and do the same as the year before. If he had any questions, Sally was next door. Both families used the same garden site and he was expecting it would take two good half-days to do it all. He unloaded the tractor with no trouble and it started right away. While it was warming up, he walked out through the garden looking for any problems: scrap lumber, wire, or other obstacles for the tiller. The ground was clean and looked well-drained. He went back to the truck, poured some coffee from his thermos and picked out a tape for the small player he could wear on his belt. This was a new thing for him this year and a great leap forward: earphones and a cassette Walkman that kept out most of the tiller's engine noise and replaced it with his choice of music. It seemed like a Bartok day, a seemingly simple and systematic kind of day, but one with enough potential for the unexpected that you couldn't afford to completely relax into it.

The first pass over the whole area took almost two hours, but the ground was just right. He stopped to eat lunch and topped it off with another cupful of coffee. It still didn't seem like it wanted to rain again, so he decided to leave the site alone overnight, and give the ground more time to dry out now that it was roughly broken up. That way the next two more passes would go faster and easier.

He secured the plastic cover over the tractor, just in case. As he drove away, he could almost imagine Andy's smile when he got home and saw the work in the garden. It did look good, and he looked forward the seeing the man next day.

It was already after four o'clock when Peter drove up to the little spur road where he could stash the truck. The tire tracks wouldn't show and, besides, anyone working in the woods would be gone by that time of day. He changed into his high-top boots, grabbed a machete and shovel out of the back of the truck, locked the cab, and hiked off down the road a half-mile or so to the overgrown logging landing. He had enough daylight left down in the patch to either dig all the holes or move the fertilizer. He would've been happy to get either one done, but it probably made more sense to do some of each, use different muscles and spread the pain around. He was working out this compromise with himself as he uncovered the pile of damp bags of soil mix and manure. He'd carry down the first load, dig as much as he could, carry down another load and see where he was at by then. The silence of the place filled up his ears, but as they got used to it he could make out the soft sighing of a light wind moving through the treetops on the opposite ridge, the creek below winding through the bottom of the canyon, and the occasional rasping call of a raven. No way he would think of bringing that little tape player into the natural sounds and silence of this forested world.

He shouldered the bag, picked up his tools, and set off, carefully picking his way down the treacherous slope. Although he would try to use a different route each time and disturb it as little as possible, there were a few places where a person carrying a load had no choice. Often supporting himself with the shovel, and sliding as much as walking, he made it to the bottom by the creek where the brush was thick enough he had to cut his way through. It was a risk, but he was careful to cut only the minimum he needed. There was always the chance that no one else would pass that way for years but, on the other hand, cutting anything left evidence that would be there all summer. He skirted the upper edge of the salmonberry growth as long as he could, and then finally took the plunge down toward where he remembered that first flat to be. It was now impossible to walk upright, so the bag had to be half lifted and half slid along the ground. When he reached the place he'd picked out, he was drenched in sweat, his face was scratched, and his back felt like it might not ever straighten out again. As soon as he caught his breath, he bent over and shuffled his way toward the ravine and the small creek. He drank deeply, splashed cold water on his face, and reminded himself that no one was making him do any of this.

The digging was easy for some of the holes except for roots he had to chop away with the machete. For others the gravel made it difficult. At the rate it was going, he could do four to five holes an hour, with a half-hour trip for each bag of soil mix that would take care of three plants. That added up to getting halfway done with his planned work before dark. His mind turned the numbers over as his feet punched the shovel into the earth. When he worked this way, he couldn't get the computing part of his mind to shut down. His thoughts repeated themselves and went through the same data time and time again; number of holes, number of trips up and down the ridge, number of plants, ounces per plant, dollars per ounce, dollars per trip up and down, highs per hole, and all the time reminding himself not to count on anything until it was all done and in the bag.

He made another trip back down with a bag and then decided to grab another one right away. As he neared the area of the patch, he stumbled and his foot dislodged a small cascade of rocks that rattled and tumbled down into the brush near the edge of the creek. Instantly he heard a loud, sharp slap on water. If he hadn't known better, he might have thought it was a gunshot. He dropped the bag when he heard the sharp sound before he realized what it was. *Shit*, he thought, *beaver!* He hadn't checked the creek for signs. Now he crouched down and threaded his way through the tangle until he reached the bank of the larger creek. He was sure he was right about the sound, but there was no evidence of any of their work. A dam would have been washed out by this time of year and they didn't need one yet for making a pond to cover the entrance to their den in the bank. They'd build later, in the early summer when the water was too low to afford that protection. There was always a chance of beaver anywhere there was a good-sized creek, but as far as he knew they didn't hassle pot. Yeah, but just because he hadn't heard of it didn't make it a sure thing. He sat on a boulder for a while and rested. He couldn't stop now just because there was one more possible predator to add to the risk. Hopefully the patch was farther back from the creek than they usually went. He'd heard of a couple of growers who trapped as more of a sideline, but never just to protect their plants. As he climbed back up through the brush he was thinking that maybe there's always a risk to anything worth doing.

That night as he dragged himself into the one comfortable chair in his tiny trailer, he was almost too tired to eat and too hungry not to. Grilled tuna and cheese sandwiches would have to do. When he could get himself up to it. He imagined having a tub to soak in instead of a shower with barely enough room to turn around in. In moments like this, he could find a lot wrong with the way he was living, with no one here to take care of him, no jacuzzi, no this, and no that. He laughed at the thought that he still had his principles, and his privacy. Things could be much worse, so he got up and started grilling the sandwiches.

The election was still five months away when Bill Reynolds called a press conference to officially announce his candidacy for DA. Normally it would have been a rather routine affair without much media play, after all he a new face in this, but this time there was a lot more interest. He had leaked it to the press that there would be an additional statement regarding policy steps his office would soon be taking. Surrounded by lights and microphones, Reynolds looked every bit the distinguished public figure he wanted to be known as. He joked with a local TV reporter, lit a cigarette, puffed a couple times, stubbed it out and stepped into the spotlights.

"Distinguished representatives of our local government, members of the press and media, and citizens of Chinook County...While it may come as no surprise, I feel it is necessary to officially announce my candidacy, and to state some reasons why I want to continue serving you in the position of responsibility I have held for the past seven-and-a-half years. By seeking re-election to the office of district attorney, I am also pledging myself to continue working as hard as I can to deserve another term. My record is clear, and I think my dedication to promoting public safety and the protection of our citizens is apparent to everyone, on both sides of the law.

"However, today I feel it is also necessary to warn the public that we are facing economic hardships in this county that are affecting all areas of society, none more significantly than the arena of crime and law enforcement. My office has prepared a table of statistics comparing the three items I see as being most important and interrelated in our local area: the number and severity of crimes committed over the past five years, unemployment and business closure data, and public funding for law enforcement and prosecution.

"The reasons behind this study are many, but the main one, and I must emphasize this, is that there are those who would suggest we curtail law enforcement and its support at the very time we should be increasing, yes increasing, our efforts to protect the public and the property we all work so hard to earn and accumulate. The county commissioners must be shown that not only is there nowhere to cut spending in these areas of enforcement and prosecution, but that more is urgently needed and must come from somewhere. Criminals must be shown in no uncertain terms that this is no place for them to set up shop, that we are not soft on crime around here, and that we will not back down from the long-held values that drive our economy and our society."

There was a small round of handclapping from the audience.

"You know, sometimes I think the criminal element knows more about our government budgeting than some of the people who are responsible for it, and that's why our citizens must be made aware of this looming crisis in public safety. Everyone who gives a damn about their lives and property needs to understand that their support is vital now in these times. Not just to maintain the status quo. That status quo is not good enough. I wouldn't be saying any of this if I didn't know that we have no choice but to demand an end to this lopsided thinking by individuals who are more concerned for the criminal than for the victim of the crime.

"We admit to some inconvenience for the prisoners in some of our facilities. Some soft-hearted liberals refer to this as overcrowding and say it violates civil liberties. Whose liberties are they talking about? I'll tell you that when somebody breaks the law and causes pain and suffering or property loss to someone else, they're extremely fortunate that the law continues to care about them at all. As long as I hold this office and Sheriff Johnson and Police Chief Glendover continue to serve by my side, the temporary discomfort of criminals will never deter us from vigorously upholding our sworn duties to protect the people and punish offenders.

"The last point I wish to make today, and I appreciate your patience, concerns the national problem of drugs and drug law enforcement. Although this office and this campaign are technically non-partisan, I am proud to say that I, personally, am a member of the party of the president of these United States. He and his wife Nancy have raised the issues about what illegal drugs are costing this country in terms of human potential and wasted resources, raised it to the top of their agenda and the forefront of their concerns. I hope all decent Americans share their commitment to solving this crisis. I don't have time today to go into the details of declining performance in the schools and lost productivity in the workplace directly related to both chemical and garden-variety mind-destroying substances, but during this campaign those matters will not be ignored.

"Now, just as in other issues I have already mentioned, there are those who will play down the impacts of these drugs on both their users and on the public good, and there are even those who will say to us: just look around at the economic realities and potential benefits of the drug trade. But I don't want to hear that crap. If the voters continue to support me and my eradication program, they can be assured that we will not let up in our continuing fight against illegal drug production and trafficking in this county. Today, I am issuing a warning to those who grow and sell marijuana, and those who make or sell any other illegal substance within our county's borders. These criminals can consider themselves in a war and we on this side of the law will use every means at our disposal to eliminate this form of crime from our county, before it's too late and we face a situation like those that have already taken their toll on other communities. I repeat, we will work harder than ever before to smash this threat to public safety and decency.

"In conclusion, let me say this, I am proud to serve the people of this county. I have enjoyed the support and time that I have had as your public advocate and the opportunity to fulfill your trust in me. Over the next few months, I will be very busy with the functions and obligations of my office. If I don't seem to be campaigning as much or as hard as other candidates in the coming election, I can say, like our president, I already have a job to do, and it is not something that can be neglected or ignored. Therefore, at this time I would like to announce that my wife Madeline has consented to take on a role in this campaign, serving the public and the press when I am not available. Ladies and gentlemen, to those of you who don't already know her, let me introduce my wonderful wife and now media coordinator. Madeline, please come up here and join me."

Mrs. Reynolds took her place beside her husband, appearing nervous and a little out of place. As he leaned over and placed a kiss on her cheek, flashbulbs popped and she smiled brightly. The two of them lifted their held hands above their heads for more flashes and they stepped away from the microphone.

"Any questions allowed, Mr. Reynolds?" a reporter called out.

"All right, Phil. What is it?"

"Well, I would just like to ask, in light of the decreasing law enforcement budget, how you think you can afford to increase spending as you emphasized today?"

Reynolds lit a cigarette and addressed the question after a moment of thought. "Phil, when I mentioned drug law enforcement, I was talking about it as a national problem. In this case, there is going to be a certain amount of federal aid available. Let me add that this money is designated for this one purpose only and can't be used for any other aspects of our program and problems. Anyone else?"

"Cindy Chadwick, Channel Eight. I'm wondering how you feel about your opponent this time being a woman. Do you think that will have any significant effect on the election and its outcome?"

Reynolds glanced at his wife and then back at the reporter. "I think my wife would be the best one to answer your question. Madeline?"

"Oh dear, all right. First of all let me say I think it's a good thing to have more women running for public office. However, what's most important is how a candidate stands on the issues. My husband has made it clear, throughout his career and in his statements, how he stands on things. I think we'll just have to wait and see what Ms. Lehman has to say before we can say what her being a woman will have to do with this campaign."

A young man toward the back waved his arm and said, "Mrs. Reynolds, Terry Lindsay, from the college radio station. I'd like to know if you plan on any face-to-face debates in the campaign, and, if so, would you or your husband be most likely to debate Ms. Lehman?"

"I won't comment on that. I think we'll just have to see how things develop. Positions on the issues will decide whether there is any need for a debate to clarify anything by having a debate. I'm sure that if it's in the public's interest, we'll do whatever is necessary."

Bill Reynolds broke in at that point, saying "Perhaps Madeline and I would both debate Ms. Lehman and her husband. A bit of a tag-team match, so to speak. But really folks, I think this is enough for today. Be sure to pick the information sheets we've provided, if you haven't already. Thank you and have a good day."

He and Madeline quickly stepped out the door behind the small stage. "Great," he said, "you were great."

"Thanks. I was so scared. I don't know if I like doing this."

"Hey, relax, you'll get used to it. You'll even get to like it, you'll see." He held out her coat for her and turned that move into a tight hug. "You're going to do fine."

"Thank you, sir," she said and smiled. "Bill, I thought Sonya Lehman was divorced."

"She is. But now we've brought it up without having to mention it. Right?"

"I guess so."

"You'll learn these tricks, no worries. Now, we need to go meet Jensen."

They hurried through a light rain to a bar and restaurant around the corner from the courthouse. As their eyes adjusted to the dim light, they were hailed by a loud voice from the back of the booth section. It was Harry Jensen, one of Reynolds's biggest financial supporters.

"Come on, come, you're already way behind."

They made their way back to the booth, where a younger woman was seated. Jensen introduced her as his secretary, Anita. They all ordered drinks from a waiter who appeared almost immediately.

"So," Jensen said as he reached out to shake Reynolds' hand, "you're off and running. How's it feel?"

"Good, not much to it anymore."

"And you, Madeline, are you liking your newfound prominence?"

"Well, it's really too soon to say. Bill says I'll get to like it, but I'm not so sure."

The drinks arrived and Jensen immediately offered a toast: "To success and glory. And to a big landslide in the fall."

They all took varying sized sips of their drinks. Madeline was not at all used to drinking in the afternoon and was very careful. Jensen had slipped an arm behind Anita's shoulders. She didn't seem to mind and still hadn't said anything. He leaned forward, pretending secrecy.

"Well I guess you sure put the spotlight where they want it."

"I hope so."

"Now we just have to make sure those boys in Washington find out what a dedicated and effective crusader you are. Like they said to me, they want a couple of showcase counties where they can count on results for their money. I'm glad you had me check it out, because the timing was 'exacto' and very much appreciated."

"Thanks Harry, thanks for your connections. You went out of your way, I know it, and I won't forget."

"Bill, you and me go back far enough that I don't want you keeping track. You'll get your chance in the big game, don't worry."

Reynolds looked sideways at his wife, realizing she didn't know what they were talking about. "Madeline, there are going to be a lot of things in this business you don't have to bother with. At the same time, you need to know who our best friends and supporters are, and

Randall Jensen here is one of the best. He was able to get straight through to Washington to get us some help in this year's marijuana enforcement money distribution. We've promised to spotlight our eradication campaign in exchange for this added help, and that's the money making up the difference in my budget between a good solid performance we can be proud of, or halfway measures all the way down the line. So, if he ever asks for anything from us, we just have to hope we can come up with it as quickly as he came through for me."

"Wow," Jensen said, "I better come up with something quick. Seriously though, it goes both ways. Mrs. Reynolds, this man has served the public better than anyone I know, and we have some pretty high hopes for his future."

Madeline glanced at her husband to see how this mention of his future affected him, but he didn't seem to notice. He asked if she wanted anything to eat. She turned it down but urged him to order something for himself. He and Jensen both ordered the special, Cajun salmon. And another drink. Both women turned down anything else and excused themselves for a trip to the ladies' room.

As the men watched them walk away, Jensen asked "How do you like my new secretary?"

"Can she do office work too?"

"Now Bill, you know me well enough. I can't afford incompetence."

"I do know. That's why I only asked about office work." He smiled.

"You lawyers are all too subtle, you know that. By the way, speaking of subtle, the other thing my friend in Washington emphasized is that they're particularly interested in evidence that the growers are moving toward violence, violence that endangers the public, you know, booby traps, guards, dogs, guns, whatever. They know it exists, but they want examples. So, anything you can turn up will 'fatten the kitty,' so to speak."

"I'll bring it up to the sheriff. I'm sure we can find something out there."

"Good. So, by the way, how's your secretary, I mean, at office work?"

"Hey, very good. At office work. I don't know about anything else."

"Never can tell. All right, here's lunch."

The two women returned as the food was being arranged on the table. They were still acting as if they didn't know each other.

Dan Neiman, campaign manager, and Terry Lindsay, media coordinator, were sitting with Sonya in the living room of her small house, waiting for the news to come on. They knew what had gone down at the press conference because Terry had given them a full report from his notes. What they didn't know was how the local station was going to play the story.

Dan had already expressed his feeling that it was probably a better tactic to let the fallout from Reynolds' announcement of his campaign for reelection to settle before responding. Especially in light of the fact that nothing had been decided about the possibility of a lawsuit concerning conditions at the jail. Sonya had informed him that there was some hesitation at the regional level due to constraints on the State ACLU's budget. Also, on her own side of things, given that she was still waiting for Ron Olsen and his wife to decide if they were moving to Dixon City.

Terry, however, argued for getting her into the public eye as much and as often as possible. He reiterated by saying, "He's given us the opportunity. He's creating attention for us, for you. As a previously unknown candidate, you need to take advantage of every chance you get to gain media momentum and recognition. This is perfect."

"Let's wait and see how they handle it. In the meantime, I'll get us a snack of some kind. Coffee, beer, wine?"

Dan indicated coffee, and Terry passed. She stepped away to her kitchen.

"Listen Terry, I really respect your enthusiasm and I think you're going to be a really big help," Dan said. "But one thing I've had enough time to learn in this business: bad timing and over-exposure are just as great a liability as the underexposure you're referring to."

"Sure, sure, but when they hand it to you on a platter, it's kind of dumb not to grab it, don't you think?"

"Depends on what you've got to come back with. Right now, we really don't have that much. It's a smart move on his part, and a bit of a trap. If we react right now, all we can do is sound like we're the ones he's talking about who care more about the comfort of the criminals than in stopping crime. By the way, thanks for your really good notes. And as far as the marijuana issue, we've got to be especially careful not to get locked into any position we can't adjust as things develop over this coming summer. See what I mean?"

Sonya came back with two coffees and a plate of crackers, chips, and dip. "Are you two still agreeing to disagree?"

Terry laughed and answered, "That's one way of putting it. Hey, here it comes. Six o'clock." He knelt down in front of the TV and turned the sound higher. There would be the usual international, national, and statewide headline stories, and then the local news. The announcer did mention that day's courthouse press conference in her program preview.

Dan reacted to the presidential primary news with, "Wonder if any of the democratic candidates will come out here…That could help us out if we got a rally with Mondale's wife."

"Now you're talking." Terry's eyes lit up as his mind dealt with the multitude of details he'd have to contend with in a case like that. "You're sure it's going to be Mondale, are you?"

"He'll be hard to beat once it gets to the convention. Primaries favor dark horses sometimes, but they get washed out when it gets real."

Sonya tried to imagine herself standing on a platform with a presidential candidate. Her mother would've been so proud, except it probably would have upset her if it wasn't a Republican on the platform with her.

The story on Reynolds' press conference was the lead in the local news. The camera panned across the public meeting room and the reporters as the station's commentator introduced the event. Terry laughed and pointed himself out on the screen. The newscaster finished the introduction and cut to the DA making his announcement.

"I do seek reelection to this office and I pledge to continue working as hard as I can to deserve reelection. I believe my record is clear and I think my dedication to promoting your public safety and the protection of the law is apparent to everyone, be they be a good citizen or a career criminal. So, to everyone on both sides of the law, I'm in this for you and to win."

The newscaster went on, "DA Reynolds emphasized that economic hardships affect all of us at this time, that crime does increase in hard times, and that more funding is required just to maintain a level of adequate law enforcement and prosecution. He spoke out against those who show more concern for the rights of criminals than for the rights of the public, and he declared war on those who grow or sell marijuana or other drugs in Chinook County. Here he is again."

"...they can consider themselves in a war in which we on our side of the of the law will use every means at our disposal to eradicate this type of lawlessness from our county before it becomes too late and too widespread..."

The announcer spoke again, "The DA went on to introduce his wife, Madeline, as his campaign's Media Coordinator, and to answer questions from the press. And now turning to the weather..."

Terry reached out and turned down the volume, looking over at Sonya and Dan, "Well, they didn't use the crack about the tag-team match with you and your ex."

Dan smiled at that, and said, "No but that was smart of him. He brought it up without having to mention details. It'll come up again, but these days divorce is not such a stigma, not something to worry about—politically that is. But it did show us something about his techniques and boundaries or lack of. He's pretty shrewd, experienced, and knows what he's doing. Sonya, what do you think overall?"

"I'm really not sure yet. He's obviously trying to steal the thunder from us by bringing up the jail conditions, but it makes me wonder if people really do equate concern for prisoners' rights with being soft on crime."

"I think we need a poll," Terry put in, "right away. To see what the reaction to his statement is, and to find out what voters think about the issues he raised. I'm beginning to see your point Dan, about being careful in our responses. But I still think we need to respond sooner than later."

"You want to take a shot at putting together a set of questions by tomorrow afternoon? We were already planning something along these lines, but I agree that he opened some doors and we've got to get moving on our focus and our platform."

"Sure, I could give it a go, nothing final, but some questions. The most important thing I've found out is the way the question is put has a lot to do with the answers. We'll have to work together on sorting that out, but I'll take a whack at identifying the main issues."

Sonya stood up and walked over to turn on a couple of lamps, then turned and faced them with her hands on her hips. "What about the drug thing? Sounds like he's making it into his main issue."

Terry was writing while Dan was looking through some notes and didn't answer immediately. When he did, he looked up and said, "That's going to be a tough one. He obviously plans to maximize the publicity value of the issue. Each year their raids are getting more and more coverage in the press. It's hard to tell whether he's just using his identification with all that publicity or if he truly believes this is an issue that backs his stance with a clear majority. Ah, here it is." He'd found the paper he was looking for and began reading: "State-wide petition drive has already collected 24,000 or more voter signatures. Sponsors of the initiative are confident of placing the measure on the November ballot. That was a couple of weeks ago. I think they'll need about 70,000 good signatures to do it. You know about this marijuana legalization measure, don't you?"

Sonya nodded yes and sat back down. Terry answered. "That's a good way to bring up the issue on this poll we'll be taking. That way it's not our issue, but us looking for opinions on someone else's proposition."

"That's good," Dan said. "However, we'll still need to work on a strategy for dealing with this stuff if Reynolds is going to push it all through the campaign, and it sounds like that's what his plan is. He could be misjudging somewhat, not considering the economic impact of marijuana and the serious downturn in the timber business. A lot of people look the other way when it comes to their pocketbooks. But Reynolds obviously thinks he's got a handle on this issue."

"So, that takes us back to what should we be doing?" Sonya asked.

"Well, hard to say at this point. We need to either ignore it and try to keep it in the background by finding more important things, or confront him with a position of our own that is neither a carbon-copy of his nor an endorsement of law-breaking. Like I said, this is going to be a tough one. Sonya, can you tell us what you're thinking?"

"I'll be right back." Sonya gathered up the cups, and Terry finished off the snacks. When she came back, she spoke thoughtfully, saying, "I really don't even know where I'm at about this, and that just shows me I need to be very careful, because I can't just take a position on something if I don't believe in it myself. Personally, I haven't smoked myself since the early seventies, but I don't think it's all that harmful. I also think the amount of effort that goes into trying to wipe it out is probably wasted. Then there's all the effort that goes into growing it illegally. Maybe I kind of feel that if it were decriminalized and regulated it would be less attractive to grow and a lot of the trouble it causes would be eliminated. I guess you can tell, though, that I haven't thought this through."

After a pause, Terry spoke up, "It seems to me that it falls under the personal freedom issue that we've already talked about at our first campaign meeting. Most of the demonstrating and activism these days, except the anti-nuke stuff, is about that, whether it's abortion, gay rights, this new 'right-to-die' debate…smoking pot is just part of all that. It's about the right to eat, drink, or smoke whatever you want to if it doesn't harm anyone else. I mean look at cigarettes. They print the warning right on the label and then go ahead and let people smoke themselves to death."

"Terry, that might all make good sense to us, at least to me, but this is a race for the district attorney's job and we have to be really careful not to be seen as supporting anything that's still against the law. Maybe we could somehow imply that it won't be a priority for the DA's office if I'm elected, given that it's a so-called 'victimless crime' and it's taking up a lot of court time and effort and jail space. But I know we can't come right out and support it, since it's against the law, and I wouldn't want to go that far in any case."

Dan agreed, "We don't have to nail it down quite yet. Let's go ahead and put a question in your poll, and let's also see if we can get some kind of estimate of numbers of people growing it and how much business is generated supplying them with fertilizer and whatever else goes into it, everyone who gains from the proceeds in some way. I'm sure that's going to be difficult due to the secretive way it's done, but maybe the sheriff's department has some useful estimates. In the meantime, I like the prioritization solution you just mentioned. Marijuana does fall into the category of victimless in most of its aspects, and maybe we can suggest that until all crimes with victims, until that case load becomes manageable, marijuana shouldn't be a priority for law enforcement operating on a limited and shrinking budget. That sound okay for now?"

"I think it's our best way to go," Sonya said. "I'm comfortable with it. I'll talk to my new friend Corinne next time she's in the office. I know she has contacts from being involved in it. Maybe as the summer progresses, we'll find out more facts. Reynolds may even have to publish some estimates in his attempts to get more money. I think it's significant that he used the word 'war,' although I'm not sure how that fits into our potential position."

Dan gathered up his papers and stood up to go. "Listen, I've got to run, expected for dinner half hour ago, but this has been important. I'll call you in the morning once we've seen how it plays out in the newspaper. I think we're doing really well at this stage. We've forced him out in the open on the jail issue, and he's taking a hardline on something that may not be so clear-cut as he thinks it is. So, let's just keep moving ahead. Terry, call me when you've got some of the questions mapped out. Make it as brief as you can and still be worthwhile. These things all cost money. Have a good night."

"Can you drop me close to the campus? I want to get started on this right away."

"Sure, it's on my way."

Sonya followed them to the door. "I want to thank both of you. You're really helping to make this a good experience for me already, whatever the outcome."

"Don't think about outcomes now," Dan said, smiling. "Maybe think instead about the old story of the hare and the tortoise."

"Are you comparing me to a turtle?" she laughed.

He smiled and shook his head, "Not exactly."

After they left, she walked slowly back to her living room, sank down on the couch, and kicked off her shoes. She thought back to Reynolds joking about her being divorced. So, it would get brought up, be a part of the campaign. She'd have to ask Janet if she knew of anything her boss wouldn't want brought out into the open. Just for self-defense, of course.

She was hungry, but neither fixing anything nor going out interested her. There was some work she should get to before the next morning's meetings, but the thought of going over any more legal documents that night gave her a most negative feeling. Face it, she thought, you're busy but you're bored and bummed, and there's not much you can do about it. At this point she was glad she was tired and had an excuse to just take a bath and go to bed early. She could work a little in the morning if she woke up early. As she forced herself up off the couch, she had a silly thought, remembering the so-called "munchies" and thinking maybe all she needed was to get good and stoned. Not really, of course, just a thought brought on by the day's conversations. No, she was all grown up now and just had to face it. Face what? Her life, her very own life? Actually, if she thought about the hassles and uptightness she used to have to put up with, it really wasn't so bad now. It was just when she compared herself to other people who weren't alone tonight, probably even Mike…

She walked the few steps into the kitchen. On the way she managed a shaky pirouette, stopped and bent over to touch her toes and stretch. Was it getting older or just lack of use that made her muscles so stiff? She really knew she better deal with her body as she ran through some old barely remembered warm-up moves. Tomorrow is going to be such a full day. How did I ever get myself into this?

When Peter and his tractor arrived at Tom and Leslie's the next Saturday, the sun was just beginning to burn off the morning mist.

He thought it might prove to be one of the warmest days of the season so far. He unhooked the chains that held the tractor in place and was nearly ready to unload when Tom appeared, coming his way.

"Morning."

"Hey, Tom. Beautiful one, isn't it?"

"You think this is it? Finally, spring?"

"Could be, feels like it, unless we missed out and this is the beginning of summer."

"I kinda hope so. Damn it's been a long, rainy one. How's it coming for you?"

"Fine. Everything's running late this year, so I don't feel bad about being behind. Seems like the whole world's behind schedule."

"Yeah, it is, but there's still plenty of time." Tom helped him shove a couple of blocks under the rear of the trailer so it wouldn't tip as he backed off. He climbed up into the seat and turned it over. It started easily. He moved the lever to lift the tiller attachment and slowly backed down the ramps. Perfect. He shut it off and checked gas and oil levels.

Tom asked, "How many horse?"

"Sixteen."

"Sears, isn't it?"

"Yeah."

"Ever had trouble with it?"

"Not really. Sometimes I wish it was a little stronger, especially in wet ground, but it works great when conditions are right."

"Want to come up to the house for a cup of coffee?"

"No thanks. I've got a thermos full. And I want to get started while it's still cool."

"Yeah, it'll get hot. Hey, did you happen to hear what the DA said the other day?"

"Sort of. Just a blurb on the radio. Declared war on us or something." Peter stepped over to his truck, pulled out the thermos and threw his jacket inside. He poured a cupful and watched it steam, then offered it to Tom, who took a sip and handed it back.

"What was last year if this year's going to be a war?"

"No shit. You putting much in?"

"Not so much. Busier and busier with the business, and growing this stuff gets harder and harder every year. And then if they start using helicopters around here..." He paused. "I've heard rumors. Think they will?"

"Sure, they will. Maybe not this year, but the way Reagan's talking, this is the only thing besides defense that's getting an increase in budget. You hear the talk about them using spray down in Georgia and Florida?"

"Yeah, heard that, too." Tom said. "Guess we should consider ourselves lucky. You were in Vietnam. Been up in helicopters?"

"Yeah, a lot."

"What can you see up there, besides everything?"

Peter finished his cup of coffee and screwed the cup back on the thermos. "Yeah. You can see a lot, if you know where and what you're looking for. But it's a slow way to check out a lot of territory."

"Maybe they'll have some kind of photography, help them out, and then pick out areas they want to come back to."

"Probably." Peter was getting a little uncomfortable with the conversation.

"Well, I'll let you get to work." Tom waved and said, "Anyway, you seem to do all right. You always seem to. Good luck."

"Thanks. I hope so." Pete settled himself onto the tractor seat. "Same space as last year?"

"Yeah, maybe a little more at the top there if you get the rest all done."

"Should have time. I'll have to come back for some of it tomorrow anyway. We'll see."

Tom started away and then turned back. "Almost forgot. Leslie said to invite you for lunch with us. Kind of a picnic down by the creek. First one of the year. Her brother and sister-in-law are coming out. You've met them, just moving here from Denver?"

"I don't know. I brought lunch."

"Save it for tomorrow. We won't be here then. How can you pass up my very own deluxe barbeque chicken?"

"Guess I can't."

"Good." Tom turned and walked away as Peter started off on the tractor, letting it warm up for a minute, then turning into the large garden space. He knew for a fact that it was one of the biggest gardens in the area, and that Leslie was one of the best gardeners. She always had plenty left over to sell at the South Fork Store, and even some for the farmer's market in town.

The ground was good, still somewhat easy to till from the extra tilling he'd given it last fall when the garden was finished. By the time he'd finished the first row, birds were already pecking along behind him. The vapors from the dark soil rose into the air and hovered above the ground. He liked this part of the job best, the early part of the day when the mist gave mystery to the land. By the third pass around the perimeter, he could feel himself settling into the rhythm of the work. He had to look behind as much as ahead, and the constant twisting always got to him by the end of the day, but right now he felt good and relaxed by the familiar and satisfying way the clumps of soil rolled out behind him, raw earth giving the space an open feeling, a ready and waiting look.

As the long lines of broken dirt fell away behind him, his mind drifted away from the job and back to the conversation he'd had with Tom. He was a strange kind of guy in some ways, and seemed to have it made now, but there was a hint of restlessness about him. He'd moved out here maybe ten years before, with Leslie, when their first boy was still a baby. They started out renting a place near the store, Tom planting trees in the winter and growing a little pot to get by on. He'd brought some old tools with him, fixed them up, and then got started replacing broken handles on tree-planting tools. They moved out to this place as caretakers and must have had a couple of good crops because they were able to buy it and set up his wood-working shop in a garage building. Now he made handles for all kinds of tools, both custom and in production batches. Peter knew he had two employees on a seasonal basis and as much work as he could take care of by himself the rest of the year. When she wasn't taking care of kids and gardening, Leslie looked after the mail-order and accounting end of their business. Peter admired the way they seemed to fit in, both to the area and in using the opportunities that came their way. He smiled whenever he thought of their company motto, "We Can Handle It."

Tom was probably being straight with him when he said he might not have time for a pot crop this year. Why take the risk if you didn't have to, especially with a family? It was a little strange to watch the longtime growers branch out and then get beyond the need for a crop. Peter didn't exactly envy them, but it was nice to know it was possible. On the other hand, there were the folks he knew like Jerry, who five years ago had been a semi-redneck logger, graduated from the woods to mill work, and was now, with the timber business decline, out of work and finding himself needing to grow. Ironic how the heavier things got with this stuff, the more guys like Tom could afford to kick back from it, while Jerry and a lot of other guys like him were just getting started.

The mist completely burned off and the sun climbed higher into the sky. More birds found the fresh turned ground rolling out behind the tractor. When he finally stopped for more gas, their cries were the only sounds penetrating the silence of the morning. It felt good to climb down off the vibrating seat and stretch, reaching first for the ground and then for the sky. He pulled off his sweatshirt, stuffed it under the seat and shook his hands vigorously. The one drawback from this work was that the vibration of the steering wheel seemed to mess with his circulation after a while, and he had to take breaks to shake off the tingling feeling. He walked over to the pickup for the gas and some coffee, his feet sinking into the clods his machine had just turned over. He kicked a few for the fun of it.

He decided to keep on going without the tape-player to keep him company. When he started up again, his thoughts turned to the question of where exactly he fit in. Probably somewhere on the spectrum between Tom and Jerry. Funny coincidence, their names and the cartoons. Anyway, he wondered if he was truly in between them or was he a third kind of grower? Three years ago, he'd taken a few pounds and turned them into the tilling outfit, more for a cover than because he needed the income. Now at least there was something else he did that people could point to when they wondered how he supported himself. The garden work and the firewood hauling he did with his old truck couldn't account for the piece of land he'd almost paid off, and some of his other expenses, but if someone didn't look too close he could dummy up an accounting for most of his visible needs. And he sure wasn't one of the grow-and-go guys, the ones who vanished to the tropics as soon as they'd turned their crop into cash. They were like the birds, always leaving and then coming back for the growing season, and not worrying about how it looked or what kind of questions were created. Actually, if he really thought about it, there weren't any hard and fast categories. Each person had their own relationship, both to the land and to their own crops.

Once in a while, he had to stop and get down, raise the tiller unit and untangle a built-up bundle of roots, sod, and sticks that always accumulated no matter how many times a field or garden had been gone over. Wire was the worst and he was sometimes hung up for quite a while as he unwound it. When he was moving again, he went back to his line of thought and put it together with the only thing he knew about communism, thinking also that riding this tractor must be tripping him out if he was thinking like that. What was it they said? Your relationship to the means of production decides your place in society. But how did that fit this pot thing? Him, Tom, Jerry, and all the others? What's the means of production, the land, or the seed and shit mixed into the dirt? Did it make a difference if there wasn't any industrial production? If you plant on government land you don't even own where the production happens...What would old Marx say about the black market for selling the stuff? Maybe it was time for a new Marxism, "Stoned Marx." Probably it was the heat of the day starting to get to him and playing with his mind. It was definitely turning out to be the hottest day so far and sweat was beginning to run into his eyes and down his back. The salty lick of his lips was a foretaste of the season ahead, and he suddenly realized he was thirsty.

He was almost done with the first pass over the whole of the old space. Might as well let it dry a little before hitting it again and instead move on up to the new add-on space for a bit. He stopped at the bottom of the row and climbed over the low fence where he could get to the small tributary of the creek. It was cool down there under the shade of the trees, cool and damp, and he knelt and bent over to drink from the cold water. The sun, shining its dappled way through the new leaves above him, sparkled on the water as he dunked his forehead in and out several times. So refreshing. For that one moment he knew everything was perfect. But then any one moment can be perfect by itself. It was when you try to string those moments together that they interfere with each other.

When he got back to the garden, he saw a fairly new car in the driveway. People were walking up to the porch where Leslie was waiting for them. He recognized the brother and his wife but didn't know the other woman and the child with her. They didn't exactly look prepared for a day in the country, but maybe it was just because their clothes looked new. Tom hadn't mentioned anyone else coming out. He climbed back on the tractor and waited until the people disappeared inside. He could see the smoke rising from Tom's barbeque down by the larger creek. As he drove up toward the top of the clearing, a new thought jumped into his mind. Damn, he hoped this wasn't a Leslie plan to get him to meet some wonderful lonely woman who was just "perfect" for him. Well, so what? He could still make some kind of excuse and get away by himself and eat his own lunch in the shade and the quiet.

The new ground was rough enough that he had to get off frequently and toss rocks that came to the surface. He was also getting tangled more often and it was really getting warm. If it keeps up like this, he thought, I'll take a dip in the creek before I'm done, no matter how cold it is. Brrr. He was just climbing back in the seat when he saw Leslie coming across the fresh-tilled ground. He waited.

"Looks beautiful. Just the first time over this?"

"Yeah, gets better every year."

She came closer and leaned against the one old stump that hadn't been removed from the site. "Isn't it a great day?"

"Perfect."

"The boys said they're going in the creek. I told them it's still awfully cold, but they said they didn't mind. I think it's because there's a girl here for them to show off for. Makes them more daring."

"Yeah, of course."

"The woman is someone Ron's going to be working with, and the little girl is her friend's daughter. They wanted a day in the country, so Ron brought them along. We didn't even know they were coming."

"Hey, I brought my own lunch anyway."

"Don't be silly. Tom cooks so much there's always leftovers. There's plenty. Come on."

There was a short silence between them as he wiped his hands on a rag. They watched the boys running down to the woods by the creek. The others were walking behind them.

Leslie asked, "So how're you doing these days?"

"Me? Fine. Doing fine. Behind as usual, but if this weather holds, I might catch up. How about you?"

"Oh, you know. I'm doing all right. Things here are about the same. I think we're a little more comfortable every year. Sometimes that worries me." She smiled. "When I think of where we came from, I can't believe how little we knew about all this. Now Tom and the boys want one of those satellite dish things. I don't know. Everything's real fine the way we are."

"That's good." He didn't know if she wanted to go on or not.

She did go on. "Sometimes I wonder what I'm really doing here. I mean, it's good to have the business going so well. At least we don't have to go through all that paranoia every summer of whether we'll have anything to live on. And the kids are growing so fast. They're really doing well here, I think. But I wonder how they'll feel about this small of a school when they get a little older."

"Hard to say. They don't really know anything different."

"I know, and that bothers me sometimes too. They haven't had any exposure to all the things we went through, good and bad. I'm really split about it all."

Peter looked over at her carefully. He didn't remember her ever talking to him like this before, not in the years they'd known each other. "Feeling split for them or for yourself?"

"Oh, I guess both."

"Well, maybe you'll find something to get involved in that gives you more of a combination. Hey, I need to wash up if I'm going to meet company."

Leslie laughed. "Okay, and then you can help me carry things down there."

"By the way, what's your main crop going to be out here?"

"I think I'll concentrate on cabbage and winter squash. They keep so well it gives me a longer time to sell them. Come on."

At the porch she pointed him to a large sink. "I'll get things together in there."

He washed and went inside where she had a hamper and a cardboard box ready to go. He brushed his wet hair back with his fingers and moved to pick up the larger of the two loads. He noticed the curious look she was giving him.

"Do you have any women friends?" she asked. "I don't mean lovers, I mean friends."

"Um, not really, I guess. Not really."

"Well, you should," she said. "We're not so bad, as friends"

"Yeah," he smiled and picked up the box. "Is this everything?"

They went out the back door and into the hot sun, heading for the creek and the picnic area. The children sounded like they were having fun.

"Oh," she stopped. "there's something I forgot to tell you."

"What's that?"

"The woman that's here, with my brother. She's running for DA."

"What? For real?"

"Yeah, for real."

They started walking again, coming into view of the picnic area. Tom called out, "About time." Chickens were sizzling on the grill.

Leslie went to the table and set the hamper down. Peter followed more slowly. Theresa and the other woman were sitting at the table, and Ron and the boys were down by the fast-flowing creek. The girl, who looked to be between the two boys in age, was leaning against a tree watching them. Peter set down the box of utensils and plates and started over to the grill.

Leslie stopped him by saying, "Theresa, you remember Peter. He was at my birthday party."

"I do remember. Hi, Peter."

Leslie went on, "And this is Sonya, she works with Ron, or should I say he's going to be working with her."

He lightly shook her offered hand, suddenly conscious of the dirt under and around his fingernails. Her hand was so clean. That was the basic impression he got from her, so clean, but that was probably all just town. "Pleased to meet you," he said softly.

"Peter's tilling our garden for us. He does it every year."

"I was looking at it. Looks great."

Theresa asked, "Isn't it a little late to be starting a garden?"

"Not this year. It's been one of the rainiest springs on record. We start everything in the greenhouse anyway, and we don't move it outside until the weather changes. I'll show that to you later. You'll see. Most things are more than ready to go out, but we had to wait. It was still muddy until this week."

Tom called Peter over to the cooking. "Here could you watch this while I get some more sauce? Use this squirt gun to douse the flames from the grease."

Leslie called out to one of her boys, "Aaron, come and get a bowl and pick some sorrel for the salad." She and Sonya started cutting up vegetables for the salad and both boys ran up for the bowl.

Sonya spoke to the girl, saying, "Kristi, why don't you go with them and see what they're getting?"

"I can see from here."

Ron came back from creekside and sat down at the table "Well, how do you like it out here?" he asked.

"Oh, it's perfect," Sonya said. "Hard to believe people can still find a way to live like this. It's like somewhere you save up all year for, for your vacation."

Peter smiled to himself when she said that, thinking how far from a vacation it really was. True, you were always surrounded by nature's beauty, but everything else was plenty hard enough for the people he knew. He glanced over at the woman, whose back was to him as she cut celery at the table, and he found it hard to believe she was a politician, especially a candidate for DA, top cop in the county. Too much of a coincidence going on here. It was like she was his potential enemy or something and here she was, cutting salad like a member of the family.

"I know what you mean," Teresa said, wiping her eyes from cutting onions. "Compared to Denver, even Dixon seems like taking a break in a small town. And we're so lucky to have already found a place to live. So, Les, since it's not too late, if you have any of your plant starts left over, I'd like to get something in this year. The last people who lived there had a small garden and it looks like it's in pretty good shape."

"Sure, I've got more than I can use of most things."

Tom was back to take over flipping the chicken, and mumbled to Peter, "Leslie tell you who our honored guest is?"

"Yeah," Peter mumbled back. "This some kind of a trap?"

"No man, just the New Age. Hey, can you get a platter before this burns?"

Peter got the plate just as the boys came running back with a bowl full of fresh clover-like plants picked from the woods. "Hi guys," he said. They both said hi, set the bowl down and started off again. Their mom stopped them and said to sit down and get ready to eat.

Ron asked, "Who wants a beer?" and got yes from Tom, Peter and Leslie. Sonya and Teresa said they'd pass. Ron went to the creek to fish out the chilled bottles.

Tom held his bottle up in the air and said, "To the first bar-b-que of the year and may there be many more."

Leslie started making up dishes of chicken and salads, and poured out glasses of fruit juice for those without beer. They all fit at the table and for a moment there was silence as they got busy eating.

Then Tom tried to start a conversation with Sonya and Ron about their work, but neither had much to say.

Sonya said, "Out here it's so easy to forget about all that, at least for a little while."

Peter was seated across from the young girl and wondered what her story was. She seemed quiet, but not at all shy, more just being polite. He looked over at Sonya and was surprised to catch her eye. Now he was the one who felt shy. She had a very direct look in her deep brown eyes. She probably practiced it for looking at judges and juries. He told himself he wasn't going to dislike her just because she was almost the same as a cop, but he was going to have some words with Tom when this was over for getting him this close to someone like her.

The chicken was very good and everyone complimented Tom. The boys raced through their food and took off again after making sure someone would call them back for the pie. This time the girl ran after them. As the rest of them finished eating, Teresa and Leslie talked gardening, and Ron and Tom debated the relative merits of the Seattle and Denver football teams. Sonya seemed content to stare down toward the creek. The sounds of birds filled the spaces in the music of the rushing water. It truly was a perfect place for her to unburden herself from all the past week's tensions and uncertainty. She was already hoping to come back if she could get invited again.

Peter finished his beer and Ron pointed toward the creek where there were more, but Peter thanked him and said, "No, I've got to get back on that tractor, and keep all those rows going straight."

"Take it easy. Relax," Tom said. "You can't finish it all today, and what's left won't take all day tomorrow."

"Yeah, but I've got other stuff to get to, if it stays dry." He wondered what Ms. DA would think about his other stuff.

"Well, if you're in such a hurry, guess I better serve the pie," Leslie said and called out, "Aaron! Timmy! Run to the house and get the ice cream."

They took off at the words, "ice cream" and Kristi came back to the table and flopped down next to Sonya. "I love it here," she said.

"Me too." Sonya said. "Maybe someday we can bring your mom out here. At least to drive around." She turned to Leslie and said, "Kristi's Mom works on the campaign committee. She also works in the DA's office."

Ron commented, "Which side is she spying for?"

"Shhh. Ours of course."

The boys came back with the ice cream, and Leslie dished out large servings of cherry pie a la mode.

"Did you can the cherries?" Teresa asked.

"Yes, and it's almost cherry season again so I thought I better use them up. As a matter of fact, why don't you both take some with you? I don't know why we have so many left over."

Tom laughed, "I do. It's because we hardly got any cherry pie all winter."

"I guess that's because you didn't make any," she said and smiled at him.

"I guess so. Now I see what I was missing."

There were ohhs and ahhs and everyone agreed how good it was. Leslie brought out a thermos of coffee and poured cups.

Tom took another scoop of ice cream, stirred it into his coffee, and looked over at Sonya. Then he asked, "So, how did you end up running for DA?"

Sonya set her own cup down, stirring idly and smiled. "I should really have a good answer for that one. I've known it's going to keep coming up, but I don't know exactly why. I've been on the fringe of politics since college, demonstrations against the war near the end of it, this ACLU work, helping to gather signatures for this or that. Since I grew up near here, I knew a lot of the people in the democratic party. Mostly other lawyers and public officials. I think somebody just put my name down, and since it's such a long shot, they couldn't get anyone else. I don't know what I was thinking when I said yes. We're not supposed to be able to win, so…"

"How do you feel about it now that it's happening?" Leslie asked.

"Funny, but I'm starting to get into it more. It was hard to accept at first. I think if I was really serious about a public office I wouldn't have done this one, but now I see so much that could be changed and needs to be changed. And the people who are working on the campaign so far are really nice."

"Good reasons. I wish you luck. We wouldn't mind a little change out here ourselves." Tom glanced at Peter who looked away. Leslie got up and started gathering things to be carried back to the house. Peter got up and stretched a little. He asked if he was needed to carry things back up, but Leslie said no.

"Guess I better get back at it then."

Sonya asked, "Could we come with you and see what you're doing?"

Kristi looked up at him expectantly, so he said yes, and the three of them started off to the garden. The heat of the sun hit them as they stepped out from the shade of the trees. They were silent as they walked across the grass between the creek and the tilled-up ground. As they approached, a flock of crows lifted from the fresh-turned soil. There must have been at least thirty of them and they flapped away to the nearest trees, complaining loudly at being disturbed in the banquet he'd provided for them.

Kristi asked, "Do all those birds live here?"

"Pretty close to here, I'd say." He held the gate open for them and they picked their way across the clods and clumps of dirt until they got to the tractor.

"Is this your tractor?"

"Yep, it is."

"And does this have to be done every year? For a garden?"

"Around here it does. The rain packs the ground some and there's a lot of sod that grows back in between gardening seasons. Also, it sets the weeds back some to have their roots chopped up, turned over and dried out. That's why you want to do it as late as possible, but still early enough to get the garden off to a good start. It's really late this year, though."

"Does that mean certain things won't have time to grow?"

He checked the oil stick, which was okay. "Depends how much more rain we get, how many more cloudy days. It's late for corn and tomatoes, but most folks start their tomatoes in the greenhouse. They'll make it if we don't get an early freeze."

"There's a lot to learn out here," she said. "How long have you been living like this?"

Too many questions, he thought. He looked at her for a moment, and decided she was more than likely just curious "Seven, eight years, around here."

Several of the crows gave up waiting for them to leave and flew off toward some other project. Kristi was looking at the sun with one eye through a piece of blue glass she'd found.

"Oh my," Sonya said, "I guess we're holding you up. Any chance you could give Kristi a ride before we go?"

"I could do that." He climbed on and started the tractor. "Here, Kristi, you have to fit in here." He sat up on the back of the seat so she could sit between him and the steering wheel. He put it in gear and they moved away, slowly.

Kristi turned her head and gave him a big smile. "This is fun."

"Maybe if you don't have to do it all day."

"I wouldn't mind. Can I steer now?"

"Hold on and keep it going straight." He let her work the wheel and it jumped around in her hands as they bumped over the rough ground.

"This is hard," she said.

They made a wide circle around the garden space with him helping her a little, and then he took over the steering and headed back to where Sonya was waiting. "Now me," she laughed.

"You'll have to take it yourself. No room for both of us."

"No, that's okay. Some other time, maybe." She helped Kristi to the ground. "Nice meeting you. Have a good summer."

"Yeah, you too. Good luck on your election."

"Thanks. I'll need it." She reached out her hand as she said, "Goodbye. Did you say thanks, Kristi?"

Peter looked at her outstretched hand, took it, and shook lightly. No ring on the other hand.

Kristi waved and said, "Thank you."

They turned and started off toward the gate. He put the rig in gear and dug in. Back to work. By the time he came around again, they were almost to the house. They both turned and waved. He waved back and kept tilling. Pretty woman, he thought, too bad she's a kind of a cop.

Detective Stockton hurried into Sheriff Johnson's office. He still couldn't believe this news about the add-on funding for the grant and the media coverage coming the same day. Now they would really have to produce results. Johnson wasn't in so he sat to wait, impatient to find out more than he'd been told on the phone. The sheriff came in and closed the door behind him.

"Morning. How's it going?"

"Fine. What going on? Tell me more."

Johnson sat down and leaned back in his swivel chair, hands behind his head and feet on the corner of the desk. He enjoyed keeping his subordinate in suspense. Stockton was always a little too gung-ho. "Well, it looks like we got what we wanted this year, plus some."

"That's what you said on the phone. But how?"

"Reynolds. He must've pulled a string somewhere. But it's not without some payback. We've got some hotshot California reporter going to be doing a season-long series, covering the 'Pot War' on the West Coast, and we're one of the counties he's going to spotlight."

"That's great. When do we start?"

"What's so great about it? Just going to increase our reputation as a good place to grow the stuff. If we make a mistake or blow it somehow, the whole damn country will hear about it. Maybe you want to be a star, get your face in the news, but I'll tell you what I think. I think it's more hassle than we need, and I'd just as soon…Hell, I don't know, I don't know what."

"What about the funding? How much more?"

"That's not set yet. Matter of fact, as long as we're getting results, we can keep getting more bucks."

"Great."

"Yeah, I know, everything's great for you. The key word here, is 'results' and that might mean different things to different people. To Reynolds it means convictions and you know how much work that is. To the feds it means statistics, numbers, violence. They want violence, or at least the potential for violence. They have to justify their budget too, and their big thing this year is that the growers have become a threat to the general public. Right? Nobody, no fisherman or hunter is safe out in the woods anymore. Backpacker raped and murdered, so on and so forth. For you, sure, it means advancement, a reputation to build up, maybe a promotion to the big time, DEA Special Agent, Tony

Stockton, terror of the international drug trade. But for me, it's just one more can of worms that's going to drag this department through the shit for the next six months, at least."

Neither one of them spoke for a moment as they both sorted through their thoughts, realizing just how deep the differences between them were. Finally, Johnson lowered his feet from the desk and handed a folder of papers to Stockton.

"What's this?"

"The grant rewrite, from their side. And here's the advance stuff from 'our' journalist. Hell, he's not just a reporter, but a journalist, for Christ sakes. He'll be here next week to gather background, with a photographer."

"Hey Marty, this isn't so bad for us, you know. And don't think I'm only in this for my own benefit. I want this department to be good. I want these growers out of the county, and I want you to get credit for the job you're doing, no matter how much you don't like it."

"Who says I don't like it. Hell, I've wanted to be a sheriff since I was a kid playing cowboys and outlaws. I've always wanted to be a sheriff, didn't you?"

"I don't know what to think about you, Marty. I'm not after your job if that's what you're thinking. So, what's this all about, for you?"

"Sorry, Tony. Sorry to take it out on you and you're right as far as you go. Maybe I'm just not cut out for the stress of all this high-pressure outside interference in what used to be a pretty simple job. Now, I've got overcrowding in the jail, budget hearings with the commissioners, and now the DEA and the media, not to mention all the decent law-abiding citizens who are getting ripped off, mugged, and losing out to frauds, and we can't deal with it all, because we don't have enough money to do our job except if we're out chasing around after invisible dopeheads and capturing fugitive plants."

"Hey, Marty, I hear you. When was your last vacation?"

"I don't need a goddam vacation. Now get out of here and go read all that stuff. Come back in here as soon as you can with an adjusted budget and an itinerary for those newspaper tourists. You're going to end up busting your butt this year and I know you'll love it. Go on now, and I promise when you get back in here, I'll be fine, and we'll forget all this crackpot moaning and groaning I've put you through. I don't mean even half of it. I really don't."

"I know you don't. See you in the morning. Take me at least all day for this."

When Stockton had closed the door, Marty sat quietly for a while, cradling his head in his hands. When he looked up, he was smiling. He got up and walked over to one of the pictures of himself and the kids on the baseball team he coached. He hunched over in a batting stance and took a couple of swings in the air. He was glad the season was only half-over and the league was getting exciting. He knew he needed those kids and the game itself to compensate his blood pressure for this job.

Terry was trying hard to downplay the excitement he felt from the way the telephone poll was going. Here he was, already a couple of years ahead of his most optimistic life plan, running the campaign polling for a real candidate, and really getting into it. More than once in the past couple of weeks, school came close to getting lost in the hustle. Fortunately, his finals were all oral exams and classroom essays, the formats most suited to his brand of spontaneous verbal skills. He was afraid he would have flunked out if he had to do any real studying or in-depth research papers. Anyway, the term was up, and he could afford to devote himself to his dual functions as radio reporter and campaign media coordinator. The main problem would come in maintaining a semblance of objectivity in his role with the campus radio station, but he couldn't see that being much of an issue. He doubted it would matter much to anyone at the campus radio level. He did plan to check out the boundaries with the station's staff, because he for sure didn't want to lose his press pass and its privileges.

Corinne and Florence had helped him compile a list of 1,000 names for the survey and now they were out coordinating a crew of volunteers for the actual calling process which would take a couple of days. Some were working out of their own homes and a few others were using the campaign office lines in the evening. Terry was busy totaling, computing, projecting and evaluating. So far, as he had already informed Sonya, it was looking better than they ever would have expected.

Corinne came into the room where his personal clutter was all stuffed into one desk and a couple of boxes. He was just clipping out an article from the day's paper concerning a request from the State Prosecuting Attorneys Association for a reorganization in the way counties ranked and paid their trial lawyers and deputy prosecutors. He shoved the paper out of his way and reached for the note cards she was bringing to him.

"How're we doing?"

"Well, we're more than half done one time through the list. These are the results from the western part of the county. Those folks say they should have all of theirs done by next Monday if it keeps going like it has been. One thing that came up is they want to know how many times we keep trying a number if we don't make contact, and how do we keep track of those that don't answer?"

"Three times is enough. Especially if it's done at different times of the day so we're sure it's not their work schedule or something. Just make a check off on the master list, by geographical sectors, and we'll decide later if we have enough first-time responders to use when we go around again in a month or so, or whether we'll have to add new numbers. What's the percentage anyway?"

"Maybe twenty per cent don't answer by the second call."

"That's good, not bad at all. Just have them try one more time on all those."

She started to leave and then commented, "It's kind of fun, but you know people ask us a lot of questions after we're done with ours. I mean some people, not everyone. Like, how do they get something taken care of by the county, like a legal question, or whatever. I think most people assume we're calling for the government."

"I wonder if they're more careful how they answer if they think that. But it's probably better than if they think we represent any particular group or individual."

"I guess so, but none of us know how to answer most of the questions we get."

"Good point." He reached down, grabbed a phonebook from the floor and flipped through it until he found the county listings. "Here, give everybody a copy of the main numbers for the county and state tollfree lines and they can just refer people."

"Okay. I'll see you, have to pick up my little one now."

"Sure." He was already transferring the new results to the combined totals. The one question he liked best was "name familiarity," where the caller was given four names and asked which of those names was either a public official or a candidate for office. Reynolds was obviously ahead with a 40% recognition factor, Sonya was at around 15%, which was okay for the stage they were at, but one of the names he'd made up for the survey was also at 15%. That didn't bother him, though, because the question was really for comparison to results in later surveys to see how much difference their campaigning made, once they started using the media. He went back up to the top of the list and began making the tallies.

REYNOLDS' JOB PERFORMANCE?
63% Approve, 20% Disapprove, 17% No comment
DOES DA OFFICE NEED MORE MONEY?
25% Yes, 68% No, 7% Don't know
ARE YOU AWARE OF PROBLEMS IN LAW ENFORCEMENT AGENCIES?
81% Yes, 15% No, 4% Don't know
TREATMENT OF CRIMINALS?
48% Too good, 20% Not good, 32% Don't know
TREATMENT OF VICTIMS?
31% Adequate, 58% Inadequate, 11% Don't know
SHOULD SCARCE FUNDING BE SPENT ON CRIMES WITHOUT VICTIMS?
57% No, 38% Yes, 5% Don't know
HOW DO YOU FEEL ABOUT INITIATIVE TO LEGALIZE MARIJUANA FOR PERSONAL USE?
Never 53% Approve 20%, Maybe 27%
DO YOU VOTE FOR ISSUES, PARTY, OR CANDIDATES?
44% Issues, 32% Party, 24% Candidate

When he finished adding in all the new results there wasn't a whole lot of change in the cumulative data, although he could now begin to see that the final analysis should be broken down by urban and rural sectors for effective campaigning. At this point there didn't seem to be anything insurmountable for Sonya. A lot of the data was pointing toward her side of the issues.

He purposely left out any mention of national issues or candidates to keep from confusing the respondents or his own opinion-recorders. That didn't mean he didn't know a Reagan landslide could affect the entire ballot. He already knew this campaign needed to focus on local issues and hope that Sonya could be portrayed as both competent and human. Perhaps the best indication of the possibility of strengthening her positions was the disparity between Reynolds's job approval and the public's rejection of his assertion that he needed greater funding to do his job. Terry could hear Sonya now, proclaiming that everyone she knew needed to live within their means and tighten their belts these days, why should the DA's office be any exception? He agreed with Dan that now they had time to clarify their positions before rushing out in front of the media or the public. He was catching on, he thought, and now he would have something for them to learn from when he explained the results of the poll.

Peter was feeling like he could finally enjoy the irony of the weather and his disrupted planting schedule. First, he'd needed to wait all spring because of the rain. Then when it did finally dry out, he had to wait for a damp gray spell to do the final transplanting into the patches. These last plants were the largest he'd ever moved and replanted, averaging two feet tall with multiple side-branches already well established. Definitely late this year, but the rest had all survived during the past couple of weeks, so he had high hopes these would withstand the shock. He carefully removed each plant from the cold frame and pot, shook some of the loose dirt from the roots and dipped the whole mass of the root-wad into a solution of water and an organic product called Root-Food. Some guys were using one of the 'B' vitamins dissolved in water as well, but he didn't think it was needed.

Once the roots were soaked, he wrapped them in wet burlap and laid each plant down next to the others on a sheet of black plastic that he could bundle and carry. He'd saved the boxes from a new stovepipe which were the right height to handle about a dozen plants a piece. He could then strap the boxes onto a pack-frame for hauling down the clear cuts to the locations below. This was the last batch of the year and it felt so good to have this stage done. Almost, that is. Now it would be up to the weather, the predators and fate or whatever there was to believe in.

He had three bales of straw in the pickup for use as mulch in his own garden. He arranged them so the narrow boxes holding the plants were completely concealed between the front of the bed and the bales. It was almost four o'clock, and he took a break to go inside and make a pot of coffee for his thermos. Be safe to head up any time now, nobody working up there this late. Except for maybe some other grower. He stuck a trowel in his back pocket, grabbed the backpack frame from its hook, and went out. As he started up the pickup, he thought he'd better get some gas on the way and maybe grab milk and eggs as well. It would probably be too late when he came back.

He let the kid fill up the truck, parked over out of the way, and checked his hiding job in the bed. He was almost done shopping when he heard his name called from the end of the aisle. It was Leslie. She looked dressed up from the way he was used to seeing her at their place. He thought she must be either coming from or going to town.

"How are you?" she asked. "You did a really great job on the garden. When we got home that Sunday, we were both really impressed. Did Tom pay you?"

"Yeah, he sent a check. Thanks. Where you going dressed so nice?"

"Not going. I'm coming back from town. This really neat thing happened. You met Sonya. Well, they were doing this phone survey for her campaign and they wanted someone from out in this part of the county. So, I volunteered. They said I could do some of it from home. Mostly I was calling up strangers and asking them questions about law enforcement, and all that stuff. Anyway, there was a meeting today after I turned it my results. Corinne from over on Bobcat Creek was there. She's actually living in town now and working at the campaign office. At this meeting, they asked me if I wanted to work part-time for them. Of course, I said yes, even though I didn't tell Tom yet. It's going to be exciting for me, and I think it's just the kind of thing I needed. Something fun to do and no long-term commitment. I probably won't get paid very much, we didn't talk about that, but enough for my driving expenses and whatever. But it gets me out like I said I wanted, remember, when we were talking? So, what do you think about that?"

"Wow, uh, which part? No, really it sounds good for you. Maybe you can find out some stuff," he lowered his voice and looked around, "like how things work downtown."

"Maybe, and then if Sonya does win, there could be something more part-time if I wanted it. Either with her or with Ron if he takes over her job."

"You really think she can win?"

"Nobody seems to think so, but the pollster guy, a young person from the college radio station, said a lot can happen between now and November."

"No kidding. A whole season to get through." He smiled.

She reached out and gave his arm a squeeze. "Listen, I have to go, still have to make dinner for Tom and the boys. Maybe we'll have you over again soon. We'll probably be having barbeque every weekend when the weather's nice. Maybe even something for the campaign. I'm really into it now. P.S. Sonya said she thought you were nice, and to tell you she's definitely not a cop. Isn't she nice?"

"Yeah, I guess, for a cop." He laughed at Leslie's expression. "Hey, do you know where the Worcestershire sauce is?"

"Yeah, right over there. See you soon."

She pushed her cart to the checkout, and he looked out the window to check on his truck. It looked okay.

A light drizzle began as he started climbing uphill on the main logging road to the patch he was headed for, perfect weather for what he was doing. He hoped it would stay cool for another couple of days. And then he'd be ready for the heat. Solar heat that is, he thought.

He turned off the road onto another, less travelled one, only a few miles from his final turn-off. It was definitely a lot longer going by way of the store, but it was good to see Leslie and hear about this new thing she was into. The road looked more heavily travelled than it had the week before. He felt himself keying up, more alert, even though he doubted anyone would be up there now unless they were doing what he was. But you never know, and you never know how you're going to react until you hit the real situation. That was the lesson of combat: you train and drill and deal with all of your possible expectations, and then the real thing comes along and you've got no time to think, just react and hope everything you learned and drilled will work in the real situation. Now he was noticing that somebody had been on the road with some pretty heavy equipment. The tracks were fresh and wider than those from the regular logging trucks.

He rounded a corner and suddenly there it was, a whole operation on the move. It was a road-building outfit, a giant cat, grader, two gravel trucks and a trailer for hauling the cat. It was all strung-out along the shoulder of the road and he could see downslope where trees had been cut and the road was being punched through to the spine of the connecting ridge. He stopped and looked it over. The was nobody around that he could see, all gone for the day most likely, not even a guard or anything. He could see where the blue strips of marker tape was fluttering from tree branches, lining out the path of the project. Close, but not really close enough to threaten him unless any of the loggers got to exploring around the area, and that was unlikely any time before fall hunting season. Hopefully. He knew this was paranoia combined with caution, but he did have a kind of territorial feeling about anywhere near where his stuff would be growing. Plus, this would make his coming and going much harder. Nighttime might be the only time it would be safe to be up here, and even then, they could have a night watchman for all this equipment. Better if he could find the way in from the other side of all this. Shit, it was always something: loggers, hunters or dee…But once you start it, doesn't do any good to have too many second thoughts. You either keep going or quit. No halfway.

He started up again, tires sloshing through the torn-up roadway. At least it would hide his tracks. And he was going to have to get a bike for sure, a small 125 cc dirt bike or something like that. He'd known that day would come, but it was another case of putting off anything that doesn't scream "Now!" loudly enough.

He got to his spur road, turned off, checked for any tracks, and was glad there weren't any. If he got out before it rained any harder, his wouldn't be there in the morning either. He wheeled around and backed as far off the road as possible. Then got out, stretched, and poured a cup of coffee. Fortunately, all these plants had fit into two boxes easy enough, so there would only be one trip down the side of the ridge. He yanked the pack-frame out from under the groceries, drained the coffee from the cup and locked the cab, then started down toward the three-year-old clear cut. The drizzle was coming faster, but still wasn't enough to get him or the ground very wet.

The pack was light but bulky. He hitched it higher on his back, readjusted the buckles, and went out onto the road, walking where the gravel was thickest. There were already a few puddles forming along the edges, and then he saw a single large hoof print in the mud, stopped and looked for others. Somehow the deer must have jumped across the road only touching down with the one foot. It was big track, maybe one of the biggest he'd ever seen. Just one more thing to add to the list, he thought. Deer don't usually eat the pot, probably because it grew at the same time as there was plenty of other things to munch on, that and they weren't used to it. Pity the poor growers once some mama deer got hip to how good the soft green leaves of her neighborhood weed plants were and taught her twin girl fawns to eat it with her, and then they had their babies, and so forth and so on.

He reached the old landing where the clear-cut fell away into the mist below. The rain continued falling softly, and he slipped a few times as he traversed the steepest part of the climb down. This was not the time to take a fall. He could see the smashed cardboard boxes now, or the tumbling pack disappearing end over end into the brush below. Using huckleberry bushes for handholds, he carefully lowered himself over an abrupt edge and from there on found the going easier as he angled across the slope. Thoughts of the road-building operation flitted in and out of his mind, but he dismissed them with his standard "once you start you don't turn back" logic. He was almost into the thick brush of the bottom alongside the creek when he heard the loud slap of a beaver tail on the water below.

The last twenty yards had him on his hands and knees, pushing the pack ahead of him through the tangled stems of salmonberries. The bushes had their new year's crop of stickers out in force, and he hated to think what his hands would feel like without the gloves. Small showers of rain fell off him as he jostled through the bushes, and every few feet a cold shock would quiver through his back as a particularly well-aimed drop found the bare skin between his hair and his collar. This was the kind of work you love to hate.

He reached his first set of holes and was finally able to stand upright and unkink some of his body parts. He stretched his arms toward the thick, gray sky hovering just above him. He couldn't see the ridgetops at all and what trees he could see on the opposite slope seemed to fade in and out of reality as the drizzle and mist swirled through them. Something he'd read once was that when this mist moved through the branches on this type of conifer, even if it wasn't raining, the tree's needles acted like a comb and collected moisture which would build up, form droplets and drip to the ground beneath the tree. They said this could produce up to twenty inches of additional rainfall.

He pulled a half-smoked joint from the dryness of his shirt pocket, lit it with the second match, and offered smoke to the four directions, mentally requesting protection and good luck. It couldn't hurt, he told himself, and anyway he always blessed the plants when he put them in the ground in a gambling mood of assurance that it might help and seeking this insurance if it does. He tucked the remnant roach under a rock and untied the boxes from the frame. He opened one, carefully unwrapped the plants and chose one to get started with.

Using the trowel, he dug a narrow deep hole in the waiting soil mix of the prepared spot. Unwrapping the burlap from the root ball, he shook it out and eased the roots into the hole, gently pushing at them with the trowel handle until they hung straight down, then nudging the soil in around them, and packing it tightly enough to make sure the plant was stable and would stand erect in wet soil. Every time he did this trans-planting he found himself starting out wearing gloves, and every time he ended up taking them off. They always got in the way and there was no choice but to pull them off and trash his fingers and nails in the cold ground.

By the third hole he was into the rhythm, a kind of controlled frenzy halfway between a dog digging a hole with both front legs and a child playing in a sandbox. There was a hypnotic quality to the process: dig, dig, plant, rest, move, dig, dig, plant, and rest again. His mind seemed suspended above him, watching. His thoughts were random and repetitive. Playing music was the only thing that compared with this, how he could get lost in it while still being conscious of what he was doing, as if he were observing or listening to himself.

He finished the last hole of that group, gathered the pieces of burlap, pack frame and boxes, and struggled through the brush to the next little cleared spot. The plants in his other two patches were protected by small chicken wire fences, guarding against rabbits and boomer chucks. Here, in this one, he was counting on the size of the plants and the lateness of the planting to get him by. It was one more gamble, but the chances were better now that there was plenty of other stuff to eat…Leave it to beaver, he thought.

The second batch went into rockier soil a little higher up the slope. His hands were truly cold and he knew the hard rough edges of small rocks were doing more damage than he could feel through the numbness. It was like when you walk barefooted on rocks in an icy creek and you don't know your feel are hurt until they warm up. As he planted, he kept thinking about how each of these plants was now on its own in terms of luck or karma or whatever you call it. Like what he was feeling, maybe it was like when your kid grows up enough to leave with so much of their life left to live, so many chances and risks to take, their parents relieved at having gotten them that far, but freaked out now that the child has passed on out of their realm of responsibility. He'd never had a child so how would he know? But then maybe he knew something because he'd been someone's child. Knowing a little of what his own mother felt when he left home and said goodbye quickly before she could break down, as if it was going to be forever, and really it was a kind of forever, because from then on she was his mother in name, but no longer in being there.

Planting the last of the second group was a relief. Only one more set to go, just down the rocky ravine and up again, one more batch and this year's kids were on their own, and all he could do now was bring them water and pray. Suddenly he was wondering how Jerry's small crop was doing. Probably through the transplant stage and must be taking off by now. Hadn't seen him since he dropped by to pick up the plants. Busy time of year for everyone. Be glad to be done with this part, only four more holes to go. The daylight was beginning its slow withdrawal from the world. It would be dark by the time he was out of there. Meanwhile the drizzle had turned to rain. If he were looking for good omen, it was a good one, just what these plants needed to withstand the shock of the move. There were six plants left for four holes, so he paired the runts each with one of the bushier ones, hoping that would result in a male and a female in those holes. Some guys planted two in every hole for that statistical reason, or had their plants completely sexed beforehand by using light deprivation techniques. Peter preferred to plant closer together, let the males come on through and then cull them. This would give a little more random pattern when just females were planted and remained.

As he reached for the last plant, he heard the low, hoarse cry of a raven from somewhere close above. Ravens are good, he thought, long life, live in isolated pairs, can see far, and just good medicine to have around. "O great Raven," he said aloud, "fly over my patch and add your magic shit to my plants. We need all the help we can get. Tell me what you see. Could you see these plants if they were ten feet tall and you were a cop in a helicopter?" That was still just a rumor and he wondered if they really were going to bring in choppers this year. The sound of one was still enough to give him the shakes, still too close to his memory cells.

Maybe that woman Sonya could find out. Need all the help we can get. He'd have to ask Leslie if there was any cool way to find out.

What had she said? Sonya said she thought you were nice and to tell you she's not a cop.

How could she tell if he was nice? She was nice looking, but he'd have no way of knowing if she was nice or not. They didn't even know anything about each other. Maybe it was because he gave the little girl a tractor ride. He finished putting in that last plant for the season. He still had a few spares stashed out behind his place in case he needed replacements later, but this was the last hole of the year. He pressed down on the soil around the plant's stalk. He stroked its leaves and the brighter green of the new growth at the top. Somehow, he'd saved one of the best for last, a many-branched, thick-stemmed beauty with wide leaf-fingers and the beginnings of its secondary branches. He watched it closely in the dimness of the coming dusk as raindrops hit the leaves and made them bounce. He was almost reluctant to let this stage of the season go now that it was over.

He knew he had to hurry to get to the truck before the darkness closed in completely. Still he lingered for a moment before moving away, stepping carefully through the plants and ferns. Who could say what kind of changes he was bringing into this space. He had added and subtracted, altering the mini-ecosystem, turning it from something unused into itself into something potentially useful to himself. He had interrupted its flow and imposed his own needs. But this was an age-old process, he and all the crop-growers, farmers and peasants, transforming the earth and themselves, sometimes in harmony, sometimes in error. Such big thoughts for such a small spot. He made the gesture of a blessing and pushed off into the brush.

When he reached the truck, it was almost too dark to see it there. He threw the empty boxes in the back and climbed in. Coffee and chips waiting for him in the cab, great dinner. He considered rolling a joint but decided to postpone until he was home and cleaned up. Pretty impossible to do anything with the muddy stubs at the ends of his fingers. He wiped his hands with a rag from under the seat, started the engine and let it warm up. He took the same road back and relaxed back against the seat. "Home again, home again, jigged-jig…" That's when he saw a light up ahead, like in a window, but there were no buildings anywhere around. He slowed and drove past the shadowy shapes of the parked heavy equipment and the window light just beyond them. Shit! It was a camper rig parked just in front of the giant bulldozer. Obviously, the night watchman, someone getting paid to stay up here nights to protect against theft or vandalism from who knew who. Maybe they were worried about environmentalists. Peter knew they would have seen his lights, no sense trying to turn around. At least it was dark enough they couldn't make out his rig as he moved past. He accelerated to get by, thinking this was almost too much hassle for him to deal with. And yet, par for the course…Really, whose forest was it anyway? Multiple-use, that's what the National Forest Service signs all said on the boundaries of the federal lands. Multiple-use, huh, him, them, the trees, the animals, all just trying to get by. He didn't want to think about it now, what it would mean for his next few visits to this patch. He'd just have to hope it would rain enough in the next couple of weeks so he wouldn't have to drive out here to water. And who knew? Maybe they'd be done soon and move on out.

CHAPTER FIVE

July

At last, and finally, July brings the dry days. When they come, it's an extreme as seemingly endless as the rain they've replaced. Within days after the last drenching rainfall, dirt roads begin to turn to dust and animals are beset by teeming populations of flies. Mosquitos who have barely tolerated the coolness of spring now accelerate their cycle to make use of the receding and evaporating sources of standing water. Heat returns to the ridges and valleys, and shade becomes a kind of a treasure. If someone came into this country only in the wet season or just for the dry months, they would have trouble imagining the opposite season they'd missed. The middle part of the summer is as bright and green as the winter is dark and gray. The vegetation sports its new garments of leaf and vine with such excess that the sturdy evergreens seem to take on a much darker color by contrast with all the rest. Berry vines and wild cucumber plants grow at a rate that is almost visible, and the droning of inconceivable numbers of insects hums along in the background of it all. It's the time between blossom and fruit for the orchards, between sprouting and making seed for the earth's carpet of weeds and grass. July, with its days so long that it seems like twice a month, and with its heat so intense and its stars so brilliant, it's like it could never end. July is the whole year hovering at one of its extremes, a time without motion as days repeat themselves with blue skies and shining campfire evenings. This is the time when the rainforest first feels the taste of thirst, and water itself becomes scarce and valuable again, when small salmon must move from the creeks to the rivers to find coolness in dark pools, when leaves must wilt to conserve moisture. This is when those who have taken on the dependencies of garden and patch must focus their energy on the transport and distribution of water through hose and bucket, barrel, pipe, and sprinkler, when the sun drinks as much or more than the plants, and the people must do the work the clouds have done during the rest of the year.

It wasn't an easy choice. On the weekend following the mid-week Fourth of July, the Democrats were holding a county-wide picnic and dance at a state park just three miles from Dixon. Candidates for all levels of city, county and state offices would be there with booths, buttons, and patriotic speeches. Sonya had gone to one of those picnics two years before when she and Mike were minimally involved in an associate's race for the state legislature. She remembered it being a rather bland experience with no notable new acquaintances or insights.

On the other hand, the holiday weekend was also the occasion of the annual Sachute River Jamboree, a combination craft fair, rock festival, and old-timer's rendezvous, which would be going all out for its sixth time around. She'd attended that the year before, more as a tourist than as a customer or participant. Her main memory of the event, unfortunately, was the impasse between her and Mike over whether to go with some of his friends or by themselves. Since their free time was so scarce, she was in the habit of spending a great deal of energy trying to get the two of them to do things alone together in the hope that it might rekindle some of the old flame. What it usually did, however, was dampen what coals there were in a repetitive round of accusation and defense.

In any case, those memories aside, this year there was a clear-cut political decision to be made, and differences emerged within her campaign organization over the choice. She didn't understand some of the intensity generated by the discussion, but, as had been the case once or twice before, she needed to intervene and settle things. This time it was Dan's loyalty to the Party and its processes that gave his opinion emotional content, and Terry was coming from his attachment to his polling results, which he used to drive home his position. Sonya was a bit apprehensive that her own desire for a good time might have tipped the scale more than it should have, but practically speaking, there were very few votes to be gained from the party faithful at this time. In the end, Dan was satisfied to take responsibility for the picnic event and to speak on her behalf. Sonya couldn't help thinking that he might have welcomed the opportunity to get himself in front of that audience, and she wished for him the best if that were the case. They divided the whole committee into two teams for creating the booths and literature for the events, and that previous week had been a full-on hurry-up time for everyone.

Sonya also went through two lengthy photo sessions, and then an uncomfortable and tedious exercise as they all scrutinized first the contact sheets and then several blow-ups, trying to choose the version of her face and expression that would best convey her unique qualities to the undecided voter. It was all a bit embarrassing to sit there in a conference while they discussed her "seriousness balanced by obvious good-natured concern" or a "real sense of good feeling beneath a calm and professional exterior" and so on. Sometimes these days it seemed like she was losing sight of herself and beginning to accept a level of objectification she never before suspected existed. Eventually, they had agreed on a full-face shot for posters and the voter's pamphlet and a different sideview for the billboards. Billboards, yet. Of all the things she had to get used to this was going to be the hardest. She couldn't imagine how it was going to feel the first time she was driving down the street and looked up to see her own face twelve feet tall with an unchanging smile and unmoving eyes that just stared out into nowhere.

She and Janet were spending more and more time together, and both Kristi and Janet's Mom were looking forward to the big weekend ahead. The women had talked about how fast their friendship grew, and how unusual this was for them both. Sonya realized that almost all her acquaintances during the Mike-era were either his friends or couples with whom they hadn't been very close. Once she was on her own again, there hadn't been anyone who filled the role of friend and confidant until Janet came along. For both, a great part of this obviously had to do with being single. Their age group was largely paired up already, and neither were swingers in any social milieu. Sonya thought maybe Terry should run one of his polls to find the breakdown between couples, singles, and swingers in their baby boomer generation. It might be interesting to find out.

When she arrived at the office for the regular Tuesday evening session, she had to confront a six-foot tall poster of her face on the front window of their building. It was certainly a shock, but not quite so bad as she'd expected it would be. Her teeth looked nice and the make-up she worried so much about mostly disappeared under the bright light of the studio set, just as they said it would. All in all, it wasn't such a bad picture of her—even if this head was taller than her whole self, standing there looking at it.

Corinne walked up, stood with her for minute and said, "Nice, huh?"

Sonya looked sideways at her and felt herself blushing slightly. "I never thought about this part of it last spring when we started all this."

"You'll get used to it."

"I guess I'll have to. Are we early?"

Corinne opened the door with her key and said, "Not by much." They went into the ground floor space, turned on lights and the coffee maker. Sonya went to her alcove and started reading through the return addresses on the stack of mail in her basket. None of it looked very important. She sat at one of the other desks and began going over Terry's recent polling figures again. It was hard for her to get as excited as he did when he explained them, but somewhere inside she could feel a faint glimmer of optimism. After all, upsets weren't all that uncommon in politics. The most hopeful result was that nearly half the respondents said they voted on the issues more than for a party or person. If they could figure out ways to capitalize on that one factor and find a way to do a better job in that office with the same budget, then she might really have a chance. Of course, the bottom line was that even if she lost this time, name recognition and experience would give a big boost to a second candidacy. Besides, Reynolds might not run again or might try for something bigger next time. Then again, she didn't want to be looking at it that way because it seemed to deny the value of what they were all doing now—and the people on the committee were working so hard. Besides, did she really ever want to do this again anyway?

Corinne came over with two cups of coffee and sat down across the desk from her. Sonya thanked her and asked, "How's Dave doing?"

"Pretty good. He might even get an early release hearing in September."

"That would be early."

"I think they're crowded up at the state pen, too. He said his lawyer would have to get some kind of concession from the DA's office here, but that the state level was okay with it, at least for the hearing part. I hope they don't know I'm working for you."

"That really shouldn't matter."

Corinne drank some of her coffee and seemed to be thinking about saying something, and then about not saying it, and then finally said, "I hope I can wait for him. I'm starting to get pretty lonely. I know I need to wait because our little boy needs his daddy, but it could even be another year-and-a-half or more. That's just so long."

Sonya nodded without commenting, thinking about the similarities and differences between them. Corinne went on, "It's not like I have anyone in mind, it's just that if anyone did come along, like this weekend at the Jamboree, it would be really hard to pass it up, and if I did get involved I would feel so guilty for Dave. I've never been someone who could just get casually involved. I mean, how is it for you? It must be different, because you wanted to be out of what you were in, or whatever."

"It's not exactly what I wanted or would ever choose. Just because we couldn't stay together…I still miss my husband and think about him often. And I do wonder what's going on with my life, what's ahead, I really do."

"Yeah, I didn't mean it's easy for you, just that there had to be some choice involved in how you got separated. It's funny, Dave and I used to have a lot of problems, but we were starting to get along really well when the bust came down. I don't know…Maybe that's just warped hindsight, and it wasn't that good, but it sure seems like it was."

Terry came in through the front door. They exchanged greetings and he went straight through the space to his own file cabinet. He was clearly intent on something. Corinne stood and picked up the empty cups. She bent close to Sonya and whispered, "What I mean is, even Terry is starting to look good to me." She laughed and went off toward the backroom kitchen.

Janet and a couple of other volunteers came in together. They made several comments about the poster in the window, and Sonya tried to laugh off her embarrassment. Janet caught her eye and Sonya could tell right away that something was bothering her when she came to where Sonya was sitting. She sat down and started talking right away.

"Sonya, something's happened at work. Not sure what, but it's important and I don't know what it is."

"Whatever it is, slow down, catch your breath. You want me to get you a cup of coffee?" She reached out and put a hand on Janet's arm.

"No thanks. Anyway, this afternoon I was running off copies of a transcript. I was alone in the machine room and I didn't hear him come in because of the noise. I felt a hand on my shoulder and it scared me. I jumped and turned around. It was Mr. Reynolds. He was smiling, and he reached over and turned off the copier. Then he just looked at me for a while without saying anything. At first, I thought he was going to come on to me, but he backed away and was actually very polite. He said he had a kind of extracurricular proposal for me. I must have given him a funny look, because right away he said no it wasn't personal. He said there was a chance for me to do something for the Office, something that could be important for the future. Both the future of the Office and for my own job. I asked what he meant, and he told me he was sure I knew there was no chance of him losing the election, but it never hurts to do everything possible when you're involved in something as unpredictable as politics. Anyway, I don't have any idea if he knows anything, but he asked me if I would go to work for you in your campaign organization." She paused as if there were more but wanted to make sure that Sonya was following her.

"As what?" was Sonya's surprised reply.

"He didn't specify anything, just went on to say it was always a good idea to have a source of information in the other camp, and he was suggesting it to me because he thought I would best fit the role."

"Well, well. Did he seem to have any idea about what you're already doing for me?"

"I have to tell you, I don't know. I got real worried, and then he started talking about how he hoped he wouldn't have to let people go if we didn't get any more allocations this year, and he said he knows how important my job is to me and my daughter, and that he was going to do his best to keep me on. It was so weird, and I was too uptight to hear everything else he was saying, because it was mostly small talk after that. He said to think it over and let him know how I felt in a couple of days. Oh, and he said it shouldn't take a lot of my time, and there would be a bonus if I did it because he knew I could probably use the extra help. I don't know what to do. I thought there might be trouble when I started all this, but I never thought it would be anything like that."

"No, me either," Sonya said, "and I don't want to be responsible for you losing your job. We'll just have to figure out what's safest for you. I think if you can stay after we should talk to Dan about this after the meeting. Cheer up! Maybe it'll turn into a good thing. Already it's better than if he caught you doing what you're already doing and fired you for it."

"Maybe that is what's happening."

"I don't think so." Sonya wanted to reassure her. "I think you're in a better position now whether or not he knows. Sounds like he needs you for this. Though if he did find out what's already going on with you, I'd wonder how it happened?"

"Maybe there's already somebody else working with us and for him, too."

"Not likely, but it doesn't matter, does it? I mean, we're not doing anything wrong and I doubt there's anything we're doing that needs to be kept a secret. No, I just think he said where he's at when he said politics is unpredictable. And the more you know that the better off you are. Besides, you already are working for both of us. It won't change anything, and maybe you'll make a good double agent."

Janet smiled and said, "I hope so. Because, from what I've heard, double agents don't last very long unless they're pretty good at it."

"Come on, let's get this meeting started."

The meeting went smoothly. Everyone knew what they were doing for the weekend events, and the main piece of new business was Dan's announcement that Joan Mondale, the presidential candidate's wife, would be coming to town at the end of the month for a rally with state and local democratic office-seekers. "Her advance people said they really want to work with Sonya since she's the only woman running for anything in this part of the state. It would mean secret service clearance for anyone on the committee who would be up on the platform, or in the special cars if they decided to have a motorcade." He went on to say they had time to figure all that out at the next meeting and by then he would have the resume forms for them.

They broke up into small groups to collate literature handouts for the two weekend happenings, and to make final plans for the booths and displays. Dan took Sonya aside and asked her how she felt about sharing the spotlight with Mrs. Mondale.

"I'm sorry I didn't let you know before this meeting," he said, "but I just found out myself.

She's doing something in Eugene because she grew up there or lived there at some point. The state party people must have told her about you. She says she wants to help if she can. Her visit is before the national convention, but we'll keep from tying you to any of the candidates by focusing on the party and the role of women in politics. We can ask her to do the same. I think it's a great break."

Sonya was still getting used to the idea, but she said, "Sure, I think it's great too. Anything that helps us is great."

"I wonder if we should at least announce it, this weekend? I think it's pretty much set."

"We should make sure, and you probably need to ask the party folks what they say. And Dan, now if you can, Janet and I need to talk with you about something that's come up at her job."

"Sure, we'll wrap this up in about an hour, and go out somewhere, okay?"

"Okay." As he walked off, she thought once again how fortunate she was to have these people working with her and how much they were all giving. She had the sudden notion to get a picture of the whole committee and put it out in some of the publicity. It seemed unreal to just put her face out there as if she were doing all this herself. Then she thought about this thing with Janet and how maybe that wasn't such a good idea if it exposed people in ways they wouldn't want.

Early in the morning, Detective Stockton picked up the journalist and photographer at their hotel. After a briefing at the sheriff's office, they stopped for an early lunch and then went to board a small plane. The plan was for an afternoon flight over pre-selected areas of the county. Their pilot was already acquainted with Stockton from previous seasons, and the two of them greeted each other with gusto and "here-we-go-again" camaraderie. The journalist, Randall Kincaid, seemed nervous, although he'd told the detective that he often flew in small planes for his assignments. Stockton promised they wouldn't be doing any searching or circling, so there really wasn't anything to be worried over. The photographer was a silent professional woman whose main concern was getting the seat best for taking pictures.

They settled in as the plane warmed up, then taxied and took off. The small city of Dixon dropped away behind them as they headed west toward the coastal mountains and the ocean beyond. Stockton and Kincaid put on earphones with microphones so they could talk without having to shout over the roar of the engine. It was a warm day with huge white clouds suspended from the deep blue of the sky. The clouds cast giant shadows on the ground below and gave a constantly changing pattern of light and dark to what seemed to be an endless carpet of trees and clear-cuts flowing by beneath the plane.

Stockton kept up a steady commentary of local tourist information and pointed out landmarks. Soon they began flying over small valleys with farms and properties strung out along the waterways.

He pointed out these narrow bands of development and said, "This is about the only way people have settled out here, down along the creeks in the bottomland. All this was homesteaded only a couple of generations ago. Folks logged off their land and then tried farming what they'd cleared and working in the mills or the woods. Never made much of a go of it, though. Now you've got mostly old timers or pot growers on these places. Many of them are abandoned. We'll drop down and I'll show you something. Steve," he said to the pilot and pointed out the side window, motioning to go down. "There's one from last year. Just cross over it slow. Not too low."

The pilot banked the plane and came around. Lowering to about 1500 feet altitude and coasting above the trees on the ridge a hundred feet below them. Stockton pointed to a small collection of buildings and vehicles and said, "We got that one last year for almost three hundred plants. They were scattered up both those draws on either side of the main creek, none of it on their land, but there were plenty of trails leading to the plants in small patches. One person took the whole rap when we moved to indict all five adults who lived there. Look, next to that big snag, bare ground next to it. That was the only spot we could see clearly from up here. We got two more like that from blow-up photos and the rest were rounded up on the ground during the raid."

The photographer was snapping pictures, and Kincaid seemed more concerned with his notes than with looking out the windows. He asked, "You say someone took the rap, could you have gotten a conviction if they hadn't?"

"Probably not, but we didn't tell them that. It's hard when the stuff's not on the actual property, but I don't think they knew that, so that one guy confessed that it was all his. Had one case in the next county over where there was no other access to the plants except through the property, but that was pretty hard to prove. Okay, Steve, let's keep going. We've probably got them all upset enough down there."

They flew on, passing over several small valleys with farm settlements, and vast sections of national forest in between. Occasionally Stockton would spot a likely flash of bare earth and have the pilot make a circle to check it out, but that wasn't really the purpose of this flight and they didn't find anything of any significance. The sun was directly overhead when they reached the coast and the pilot took them down and around several of the lakes between the forest and the dunes.

"These lakes have been used a lot by the growers. Usually the access road only goes along one side of the lake and they use a small inflatable to boat their stuff to the other side, then hike up the hidden creeks that feed the lake."

"Tell me, Mr. Stockton, have you yourself ever encountered a boobytrap or any evidence of lethal devices in any of these locations?"

"I've seen devices that were captured in raids, some crude, some pretty sophisticated."

Kincaid rephrased his question, "I mean, have you yourself ever run into to any of these deployed in the field?"

"No, not exactly. Twice last year I was with one of our units when we came across trip wires on trails leading to plants. On investigation, it turned out that the devices were removed before we got in there."

"Or perhaps never installed. Maybe the wires were just there to scare away thieves or wandering hikers."

Stockton replied, speaking louder, "Possibly. In one case that might have been true. In the other case, there had clearly been something nailed to a tree where the wire ended, and it must have been removed sometime close to when we got there."

"I'm just curious, Detective. After all, we're hearing so much about the violence and the threats. We want to confirm this in our coverage. In some of the areas further south, armed guards are not uncommon, but the actual use of traps and deadly devices just doesn't seem as widespread as we hear it is."

Stockton didn't answer and signaled to head back inland. It was truly beautiful along the coastline, but they needed to get back to town. He spoke loudly to the pilot, "Steve, let's take them over the Jamboree site. It must be starting to fill up by now."

The pilot eased the plane into a more southeasterly direction. "Come up the South Fork?"

"Yeah drop down fairly low but keep it on a straight line." He turned to the photographer and asked, "How close-up of a lens have you got?"

"Anything you want." She hollered back, "Standard telephoto?"

"Okay, keep it handy, we might see something interesting up ahead here."

They crossed over a series of close-packed ridges, and then a valley opened up below them. It had the rough shape of a star with a large central area and five feeder valleys narrowing as they led away from it.

"Here's where most of the rural activity is on this side of the county. The only real farming is down in there. You can see a mill, and at that crossroad there's the school. I figure nearly half these people down there are involved in some part of the growing business, mostly the ones not working in the woods or the mill."

Kincaid spoke up again, "Of course down south of here water is much more of a critical factor for them and ponds or streams are the best tip-offs. What do you look for here?"

"Remember this morning at the office when I was showing you the photos? Too bad they weren't in color because it would have made it clearer, but here we're mostly looking for the bright green color which stands out from everything else toward the end of the dry season. They have to keep watering and the stuff keeps that color. Or we're looking for gaps and signs of clearing in the thick vegetation. Most of the regrowing forest area here is twenty to forty years along since it was logged and planted, and the brush and leafy trees have filled in and grown enough that these guys have to clear some of it to get sunlight down to their plants. Steve," he called out, "head into that canyon pretty low." He resumed talking into his mike to Kincaid. "Look over there, see that small flat place most of the way down the ridge? And that other one over there? Now look along the bottom where the creek runs. See those fallen trees?" He turned to the woman. "Can you get a shot of that down there?"

The photographer braced herself right up against the window and began snapping photos.

"Circle it again, Steve. Okay, now can you see how much they had to clear down near the bottom compared to further upslope on that terrace? We got those last year. No idea whose they were, but if there was pot growing down there now, you'd see some green brush in the middle and north side and then some bare dirt between that and the brush. In kind of a circle, sort of like a brown donut with a green center." He chuckled, "We actually call it the 'donut profile.' Also, if the land had just been cleared this spring, you could probably see a lot of brown leaves on the downed trees. Then if the pot is growing on the side-hill we get low enough to see it from a side view, and nothing else here grows in that color and shape. We call that the missile shape because they look like nose cones sticking out of the side of the hill."

"So, Mr. Stockton, basically you're out here looking for donuts or missiles." The reporter smiled carefully at the detective, not wanting to appear to be taking it too lightly.

"I guess that's one way of looking at it."

They flew on in silence until Kincaid spoke up again, "I assume the reason you're not showing us any actual plantings on this flight is because you haven't found any yet."

"Yes sir, it's much too early to see any from the air. The plants themselves are probably not much more than knee-high, and the rest of the vegetation is at its brightest green of the season. Plus, we're not mobilized to follow up yet, so we don't want to risk tip-offs by flying too close."

"Of course. Well then, I believe we've seen enough. You certainly do have your work cut out for you. There must be a thousand square miles of potential growing land out here."

"And that's just this half of the county. Now, if you take a look over there, we'll fly a couple of circles around the campground and Jamboree site. Every year now, there's a big gathering out here. You might want to take it in if you're here this weekend."

"I'm afraid we're headed out tonight. But what exactly is it?"

Below them, a series of pastures and fields had been turned into parking lots with a dense scattering of tents and vehicles of all sorts.

"Well it's supposedly a crafts fair, but also a rock festival, and if you can believe it, a frontier days rendezvous, miners and cowboys play-acting. Mostly hippies, some rednecks, locals and tourists, who knows what all. Most of the growers will be there, and most of our narcs too.

It's one big party, but if the whole thing got wiped out by an act of God, I don't think society, or this county would miss it."

They flew another circle and then headed back to the airport.

The Jamboree grounds were divided into three distinct areas. The Rendezvous with its tipis and trapper/frontier lore and paraphernalia was off to one side of the main parking section. There would be shooting ranges there, as black powder and cap-and-ball enthusiasts showed off the skills and vintage arms and competed for cash and prizes. Some of the displays included home-tanning kits, guns, Indian and trapper clothing and patterns for making them, along with food booths selling old-timey eats and drink.

On the other side of the parking area, near the winding creek that flowed through the grounds, there was an entertainment amphitheater and a few smaller stages for puppet shows, juggling acts, and all sorts of other amateur performances. At night there would be big-name music acts.

The remainder of the grounds were laid out in a labyrinth of lanes and paths lined with booths featuring all manner of food, crafts, and even politics. Most of the food options were concentrated near the main entrance, and the world seemed to be represented by fluttering flags and signs representing a fantastic array of imported and regional delicacies and homemade goodies. A person could pretty well eat their way around the world if they had the money and a big enough appetite.

Politically, too, it was possible to sample ideologies, issues, and representatives of opinions and literature from every stripe of the spectrum. These issue-focused booths were arranged into a wide circle that had come to be known as the "OK Corral." Some said the name came from the heat of the arguments that sometimes erupted between divisive faction of the potpourri of loud and competing points of view assembled in such tight quarters. Others said that name came from the amount of manure that was generated in these debates. In any case there was a small platform and a microphone set up for a rotating schedule of candidates and spokespersons for the various causes represented by the booths.

The crafts market actually took up the largest area on the grounds, as booths and artsy stands thrust every sort of home and cottage industry product into the public's eyes and hands: clothing and jewelry were the most common, but furniture, smoking paraphernalia, artwork, candles, and tools were also in good supply. The requirements of the Jamboree stated that all crafts must be produced either largely by hand or at home, and the people selling them had to have some involvement in making them. This regulation kept the event from turning into a flea market, but it also excluded some people's work that had started out as a home business, and then developed into small, local production operations, often with several employees.

Although the opening was Friday at two o'clock, it was already crowded and traffic was congested by mid-day. Sheriff Johnson drove his patrol car slowly down the shoulder of the state highway leading to the grounds. Traffic was at a start and stop pace as the parking attendants did their best to direct the arriving drivers in as many directions as possible to keep them moving to open parking spaces. The sheriff enjoyed checking driver expressions as he moved slowly past them, noting many tight jaws and twitching steering wheel hands. This was the real work to him, safety and maintaining order in public places. It was a service to the public and noncontroversial, usually danger-free work, and he always enjoyed getting out into the crowds, whether it was this event, a football game, or whatever.

As he waited for a snarl ahead of him to unravel, he was remembering the not-so-safe mini-riot that had occurred four years ago at this thing when some of the so-called fur trappers got into too much of their own firewater and went on a raid into hippie campsites. When the Jamboree security crew tried to break it up, they were forced to use firehoses which failed to dampen anybody's craziness. Both sides seemed to resent his arrival with a small force of deputies armed with tear gas, which they threatened to use but ultimately didn't need. Fortunately, no one had been really hurt, and at the peace talks the next day the different sides came to understand that the gathering itself was on probation with its permit in jeopardy if anything like that occurred again.

It was getting hotter and dustier as he threaded his vehicle through the parking area and eased toward the main entrance. He passed literally hundreds of people carrying burdens of blankets, instruments, small children and baskets with who-knew-what inside. His radio crackled with traffic reports and calls for more help at various intersections. There had been a two-car accident earlier in the day, but it wasn't serious and should have been cleaned up by noon. As far as Marty could tell, the day was off to a good start. He parked in a space to the left of the main gate, got out and leaned his back against the car to watch the parade of widely differing types swirling through the gates. At some point during the day, he planned to go inside and cruise the whole scene. He knew his uniform wouldn't make him the most welcome visitor, but it would be a reminder, a way of keeping the lid on a bit.

Corinne had just checked on her little boy at the daycare center set up for people who were working in booths. He was napping so she had a little time to wander through the exhibitions before coming back for him, and before her next shift at Sonya's booth. She was trying on some earrings when she heard her name called out from across the lane. She looked in the direction of the voice coming from among racks of brightly colored dresses and shirts and didn't recognize the face of the woman who was waving excitedly at her. She removed the earrings, returned them to their case and walked across to see who it was. Then she knew. Of all people, it was Monica. How unbelievable! They been in high school together and went to Hawaii years ago. She was from those old days, good time days, and now here she was today. They hugged tightly, not letting go as the years since their last encounter flowed back and forth between them, and they just held on to each other and laughed. When they could finally talk, they both started at once and then just had to laugh some more. It was a scene that was probably repeated scores of times during the rest of the weekend as people of similar cultural niches and widely separated geography indulged in these unexpected reunions.

They exchanged news and updates on their lives, loves, and children, talking fast, being interrupted by browsers looking through the clothes

Monica and a friend were selling, and all the time reestablishing some of the best friend energy that had been dormant for so long. She was sorry to hear about Dave and the law and countered with a story about her own near-bust and the growing climate of militancy and fear where she'd been living.

Too soon, Corrine felt she had to leave to check on her boy and get ready to return to the booth. She urged Monica to drop by and see her in her new role as a political worker, and they promised to get together again before the weekend was over.

Corinne, still smiling from the happy run-in, picked up Robin, and started back for the booth. She stopped and bought fresh-squeezed orange juice and a burrito, and they sat beneath a convenient tree. She alternated the juice and the burrito, accepting some mess in exchange for letting him do what he could himself. He was turning into such a chunky kid, not fat, just thick, and she loved the way his eyes just kept moving, looking everywhere, trying to see everyone and everything that was passing by. He didn't want all the burrito, so she finished it for him and let him throw the cups and napkins into the waste barrel.

"Mama, I want a balloon," he said, pulling on her hand and pointing to several kids with helium balloons on strings tied to their wrists.

"Okay, we'll see if we can find where they have them."

She picked him up and began weaving her way through the crowd. When the boy needed to be carried, she particularly missed Dave's help. Robin really was getting too big for her to carry. They found a clown with a cart and an air supply. He was singing a nonsense song as he filled multicolored balloons. Her boy reached out and waited until one was tied onto his wrist. He stood there staring up at the balloon and making it bounce in the air by tugging up and down. His expression was something between joy and awe and he said thank you to the clown at Corinne's reminder. As she came into the political circle, she could her a singer at the microphone. His voice was strong and clear, and the song was "America, America." A crowd had gathered, watching the old man with the guitar. As be began the chorus, many in the crowd joined him, and the old song rose over the audience in a way that could send chills down your spine. Corinne slipped into the Sonya booth and apologized to Leslie and Janet in case she was late.

"No problem," said Leslie. "We're having a great time, aren't we?"

"Yes, it's been a lot of fun," Janet added, "and I've learned some things."

Leslie nodded in agreement, "Some of the speakers have been outrageous."

Corinne settled Robin into the back among boxes and posters, got out his toy trucks, and sat down to rest. "God, he is getting so heavy."

She reached back and untied the balloon from his wrist and wrapped the string around a handy post. He complained at first, but when he saw it floating above their booth he was happy and went back to digging dirt for his truck.

"Who's the singer?" Corinne asked.

The song finished, and people were cheering for the old man and calling for more. Janet answered, "He says he's running for president as candidate for the True Patriot Party. He says a true patriot is someone who refuses to work enough to pay taxes, breaks as many laws as possible without getting caught, and supports the military because it keeps so many 'gorillas' off the streets. He also claims to be a direct descendant of Johnny Appleseed, but instead of apple trees, he travels around the country planting marijuana. He might be connected with the legalization people, but I'm not sure."

The singer now launched into "Yankee Doodle," after explaining that in the original version of the song, the feather was a marijuana joint stuck in Yankee Doodle's hat, which he could prove because George Washington once referred to the hemp growing on his plantation as the macaroni of the plant world.

The way he strutted and the obscene hand gestures he made for the words "and with the girls be handy" were drawing a crowd and causing lots of laughter. Suddenly he stopped singing and pointed the neck of his guitar straight over the crowd and spoke loudly into the mike, "Sheriff, good to see you here. Always like to see my freedom of speech is protected, and I hope you enjoy the show today. And hey, Sheriff, I want to ask a favor. Listen, your boys got my whole crop last year and I don't know what you did with it, but if you could front me just one little joint I promise not to turn you in. What do you say, Sheriff?"

Sheriff Johnson smiled and held up both his arms in an empty-handed gesture, waved, and turned to leave.

"Wait a minute! If you're fresh out, sheriff, don't be embarrassed, maybe someone here in the crowd has some they could turn you on to. I didn't realize you'd be dry too. Hey, anybody out there got a joint for our Sheriff? I mean he deserves a good time, too. You-all don't think he rips off our stuff because he doesn't like it, do you? Folks, the Sheriff and his boys probably smoke up more weed in a year than all the rest of us combined. Right, Sheriff?"

"That's right," Johnson yelled back and turned to leave. As he was walking out of the round enclosure he nearly bumped into Sonya and young Kristi, who were returning from a food and browsing tour of nearby booths.

Sonya spoke first, "Well, hello Mr. Johnson. Enjoying yourself?"

"Ah, hi, Mrs. Lehman. I'm fine. Crowd seems pretty good today, weather's nice, and you look prettier every time I see you."

"Thank you, Sheriff. But why the flattery? Have you seen some poll results I haven't?"

The old man on the stage was finishing up his act with a perfectly off-key version of the "Star-Spangled Banana," and it was hard to have much of a conversation as they moved apart.

The Sheriff stopped and called back, "It's not flattery, it's the truth. You should come down and see me again. I emptied the jail, and there's no more problems."

She stopped and said, "I'm sure something else will become a problem, don't worry. And don't you still have to spend all that DEA money?"

"Yeah," he answered, smiling, "but that's not a problem. A lot of these folks here give us plenty to do with it. Actually, I better move along. I could get lynched here if that old guy gets any more carried away. Have a nice day, Ms. Lehman." He touched the brim of his hat and moved away through the opening aisle the crowd automatically formed for him. Feisty was the word that stuck in his head as he strolled along not really looking at anything, mostly just being looked at. She was definitely feisty, and pretty.

Sonya and the girl reached the booth just as the old performer finished his act and stepped down from the platform. "I'm sure glad I don't have to follow him," she said to Corinne as she scooted in behind the counter.

Leslie stood and offered her chair to Sonya as she gathered some of her things. "I have to see how Tom is doing at our booth. He might need a break. Anyway, there are volunteers to leaflet the crowd when you do get up to speak. That should be right around six o'clock if things are anywhere near on schedule."

Sonya declined the chair and urged Kristi to take it. The girl was telling Janet all about where they'd been and how much they'd seen. She'd found something she thought would be good for her grandmother's birthday but needed her Mom to go look at it first before she bought it. Corrine told Janet to take off if she wanted to, that she would be around at least until the speech. Sonya wondered out loud if there would be anybody still there at six.

"You mean the crowd or any of us?" Corinne asked.

"Oh, I mean the crowd. Maybe there won't be anyone around by then. That's okay by me, but not good for what we're supposed to be doing here."

"Terry said he'd have runners going through the crowd in the booth area outside of here a half hour ahead. He also wanted to explode some fireworks here, but I'm sure they won't let him."

Corinne handed posters and a packet of push pins to Janet. "See if you can find anywhere to put these up."

Janet and Kristi moved away into the crowd and Sonya straightened up the chairs and boxes and began restocking the counter with position papers and leaflets about the end of the month rally with Mrs. Mondale. She still wasn't comfortable seeing her own face on so many pieces of paper. Although, as she was sorting and laying out papers, she found herself acknowledging greetings and comments. It was kind of fun, and people couldn't seem to resist saying, "Oh, you're her." As they pointed up to the big poster atop the front of the booth. She would say, "Yes, that's me" as nicely as possible and hand each person a sheet of paper with the same picture and a list of her qualifications and promises on it. Occasionally someone would look it over and want to argue a point with her, but she didn't see much to gain from that. She just tried to skirt those issues with a promise that she would look at alternatives to what she was proposing in her campaign.

She had just returned back to the counter from getting a drink of water for her dust-coated throat when Peter appeared.

"Hi," he said, looking away. "Leslie around? Tom sent me over with a message for her."

"No, she actually just left for their booth."

"Bummer, he said to tell her she didn't need to come there because someone who works for him showed up, and he would meet her here as soon as he got the boys something to eat."

"I guess she'll find that out when she gets there. You want to come in and sit in our shade?

The dust out there is terrible and all we've to drink is water, but you're welcome to it. Or are you still too suspicious of me?"

He looked at her carefully to see what kind of challenge she was making, but her face showed nothing but friendliness, so he considered accepting her offer. It really was getting hot in the afternoon sun. He suddenly remembered he'd need to water all his plants before this weekend was over, Jamboree or no Jamboree.

"I'd accept and come in, but what if someone sees me? They'll think I've gone over to the other side." He smiled to take the sting out of his comment, not wanting to offend.

"I guess that's just the risk you'd have to take."

"I suppose I could hide my face behind some of this," he said, waving his hand over the piles of her campaign literature. "I haven't seen any of it yet."

There was a lull in the passerby traffic as a woman began a speech at the microphone and the crowd gathered quietly. It was a pro-legalization rap being put forward by one of the organizers of the statewide petition drive. She was describing the legal process of the initiative and what would happen to the bill if they could get enough signatures.

Peter slid around the counter and slouched down into a chair. Corinne finished a conversation with someone, gave them a packet of papers, and turned to look at Peter.

"Sonya, you could introduce me, even though I think I know who he is."

Sonya hesitated and then said, "This is Peter Something. A friend of Tom and Leslie's. Peter, this is Corinne."

"We've met somewhere. Don't you live over on Bobcat Creek?"

"Used to. Moved to town when I started working with Sonya."

Sonya turned back to the counter to deal with some questioners there.

"Mind if I ask how you guys came out in that trouble over there last year?"

"Okay, I guess you could say. My old man's doing some time in the state prison, but he might get out this fall."

"Sorry to hear that. So how come you're working for the future DA?"

"She helped me out with all the trouble I was having, welfare and stuff. And what happened to Dave probably wouldn't have had to if Sonya was DA."

"Or if that initiative ever gets passed," he said. "But which is more likely? Probably neither."

Sonya heard him as she faced back into the booth again. "Probably neither, especially if no one works for change."

Peter looked back at her, carefully. "Sorry, but do you really think you have a chance with this county's slanted politics?"

"I don't know. I really don't know, so I don't ask myself that question."

"Yes, she's got a chance," Corinne said in a raised voice, "more chance than all the cynical, anti-politics copouts who will benefit if she does win." Then she laughed and turned back to her work.

"I think I better get out of here." He stood up and covered his head with a campaign brochure.

Sonya reached toward him, saying "Wait, don't go. I need to ask you about a couple of things. I'm going to get up there and talk to whoever shows up at about six, and I'm not sure what all I'm going to say, like about that petition she's talking about. How do you think most people feel about it?"

"Don't know. For some people it would be a good thing, for others, not so good. Hard to say at this point."

"Who would it be bad for?"

"Should I sit back down?" he asked. She motioned him to do so. "Some growers feel it would cut into their market if everybody in the state could grow their own."

"Then it stands to reason the consumers of it would be in favor, doesn't it?"

He looked up at her and motioned her to the other chair. "I don't know anything. Politics is your game. Don't you take polls on this stuff?"

Robin, who had been playing quietly with his trucks for the longest time suddenly let out a cry as he stood up too fast and bumped his head on the corner of a table. Corinne scooped him up and tried to comfort him. He kept screaming so she said she was going to take him for a short walk.

Sonya and Peter were quiet after she left, and no one seemed to be passing by the booth. The speaker was describing when patriot Thomas Paine was exhorting the American colonists to increase the production of hemp as their citizen's duty to help defeat the British navy, and Thomas Jefferson writing in his diary, keeping careful records of his breeding experiments with new strains of cannabis.

"Is that true?" Sonya asked. "How could marijuana help defeat the British Navy?"

"Hemp was the best fiber for rope and all the ships were sailing ships. They required huge amounts of lines for their rigging. The colonists had plenty of wood for shipbuilding, cotton for sails, iron for cannons, powder for ammunition, but not much rope in the beginning of the war."

"I never heard that in history class."

"Hey, this stuff, at least the kind that doesn't get you very high, it was important in a lot of the world's history. Spain controlled the sea for a while because of their colonies in North Africa, like Morocco. It grew really well there. Then when the British got hold of India, they were able to import enough rope to build a big enough navy to defeat the Spanish Armada."

"Where did you get all this?"

"I don't know," he said and smiled. "Probably just made it all up."

"Sounds like it, but it makes some kind of sense, too." She didn't know him well enough to tell if he was making fun of her or not. But he seemed serious and it did sound plausible. He looked like he was getting ready to leave again, but she wanted to talk with him some more. He was a good source of information about just the kind of people whose support she needed to beat Reynolds. She could feel how reluctant he was to talk with her, and Leslie's description of him as a loner popped into her mind. She wondered why that was so.

"Listen, if you could wait just a few more minutes, someone else will be back here, and I'd really like a chance to hear some more of your opinions, I am seriously trying to figure this out."

He didn't have anything else to do until the entertainment that night, and her naivete about the pot issue, for someone running as potential top enforcer, interested him. It seemed like she was running for the job without much of a program against growing. Maybe she wasn't a threat after all. Maybe she could even be used, he thought, chuckling to himself that she probably thought she was the one using him.

"Okay, I'll stick around a little longer, but you can't quote me."

"Thanks." She turned back to the counter where some folks were waiting to ask questions, and he buried his face in some of her literature. He wondered what she'd do if he stepped out behind the booth and lit a joint. He could also just step out into the crowd, but then one hit and it would be gone, being passed around. Better wait for Corinne to come back and ask her about a good place to hang out.

Leslie came back to the booth with her boys close behind her. "Oh hi, Peter. What are you doing here?"

"Getting indoctrinated. Actually, I came to give you a message from Tom, but it looks like you already ran into him."

"We all got something to eat. Thanks, though. Sonya, the boys are going to walk around carrying those posters about your speech. Do you know where they are?"

"I think Terry left them in the van, over there by those trees."

"Shouldn't we get them now?"

"We could. I'll go find out what time they say I'm really supposed to speak, so we can write it in on the signs."

"I'll get whatever it is you want, if you tell me what," Peter volunteered.

Leslie pointed over to where a tan van was parked, poking out of a clump of trees. She said, "Good, I'll stay here with the booth and you can get the big posters. They're on short poles with Sonya's big picture. You can't miss them." She tossed him a set of keys.

Sonya was already gone to find someone who knew about scheduling and the boys were down by the small creek that ran behind the booth. Peter walked through the crowded pathway toward the van. The sun hit him hard as he stepped out of the shade. When he got to the van it was a furnace inside. He quickly shouldered the bundle of posters and locked the door. On the way back, he glanced down to where Leslie's sons were playing. There was a nice patch of tall grass in the shade and rocks leading to the water. The spot couldn't be seen from the public side of the booth walkway but was close to the back of theirs.

Corinne had returned to the booth and so had Sonya. Corinne pointed to Peter and commented that it looked like they had recruited another campaign worker. He pretended to drop the posters as if they were contaminated. Sonya laughed and told him not to worry, they weren't dangerous. Leslie asked what time they should mark in the space on the signs.

Sonya answered with, "They said any time after 5:30. That's only about an hour from now. I think we need at least until about six, but maybe I'm just nervous."

"No. Six makes sense, more time to gather a crowd before they start eating, and it might even be cooling off by then. We'll finish up the signs and get the boys to walk around with a couple of them. Terry should be here pretty soon with some volunteers to carry around the rest. So why don't you take a break and rest up for your big debut?" Leslie smiled and flashed a finger 'V' for Victory sign.

"I'd like that. I still don't know what I'm going to say out there." She turned to Peter. "Want to take a walk around?"

"If you really want to rest up, get out of the dust and heat, there's a nice spot down where the boys are." He pointed down toward the creek.

"That would be nice. It's so hot everywhere else."

Leslie smiled at the two of them, but they didn't seem to notice. She said, "And tell the boys to come up now, okay?"

"We will." They walked out through the heat toward the creek.

Corinne said to Leslie, "Well, how do you like that?"

Leslie looked over at her and said, "I like it. Here, let's get these cords tied onto these posters and fix them to the poles. I think it'll work."

As they climbed down the slope to the water, Peter called to the boys that their mom wanted them back up with her. Aaron, the oldest, had his shoes and socks off and was holding up a crawdad by its tail. It was writhing around his fingers, and he was thrusting it at his little brother.

Peter said, "You better go, she's got work for you to do."

Sonya eased herself down to the water's edge, sat down on a large rock and removed her new running shoes. She'd only had them for a week, and hadn't been jogging yet, but they turned out to be just right for standing around in the booth all day. She stuck her bare feet into the water and was surprised by how cold it was. Still, it felt great. Peter sat down cross-legged on the grass a short way away, pulled out a pouch and some rolling papers from his shirt pocket and began carefully cleaning a bud in his hand. He rolled it into a well-tailored joint and held it out to her.

"No thanks." She looked away. "Besides, what happens if I get caught?"

He slipped the joint back into his pocket, and said, "Might make your campaign more interesting. Do you ever smoke it?"

"I used to. Seems like a long time ago." Her feet were getting used to the cold water and she rolled her jeans higher to get more of her legs into the water. "I can't really remember what it's like."

"Hard to describe. I used to try and figure it out," he said, "but I always got lost in the words if I was stoned, and I couldn't remember how it was when I wasn't. Maybe it's just too much of a feeling to be talked about. Think you'll ever try it again?"

"I don't know. I don't mind if you smoke that if you think it's safe here."

"It's okay. I can wait, even though I don't think they ever bust anyone as these things."

She looked around, thinking about the implications of who she was now, and said, "You know, I'm in an odd position with the laws these days."

"No shit."

"I mean, I can't afford to endorse anything that's actually illegal. On the other hand, I can't in good conscience promise to enforce what I consider to be mistaken laws."

Peter lay back against the grassy slope and stared up at four huge white clouds in the bright blue sky. "Sounds like you're in a hard place."

"What would you do?"

"I'd stay out of that kind of mess."

"Yes, I've heard you stay fairly uninvolved."

He sat back up to look at her, to try and read her expression. "Is that bad?"

"I guess it depends on your reasons."

"What did you want to ask me anyway? You've got to get to work pretty soon." He eased over to the creek and splashed cold water on his face.

"Right, let's avoid the personal side at all costs. Sorry. Well, as a representative of what we might call the free choice segment of society," she said in her courtroom tone of voice, "I'd be interested in your recommendation as to how a certain candidate for chief legal office in this county should approach the electorate concerning the proposed initiative to legalize the personal cultivation and use of marijuana."

"You want my answer as me, or as a representative?"

"Are they different?"

"Might be."

"Then first as yourself."

He splashed more water on his face, shook it off, and looked directly at her. "I don't know if I can or even want to help you out. You seem okay, but who can say what you would have to do if I get busted for possession and my trial came up after you got elected. You might be able and possibly willing to make a difference." He looked away and paused for a long moment before going on. "So, I'll take the risk and tell you what just came into my head, and if it's crazy, just say so. It seems to me that you can say that even though this initiative is a statewide vote thing, that you would use it as a guideline for determining the desires of the voters in this county."

"Can you explain that a little more?" Sonya splashed water with her feet.

"What I mean is that even if it fails on the state level, you could follow the local results when making decisions on which cases to prosecute locally. Still don't understand?"

"I'm beginning to. You think if it wins in Chinook County and I win, I could act as if it's the law here."

"Yes, I'm saying that might get support from people who might not otherwise vote, or are only voting for the initiative. They might vote for it and for you, together, and if it doesn't get enough signatures to make the election, you're off the hook on your promise, same as if it fails here. Now you see how I think about this stuff? But I'm sure they're just wild thoughts."

"So, actually I could make the promise, but I would have to win the vote and the initiative would need to pass here for me to have to make good on it. And what are the chances of that? It makes a kind of sense, even though you think I'm wasting my time on all of this, don't you?"

"No, I can't say that." He paused. "Not if I don't know what else you would be doing with yourself."

This time she kicked some water in his direction. "Probably growing pot."

"Good answer." He laughed and then looked away.

"Are you serious, do you really want to know?"

The silence between them thickened slightly, becoming almost a feeling, a moment in which a lot can happen, or maybe nothing. She wondered if he really did feel threatened by her. In a way, it didn't matter. There wasn't anything between them anyway. She told herself she was just picking his brain for political purposes, and whatever was in it for him was probably no more than curiosity about her involvement in this campaign. As it stood, according to Leslie, he was known for not involving anyone else in his life. She kicked her feet to break the quiet with the sound of splashing. He was so different from Mike, who never gave much thought in his life to answering her questions. She'd always let that bother her, that he could be so sure of himself that he'd give you the first thing that popped into his head and be so convinced that it was right you'd better not disagree or you'd find yourself having to defend anything you said. Peter didn't seem unsure of himself, but he was more careful with his thoughts, more like he didn't want to share them because they weren't ready enough. She wondered what he was thinking right now. About her? And what difference did it make when she had so much else on her mind?

Peter plucked a wide blade of grass and held it between his thumbs, up to his lips. He blew hard into his cupped hands, producing a shriek from the grass. He glanced over at her, thinking how absurd this had gotten, knowing she was waiting for an answer to her question even if there wasn't one. How can you tell someone you don't want to know about them, even more how can you not want to know about someone who wanders into your life and seems to fit into some space you didn't even know existed?

"Yeah," he said. "I guess I might."

She couldn't hold back the little laugh that spilled out of her for almost having forgot her question. "Well, thanks, thanks a lot." That was her first reaction, like one of Mike's, she thought, but when she saw how quickly he looked away when she'd laughed, she realized that maybe he was giving something up by admitting any interest in her, that maybe something that sounded like nothing to her really Could be a lot for him. "I'm sorry," she said, "it just seemed like such a vague answer."

"I'm pretty vague when I have to be." He gave her a quick smile and then took the unsmoked joint out of his pocket. "Shouldn't you be doing something to get ready?"

"You're right," she said, looking at her watch. "What about later? Are you hanging around later?"

"Probably. There's a good band tonight."

"Well, maybe I'll see you." She dried her feet with the socks, slipped on her shoes over the bare feet, and pushed herself up.

He looked up at her and said with a smile, "Guess it depends what you say in your speech."

"Come on, you don't care about that." She turned away and headed back to the booth.

"Hey," he called after her, "you'll do all right."

"Thanks, you too."

He watched until she was out of sight near the booth before lighting the joint, inhaling deeply. He lay back and took another couple of hits before carefully snuffing it out into a good-sized roach. The bright blueness of the sky made him squint. The sound of the creek grew louder in his ears and he though back to one time when he was tripping and the sound of his own blood running through his body sounded like a river, with him thinking it was all running out of his body and into the ground. As far as he could remember now, it hadn't been a bad feeling at all. He rolled over so he could dunk his whole head into the small pool at the edge of the creek. Shaking off the water, he ran his fingers through his hair, squeezing out the excess. Suddenly the sound of long blasts on a car horn repeated from the direction of the crowded area. He could also hear the thumping of what sounded like a bass drum and other noises he couldn't identify. He nodded goodbye to the moving water and climbed up the bank to rejoin local civilization on its holiday.

The car horn belonged to a Volkswagen bug leading a parade of strangely dressed musicians beating on drums and banging cymbals and other noise makers. There was a tuba and a trombone in the entourage, and above it all was a guy on stilts carrying one of the six-foot tall posters of Sonya, twirling it slowly so that the words "6 PM Rally, OK CORRAL" could be seen by everyone he passed. A large group of people followed the ragtag band as it turned into the big circular space in front of the stage. Terry was driving the VW, and now he parked and jumped out and up onto the platform where he began adjusting the microphone and setting up posters for a backdrop.

Peter worked his way around the back of the gathering crowd and into a shady spot far from the stage. He noticed a couple of officers, maybe even the sheriff himself, over on the other side of the haphazard arena. He was glad for Sonya that there a turnout but wondered if she was prepared for this many. There looked to be at least two hundred adults and several dozen children.

The band arranged itself along the front of the stage and proceeded to put together a pretty good rendition of "When the Saints Go Marching In." Terry opened a big box behind the stage and about fifty balloons went floating skyward. They were all tied together and kept tangling in different formations as they sailed away above the crowd. Sonya was glad for the distraction as she watched them go, trying not to look at all the people probably expecting her to live up to all the hoopla. She felt totally anticlimactic and wondered if Terry's unexpected enthusiasm and show hadn't been good for collecting a crowd, but bad for her to follow. There wasn't anything to do about it now, though; this was politics and she was in it and could only get out of the campaign by either winning or losing, so she might as well try to win. Unfortunately, as she tried to talk herself into getting used to this, her mind seemed more blank than at any other time in her life. And this really was only the beginning.

Leslie had been chosen to introduce her and Terry was calling for her. Here goes, she thought, it's about to start. She looked around, trying to catch a glimpse of Peter, but couldn't spot him in the crowd. Maybe still at the creek.

The crowd settled down a bit as Terry introduced Leslie, who approached the microphone and immediately began talking about the candidate's record as a lawyer for justice and as a civil liberties advocate. She talked briefly about how good it was to see a woman challenging the good old boys of the county. Then she called on Sonya to come up on stage.

As she reached the small podium and turned around to face the audience, she was strangely conscious of the big posters behind her, looking over her shoulders as it were, some with her face six feet tall. She let her eyes wander across the crowd, many with sunburned faces from the day's activities. The crowd grew quiet and she knew she had to say something, something, but still she kept looking at all the people. She noticed Sheriff Johnson and another officer, a small group of men in full fur trapper garb, some of her volunteer campaign workers with armloads of leaflets ready to give out at the end of her talk. She looked across at her booth and saw Corinne give a wave and a victory V and move her hands in a hurry up motion. Sonya waved to the crowd, finally accepting that this was really what she was doing, so she better get on with it.

"Hi everybody, thanks for coming. Welcome! I'm Sonya Lehman, the real Sonya. You can tell because I'm not nearly so big as all the other ones behind me." She gestured toward the posters backing her up. "And I'm the one who's actually alive. Can you tell?" She pinched her bare arm and there was a ripple of laughter.

"I'm here today because you're here today, and you're the people who inspire me to be running for office in this county. I grew up near here, and I just love it here today. This truly is a great event and one that demonstrates some of the very best things about our country as we look around ourselves on this, America's 208th Birthday. The variety of people here today, and the things they've brought to sell and come to buy are incredible in their diversity. If freedom means nothing else, it is about all our differences and the unity that holds us together.

"I'm running for the office of your District Attorney for two main reasons, and if you'll listen to me for a few minutes I'd like to tell you why someone like me thinks we can all work together and make things better here in this county, and hopefully throughout this great country. I'm an optimist. I haven't given up on America, on freedom, or on the political process, although it's hard sometimes. I know it can seem absurd to even try to change the status quo or to challenge the powers-that-be, but that's not the tradition in this country. A handful of people can start the changes that ultimately lead to a major renewal of the whole people's spirit, and that is what I hope is happening again and what I want to be a part of.

"Since we're celebrating our country's independence this week, I want to take this opportunity to say that I don't think patriotism has to be a bad word, and I think that one of the highest duties of patriotism is to question, and, when necessary, to criticize one's own government and those who govern. It's frightening to me to look at the calendar and to see that this really is 1984, and that we have leaders in this country who are calling for an end to any and all criticism, who call for unity first, and questions later. We have an administration that just invaded Grenada, a tiny island nation, and then prevents the press from having access to the scene of the so-called Goliath over David victory. I think we must look carefully at any government that demands unity and prevents criticism, and I think this is one of the main issues in this election year, and that this is asking a question we all need to be thinking about. This question bears directly on the amount of freedom that we have both on the national level and here at home on the county level."

There was the beginning of some applause which Sonya quieted with the motions of her arms and by talking over it.

"Tell you what, please save your applause until the end or until you're tired of what I'm saying. If I go on too long or stop making sense, let me know, and I'm going to try and keep it short, but if you want me to stop that's when you need to start applauding. Okay?"

Several voices answered with shouts of "Okay!"

"I want to spend some time telling you why I'm running for this office and I want to ask for your support if you think I can be an improvement over what we have now. Let's face it, I don't think there's anybody who thinks I can win. As a matter of fact, my opponent, Mr. Bill Reynolds, doesn't even think he needs to campaign for your votes. But I think with your help we might just be able to come up with a surprise for him. I really am starting to believe that we have a good chance to win.

"The first thing that makes me want to serve you in this position is the way Mr. Reynolds and his crew of assistants are currently handling that office and their responsibilities. I want to eliminate and prevent abuses of the system and to show that it can work for justice and fairness. Today in the county jail there are three prisoners for every two-person cell. This is illegal and borders on being inhumane. I've been there to observe, and I've seen just how bad it is.

"The reason this is going on is not simply a lack of funding as Mr. Reynolds would have us believe, but it is directly tied to a policy which discriminates against poorer citizens who are waiting for their trials and caters to the few well-to-do criminals in that same situation. For example, there are fourteen inmates who are in some stage of the pretrial process and cannot afford the bail which has been set for them. Not one of them is accused of a crime involving more than five hundred dollars. On the other hand, one of our former county commissioners, and presumably a friend of Mr. Reynolds, is appealing a conviction for defrauding the public of nearly a quarter of a million dollars. He is out free on his own recognizance. This is a total imbalance of justice with the scales tipped all the way to one side. If I am elected, bail will be requested and determined that is directly related to the degree of the crime committed, and never based on the suspect's credit rating, bank balance, or community standing. In the meantime, the ACLU, which I worked for up until I became a candidate, is currently filing a class action lawsuit against the county to reduce the number of inmates and to require the district attorney's office to set bail amounts based on each person's ability to pay it if they are qualified on all the other criteria.

"I hope I am not boring you, but some of this stuff is very important and affects many people. Along with this issue, I want to bring up the constant complaints and poormouthing of many of the county officials in charge of certain departments. I don't believe it's the fault of the overtaxed public that vital needs for service are not being met. It makes me sick to hear elected officials blaming the public for their own inefficiency while they continue to maintain bloated, high-salaried staffing which has more employees than would ever be allowed in private industry, and then don't hire enough people at lower levels to get the basic work done in a timely and professional manner. With our economy in this country in as bad shape as it's in, and with all the budgets growing every year, I think it's a shame we still have to listen to Mr. Reynolds and his cronies making excuses that they can't do the jobs they are being paid to perform. I would like you to give me the chance to prove that effective protection of the public's rights, safety, and property can be carried out and maintained within the public's ability to pay. I know I can do this with all of you helping me.

"There are other abuses of power I plan to address as the election draws closer, but those were the main ones I wanted to address today. The other area of concern I want to bring up today and throughout my campaign is the pressing necessity to safeguard the freedoms we still have today. Fifteen years ago, many of us were younger and more likely to march in the streets over issues we were passionate about, like the illegal war in Vietnam and the institutional racism of this society. We were demonstrating for change in the way that large groups of people were being affected by the American system of international imperialism and the national shame of inequality. Since that time, we've seen the issues themselves change, beginning with women's recognition of their own needs for a better share in our culture and economy. We've seen the rights of individuals called into question and these rights need to be defended. Freedom of choice regarding one's own body has become a major issue of these times. The right to decide about pregnancy and abortion, the rights of gay people to freely relate, the rights of terminally ill people to end their suffering and their relatives' anxiety, and even the right to ingest or inhale whatever a person wants to put into their own body..." She was interrupted by loud cheering. She went on, "These are frontline issues, and, along with the huge concerns over our environment, these matters are beginning to move people to once again join up together to try to make a difference. What I'm getting at is that we are now being confronted more and more with the situation where freedom over one's own self is being questioned and even prosecuted by those who think they know what's best for everybody, and we now need to protect ourselves from those who would legislate private and personal behavior based solely on their own narrow views of life and death.

"What does this have to do with Chinook County and the DA race? I hope it has a lot to do with it because I hope you realize that if we don't safeguard our own freedoms no one else will, and then they'll be gone when we really need them. I hope you realize that when our current elected district attorney declares war against any segment of our population then he is violating the Constitution where it says that the government shall not use military measures against its citizens without a declaration of martial law and a definition of the emergency. The Drug Enforcement Agency has become a militarized arm of the US Government and our current county administration has accepted funding for a military-style crusade against the cultivation of marijuana in this area. At the same time, citizens throughout the state are signing petitions to allow legalization of personal growing and consumption of this substance. I want you to know that I don't believe that any public official, from president right down to the local librarian, has any right to declare war on any segment of the population—no matter what the issue. Civil war is not the answer or the solution when an issue revolves around personal choice and crimes without victims, and this is exactly what the marijuana issue has become today.

"In conclusion, (did you think I'd never get here), I will make this promise to you and to the people of this county. First, that part of the county budget allocated to the District Attorney's office will be prioritized to deal with the seriousness of the crimes and the effects they have on victims and on society as a whole. If there is enough money, then all laws will be enforced. However, if there are shortfalls such as those Reynolds is always complaining about, those crimes without victims will be the first to go unprosecuted. It seems to me that this only makes logical sense and should already be a matter of policy. Secondly, and this goes along with all the rest of what I have been saying, if the Marijuana Initiative gets on the ballot, and if it passes in this county, then no matter what happens in the rest of the state, I would carry on my duties as if it were the law in this county. Meaning this: that the provisions of this initiative, here in Chinook County, would be considered the law if our voters approve it." She paused to look across the faces of the crowd, and then said loudly, "Would that be all right with you?"

There was a great roar of approval and applause which lasted more almost a minute. Then, once again, Sonya gestured for quiet. When she got it, she went on in a voice that was both hoarse and excited.

"Thank you, thank you! Now don't tell anybody I said that unless they're willing to vote for me. I do need your help, all of you. And I appreciate you coming here today. There are leaflets and other information being handed out by our volunteers, and our booth is right over there and will be open all weekend. And remember, this is the United States of America, where freedom and human rights are still the most important reasons we have for existing as a nation. Have a fun and happy weekend and thank you so much for your attention."

There was another loud burst of applause and cheering. Terry began jumping up and down in front of the band and they played a rousing approximation of a march. A woman with an American flag moved through the crowd to the front, waving it back and forth over her head. Sonya raised her arms high above her head, making victory signs with her fingers and smiling even brighter and wider than in any of the giant photographs behind her. Someone set off a string of firecrackers in the open area behind the booths, and the noise of the rally built up and up, until it peaked. As Sonya left the stage, the band marched out through the crowd, and folks began to gather up their children and belongings and drifting off toward the food, entertainment and whatever else was going on.

She was surrounded by well-wishers and her campaign workers as she worked her way slowly back to the booth. What she really wanted was a drink of water and some quiet, although neither seemed immediately possible. She was amazed by the response and was still shaking from the effort. It was her first success, in front of a friendly and supportive crowd. She knew she'd targeted her remarks mostly at their interests, but she hoped it was good politics and not seen as opportunism. Maybe she got carried away. What were Dan and the party going to say about her promises? These thoughts raced around in her mind as she shook hands, kept smiling, and continued to work her way through the crowd as it moved toward the exit, all the while edging her way toward water and a private resting place in the early evening shade. At the same time, she was nearly overwhelmed with the euphoria of it all. Her logical side was reminding her that this was only a small fraction of the people in the county, and only a sliver of the wide range of public opinion, and that most of these people were here partying rather than politicking. Still, it had been a good test of her ability to get up in front of and get a message across to the people who might just count for the most in what she now trying to accomplish.

When she reached the booth and nearly fell into one of the chairs, Janet was right there with a handshake and a big glass of icy lemonade.

"Or do you want water first?"

"Anything wet. Both. Thank you." She gulped at the cold lemonade. "It's still hot out there, really hot."

"I know," said Janet, "but you were terrific. To tell the honest truth, I had no idea you could do that and do it so well."

Her throat felt smoother as she drained the lemonade and sucked at a couple of ice cubes as she reached for the water jug. "I just hope I didn't blow it too bad. Your boss is probably going to love it. He'll just have to quote me and probably three-quarters of the people will want to vote against me."

Janet handed her a cool wet rag, and said, "Don't be too sure. At least you're giving people a real choice, and maybe there are a lot of people tired of the hypocrisy of the way things are now. I know I am, and I've never used marijuana and I don't think I ever would. Anyway, don't think about it anymore today. You're done for now and can just enjoy the holiday."

"I'll try. Thanks, Janet, I'll try." And for the first time since before the speech, she wondered where Peter was, and if he heard her speech, what did he think about it?

Peter was up at daybreak on Sunday. He'd meant to get all the watering done the day before and maybe head back to the Jamboree, but he ran into problems with the drip system at his first patch and spent most of the morning running the waterline from a new collection spot farther down the hill from the spring itself.

When he stopped by the store later, he ran into Al and some other growers. Their main topic of conversation was Sonya and her unexpected position on pot. The newspaper had given a spread to her speech, branding her as the "Pro-Pot Candidate for District Attorney." Peter and a guy named Jim were the only people who'd been at the event and the others questioned them about the speech. Even after talking to her, it was hard for Peter to believe that a legitimate candidate would take a stand that would make so much sense to growers. Jim said he was sure she wouldn't be able to follow through on it even if she got elected, and most of the other guys agreed. Al was more optimistic, calling it a crack in the egg. In any case, they all agreed it wouldn't make any difference for this summer's growing season.

Peter mostly listened to the comments, saying only that taking a stand like that would probably lose her the election, if she'd ever had a chance in the first place. Still, he added, it was the first time he'd heard of someone running for office who you could get behind and believe might have any chance of improving things.

The talk drifted away from politics and on to the realities of how the plants were coming along, how well the water was going to hold out if it didn't rain again until September, and whether helicopters would be used in this county. Jim said he hoped it was all just a rumor.

Al walked Peter over to his truck and asked him if he was going back over to the Jamboree. Peter said no, not that night, but maybe the next day for the last of it. Al told him he could move a pound for him if Peter still had that much for trade. Some friends of his at the gathering were looking for some and had the money with them. They agreed on a half and arranged for Al to drop by Peter's place before noon the next day.

Peter was just parking his pickup in a turnaround when the sun climbed over the treetops on the opposite ridge. He'd come in the back way, making it an extra eight miles of gravel road, but it was worth it and necessary if he wanted to avoid that road-building operation and the possibility they had a watchman on duty. It might not even still be there, but he hadn't had the time to check that out. He planned on getting a small dirt bike. It would be easy to hide in the brush and wouldn't look suspicious if someone did spot it. Plenty of folks just cruised around for fun in the summer. He would use the money from this half-pound deal with Al if he could find the right bike.

He shouldered a bag of fertilizer and walked up the road to the landing above the patch. He dropped down at a different place from last time and worked across the clear-cut on a long zigzag that brought him down just above the first of the plants just as the sun reached the bottom of the canyon. It was still cool and damp in the shade near the creek and had the fresh smell of lush growing things. He crouched and moved through the thick brush, dragging the bag, until he reached the first couple of plants. He was happy to see they'd started taking off and were growing like crazy since their recovery from the shock of being moved and transplanted.

He sat by the nearest plant and rested from the long descent. These plants had been stunted by spring's endless rain and clouds, but they were strong and branching out well. He reached over and stroked a plant's top leaves. He never stopped being fascinated by the mystery of their growth and the brilliance of the fresh new green color. He tore open the top of the bag of plant food and spread a couple of handfuls around the base of each plant, where it would be dissolved by watering and seep into the ground to mix with the all-natural soil additives he'd used for the earlier planting.

He recovered the bucket from its hiding place in the nearby brush, turned on the spigot from the water line, and began carrying half-buckets to the seven plants spread around this site. The sun was turning the moisture of the creek-bed area into steam that rose up and vanished above him. When the plants were all watered, he grabbed the bag and plunged through the thickening brush to the next set, located on a small bench above where the creek took a bend. A berry bush latched onto his arm; as he gently removed the thorns, he thought again about the relative insanity of this way of life, wondering if Sonya really could make any difference, or if the legalization process would ever succeed. And what would the pot be like if it ever got easy to grow? Would the high lose its edge and just become a numbing of the mood and energy of the person taking it in? He tied a bandana around his head to keep his free flowing sweat out of his eyes, spread more fertilizer, and lugged more water.

He kept wondering if legalization would commercialize the whole business, or would there be a backlash and even stricter and higher-tech forms of eradication with satellite detection and poisonous aerial sprays? It wouldn't be any fault of Sonya's if his outlaw ways became obsolete—it had nothing to do with individuals. He wanted to tell her what he thought about her speech, how it amazed him she could speak so clearly about such ideas. As he'd listened to it coming through the loudspeakers, it had been very hard to put that voice and words together with the woman he'd been sitting with by the creek only a short time before.

While she was speaking, he'd glanced over at the Sheriff several times and it had seemed like he was having a similar reaction: disbelief that she was actually saying this, but also a kind of recognition that it wasn't really so off the mark. What else do you do in a county where people are taken off guard and laid off suddenly and they can't afford to move away? What do you do when the local government can't balance its budget without more taxes or drastic cuts in services? Or, in this case, declaring war on the new moneymakers and collecting federal dollars to stop something that probably couldn't be shut down without an occupying army…

Peter admired her for standing up there and trying to make some kind of change happen. And this was for sure the first time he'd ever applauded a rap by a bona fide politician. But could she seriously be called a politician? She was just a person. So, how did the person he danced with at the Jamboree later that evening after the speech, how did she fit into straight politics? It sure didn't fit into his own mind very well, and he could tell that it was beginning to affect him.

The last batch of this set of plants was farthest from the waterline, and there wasn't anything he could do about that because there was a slight rise in the ground between the pipe and where the plants could get good sun. He knew some growers used pumps, silent battery-powered units or buried gasoline models. He hadn't been able to leave behind his old ways, though this was his first season using this drip irrigation in a few places, mostly as an experiment, and he was planning a trip to town to get a dirt bike, so it was okay to just keep on keepin' on, and hand-carry most of his water in a bucket. Not for forever...Hell, someday he was going to retire and just grow a stash for himself, maybe every other year, go to Alaska for the summer, be free to travel, go to serious music festivals where accomplished orchestra musicians held workshops and teaching sessions in a resort-like atmosphere. Maybe sign on to a sailboat for a long voyage. Maybe, maybe...but in the meantime, I better get some water to the rest of these plants.

When he finished hauling and dumping the last bucket, the sun was already about one-third high, ten o'clock. He still had plenty of time before Jerry and Carla were going to drive him to the Jamboree, picking him up around noon. He hadn't seen them for a while and when Jerry had waved him down to invite him, he could tell they were feeling a little like they thought he might have been avoiding them. It wasn't that at all, it was just that he'd been so busy or tired, trying to catch up with the season after the rain delay of the spring.

Sonya would be there again, but she said no speech was scheduled on Sunday because the crowd and the booth-people would all be trying to wrap things up. He and Jerry were planning to take in the finals of the marksmanship contests at the Fur-Trapper Rendezvous. Jerry was known to be a crack shot, but he hadn't had any time to practice this year.

Peter crawled his way down the bank to where the brush opened out onto the small creek. He jumped across to a big rock, stripped off his soaking shirt and bandana, laid across the rock so he could dunk his head into the water, and then splashed it all over his upper body. He lay back on the warm surface of the rock as the sun massaged his muscles and skin, lying there on the drowsy edge of dreaming. He twitched his arms and his body jerked with the reflex that must be why this is called "falling asleep."

He thought of Sonya, maybe sitting on another rock in the creek behind the booth, and he felt something he'd long ago forgotten about. But clearly he couldn't, wouldn't, and shouldn't be thinking about her like that, about the way her hair bounced on and off her shoulders when she was dancing, or...Thinking about how they both laughingly confessed to not having danced like that for years, how they were both awkward and inhibited, and so similar about it all that it hadn't mattered. He wondered how she felt about the way he split so fast when the music stopped, almost afraid to stay, and have to talk, or say goodnight. He was sure that she only hung out with him because she was lonely and feeling kind of conspicuous or out of place, and he was just someone convenient to be with. It was strange, although he hadn't thought he would ever be affected quite like this again. Like once you accept your immunity to such feelings, it can come as a shock that at least the mental side of it can happen again. And, dammit, he knew he wanted to see her again, but he knew there was no way she could understand him or where he was coming from and what was behind him. If she was smart, she would just thank him for his ideas and ask him to keep in touch. If he was smart, he wouldn't go straight back there and be looking for her again. But he did want to at least see her, look at her again, and maybe set up some time to see her in some neutral situation. He splashed more water on himself, pulled on the sweaty shirt for protection against the brush, and start climbing back out the way he'd come, smiling at the thought that it was getting harder and harder to recognize himself without a mirror

By the middle of the month, the sheriff's office was beginning to get their yearly influx of tips about growing operations around the county. Most of these calls were anonymous and vague, and were filed away for later aerial confirmation, but in a few cases the caller felt strongly enough to insist on filing a complaint and making it possible to obtain a warrant for a search. Most of these cases were backyard in scale, and not worth much in either publicity or results. It was, however, enough to get the wheels rolling in the law enforcement offices, and to start coordinating the paperwork and logistical cooperation that would become necessary as the season moved along. Detective Stockton was waiting for a duplicate signed copy of a warrant when Bill Reynolds came through the office. They exchanged greetings and Reynolds asked the other man to step into his office.

"Sit down. Coffee? How do you take it?"

"Just black."

Reynolds buzzed and asked for the coffee, and then turned to study his visitor. He hardly knew Stockton other than by his reputation for bringing in a lot of the pot they captured, but he liked to think he could take the measure of someone from the way they sat through a short silence without knowing what was coming. The detective seemed quite at ease, looking around the office and settling more comfortably into the big chair. He looked like a man who enjoyed his job, but who wouldn't let it pressure him outside of work. He also seemed to be of the patient sort, and this was one of the things Reynolds counted highest in forming his judgement about someone he didn't know very well. A patient man could be useful, especially when the rewards were long-term rather than immediate.

"I'll call you Tony if you call me Bill," he said. "So, how's it going for you this time around? What stage are we at with all that rain we had?"

"I know there's a lot out there, and I think we're ready. With some of the new methods, I'm expecting we'll do pretty well. We've already got more tips than in years past, and I think a lot of the growers are gambling on us sticking with planes for another year. The copter is going to change a lot of the rules of the game."

"Good to hear. How about prosecution, any increase on our end of it?"

"Less and less on private land, other than the small home garden stuff. I don't know. Of course, any time we can find anything to tie a grower to his plants, we'll bring it right in here to you."

The secretary came in with the two coffees. "Anything else?" she asked.

"No thanks, Sally. But would you have Janet ready to come in here when Tony here leaves? And tell her it won't take long."

Sally nodded yes and backed out.

"Well, I'll tell you what, Tony, just between you and me, we do have a small problem, but I think it's something you and I can work on. As you know, we've got pretty much cart blanche on the money this season. That's great for us and couldn't come at a better time. We'll need everything we can confiscate and make a detailed record of to prove just how serious the problem is, and to let people know that this crackpot idea of legalization or decriminalization isn't going to work around here, not in this county. The election is a little more important now since this Lehman woman put her campaign in line with the pot people. Basically, that should help us, but only if we can keep showing what a menace this so-called business really is to the public. How's your coffee? Wish I could offer you something stronger. Maybe we'll get away from the office and have lunch someday soon."

"Coffee's fine. Why do you think she did that?"

"Can't figure it. The polls show the initiative losing in every county in the state—if it even gets on the ballot. I think she's nailed the lid on her own coffin, but she never had much of a chance anyway, so maybe it made some kind of sense to take this gamble. But I really don't know, never could figure Democrats. What I do know is that the more we can keep this issue in front of the public's face and the more we show just how dangerous it's become, the better it is for us all the way around. Better for our relations with the DEA and the feds, better for us when local tax elections come around, and better for me when this election comes around, or any others we might be involved in later on."

"Did you see the first article from that Kincaid, the journalist?"

"Yes, I did. Just the kind of thing we need more of. Good quotes from you, by the way. When are they coming back?"

Stockton glanced up at the calendar hanging on the wall next to the clock. "Should be up again middle of next month. Unless something breaks that they want to cover. They're pretty much on standby for this one."

"Tony, I think we've got an opportunity here, a big one that's too important to pass up. I don't know what you're planning for your future, but I'm sure you've thought about it. You've shown excellent ability around here, and I'm afraid we'll have trouble keeping you if you continue doing such good work. Somebody else is going to notice and try to grab you away. No, I mean it. But I want to level with you, and this absolutely can't go beyond you and me. I believe our sheriff is beginning to, how can I say it nicely, to run out of gas. As far as being able to keep up with the demands of the job, and as far as his enthusiasm goes, it's looking like he'd rather be doing something else. I think he can handle the next two years, but I don't see him sticking it out much longer. And this County of ours has some pretty sweet early retirement incentives. So, here's what I'm getting at: we're going to need someone good, and someone with experience to step up here. I just want to plant the seed here with you, today. As far as I can tell, there's no one else in the department who's got either the drive or the qualifications to move into the top spot. And, frankly, we're not the kind of county that attracts good people from other jurisdictions. In any case, there's food for thought and I'd be interested to hear what you're thinking."

Tony paused before answering. These were not new thoughts to him, but it was the first time he'd heard them from anyone else. He wanted to be careful and not appear over-eager.

"I guess I'll just have to see how it goes. Maybe I'll start paying a little more attention to this election business. Can't hurt to learn a little about every aspect of public service."

"That's a nice noncommittal answer, Tony. That's the most important thing we learn in politics, you know, how to stay noncommittal, as long as possible. It's all about maximizing your options. Well, there's one other thing I want to bring up before I let you go. I'm sure you can tell that the people behind this grant and these news stories have their own needs and expectations, reasons why they can help us out, and results they need in order to continue their programs and aid. Cards on the table, we've got to come up with proof of marijuana-related violence. We know it's out there: armed guards, boobytraps, the whole works, but what we know and what gets printed in the newspapers isn't enough anymore. We need the guns, the explosives, the trip-wires, whatever there is. We need documentation, and we need it soon. I'm not talking so much about the individuals behind all this, but we need the hard evidence."

He stopped long enough to see if Tony had anything to say, and then he went on, "Now, like I said, I don't think Marty Johnson's got what it takes to grab hold of the initiative in this, so I want to tell you, and only you, what I think we might need to do about this."

"I'm not quite sure I know what you mean. We'll find it if it's out there, and it'll certainly get coverage."

"Fine, fine," Reynolds said, "but what I'm saying goes a little further than that. We know it's out there and if we find it that's great. But I'm talking about what we might have to do if you can't find a smoking gun. See what I mean? If it's there and we don't find it, that doesn't mean it isn't there. So, what it comes down to is that we need to find something, one way or another. Understand me?"

"I think I see what you mean. How much time have we got?"

"As much as it takes, as long as there's time for major coverage before your raid season kicks off in earnest. We want people to know why we're doing what we're doing, and we want them to know it's for their protection. Enough said?"

"Yeah, I think we understand each other, and I'll be thinking about the other things you mentioned as well. Anything else?"

"Not that I can think of." Reynolds loosened his tie, stood, and leaned across the desk with his hand outstretched. They shook and the younger man turned to leave. Reynolds spoke again, "Be sure you let me know if you need any help over there and by all means, keep in touch."

"Sure. Thanks again. Good coffee."

As the detective was leaving, Reynolds wondered if he'd left things too open by not heavily emphasizing the private nature of their conversation. He didn't think he'd read his man wrong, but it could get very ugly if Stockton were to carry any tales back to Sheriff Johnson. The chime on the intercom rang softly, and he acknowledged it by tapping a button.

"Janet Clark to see you now."

"Send her in." He sat back, tightened his tie and made himself look as comfortable as possible. He didn't want this woman any more nervous than she probably already was.

Janet let herself in and quickly took the seat he motioned her to. She'd only been in this office a couple of times, and mostly when he wasn't there. The feeling reminded her of going to see the principal. You only went there if you had been especially good at something, or very bad. With Mr. Reynolds she was afraid she was in trouble for doing nothing.

"Well," he said and smiled. "Good to see you. How are you today, Ms. Clark?"

"Fine, fine." She glanced around the office. He didn't seem to be particularly threatening or upset. She and Sonya had talked about what she should say when she was confronted, but now she wasn't at all sure of how she should react.

"What case are you working on these days?" he asked.

"Oh, I'm just indexing all the research on the new county liability policies. I never knew there was so much to need protection from."

"Or to be bored by. Listen, I think you can finish up whatever stage of it you're at and hand it off. We're possibly facing a class action suit arising out of the jail's population limits. If we're going to have a chance to head it off before the hearing process kicks in, we need some good research done quickly. We'll have Mr. Myers fill you in and get you started. I might as well tell you right off that Sonya Lehman is behind this thing, her and some ACLU flunkey she's got doing her work while she's campaigning. It's an obvious election stunt and it's being directed at the media, but I think we can take it away from them before it gets much further. Would you like me to have coffee or tea brought in?"

"No thank you."

"And speaking of Ms. Lehman, how's that going? Have you gotten to meet her?"

Janet made a quick decision to go ahead with the truth as far as she could. It was clear that he could find out anything he didn't already know, so it was only a case of hiding her loyalty to Sonya. She answered, talking slowly, "Yes they need workers quite badly. They have so little money that it's almost all volunteer help. They couldn't afford to turn me down."

"So, what's she like, up close?" He leaned forward, elbows on his desk.

"In what way?"

"Oh, is she running her own show, or is she being pretty carefully handled?"

"She seems to be in charge, of herself. There are party people around her, but I don't yet know how much influence they have."

"Who do you think is responsible for her radical stance on the pot thing? Personally, I can't see the Democratic Party going out on a limb like that."

"I honestly don't know." She was able to look him in the eyes because she really didn't know. It was a mystery to her, too. She had not expected Sonya to take any kind of definite stand and was completely surprised by what her friend came out with. "She hasn't really brought it up again in public or in the few staff meetings I've been to, not since the papers played it up so big. Maybe she's having second thoughts."

Reynolds leaned back in his chair and said, "It certainly seems like a big mistake to me. But don't tell her I said so because I love it. I was almost beginning to think I might have to get out and do some real campaigning, but, hell, she's doing it for me. Have you any assignment for the rally with Mrs. Mondale?"

"Not yet. The Secret Service wants a security check for me in case I do get more involved."

"Right, they would. That's good to know. Any idea how much of her staff is getting that check? Any idea, at all?"

"No," she spoke quietly, surprised by his excitement. "Probably anyone who might be on the platform or in the motorcade, that's all I know for sure."

"Okay, good. Now, here's what you can do. If there's anybody near her, friends or workers, that seem at all suspicious, or in any way linked to marijuana, I want to know names. No reason why we can't have the Secret Service doing some of our work for us. I mean it, I want you to get close enough to her to know who she spends time with, who she gets her ideas from. She's got to have connections to the dope business somewhere, and that's going to be our ace in the hole." He paused, leaned forward, looked her over, trying to gauge what she was thinking. How much did she know? How much did this Janet woman think he knew about her? One thing for sure, he didn't want to scare her into jumping ship. At the same time, he needed her to be acting in her own self-interest.

When he resumed speaking it, it was in a dry, professional voice, "Ms. Clark, I think you may not realize or may have underestimated the problem here by not knowing the kind of people I'm talking about. We have definite information linking Ms. Lehman and her campaign to a shadowy organization of growers and dealers who are providing her with under-the-table cash and other types of help. You may not have had time to notice any of this yourself, but these people, and we think we know who some of them are, are experienced criminals who will use anyone and anything to protect their illicit income from any kind of interference. The fact that they are bold enough and wealthy enough to get a full-fledged political initiative to the state-wide petition stage shows how powerful they're becoming. We can't allow ourselves to be fooled by their legalistic cover job. These people play for keeps. I want names and I want connections, but I don't want you to get hurt." He paused and looked directly at her, "Do they know you work for me? Officially?"

"Yes, they do. I'm sure Ms. Lehman has seen me in court once or twice."

"How did you explain it?"

"I said I didn't like the ways the Office was being handled and wanted to help change it."

"Do you think they bought it?"

"Yes."

"Good thinking on your part. Stick with that story. Give them whatever they ask for about how we work here. Try to prove to them how much you want to help out. You could say you're afraid of losing your job anyway, so you really want to help them win. Whatever it takes to get in with them. Meanwhile, I'll arrange some minimal protection for you and your family, have the police put your home on their rounds late at night, and so forth, can't be too careful. I'm pretty sure there's no danger for you, but it's always good to be careful. In the meantime, your best protection will be to come up with some of those names so we can either pull them in or run them out of these parts. And I'll tell you something, when this is done with, Chinook County is going to be a whole lot safer place to live. And your part in it won't be forgotten. Now, anything else you can think of?"

"No, no there isn't."

"All right, you're doing great. And I hope this jail issue is a lot more interesting for you. I hate all the insurance crap myself. I'll inform Sally that you can have direct access to me at any time. You could become very important to me, and I don't forget it when someone helps me out."

"Thank you. If there's nothing else, I'm supposed to get off from work early to take my daughter to the dentist right about now."

"No, that's all. Hope your girl is all right. Remember, call me right away with anything you come up with, even if it doesn't seem important to you."

"I will." She stood and turned to go.

"One last thing. Find out who she sleeps with…And have a good day."

Janet smiled politely and left without saying anything more. She had to talk to Sonya as soon as possible. On the other hand, she also had to be more careful now than before. She didn't quite believe Mr. Reynolds's suspicions, but she herself had been a bit worried about the sudden emphasis the marijuana issue was getting in Sonya's campaign. As far as who was sleeping with who, she had a definite aversion to any plans Bill Reynolds might be making for her own future with him.

The day of the Joan Mondale rally came on clear and hot. Sonya wasn't quite as excited as some of her staff, but it was enough to make her nervous whenever she stopped for a moment's break in the last-minute flurry of arrangements. Dan was carrying most of the load, and he was also the one most energized by the event. It was obviously important to him that everything go off smoothly, and that he get a lot of the credit for it. This was, after all, as close as he was going to get to the big-time in the '84 campaign, and there was always the chance that someone might notice him, someone from the state or national levels of the party. His ambition wasn't the sort that wanted something for nothing, he was someone who wanted to earn recognition for a job well done, and that kind of notice is often more a matter of chance than of ability. Sonya was aware of this, and because she was so grateful for all the good work he'd been doing, she introduced him to everyone she was meeting, and put in a good word for him every chance she got.

The Mondale plane was late in arriving at the Eugene airport, but the entourage moved quickly and the caravan of two limos and several matching black rental cars sped through the countryside toward Dixon City without further delay. The two women of the day found an easy rapport in the details they shared about being in the center of the fishbowl with this campaigning business. They laughed together as they checked their makeup in small hand mirrors on the way to the rally, and they exchanged pleasantries about the local area. Mrs. Mondale had often been to Dixon as a child and was looking forward to seeing how much it had changed. Security was low-profile, and Soya hardly noticed it at all.

When they reached the fairgrounds at around two o'clock, a small crowd had gathered in front of the stage. Sonya and her people paired up with the visitors and took them into a small luncheon room where snacks and cold sodas were waiting. They had until 2:30, when things were scheduled to begin.

Sonya and Joan, as she insisted on being called, spent a little time going over the content of their respective speeches, making sure they wouldn't duplicate each other, or disagree in public about anything. It didn't take them very long to determine that there were no problems. Sonya noticed that Terry was having a hard time controlling his desire to be introduced to their guest, so she called him over.

"Joan, this is Terry Lindsay. He's our pollster and media coordinator. He's doing an excellent job. I hope he decides to stay in politics because he's already an expert at what he does."

"Hello, Terry."

"Hello, ma'am. It's a thrill to meet you."

"I'm always so pleased to meet young people who are involved in the work of the party and the process. Politics had a bad name there for a while, but I think we've turned it around, especially when I travel around and see so many young people working so hard at this."

"I'm glad to hear that," Terry said. "I'm also a reporter for the campus radio station and I wonder if I can get you to answer two questions for me, on the record. It would be an exclusive for me, you know?"

"I think that would be all right. Well, depending on the questions."

"The first one, and I'm taping now, first one is, what has him being the front-runner for the nomination meant to your husband's strategy, and has that strategy changed since he was behind in the early primaries?"

"Wow, some question. Well, I'll take a stab at it. Being the front-runner is a mixed blessing, at least in our case. While it gives you the chance to be heard on everything, you also never get a chance to let down, to take a break and relax. Of course, this is from a candidate's wife's point of view, but I think it's clear when you look at some of the others in the race, like Mr. Hart or Mr. Glenn, you can see them waiting for us to make a move or state a position, that they can then react to. This makes it so we must be 'on' all the time, while I think they get to take a breather once in a while. And no, I don't think our strategy has ever really changed. We're still doing everything we can to win the nomination at the convention, and that's always been the goal."

"Thank you. Second question. How do you personally feel that the White House would change if you were First Lady instead of Mrs. Reagan?"

"Well, I don't want to count on any chickens before they hatch, but there are a few things I might say to that. Let me first say that she has been a gracious and fascinating first lady. I think I would be a little more private than she's been, but then I didn't come into all this from Hollywood. And I guess I think my wardrobe would be a little less extravagant, probably because I get attached to my outfits and like to wear them many times. I also think that both my husband and myself would be a lot more outspoken about the role of women in our society. We feel that this is a hard time for women in all types of situations because things are changing so fast, so I think we would keep this aspect of things much more in the public's awareness that the Reagans do." She finished her ginger ale and asked, "Well, Terry, was that good enough?"

"Oh yes, really good, it'll be on both the evening and morning newscasts. Thank you so much." He shook her hand when she held it out to him.

He walked away, looking to be in a hurry, and Mrs. Mondale turned to Sonya, who had been enjoying their exchange. "He's quite perceptive, I'd say."

Sonya replied, "Yes, he is. Listen we have about five minutes. The ladies lounge is over there if you want it. I have to check on one last-minute detail with my manager, so I'll meet you there by the stage."

"Certainly." They both stood and went off in separate directions. Sonya noticed that the tallest of the silent men in the corners of the big room followed Mrs. Mondale and stood by the door of the lounge. Sonya wasn't sure she would want that kind of constant protection for herself, but then she was probably going to lose her first election, let alone climb the ladder to the world of Secret Service guards.

The heat hit them hard as they left the air-conditioned building and walked toward the stage. One of the security men told Sonya and Joan that there were about 1500 people, mostly women, and a large contingent of media waiting for them. They climbed the stairs to the platform and took seats behind the podium. Sonya looked out over the crowd and smiled, partly for the crowd and partly to herself as she remembered Dan's last words to her about not saying word one about marijuana. She wouldn't have anyway, but it was a good indication of just how important he felt the national focus on this event was for them both.

To open the rally, a trio of young women got up to the microphone and sand "From Both Sides Now," and three verses of "We Shall Overcome." An elderly woman professor from the college stepped up and introduced Sonya as a hard-working and dedicated young lawyer who was a fine example of what women can accomplish if they set their minds to it. Sonya moved to the podium as the applause peaked and then began to die away.

As she looked out over the audience, she had a flash of memory from her high school graduation ceremony. She had been one of the speakers and had never been so nervous in her life, before or since. She could feel the difference now and how she was getting more used to the speaking role. But so far, she was only appearing in front of basically friendly crowds. She glanced down at her notes and wondered what it would be like to have to talk in a hostile setting.

She began her speech with a reference to the old story of the hare and tortoise and drew a parallel between rabbit-men and turtle-women in politics. She emphasized the importance of women's common needs that go far beyond the old definitions of party or interest groups. She said her main issue was and always would be the protection and guarantee of human rights, and that people could see right now what can happen when they are ignored as under the current Reagan administration and the Chinook County courthouse and jail. She also made a strong point about the rights of everyone, especially women and children, to be protected from abuse, both physical and psychological, and she pledged a vigorous program of prevention and prosecution if she were elected. Once again, she emphasized the difference between crimes with victims and those without. She closed her remarks with a plea for people to work together at the local level to help defeat Reagan and Bush, and then she introduced Joan Mondale as a delightful and very bright woman who would be a great asset to all Americans as their first lady. As she took her seat, she thought of two or three things she hadn't said, but none of them were important enough to worry about.

As Mrs. Mondale took her place at the speaker's stand, Sonya joined the clapping and admired the calm and even casual way the woman carried herself. The potential first lady began her speech with a couple of anecdotes from when she lived in Oregon as a child. Then she talked about the hardships of campaigning for the presidency, the travel and separations of the members of her family, but she countered that with praise for all the wonderful people they got to meet along the way. She reemphasized the need for the unity of women outside of party affiliation, and the need for women to get involved in every level of society, from educating other women, to national, state, and local contests.

It all counts, she said, and the only possibility for real and lasting change lay in hard work and commitment. She called for an international show of solidarity with people everywhere who were trying to end the arms race. She reminded people that human rights had been the highest priority for Jimmy Carter and her husband and stressed that one must always place their principles above politics, even if it costs them an election.

She went on then to urge everyone, especially women, to try to work together for a better definition of strength without hardness, and respect without subservience. She said that everything she could find out about Sonya Lehman impressed her favorably and that this was an opportunity for the people of Chinook County to demonstrate with their votes that law enforcement need not require heavy-handedness, but rather even-handedness. She closed with a call for unity and action, and with a reminder that today's elections determine tomorrow's policies, and that the people of the United States deserve leadership based on fairness, and solutions based on reality.

The applause lasted more than a minute, and there was a boisterous demonstration by some twenty people with posters calling for "US out of Central America." Sonya and her new friend, Joan, shared a hug and left the stage together. Now that this was over, they could both feel the strain of the heat and commented to one another on the endurance of their audience. As they walked, they were surrounded by a cluster of microphones, cameras and reporters all trying to get their own questions answered first. Mrs. Mondale signaled to her guardians, who stepped in and cleared a way for them. Dan was shouting at the media that there would be an organized press conference in fifteen minutes, and in the meantime the two women needed a short break. He shouted that there were refreshments for all in the anteroom where the question period would take place. Sonya and Joan were able to slip through the door into the lunchroom and both sank into soft chairs and gratefully accepted tall, frosty glasses of lemonade that were handed to them by teen-age girls.

Sonya leaned over toward her new friend and asked, "How are you?"

"Oh, I'll be fine. It was hot out there. I enjoyed what you had to say. And I do hope you get the chance to try and get some things done."

"Thank you, my wish for you as well. Where do you go from here?"

"After Eugene and Portland, I'm going home for a short rest before the convention. I'll be very glad to just sit still, if that's possible, even if for only a couple of days."

Sonya thought about how tired she was some of these days and felt a real sense of concern for her new acquaintance. "Now tell me truthfully. How are you really? I don't know how you can keep up with it all."

"Thanks for the concern. I'm really in pretty good shape, and one way or another it's going to be over, the campaign, I mean. Thank God."

Just then Dan came over to them with a short explanation of the format for the press conference. They still had a few minutes in which to freshen up and then he would be back to take them into the anteroom. He asked if there was anything else he could get them. There wasn't, and Mrs. Mondale said she would be happy just to sit there for a few minutes. Sonya got up and went into the lady's lounge, smiling because she wasn't important enough to have any of the bodyguards follow her there.

Jerry was sitting on his front porch when Peter came walking up the driveway. He told his dog to shut up and called out a greeting but made no move out of the shade. He drained his beer and yelled inside to Carla that they had company. She came out right away, wiping the sweat from her forehead, spotted Peter, and said, "I thought you said it was company."

"If I'm not company, what am I?" Peter bantered back.

"We haven't figured that out yet."

Peter reached the shady steps with relief. He sat on the top step and wiped his face with a bandana. "Hottest day of the year, I bet."

"Probably," Jerry said, "and another one tomorrow."

"And the day after," added Carla as she went back inside to answer their baby's cry.

"Want a beer?"

"No thanks. Need water first. Can I get it myself?" Peter stood up and started inside. Jerry pointed to a faucet beside the steps. Peter stepped to it and stuck both hands under the stream of water, sloshing handfuls over his head and face. He drank deeply with his head turned under the spigot. "That's better." He sat back on the steps. "What's up?"

"Not much. Couple of turkey vultures over that way."

Peter looked where he was pointing and watched the two big birds spiraling in the rising current of hot air. "Looks like a fine way to relax," he said, slumping back against the porch railing.

He looked inside through the screen and not seeing Carla, asked, "How are yours coming along?"

"Great, really good. There's one big tree in the way come afternoon, but I think they've got enough sun from the rest of the day."

"Yeah, this time of year they don't need the whole day of it direct. Gives them a chance for a siesta."

"How's yours?" Jerry asked.

"Good. Drying out too fast in this heat, but it's okay—just means more work for more results." He took out his pouch and papers. "Smoke one?"

"Guess so." He untied his shoelaces and loosened them. "Not much left to do today. At least I hope not."

"Leslie told me to watch the local evening news. Said that woman, Sonya, you know, the DA candidate, said she's on. They had a rally today at the fairgrounds, with her and Mondale's wife. Thought I might come over here and check it out, if you're watching." He picked some small stems out of the palm of his hand and rolled the joint.

"What's she up to, anyway? You think she's for real?"

"Yeah, she's for real. I talked to her a couple of times, once at Leslie's. She's pretty real, but I think she's blowing it if she thinks she can come on that out front. Course they say she didn't have a chance anyway." He lit the joint, toked on it, and handed it over to Jerry.

The dog came out from under the porch, snuggled up to Jerry, who blew some smoke in his face. He crawled back into the shade underneath the steps. The vultures were drifting farther away, then disappearing over the ridge. They finished the joint in silence, brushed lazily at a couple of flies, and listened to Carla moving around in the house.

"Carla," Jerry called, "what time is it?"

"Almost five-thirty." She came to the screen door with Maya in her arms, "Why?"

"Want to watch the local news? Leslie told him that DA woman's on."

"Well, it starts in two minutes." She came out and sat in the porch swing. "You going to bring it out here? It's too hot in there."

He went inside to get the TV.

Peter looked over at Carla and the baby. "Three months almost," he said. "How's she doing?"

"Fine. She's really a good baby. Got her shots last week, but she's never had any problems. Want to hold her?"

"Is it all right?" He looked self-consciously down at his hands. They weren't dirty, but they hadn't held a baby for longer than he could remember.

"Yes, it's all right. She won't break." Carla bent over and reached the little bundle of diaper and skin as pale as blank paper over to him. He took the baby carefully and held her awkwardly next to himself. She seemed to know something was different and squirmed around, but she didn't cry. Jerry came out with the small TV, trailing antenna wire and extension cord.

"Well, Uncle Peter, how do you like her?" He asked as he set the TV on an upturned five- gallon bucket.

"She's so light. How much does she weigh, you think?"

"Maybe twelve to fourteen pounds, maybe a little more."

"Seems lighter than that." The baby was starting to fuss a bit. He glanced over at Carla who didn't seem to notice, so he started rocking her in his arms and she quieted down.

Jerry turned on the TV and tuned it in. He asked Peter if he wanted that beer yet. Peter nodded yes, so Jerry went back inside and came back with a couple. A car salesman finished his rap and the newscaster came back on and introduced the lead story of the day, the Joan Mondale rally at the fairgrounds.

A reporter filmed at the rally described the situation, and there were two excerpts from Sonya's speech. She looked and sounded good on TV, and the crowd seemed to be listening intently. Maya started to cry so Carla reached over for her. There was more coverage, of Mrs.

Mondale's speech with several excerpts, and then there was a short segment covering the question and answer period following the rally. Most of the questions were about potential running mates for Mondale. Would he consider selecting a woman? What about Jesse Jackson? Someone asked her whether she preferred the West Coast to Minnesota. "Of course, I do," she answered, "except when I'm in Minnesota and I get that question." There was a ripple of laughter.

Sonya stood quietly beside her, but there were no questions for her recorded in the news story. The last shot ended with a plane taking off from the Eugene airport, and the reporter closed with a comment that there was no way to measure the impact of such a visit on Sonya Lehman's chances in the November election. Jerry turned the sound off when an ad came on and looked over at Peter. "Well, she didn't get into any trouble this time."

"Guess not. She looked pretty straight."

Carla was nursing Maya, who was eagerly getting what she wanted. Her mama said, "That Sonya woman sure is pretty."

"Yeah," said Peter as he thought about how attractive she was in real life.

"You want to watch anymore?" asked Jerry.

"No, better get going."

"Do you want to stay for dinner?" Carla asked. "Nothing fancy, just rice and bean burritos" She put Maya over her shoulder and patted her back.

"No thanks, got too much to do before dark, now that it's cooled off some. Maybe some other time when you're eating something fancy."

"Might have to wait quite a while." She stood and smiled to him and went in through the screen door.

Jerry finished his beer. "Want to go fishing next weekend? I was going up to this lake I know in the Cascades. Maybe take a couple guys with me."

"Don't think so. Thanks, but I do most of my watering on the weekends. Seems safer."

"Yeah, hope so. Well. If I don't go, we could try again in the middle of the week."

"Maybe so." Peter drained the last of his beer, set the bottle down, stretched and unkinked his legs. "Better get going if I'm going to."

"Yeah, see ya soon. Glad you came by."

Peter felt the lingering heat like a slap as he stepped out of the shade of the house. The dog came out from under the porch, sniffed at him as he walked away, and crawled back where he came from. Jerry was moving the TV back into the house when he turned and waved.

He got home as the sun was going down behind the ridge, watered his garden and gathered some salad makings. He built a small fire under the grate in the yard, and ate a meal of smoky burgers, fresh peas, and ice cream. When he finished eating it was coming on dusk and he stoked up the fire, cleaned up after himself, and moved his speakers outside the trailer. He tuned in the classical station and settled into the chair without legs that he used beside the rock-lined firepit. He filled a carved wooden pipe with small buds, smoked it to the sounds of a Bach cantata transcribed for orchestra, and settled back for a long summer's evening. His muscles ached from the firewood he'd been chopping that morning to fill an order from an old man who lived down the road. The picture of Sonya on the TV played around in his head as he toked slowly on the pipe. She was certainly spending more and more time in his thoughts, but he didn't see any more chances to see each other now. She would be so busy with all the campaigning and he needed to stay close to his patches with this heat, and who knew when the flyovers would start. Besides the fantasy of the woman was more than he wanted to be bothered with. At least that's what he was telling himself.

Later, as the stars and satellites filled in the dark depths of the sky, he put on a cassette of the Franck's Symphony in D Minor and got out his horn. He listened to the whole first movement in silence, immersing himself in its solemnity and foreboding, thinking of his own life, the limits he faced, the weight of the past and his inability to get close enough to anyone to share himself. At the same time, he could feel the freedom he did have, the absence of anyone to drag on him or be responsible to. The stars would go on moving across the sky as they always did, and he would sit beneath them to lose himself in the silence of the land and the sounds of the music he could play along with, like he always did.

The symphony paused at the end of the first movement and he got up to turn it louder. He picked up the horn and sat down on another old lawn chair, this one with legs. He kicked some more sticks onto the embers of the fire and set himself to play along with the rest of the French horn section. The second movement translated the mystery and brooding of the first into action, into horn solos and a strident contest of power between different sections and instruments, between the striving sides of himself. He played for the stars, for himself, and maybe even for the unattainable Ms. Sonya Lehman.

CHAPTER SIX

August

August can seem to be the longest moth as it eases in with its "dog days," slinks along the side of the road looking for shade to lie down in, and spends its nights looking up at Sirius, the dog's own star shuffling across the sky. The days shorten and the heat intensifies, as if there is a set amount of it that has to get used up by when darkness comes earlier, and the days finally begin to cool down. The flies move slower, but the hand that swats at them also moves more slowly. The bright green of the vegetation takes on a fine coating of dust that dulls its earlier brilliance. Berries and vegetables flower and begin the countdown to maturing with their fruit and seed. The first cool night slips in and sends a warning through the animal world: eat more and get your breeding done. Children spend most of each day splashing and dunking, and the memory of school is pushed out of mind. In the forested lands, among the clear cuts, cultivated plants get regularly watered and begin to stand out from the drying and withering greens of their neighbors. Larger leaves must be plucked off and some branches pruned, both to free up energy for flowering and to lessen the chances of detection. The turkey vultures are joined in their constant circling by other aircraft, as up and down the coastal mountain range, large mechanical, metal mosquitos begin to crisscross the breezeless sky. It will likely rain sometime before the end of the month, but the new moisture will hardly settle the dust, and the springs and creeks will come close to disappearing. It is a month of waiting and change-over, of preparing for fall, and protecting the gains of summer. The month's last days usher in the beginning of the season of gathering, the transition between extremes and balance, marking the erratic identities of both, and the characteristic behavior of not looking back.

Detective Tony Stockton returned from a four-day training session in California to find an urgent memo from DA Reynolds on his desk. The training had been intensive and eye-opening. They'd spent one day in the classroom learning how to detect and dismantle lethal devices. A second day of lectures and films dealt with the use of helicopters in search and eradication operations. The second half of the training had been field exercises in the use of metal detectors and actual airtime in the choppers.

The memo didn't say what Reynolds wanted him for, just to get in touch as soon as he was back. Tony thought he might know what it was about and felt better prepared for that kind of thing than he had before he'd gone. He finished a cup of coffee and a butter horn and cleared his desk of the buildup from his absence. He looked over the proposed schedule of days for the combined task force of Oregon State Police, US Forest Service, and local authorities to conduct their coordinated raids in the county. Only two weeks away and an incredible amount of work to be done before then. He could feel the first waves of mounting excitement in his nervous system as he thought about the hardships and successes of the "Pot War" to come. He had missed out on Vietnam, drawing instead a soft tour of duty with NATO in western Europe, and though he knew there weren't any real enemies out here in this forest to compare with the Vietcong, he could still feel good about himself for choosing this role in the closest thing to combat you could get these days.

When he'd run through everything in the incoming tray, he opened his briefcase and began filing and putting away all the reference material he'd received at the training camp. Part of his responsibility now included organizing and presenting the information in a shortened version for the local task force. He would need to edit it down to a half-day classroom session to be held in conjunction with the rest of that day devoted to overall strategies and assignments. It was a lot like being in school again, but at least this had immediate and practical usefulness.

He called Reynolds and found he was right about what was wanted from him. He assured the boss that there were some tips that looked as though they might involve the kind of thing the DA was looking for, and that, in the absence of any hard evidence, he was going to be able to deal with it soon enough. They exchanged a few other pleasantries, with Reynolds again making a vague offer of lunch sometime. They signed off with encouraging words for one another about their different but simultaneous campaigns.

As he hung up, it crossed his mind about the irony involved in him contacting Reynolds even before he'd reported back to the sheriff, but this season surely called for high-level inter-departmental cooperation with or without the knowledge of all parties. He rang for Marty and was told he was out and wouldn't return until early afternoon. Tony made an appointment for three o'clock, and then left a message with the desk officer that he would be out until then himself. He grabbed hiking boots from his locker near the parking garage and signed out an unmarked pickup. He wanted to check on a couple of the patches they'd raided last year, and if he hustled he could make it back on time.

At three o'clock, he was just pulling into the garage, a little late, but not by much. He turned in the truck, put his boots into the locker, and stopped off at the washroom to tidy up. *I look like a grower*, he thought, looking in the mirror and pulling a couple of twigs out of his hair.

Marty was waiting in his office, studying a thick folder opened on the desk. He looked up and motioned Tony into a chair, then continued reading for another minute. The detective waited, glad for a moment's breather. He was going to have to get in better shape fast, probably need to start working out in the gym on the way home.

Marty closed the folder and slapped it with his hand, "Know what this is?"

"No, but hello. How you been?"

"Yeah, hello. Been terrible. This here's a class-action suit against yours truly, Mr. DA Reynolds, and the Board of County Commissioners, on behalf of present and previous inmates of our own local hotel. And it's goddam well put together."

Stockton wondered why Reynolds hadn't mentioned it, and asked, "What's it mean?"

The sheriff got up and started pacing back and forth behind his desk. "It means we might be up shit creek without a bat." He picked up a softball from his desk and started flipping it from hand to hand. "And you know why? Because they're right, that's why. We are in violation and we'll be damn lucky to get out of this without the County paying damages to somebody. Listen up, Tony, the buck is going to catch fire from being passed around so fast on this one, you wait and see."

Tony looked at him sympathetically, thinking how it was true that the old man really wasn't cut out for the job, just couldn't handle the politics even though he was a pretty good administrator and one smart cop. "Whose fault is it?" he asked, not really knowing.

"Long-range fault, or short-range guilt? The Commissioners don't give us enough to run even the mandated services we're bound by law to deliver. They say they don't have it, but they just remodeled the whole goddam county office building, and the whole fuckin' staff is top-heavy with do-nothings. They'll say it's my fault for not getting a proposal for a new or improved facility to the voters. Hell, the voters won't even show up once you breathe the word levy. Besides, that plan would take six years before we could put the funds on the ground and get work done on new buildings, and even if I'd started on it two years ago when it first came up, and even if it did get passed somehow, it'd still be four years, one of those other bastard's entire term. No, the short-range fix sits right over there in that courthouse: Bill Reynolds and his tight-assed boys always worrying about their won/lost record and keeping stats for their future careers in God knows what kind of political hanky-panky. They ought to find a good way to separate law enforcement from politics. I'm not saying it's not good to try for a good track record. I'm just saying there's a limit and sometimes you've got to throw some back in, give 'em bail they can afford and let 'em jump. You'll get 'em back sooner or later."

"You think this other candidate's approach would be any better? I mean, you think she'd make anything any different?"

Marty sat down, hitched his feet up onto the corner of the desk, and laughed. "I doubt it. She doesn't know a damn thing about the job. Reynolds is too political, and she's too innocent. Between the two of them, I'd rather have you. Where you been anyway, and what'd we pay for you to be doing? And tell me just how we're going to round up all the growers and put them in holding pens down at the auction yard? About the only space we've got left."

"May I give you my report, sir?" Tony smiled and began. "You'll be glad to know that the strategy from up top this year is to minimize hassle. Eradicate, but don't worry much about arrests unless some fool gets in the way or uses violent defensive tactics. In other words, not to worry so much about warrants or the paperwork for cultivation busts. However, there might be a coming attempt to confiscate some land. They're going to test it down there first, try to get hold of an open and shut case. Got to prove that the land was paid for by illegal activity. Kind of stuff they use on organized crime. Hard part is they have to connect the owners to the pot growing on the land. If they can get that through, it'll give us one more deterrent. Other than that, there's a push to find lethal devices in connection with the growing operations, educate the public about the level of violence and danger, and try to get more of the public to work with us instead of ignoring the problem."

Marty didn't respond so he went on, "The best part for me, for us, is the chopper. God, what a difference. We flew slow over some stuff down there and you can almost count the leaves when you park above it. Now, instead of only being able to look for color or profile, we look for the round shape of the plant from directly overhead. There's nothing else out there that grows perfectly round, not with that color. With a glass floor on the bird, if it's there, you see it.

"That's about it. I met the pilot we'll get. He's good, been at it for four years as a test project. Ran a spray copter before this came along. Learned in Vietnam. We'll only get five days for the whole county, but we can afford to run three ground units with the chopper shuttling back and forth between them. Should be fun."

The sheriff tossed the ball up near the ceiling, caught it, and gave his detective a hard look. “Fun, Tony? Has it occurred to you that if those guys out there are crazy enough to set boobytraps and bombs and maybe kill somebody for this stuff, they’re also capable of blowing you and your glass bubble out of the sky? And don’t forget, some of them are probably veterans as well.”

“I think there’s a difference, and it hasn’t happened yet. Hell, we’ve been flying low enough in our little plane last couple of years that if someone wanted to take a shot they could have. It’s a much more serious thing, shooting at the law, than just growing pot.”

“Killing’s killing. My point is that I think you’re still safe, but not because a guerilla grower draws the line between blowing up civilian backpackers and shooting cops. I think the only reason you’re safe is because these people aren’t ready to kill for their pot. Yet!” He took his feet off the desk and flipped the ball to Tony, who managed to catch it. “And one more thing, I personally don’t believe all this horseshit about traps, landmines or whatever, or we would have taken casualties before now. So far all you’ve found is some fake tripwires that don’t connect to anything, those and some noisemakers. Yeah, they’ve got warning systems to scare folks off, but ‘lethal devices’? I’ll have to see one before I go for all that crap. At least around here. Armed guards maybe, maybe next, but the rest of it doesn’t fit the pattern. They’re not real criminals, mostly just what they call ‘stoners’ is all they are.”

Tony tossed the ball back. “I hope so, I really do. In any case we’ll be supplied with the best metal detectors we can get, on the slim chance one of your angels out there gets tempted by how easy it is to protect a fortune in the middle of nowhere. I’ll drop you by some of the reports we looked at, at once I get them copied. From all over, Florida, Oklahoma, Hawaii, and of course our neighbors in California. It’s a war out there, Marty, and no sense taking chances. Because it’s coming here, too.”

“I hear what you’re saying, and if you find some of this stuff, I’ll feel pretty stupid, but if you do find it out there, maybe we’ll think twice about you up there in that whirlybird. In that case maybe the danger will outweigh the effectiveness.”

Tony stood up, ready to go. He'd come home late the night before and was tired. Marty reached across the desk to shake hands. "I want you to know that I have to look at all this like an officer in charge of his troops and think about your safety. I don't want to lose my best man, Tony. Take it easy, get some rest, and come in and see me before the end of the week so we can start going over rosters and assignments. We'll be using a lot of overtime this year. Hope the feds can pay for it."

"They will. By the way, how's your team doing this year?"

"I'm on my way over there now. Warmups in half an hour. We're 8 and 2, tied for second. Great bunch of kids. Need a little better hitting, but they're still improving, with six games left until the playoffs. If we make it that far, I'll get you a free pass."

"Yeah, Marty, on all fronts, like you say, if we make it that far." He let himself out.

The sheriff picked up the folder containing the lawsuit. He held it in one hand and the softball in the other. He weighed them, as if in a balance scale, then slammed the folder down on the desk, grabbed his coach's jacket, and followed Tony out of the office.

The weekly Tuesday evening campaign meeting started out as usual with reports from the various coordinators, but it began shifting into crisis mode when Mr. Campbell reported there was no money in the bank to cover incoming costs. Dan had tried to postpone any discussion of finances and fundraising until later in the evening, but Sonya said they probably needed to deal with this before going any further. Even Sonya was surprised by the news but was fairly confident it would work out since they'd planned for the bulk of their fundraising and spending to occur during late August and September.

Dan took the floor to say he had more information on the budget and if they wanted it now, he would oblige. There was agreement, so he went to the flip chart at the front of the room.

"The party's central committee was considering withdrawing its support from Sonya's campaign because they felt they couldn't afford to be linked to any position regarding the marijuana issue, since it is illegal." He added that he felt all along it was too controversial to be a part of their campaign strategy but had waived his reservations in light of Terry's most recent polls. "What the party leaders were seeing was the other side of that. They were hearing from established party backers who were threatening to withdraw their support for the party unless Sonya is dropped from the campaign. I've decided that I'll stay on board with this committee in any case, because I'm committed to seeing a change in this county, even if it hurts my own future. I do think that Sonya is ahead of the times in her rather outspoken defense of the legalization initiative, but we can argue that support for legalization is not the same as support for illegal use. But I would ask us all to do some serious thinking about this, since so much depends on how we handle it."

When he finished speaking there was a long silence in the room. Then Terry stopped ruffling through a stack of papers on his lap and moved to the front of the room. He was obviously excited, but that was not unusual. Sonya, sitting between Janet and Leslie, wondered what he was up to now. She was worried that this might split the campaign committee. She told herself that she'd known all along this was a possibility, since Dan had warned her after her speech at the Jamboree that party regulars would be upset by the media coverage of her position.

Terry turned the flip chart to the agenda notes and looked out at everyone. There was no reason for him to be first to talk, except that no one else seemed ready to say anything. "I think it's really important that this is happening," he said, "because it's going to show us where politics is really at these days, from here all the way up to the presidential level. Why did Gary Hart do so well with no help form the party regulars before he had to quit the race? Why is Mondale going to get beat so badly in November? The whole problem with both political parties today is that they're afraid to give up their constituencies of the past forty years and be bold enough to relate to the issues of these current times. Those traditional interests, the post-World War concern for normalcy and a return to the past, those interests are dying off. Now when you say post-War half the people in the country are going to think of Vietnam and many of them are even forgetting that.

"I don't want to get carried away with a whole analysis, but what I have to say is just too coincidental to overlook. I just finished the second round of polling and the figures are still to be finalized, but I'm up here talking now because we're obviously at a crossroads, and I need to present the other side of what Dan laid out." He waved the sheaf of papers in the air. "This information might seem kind of unbelievable, but it's what's happening and I truly will stand behind it. First of all, last time we had 15% name recognition for Sonya against 40% for Reynolds. Today, they're even at 45%, meaning 90% recognize one or the other or both. Why? You tell me. On Reynolds' job performance, he actually went down from 63% approval to 54% and that was before the overcrowding lawsuit reached the media. Now, and here's the big one, and I'm willing to do it all over again with all new names if you don't believe it's accurate—the initiative to legalize personal use of marijuana has gone from 20% in favor to 41%, and half of those switched from totally opposed. So, the way it stands now is 43% opposed to its passage, 41% in favor, and 16% don't know or won't say. And that's all just in this county.

"A little more, and I'll stop. There are two parts to working as a pollster. One is gathering the data, and the other is interpreting it. I know this data is good, and I'm pretty certain that Reynolds is getting the same thing, so he's going to have to start real campaigning very soon. The overall interpretation I'm getting from this is that Sonya has been a huge help to publicizing the initiative, no doubt about that. But it's also true, and this is really important, her taking a stand on this issue and the resulting media coverage good or bad, has boosted her recognition among voters and lowered Reynolds' approval rating. And we're only barely into August. If she backs down now or shuts up, she's going to keep getting asked about it everywhere she goes. If she doesn't stick to her statements, she'll be seen as shifty and wishy-washy, not to mention inexperienced. There are two pitfalls we most have to avoid because I want to tell you, here and now, we really do have a chance. We really do, and I know you probably don't trust me on this, and think I'm always over-reaching, which may be true, but don't dismiss the facts. The last number to look carefully at is the one on how people vote, and this one is looking better and better for us: 48% now say they vote the issues, 21% on party lines, 27% on the candidate, and 4% say all of those affect their decisions. Since our last poll, the issues and candidate factors rose significantly while party loyalty declined. So, I ask you, do we need the Democratic Party, or do they need us?"

There were a couple of handclaps as he sat down, but the feeling in the room was far from the cohesion and optimism they all had come together around several weeks back. For one thing, several of the older workers had come to Sonya's campaign as volunteers, directly from the party, and that loyalty was a strong element in their feelings and commitment. Small conversations started up here and there in the room when no one took the floor to continue with the discussion. After a long moment, Sonya stood and said she thought it was a good time to take a short break and let people go ahead and talk about these things in small groups. Coffee and tea were waiting on a side table. As people gravitated to one another in the informality of the situation, it was clear that there was and probably always had been a kind of generation gap among the members of the committee. Its effect, however, had never been clear as far as the issues went.

Sonya asked Dan and Terry to step into the back room with her so they could figure out how to proceed with the meeting at this point. It was clear to her that they both were feeling real attachment to their own perspectives and that they were reflections of what could become a schism within the committee. She and Dan both got a cup of coffee and followed Terry into the back.

Terry sat on a table and Sonya and Dan took the two chairs. They were quiet until Sonya said, "I very much appreciate both of you and your hard, hard work, and I do know how much you're putting into this. I think that some amount of internal struggle is healthy and unavoidable in politics, but if we can't resolve our differences, then we shouldn't pretend we're all working for the same things. I would rather quit this whole thing than have it turn into something that places us in adversarial positions with one another. These two things coming together, the somewhat bad news about the money situation and the good news about the polls, are really our first crisis as a group, and I'm not sure whether being out of funds or out of step with each other is worse. What I do know is that there are more important and potentially more tense situations ahead, and that we must protect our unity, as an organization, or it isn't worth it. I'm not saying what's right or wrong in this case, what I'm asking is that the three of us provide some leadership tonight and show that honest disagreement can be healthy when our intentions are good, and for the best. Now, about the issue itself, I have a few things myself that I want to say to everybody, and then I think it would be a good idea to hear from anyone who wants to speak to this. Do either of you have anything you want to say here just among the three of us?"

A moment passed and then Dan spoke, "I want you to know that I'm not questioning what you feel as an individual, or even as a candidate. But as your advisor, I'm only trying to make you aware of the consequences of a certain strategy, or maybe lack of strategy. And Terry, don't take me wrong, I'm excited about our results and I agree with you about the way political parties have become irrelevant to many of our citizens. Again, it's a matter of strategy rather than ideas. So I'm willing to listen and go with our consensus, even if it costs me some of my standing with the democrats down the road."

Sonia smiled to him and said, "That's good to hear. I respect what I hear you saying, and I know we all recognize that you have the most experience of anyone on the committee. Terry?"

"I said most everything I want to say, except I want both of you to know I don't use pot, don't think much of it, and wish it wasn't an issue now. But here it is right in the middle of all that's happening in this county, and it's a readymade issue that may or may not be our ticket to winning. Without it, we really don't have much of a chance against the established apparatus, and if things don't change around here, I think there will be some negative changes coming in the next couple of years, with the feds getting more and more involved in local law enforcement. It doesn't kill people to smoke it, but it might start getting them killed it they're growing it."

Sonya thanked him and then asked, "What do you think the chances are of the initiative getting passed just in this and some other counties?"

"More and more all the time. I think it's still too close to call, but don't forget the entire law enforcement network, led by Reynolds, is just now tooling up for its annual raiding season. Who knows what kind of publicity or consequences that could have?"

"Well, let's get back in there and see if we can't sideline this issue somewhat and figure out how to raise some seriously needed money."

When they were back in the meeting room, Sonya asked the folks to find their seats again and get back to the business of the meeting. Then she waited for people to get settled.

"I want to say a few words, and then let's discuss things as much as we need to, but remember we have lots of other business. What I see is this: if we don't have unity and we don't have money, there isn't much point in any of this. So, first of all, I want to review where I'm at and what I committed myself to. I have made the point that in a period of budget constraints, as DA I would rank crimes and their prosecution and sentencing in order of the seriousness with which they affect their victims. This implies, of course, that without enough funding to cover everything that goes down in this county, victimless crimes would have the lowest priority and likely go unprosecuted. This is how I'm looking at marijuana use and cultivation. It makes sense to me, and would certainly change if there were to be a large infusion of funding for the DA's office and greatly increased prosecution, but I don't see that happening in the near future. So, this makes sense to me, and if we can force the media to be factual about this position, then it isn't such a controversial stance to be taking. I think we should commission a study of where the current DA is dedicating the county's resources. I think we could prove they're neglecting some crimes with victims, such as domestic abuse or embezzlement, or whatever we find. And they're doing this just so they can put as much of their budget and people's work-time into the pot thing as they can get away with. I think the voters would be able to understand that if we can prove it in a clear way.

"Second, what I said about the initiative in Chinook County has been blown way out of proportion and that's my fault. I admit to making a spontaneous decision and not consulting everyone on that position. But I think that, if we can get it looked at objectively, it isn't all that controversial either. What I said was that we would abide by the vote in this county in our prioritizing of enforcement actions. By that I mean if it passed here even if it failed in the rest of the state. I still thinks this makes sense and fits into the rest of how I am speaking about all these issues. The problem is that it opens me up to the accusation that I condone breaking the law, which is an obvious contradiction when you're running for an office that works to enforce the laws. However, I am not just a plug-in or wind-up DA doll, and I happen to think it is the responsibility of public officials to speak out when they consider a law to be a wrongful approach to a problem, or one that does not reflect the will of the majority, and this is all that I'm really on the record for doing. Personally, I could never say, 'I will enforce all laws right or wrong,' and stay true to myself and my profession.

"The third thing is that I do believe this is an important issue because the whole situation is getting out of hand and obviously the community is polarizing just as we ourselves may be. If a middle ground isn't found soon, we will be facing a federally financed mini war right here in this county, and that really is something to be afraid of. Now, I know several of you, and maybe everyone here, has something to say about this, so let's get started and try to be somewhat brief, and I hope we can come to an agreement that allows us to move forward together."

The discussion that followed started off slowly but grew livelier as it progressed. The main argument was that the issue was emotionally charged and that if a position couldn't be clarified in layperson terms, then it would leave Sonya open to twisted and opportunistic attacks by her opponent, and by those in the establishment and the media who might be opposed to what she was putting forth. They did agree that the party was mistaken if it thought that the issue was either unimportant or avoidable. A proposal was made to:

1. Follow Sonya's suggestion for a study of Reynolds' priorities, with Janet being the obvious one to lead that effort as long as she was careful and protected herself from reprisals.
2. Come up with a position paper outlining Sonya's stated commitments and the reasons behind them.
3. Downplay any connection between her campaign and the legalization initiative, especially to deny any funding connection.

Terry and a few others volunteered to work on the position paper, which would be only one of the issues she was running on and would be presented at a press conference toward the end of the month, along with the rest of her platform. There was an obvious sense of relief evident in the group as they were able to move ahead to what was probably even more serious, the need for immediate fundraising projects and results.

Dan said he would take responsibility for trying to soothe the party people and arrive at an agreement that both they and Sonya could get along with and, in the process, get a budgeted pledge from them for the rest of the campaign. If necessary, Sonya would also meet with them as soon as possible. The leverage would be that it would look bad if they abandoned any candidate for anything less than deception or a political stance that clearly ran counter to the party line. The benefit of this approach was that the party still didn't have an official position on marijuana.

This was followed by a lively discussion about slogans and designs for buttons and bumper stickers. A subcommittee was formed to select the best suggestions by the next meeting. Everyone was encouraged to contribute ideas and Corinne volunteered to organize that project. Ed Weber, the printer, said he would solicit donations of poster and leaflet paper, but didn't think he could get the bumper sticker blanks for nothing. They all agreed to avoid linking Sonya's candidacy to the national ticket, and to downplay the Democratic Party connection in their publicity, at least in the large print. This was thought to be useful for everyone concerned. Sonya expressed that she would like her publicity to be consistently positive, and not based on tearing down the opposition. No one was able to estimate how much funding could be gained from the sales, so they planned on ordering modest amounts of materials for the time being.

Mr. Campbell said he'd done a small amount of research and estimated the basic costs for the final three months of the campaign would run to a minimum of $4,000 to $6,000, excluding television ads and any salaries. That was a bargain basement figure, he said. Terry pointed out that the return on money spent by a challenger, in terms of votes, was almost always greater than for the incumbent. However, he went on to say, it was always easier for the incumbent to raise funding. He recommended trying to gather resources for a big TV push in the final weeks of the campaign, as that would give the best results for the money spent, followed by billboards at busy locations.

Leslie and Theresa were having a whispered conversation, and then Leslie spoke up to offer a benefit picnic and party at their place on the Sunday of Labor Day weekend. She suggested that it might then be possible to get other supporters to do the same thing in different parts of the county. She said she thought she could get a band to play at their place, charge admission and parking, sell beer from kegs, and ask for additional donations from the people who showed up. She went on to say that if the group approved of that idea, it would have to be her main contribution for the month, and that someone would have to take her place working the phones as the event got closer. The idea was enthusiastically accepted, and some of the other folks promised to think about sponsoring some kind of an affair in their neighborhoods. Corinne went even further by suggesting that if these things worked out, they could think about having a big street fair and dance in town at the end of September or beginning of October.

It was getting late in the evening, so a few more ideas like raffles, letters of appeal to selected citizens, and a radio show were put on hold until the next meeting. They broke up into short subcommittee meetings after Sonya again thanked them all for the super job thy were doing. She commented that it was a pleasure and an honor to work with people who could place the unity of the effort above their own personal opinions.

Afterward Leslie and Theresa talked Sonya and Janet into going out with them for a drink and maybe some dancing. They went in separate cars and on the way across town Janet brought Sonya up to date on how the DA's staff was handling the lawsuit about jail conditions.

"As far as I can tell, the Sheriff is putting the blame on Reynolds. Says he's tried to reduce the population in several ways, but his hands are tied because he has no authority over bails and transfers. Reynolds is blaming the courts for moving too slowly, but the judges are saying that if they don't exercise thorough procedures, then the retrials on appeal would make things even worse. I don't have any idea what the Commissioners are doing or thinking. What I guess I think is that they're just waiting for everyone else to get things straightened out, so they can simply approve a solution. Anyway, it's created quite a mess down there, and it's giving me lots of work."

Sonya turned to follow the other car. They were headed out to a place near the edge of town that Leslie knew about, and it was near Theresa's house, where Leslie stayed when she was in town for the Tuesday meetings.

Sonya said, "That all sounds great for us, but when will it make any difference for the prisoners?"

"The deadline for a response is next week. After that it's anyone's guess how long it would take to issue an injunction if that seems to be called for. The one interesting thing I did overhear is that they're not going to be focusing on arrests this year when they make their raids. I heard Reynolds yelling that it was just like a bunch of liberals, to wage war and let the enemy get away, but I think he knows it makes sense, especially when there's nowhere to put anybody."

"So, it wasn't his decision?"

"No, I think it's coming from the same place as the money, the federal government."

"Has he asked for any information about us? Please don't tell him we're broke right now."

"No. He hasn't talked directly to me since the last time I told you about. But there is one thing I didn't tell you. I thought it was too weird. He asked me to find out who you were sleeping with these days."

Sonya sort of smiled and glanced over at Janet's face in the alternating light and dark from the streetlights. "For real?"

Janet answered slowly, "Yes, for real."

Sonya slowed down as Leslie's car turned into the Silver Stein Bar & Lounge. Sonya followed and pulled in next to her. She turned off the car and looked over at Janet.

"Well, for God's sake, don't spoil it by telling him I'm not with anybody."

They both laughed and got out. Inside, there was a three-piece band playing for a small crowd in the dim light of the lounge. Leslie led the way to a corner table near the back. They sat down and were waited on almost immediately by a cheerful barmaid. They ordered beers all around and Theresa and Janet left for the ladies' room.

"Some meeting," Leslie said.

"Yeah." Sonya was beginning to feel her energy draining away. It had been a hard one. "I'm beat. Didn't realize it takes so much out of me."

"I thought you were great. You didn't back down, but you made it seem like you were compromising."

"Isn't that what politics is all about? Listen, can we not talk about it anymore tonight?"

"Sure."

Their beers came, and they looked out toward the dancers. A few guys at the bar were casually looking in their direction. Leslie leaned forward over her beer and pretended to be whispering to Sonya, who laughed, and asked how it had been going for Leslie.

"Oh, I'm busier than I have been in years, but I love it. Tom is having kind of a hard time with my new routines. He doesn't like me being gone so much, but it really isn't all that much. It's good for him. How about you?"

"Oh," Sonya thought for a moment, "I'm fine."

Janet and Theresa came back to the table, and conversation turned to the party they were going to have at Leslie's, and the other parties that might be happening. Theresa commented that if she were single like Sonya and Janet she would really be looking forward to the socializing. Janet replied that it wasn't that easy, and they started talking about which was harder, being new in an area or being single, as far as social things went. Sonya quietly asked Leslie if she'd seen Peter recently.

"Not in the last week or so, but I'm glad you asked."

"Why?" Sonya said with a trace of embarrassment.

"Why? Because I'm glad you're interested. I still think there's something about you two. I can't explain it, but I can feel it."

"Well, I'm glad you think so, but I doubt if we'll even see each other again. He thinks I'm a cop, and I don't know what to think about him."

Two of the guys from the bar came over and asked if they would like to dance. Theresa stood right up and Janet looked over at the other two women. Since she was sitting at the outside, they both waved her to go ahead. She gave them a look that said she'd rather be doing anything else, but got up and smiled at the younger man who led her out onto the dance floor. The music was fast, and the space was as crowded as it was going to get that night. After a few stiff moments, Janet started looking like she was having a good time, and Theresa was obviously having fun. Leslie commented that her sister-in-law was having a little trouble adjusting to small-city life in Dixon, and that she was a real good times person.

Sonya said, "Maybe we should have a party or at least a dinner. I don't mean a big one like we're talking about out at your place, just something small, just for the committee and friends."

"Great idea." Leslie thought for a moment. "How about a housewarming for Ron and Theresa? They just moved in and have been so busy getting settled. It would be a chance for them to meet some other people and have fun with the ones they know."

"A surprise?"

"No, that would be too complicated. Besides, I'm sure they'd want to be doing a lot for putting on something like that. We could have it be a potluck for everything, except have Tom and Ron barbeque. I know they've got a nice grill, I saw them unload it."

"When so you think it should be?" Sonya finished her beer.

"How about a week from Saturday, what's that, the eighteenth or so?"

"If it's not too close to Labor Day for you."

"Shouldn't be, just like a warm-up. Have to figure out who to invite besides Peter."

Sonya kicked her gently under the table, and said, "Come on, he probably wouldn't come anyway. And if he did, he'd be uncomfortable."

Leslie laughed, "Of course he would be. The two of you make each other uncomfortable, and that's a good sign."

The band stopped playing and announced a break, and Janet and Theresa came back to the table, a little breathless. They finished their beers and everyone except Janet ordered again. Leslie started explaining their idea for a party. Theresa was thrilled. They counted the people they'd like to see there, and it was certainly enough for a party. Sonya excused herself for the Ladies room and by the time she returned, plans were nearly complete. Theresa said it would be fine to have it at their new place, and they could just hold off on unpacking so there would be plenty of empty space for socializing.

As the band began drifting back to the small stage, Janet apologized for having to mention that it was getting late for her. She needed to be up early to get Kristi off for school before getting herself to work. The others agreed it was time to go. They finished their beers and got up to leave. Theresa gave a wave to her dancing partner and they left the lounge.

The next morning, Sonya went running for the fourth time. She'd driven around the park near her home and found a route that measured a mile-and-a-half from her house and back. That was what the young woman at the sporting goods store said was a good distance to start with, even if you didn't run the whole way. She felt self-conscious in her new shoes and Mike's old sweats, thinking that anyone out there would know she was just a beginner and thinking she probably wouldn't stick with it. The first three times she'd tried, she thought the same thing herself. As soon as she got out of breath, she would stop jogging and just walk. This morning she promised herself to try and keep going the whole way no matter how it felt. Go slower, but don't stop, or walk, she told herself. It was getting easier and it felt better. It was early enough in the morning that the dew was still on the grass, although you could already tell it was going to be hot later in the day. After the first half mile, her right calf was hurting, and it felt like air was having trouble finding its way into her lungs. She thought she'd probably started off too fast, faster than she could maintain, but this time instead of stopping to walk, she only slowed down and continued jogging.

She passed other runners who gave her warm smiles, and she wondered how her own smile looked to them. Probably more like a grimace. She figured that if it felt this bad it must be doing some good. She needed to think about something beside her calf and breathing, so she thought about the party plans. She tried to assure herself it had been a completely innocent suggestion on her part, and then it turned into maybe another chance to see that weird guy she kept wondering about. It was all only curiosity, she convinced herself, since all she really knew about him from Leslie was that he'd been alone for as long as she'd known him, at least four years.

Only a half mile to go, with her mind trying to measure attraction, to separate the need to know from just idle speculation. There was something about him, something deeper than what would come out between casual acquaintances. They'd had a good time the two times they'd seen each other, but what did that count? Nothing since then and that was almost a month ago. She did wonder what he was about, at least on the superficial level, besides his tractor work. She wasn't sure he was a grower, although it was a reasonable assumption. Great. Reynolds was already curious, and it would be just perfect if he found out she was hanging out with a grower. That would finish it—for everyone, the democrats, the media, Reynolds. It was exactly the connection they'd like to find. That was one real good reason to hang back instead of hanging out, better to not even think any more about him. All the work and money for the campaign going up in smoke. She tried to laugh at her accidental pun, but her lungs were burning, and her right calf had just taught the left one how to hurt the same way. She kept up a limping jog, but told herself she could probably walk faster than she was moving along in the shuffle-step that was slowly taking her down the block, four houses to go, only three more…

As Sonya collapsed onto the rug, she reached for the stretching pamphlet on the coffee table. They advised five exercises to do when you finished your run. Now she could feel the sweat oozing out of her skin, dripping down her face, neck, and arms. How long is a marathon? More than twenty miles. Impossible. She worked at stretching her legs, making her calves burn as she tried to release the cramps that gripped them.

In the bathroom she stripped, looked herself over in the mirror and squeezed her leg muscles. Maybe a tiny bit firmer, maybe. She stepped on the scale. Her weight was fine, probably because she never ate regularly anymore. As she climbed into the shower she was thinking that this was the best reason for jogging, a shower that isn't just for maintenance or indulgence, but a necessity and a reward, like a long sigh that comes to you once you've caught your breath and realized that, yes, you're going to live to run again. She turned the stream of water to full blast, and let it play against the soreness in her back and legs. At least she hadn't been thinking about Mike very much in the past month. If nothing else, this Peter was helping her in that way. She only thought about that because she could imagine Mike was probably taking a shower at the same time, some several hundred miles south of there.

Reluctantly, she turned the water off and stepped out. She toweled the slick water from herself, powdered, lightly sprayed here and there, and crossed into her room to dress. She tried on a shirt Janet had given her. It fit well, and this made her think of her friend. *Poor Janet.* What did she need? Where was she really at? The excitement of their initial getting to know one another seemed to be cooling somewhat, and of course Janet was in a difficult place, with her job, the campaign, her daughter and all, and what was she having to tell Reynolds? Sonya couldn't tell if the woman was lonely for someone, or anyone, or none of the above. She said she was, but she seemed so self-contained. It was nice to see her dancing at the bar. Some people just don't have that knack, but she was surprisingly good once she loosened up a bit. There would be dancing at their party, and Leslie promised to bring a stack of oldies, Supremes, Stones, etc. Who would be there for Janet, who could they invite? Sonya really couldn't think of anyone.

She finished dressing and looked at the clock on her way to the kitchen. Only 8:15. Seemed like she'd already been up half the day. The exercise also made her forget what she was supposed to do next that day but running gave her a nice relaxed and awake feeling, not that she'd really recovered yet. She sliced a grapefruit and buttered a large rice cracker. She would probably have to start eating a real breakfast if she kept this up. It really was circular, exercise to stay in shape, eat more, exercise more to keep from gaining weight, eat more in order to need to exercise more. Forget it, just get flabby and forget it, but she really did feel good at this moment. As a matter of fact, she told herself as she headed out the door, she probably couldn't be feeling better.

When Peter got home from watering and pruning his main patch, there was a note on the trailer door. It was from Al and it just said that some of the guys were getting together that evening to talk over some mutual problems based on new information. Not hard to guess what the problems had to do with, but what was the new information? He let his mind wander, maybe the government decided to cancel its eradication programs and let the free market determine the role of marijuana in society, pure Reaganomics, the ultimate deregulation. No, must be something about their plans for the raid season. Rumors probably. They should be starting up soon. Last couple of years it always started with plane searches about the middle of the month. Wasn't that much they could do or see before then. If he went tonight though he'd miss the weekly NY Philharmonic concert on public radio, but it wasn't that important. The note said to be there "by dark," which gave him just enough time to clean up and get a bite to eat. He took the sack with the shade leaf pickings out to the compost pile at the edge of the woods. The shopping bag with the pruned tips went up on the roof of the trailer. He'd pinched back pretty good in the patch because it seemed it might be visibly vulnerable from the air. It hadn't been hit in past years yet, but there was always a first time.

He drove through the deepening twilight, keeping his eyes on the color of the sky above the ridges. There was one phase of the sundown transition that always got to him on these clear evenings. It was a quality of blueness that didn't exist at any other time. Sundown Blue, he called it. If he were a painter he'd spend a lot of time trying to capture that color on canvas, but he knew it was probably impossible because it was made up of fading sunlight and growing darkness, both changing rapidly. Sometimes he sat outside on summer evenings and tried to pinpoint the moment that the color left the sky, but he always missed it. Now it was gone again, and he needed headlights.

There were eight people gathered around a picnic table and some six packs when he arrived. Greetings were lowkey. They all knew each other, but usually didn't have that much to do with one another, especially at this time of year when they were all so busy with their crops. Peter knew there were a couple of grower partnerships, but for the most part it was a solitary occupation. Al was starting up a small fire a little way away from the table. The sound of a child's crying and Linda's voice came from the house. The conversation drifted from the amount of water left in the area's springs to the results of some new seed strains and hybrids that were being use for the first time. Everyone present had been in the area as long as Peter, so he didn't feel much paranoia with this group, and he hoped nobody felt that way about him. Al was glad he'd showed up and said so once he got the fire going. There was almost a need for it as the night was cooling faster than usual. It was all beginning to change again. The earth was feeling signals from within and from above. It wouldn't be long now until the leaves on the trees and brush sensed it too and started their changes. Blackberries were beginning to ripen and male plants in the patches were showing themselves and being eliminated.

The group was still waiting for one or two others to show up, and a couple of joints were passing around. A guy named Dean asked if anyone else noticed a forest service truck with a flashing light unit on the roof. Said he'd seen it twice with the same dude in it, maybe the law enforcement deputy the agency had focused on pot. No one else had seen him, but it was good to know about and keep an eye out for. Al and Jim told how they'd heard from further south that the forest service had trucks parked on high points listening for single chain saws and motorcycles. These trucks were equipped with good CBs and could get an approximate fix on locations by comparing the direction of the sounds from the different trucks and marking where the lines crossed on their maps. They'd busted some folks getting firewood illegally, but so far, they hadn't heard of it happening to any growers.

Another rig pulled into the parking lot, and Peter was surprised to see it was Tom and Leslie. He thought they were hardly growing anymore, even though they were still part of the "underground community." They walked into the circle of brightly flickering firelight and exchanged greetings with everyone. Tom took a beer that was offered, handed it to Leslie and took one for himself. She went over and sat next to Donna, the only other woman there. Al announced they could get started unless anyone knew of anybody they were waiting for.

"What we're here for tonight," he said, "is to try to get ourselves together, if we can, for what's coming. I'm sure everyone remembers last year, and I know you're all hearing stories from further south. What we're going to get here this year is probably in between, but there might be some things we can do if we can get word out in time when it comes down. I'm not talking actions, just precautions and communication. Mainly, I wanted everyone to know the stuff Leslie's been finding out, mostly from her brother who's had some dealings she can tell you more about." He nodded to Leslie and threw some small branches of the fire.

"Hi, everybody. So, there're several things to talk about, but I probably better start off with the good stuff first. My brother just moved here from Denver this year, and he's been working on a lawsuit against the county for crowding the jail over the legal maximum. In the process, he meets with the Sheriff once in a while. Says he's a pretty interesting guy, likes to talk, that's what my brother says. Anyway, last time they saw each other, they were hassling about the jail population and the Sheriff said it was going to stay pretty much at the same level for the next few months unless the lawsuit succeeded and forced them to cut some people loose. Or if some openings came up at the state prisons. My brother asked him what he meant by that, that it shouldn't change much, and the Sheriff said the DEA finally woke up to the fact it doesn't do much good to waste a lot of time trying to bust the growers. My brother said he tried not to seem too interested but did try to get the man to say more. So, apparently the strategy this year is just to go for the crop and shine on the paperwork. Over half the cases get thrown out anyway, on technicalities. So that's probably kind of the good news."

It was good to some degree, but no one there that night considered themselves personally vulnerable to getting busted unless they got caught in a patch. They'd all been growing on public land long enough to be reasonably secure about that, at least they hoped so. Someone asked, "So what's the bad news?"

Leslie looked around the circle of faces lit by the fire. They were all looking at her with varying degrees of intensity. She caught Peter's eyes and smiled briefly, then went on. "The bad news is helicopters. For sure. My brother, and I'm not using his name intentionally, so you never heard of him, was able to get the Sheriff to keep talking about pot even though that doesn't have anything directly to do with their legal business together. He thinks the Sheriff might not be one hundred percent behind all the money and energy that goes into all this pot war stuff. That doesn't make much difference, but it might explain why he's even talking about it to an ACLU lawyer who's suing the county. He said that, for the first time this year they were going to find out if anybody would shoot down a helicopter to save their crop. That's how he said it, I swear."

"I will," Dean said motioning toward the sky with a pretend rifle. There was a moment of laughter.

"Yeah, good, that's just what we need around here," Leslie said, sort of laughing, and then she went on, "The problem is if somebody does try it, that'll give them the excuse to come down really hard." A few of the folks mumbled in agreement. Dean said he hoped no one thought he meant it, and someone else said he'd seen a diagram of just where to aim to bring down a chopper if he changed his mind.

Al broke in with "I wish we could joke about this, but if it's true, then the whole game changes. They got half the crop in Hawaii the first year they used helicopters."

Leslie spoke again, "It's for real. He said the Sheriff went on to say that if they didn't get shot out of the sky, they were hoping to at least find a couple of booby traps. Of course, maybe he was being sarcastic, but it was kind of weird, and then the two of them went back to arguments over the details of the lawsuit, and that was all there was to it."

Jim said, "Guess that means we should tell everybody we can. Not much we can do about it now, except tie the plants down and hope for the best. Did he get any idea when it would be?"

"No, couldn't find that out, but they'll probably only do it for a couple of days before they move on. The Sheriff also did say they would just have a short-time turn at this."

"He did say his legal opinion was that one advantage to the helicopters, for the growers that is, is if they do a bust on private land, it's much easier to say the helicopter was searching without a warrant than if they're just flying circles much higher up in a regular plane," Tom said. "And that's the only chance to beat those charges, them searching without a warrant."

"Yeah, but who wants to be a test case?" Donna put in.

"You're right about that. Anyway," Leslie continued, "that's what's happening about all that stuff. I wanted you all to know as soon as possible in case there's anything you need to be doing about it. The other things I want to talk about have to do with the DA campaign and the initiative. I've been working for the woman that's running against Reynolds, Sonya's her name. She's good people, and I think she would make a difference if she got in, especially on the pot thing, which I'm sure you all heard what she says about it not being her priority. She's maybe got a slim chance, but there's almost no money and without a lot of paid-for media, she can't beat this Reynolds guy. So, a couple of things are happening. First, we're having a benefit picnic, dance, whatever, at our place on September 2nd, and we want everybody to come. Rainbow Junkyard said they'd play for free and there'll be an open mic all afternoon for local talent. It'll be a potluck and we'll be selling keg beer to raise campaign money. The cost is going to be $5 at the gate, and we're trying to come up with some other ideas to make money. Be careful about smoking pot in the open because we're pretty sure some media will be there, and you probably don't want your face on TV with a joint hanging out of your mouth." She smiled at the thought.

"Besides that, or in addition, I talked to a few of you and some other people about fund-raising for her. Because even if the initiative gets on the ballot but doesn't pass, she's promised to carry it out here if it wins in Chinook County. Now, I don't want to sound like I'm making a speech or anything, but the Chamber of Commerce and the alcohol industry are giving big bucks to make sure it doesn't succeed. Sonya is the only candidate to come along that deserves help from our side. So, we're trying to raise a big donation from the Chinook County Horticultural Society."

"Who's that?" Dean asked.

"You," said Al.

Leslie went on, "We've already got pledges for $600 from a couple of growers, but we need a lot more, so just look at it as taxes on your crops. And it'll for sure be anonymous. I know it's a bad time of year for bucks, but let's see what we can come up with. Anyway, that's all I wanted to say. You can get in touch with me if you want to donate."

The fire was almost out, and Donna mentioned that the meteor shower was still going on a little. They watched and got to see a couple of shooting stars and a satellite cross the dark sky. After a while, a few guys got up and left. Leslie moved over and found a place next to Peter, who was lying on his back staring up into the vastness above.

"Hi," he said. Several of the others had gotten up to stretch and move around.

"Hi. What do you think?"

"Had to come."

"Helicopters?"

"No. Organization. Didn't you notice we just had a meeting?"

"Is that bad?"

"No, just different. Next thing you know we'll be just like the Grange. Monthly meetings, officers, endorsing candidates, and entering our plants in the county fair." He pulled up onto his elbows so he could look at her. "Don't get me wrong. I appreciate what you just did and said. I'm just too much of an anarchist to let it go by without some comment."

"I'm glad you said that last part. Really, don't you think we have to start getting organized? It seems to me it's either that or most of these guys will have to move somewhere else."

He looked at her for a moment and then said, "You're right. I guess I'm just not sure which of those it will be for me." He pulled out his pouch and began the routine of rolling a joint.

"Want to talk about something else?" she asked.

"Like what?"

"Well, besides the big party on Labor Day weekend, a few of us decided to have a get-together this Saturday, a housewarming for my brother and Theresa. You're invited."

He didn't say anything while he finished licking the joint, lit it, inhaled, and offered it to her. She said no thanks. He took another hit and handed it off to the nearest person.

"Can't," he said. He looked at her carefully to see her reaction in the dim light from the house. She looked closely at him, and asked, "Why not?"

"Got a date."

She couldn't see his expression in the last flickering light of the fire's embers.

"For real?" she asked.

"Why would I joke about something like that?"

"Who is it, if you don't mind my asking?" She was beginning to think he was truly serious. Tom brought the joint back to him and sat beside Leslie.

"How you doing?" he asked.

"Fine," Peter said, exhaling.

Leslie said, "He says he can't come to the housewarming because he has a date."

Tom glanced at Leslie and then at Peter, "Good. Probably just what he needs, huh buddy?" Someone put a little more wood on the fire and a shower of bright sparks climbed skyward.

Leslie started to get up, but stopped and said, "Well, you and your date better be ready when we come by to pick you up. Four o'clock Saturday." She stood up and walked away to the house.

"She's calling your bluff."

"I know. I wasn't lying. I'll bet that Sonya's going to be there and I bet Leslie's got me all set up with her. See, that's my 'date' why I can't come." Peter took the last toke and stubbed out the roach.

"Tricky. But what's wrong with Sonya?"

"Nothing," he said and lay back down. "It's what's wrong with me." Tom lay back too, not saying anything. Peter spoke again, saying, "I was going to tell Leslie to count me in for a couple of hundred, make it three. I'll just skip my next trip to Reno."

"I'll tell her. You can give it to her Saturday when we pick you up."

"Right. Hey, it's late. I've got to go. Working man, you know."

"Sure, me too." They both got up and Tom said, "Just go along with it. I think this Sonya can be trusted, and she doesn't have to know much anyway."

"I guess I think that too. Buy it's not really the problem." He stood on his tiptoes and stretched his fingertips until they almost touched the stars. "Anyway, tell Leslie thanks for trying to help me."

"I will. Good luck with your crop. See you Saturday."

"Thanks. Sounds like we'll all need as much luck as we can get." He moved away and talked briefly with a few other people before climbing into his truck for the drive home.

DA Reynolds and Madeline were going over the schedule of public appearances for the next several weeks. They were trying to decide which events required his personal attendance and which she could handle for him. There were also two TV spots to fill, and a series of paid political advertisements to write and film. So far he'd avoided most of the campaigning, but the latest polls showed a steady increase in the Lehman woman's potential standing—certainly not enough for winning, but if she got enough votes she'd make him look weak. Madeline proved to be an enthusiastic substitute for him, but she was beginning to feel overburdened with both his PR and all the usual entertaining and hobnobbing that went along with the role of DA's wife.

There were two calendars on the table. One showed his upcoming court dates, and the other had the campaign schedule penciled into it.

He pulled it closer and said, "You can handle any of these if you feel up to it. These are mostly for raising additional funds, which God knows we need. I have at least six court appearances in the next month that can't be avoided or postponed. Half of them dealing with that goddam lawsuit. So, because of timing conflicts, you'll have to take the County Employee's Forum and the League of Women Voters."

She sat back in her chair and looked at him, wondering if he ever got tired. Even when he looked a little tired out, it seems like it was only skin-deep. All this extra work gave her more time with him. That was the only real advantage. But that time was almost always focused on the campaign.

"What about the debate challenge? You know I can't do that for you."

"No, but I'm not sure we have to accept it either. Not unless she starts doing a lot better. It would be sort of fun, I imagine, but don't say yes yet, just say we're still considering it and waiting for a proposal on the format. Keep them dangling as long as possible. We won't accept unless we have to, and maybe we can delay until it's too late to put it together."

They heard a car pulling into the driveway and both looked up. It was their oldest son coming home from his job at a boat marina some ways out of town on the lake. He didn't get off work until it got dark, but it was a good job. He was saving money so he could have a car when he went away to college in less than a month. The screen door slammed as he came in through the back porch.

"Mom, Dad." He dropped the keys on the counter. "Any dinner left? I didn't have time to eat tonight."

Madeline got up quickly, told him to sit down, and moved to heat up the remainder of their dinner.

"How's it going, Dad?"

"Good, well, pretty good. How would you like to make a speech at the Bar Association annual meeting, or maybe this one, a radio interview for the college radio station?"

"No thanks. I'd say the wrong thing for sure."

"Yeah, you probably would. How's the job these days?" He continued marking up the calendars, still trying to make a coherent schedule out of the complication of dates and places. He needed a third calendar to transfer a master plan onto.

"It's okay. Got to try out the new '85, 70 horsepower outboard. Just came in today. What a toy. Hit fifty on that eighteen-foot demonstrator we've got. Pull a skier at nearly forty. You ever been forty miles an hour on the water?"

"No, no, I haven't. Not sure I want to."

"Thanks Mom. Looks good. What is it?"

"Ravioli, and broccoli with cream sauce, and wild rice with herbs."

She watched him eat, wondering if he tasted the food or if it was all a matter of texture as he shoveled it down that fast. He'd be gone soon, grown and gone. It was hard to imagine she was already done. Retired from being his Mom. They'd always been close, she knew that, something about the firstborn, but this would be the real weaning. Someone else, some restaurant or dining hall, eventually some other woman, would be feeding him from now on. No more "What's for dinner, Mom?' She supposed it should feel good, a sense of accomplishment, a kind of completion, but all she could think of was how fast it all went by.

"Rick," she asked, "have you made a list of things we need to get before you leave, the clothes mainly?"

"Not yet. I'll get to it, maybe tomorrow. I go in early and should get off early, too, but remind me before I leave in the morning."

The phone rang. She answered it, Someone was asking for Mr. Reynolds. She handed him the receiver. "For Mr. Reynolds."

"This is Reynolds." It was Detective Stockton at the other end. "Here, Madeline. I'll take it in my office. Hang this up for me, will you?"

He sat down at his desk in the other room. "Yeah, Tony, what is it?"

"Hope it's not too late to call, but it's important."

"No, fine, glad you did. What's up?" He settled into his desk chair and lit another one of too many cigarettes for the day.

"We got one. Just got back from checking it. It's in a patch about thirty miles out, BLM land, well hidden. Got a tip from someone who wouldn't say who he is. We'll need to move fast on it, tomorrow might even be too late. Can you get loose to come along first thing in the morning?"

"What is it exactly?"

"OK, sorry I didn't spell it out. It's a pretty strung out operation, along two banks of a feeder creek. I'm surprised they went to all this trouble since it probably doesn't get a whole lot of sun. Anyway, there's at least three grenades hooked up to trip wires on the only path leading to the plants. We've got that small high-powered metal detector now. I wouldn't go there without it. Glad we spent the bucks for it."

"This is great." Reynolds stubbed out his cigarette. "Buy you two drinks first chance we get. What happens now?"

"I couldn't get in and out without blowing myself up or leaving some sign that I'd been there, so we need to move quick or they'll find my trail and have time to disappear the whole thing. I want to move on it tomorrow, leave downtown by ten o'clock. I've still got to tell Johnson and line up the interagency bomb squad. I don't want to mess with this stuff myself. I think it would be good for you to be there too. I mean, hey, it's your 'war' too."

"All right. I'll be there. Only hitch I see is that it doesn't give that reporter time to get up here from wherever he is."

"He can use the photos from the local paper. I've already contacted our guy over there. They've got a reporter assigned to us, on call, for the rest of this month anyway. Also got TV lined up. It's going to be a hell of a job getting everybody down there, but we'll make it work."

"Tony, this is fantastic. Going to make the whole eradication program look good. You're a brave guy, and I'm going to let people know it."

"Thanks. I like my job, especially this part of it, and that's enough for now. Can't think of anything else. I'll see you at the assembly area next to the garage tomorrow."

"Sure thing. Should I bring anyone else from my office?"

"Up to you."

"Tony, any chance of finding whoever did this?"

There was a short pause on the line, and then Tony answered, "No way. Unless we find something in the patch to connect it to someone. One thing for sure, it's all pretty professional."

"OK, see you in the morning, and thanks for letting me know right away."

"You bet. Good night."

Reynolds sat there for a short while as he slowly replaced the receiver in its cradle. This was it then. The missing link in his campaign. Now, let Ms. Lehman defend the growers. Now let's see what happens to the goddam legalization bullshit. He got up and started for the kitchen, reaching for another cigarette, but stopping himself at the thought of Madeline fussing at him about his smoking. She was getting worse and worse about it. He was smiling as he entered the kitchen. Rick stopped their conversation when he came in.

"Rick don't make your mother wash the dishes. Hell, she fixes the food and everything else around here. You ought to help her while you still have the chance."

"She wouldn't let me, Dad. I offered."

"It's all right, Bill," Madeline said. "Now, what's making you smile so much when you're trying to act so tough?"

"That was one of our detectives on the phone. They've discovered a marijuana operation complete with grenade booby-traps. It's what we've known all along, just couldn't prove it until now. It's going to shake up some of the hands-off liberals and show the pot business for what it really is. If it wasn't so serious, I'd say it's just what this county needs. Let's see what happens to that legalization drive now. Bunch of terrorists behind it, and we can prove it."

"Dad, you really think everyone who wants to legalize pot is violent?"

"Not everyone, no. Matter of fact, most of them are probably scared of their own shadows. The stuff makes you paranoid, you know. But they're providing cover and comfort to a small group of criminals who don't care about anyone or anything else. And that small group of hardcore criminals is in a perfect position to exercise some pretty important power around here, if we can't get the public to wake up."

"Dad, I've heard the speech. I just want to know what you think, what you really think."

"That's what I think. More than that, it's what I know. What the hell's wrong with you? I suppose you think it's a harmless recreation, like water skis? What do they call it in their ads, a 'safe euphoriant'? Bullshit!"

Madeline came over and stood beside him, wiping her hands on her apron. "Take it easy, both of you. I don't want any of those 'generation gaps' in my kitchen."

"Okay, okay, I just don't want our son going off the college with a bunch of soft-headed ideas about this stuff. Maybe he should come with me tomorrow."

"What do you mean?" She gave him a worried look.

"I'm going out with the team that investigates this situation tomorrow. Have to go, media'll be there. It's going to be a big deal."

"Why do you have to go?"

"Because, like the detective says, it's my 'war' too." He chose not to hear his son mutter the word 'war' under his breath, thinking, you raise them up, do your best, and then you have to let go. Thinking, that's why this stuff got to be eradicated, because as long as it's out there, there's no way to protect your kids from it.

Madeline took off her apron and started straightening up the paperwork on one side of the table, asking, "Is there anything else we have to do tonight?"

"I'm going to bed. Night, Mom, Dad."

Madeline said goodnight, and Bill put a hand on his elbow as he walked by. "Son, if you can't hear it from me, find someone else you can trust. But be careful."

"Sure, Dad. Night."

As he left the room Madeline moved close behind her husband and put her arms around him. "He's a good boy, Bill, and you know it. Don't worry."

"I know. He's just got to challenge everything these days."

"Of course, he does. Didn't you when you were his age? I remember you when the whole world was blind, and you were the only one who could see. How did you feel about your father in those days?"

"All right, honey, you made your point. Let's get this mess put away. I better get some rest if I'm mountain climbing in the morning."

"I wish you didn't have to go. You could get hurt, and what good would that do?"

"You'll worry, and I'll be fine, and tomorrow night, I'll take you out to dinner wherever you choose."

First thing in the morning, Marty read and reread the memo on his desk. Hard to believe. It said Stockton found a growing operation with approximately twenty-five plants in it. But that wasn't the important part. It also had grenade boobytraps. There was to be a press-attended expedition, meet at ten at the motor pool. It asked, would he be there? Hell, yes. Where was Stockton now? Dispatch said he'd gone out in the field very early with another deputy, Henderson, and they would be back by ten.

He couldn't set the piece of paper down, so he read it again. Here, right here in Chinook County, and he was on record saying it couldn't happen here. Now it did. Goddam all of them. Didn't people have any sense at all? Didn't they know it was stupid enough to fight and kill over land or religion or whatever, but over a few thousand dollars worth of plants? Two more years he had left. To serve with honor for two more years. He could always resign, take his early retirement benefits, but that didn't feel right. He'd regret it as much as he'd enjoy it.

He cleared the desk by signing a bunch of papers, then headed down to the locker room for boots and coveralls. No sense ruining a good uniform out in the brush. He stopped on the way to pick up cup of coffee to go and listened while two employees discussed this news in quiet voices. Oh yeah, this was real news. Now what next?

At ten to ten, he walked into the assembly room adjoining the garage. The TV crew and a reporter and photographer from the local paper were already there. He waved aside their questions, saying he didn't know any more than they did. Through the window, he watched as a city police van pulled into the parking lot. It was the one used by the SWAT team. Didn't get much use in Dixon, he thought. He recognized the officer trained in bomb work getting out of the rig. So, it really was a full-on mission. Well, he thought, Stockton deserved the credit and the coverage. He stuck to it and it looked like he got results. Where the hell is he anyway?

At precisely ten o'clock, Reynolds walked into the room, dressed in a new camouflage outfit and hiking boots straight out of one of those catalogues for hunters and backpackers. He smiled at the reporters coming over to shake hands with him, and waved off all their questions,.

"Looks like you scored this time," the reporter said.

"Does, doesn't it? Great way to start the harvest season."

"Well, no one should be surprised."

"I am," Marty said and looked away. "I really am."

Through the window, they watched Stockton pull into the garage and jump out of his patrol truck. He walked toward the group inside with quick steps. His coveralls were smeared with dirt and he had a few scratches on his face. He smiled at the waiting group and waved to Marty.

"Good to see you all. Pretty sure it's safe to head out there now. We made a quick run to check on things. All quiet for now. I'd like to get going right away unless there's any reason not to. You guys got your own vehicles?" he asked the press group. They said yes, they did.

"Anything else, Sheriff?"

"No, no, I'm ready."

They filed out to the waiting vehicles. The caravan shaped up as two press cars, the police van, Marty's patrol rig, and Reynolds riding with Stockton in the pickup. Marty was glad to be left alone. He wasn't sure how he wanted to react to this, but he knew he was going to have to talk to the media before the day was done.

Stockton had given each driver a map to the rendezvous point in case they got separated on the way. As they wheeled out of the garage and through the city streets, heads turned as they passed and other drivers gave way even though their lights weren't flashing. From the map, it looked to be less than an hour to get to the rendezvous at the first logging road, and then ten to twenty minutes in the hills after that. Marty was always glad to get out of the office, but this time he was sure wishing it was for some other reason.

The caravan finally reached a nearly overgrown logging landing overlooking a series of ridges stretching away toward the ocean beyond. There was a fog bank out near the coast, but the rest of the sky was a sparkling blue interrupted only by a tall column of smoke several miles to the southeast, a slash fire burning logging waste on a recently harvested unit. By afternoon, it would probably put most of the area in between under a smoky blanket of gray air and filtered orange sunlight. It was beginning to get warm out, and as they all climbed from their vehicles it became clear that this project was about to turn into some strenuous real work.

Stockton led the party to the edge of the landing and pointed down to where they would have to go. He asked the cameraman if he thought he could make it with all his gear.

"Yeah, going down. Don't know about coming back up."

"Just pretend your camera is 10,000 dollars' worth of fresh-harvested pot," Stockton said, and got a laugh from the others. He waved to the south, where another deputy was standing on a large stump waving to them. Stockton had posted him on guard. Now he started working his way across the slope to meet up with them on their climb down.

"Lock your rigs and we'll head down." Stockton was obviously enjoying his role as honcho of the operation, and Marty had to admit that he was doing a good job of it.

It took about half an hour to work their way down to the flat near the small creek. The cameraman and the two bomb squad police needed help with their equipment. The bulkiest item was the "blanket" used to cover suspected explosives. It took two men to wrestle it down, and everyone had to make frequent stops to adjust their own loads or wait for the others. Reynolds seemed to be enjoying himself, although the climb down wasn't easy for him. Marty was thanking himself for all the exercises and training he joined in when he put the boys on the softball team through their workouts. It made a difference when most of what you did was ride a desk. On the way down, he'd noted a few marijuana leaves caught in the brush. Stockton didn't mention them and no one else seemed to notice, so Marty didn't bring it up.

When they reached the outcropping of rock Stockton had designated as their staging area, Henderson joined them and reported there'd been no activity all morning. Stockton pointed to a tarp off to one side of the clearing, and said, "We worked our way around and cut most of the stuff last evening. Didn't want to take a chance of someone sneaking in here at night, noticing we'd been here, and removing it all." He went over and pulled back the tarp, showing off the bundles of six to eight-foot tall plants. "Get your pictures of this now if you want to, that way Henderson can start moving it up topside."

The newspaperman asked if he could ask a question. He wanted to know how they'd been sure it was safe to harvest those plants. Metal detector, Stockton told him. They'd been able to isolate the booby-traps and wires, and work around them using a specially adapted device, supplied by the feds. From now on, they would be using those in all such raids and investigations. He said they were sure that their destination was completely safe and clean, but that no one should get off the fresh-cut pathway. He would make no guarantees as to what lay beyond the area they'd scoped.

When there were no other questions, he led the two bomb experts along the face of the slope and down a rocky path between salmonberry bushes. The SWAT guys, Marty, Reynolds, and then the press followed them into the tunnel of sticker canes. Their line stopped moving some thirty feet down the trail, and they bunched up while Stockton pointed out a nearly invisible path that led into the brush in front of them.

"That's their trail. The first trip wire is about twenty feet farther down. If you guys want pictures, you should move a little over that way."

He stepped aside as the two cops moved forward with their "blanket" and tool kits. They wore helmets with ear-protectors and face-shields, as well as heavy shrapnel-proof vests. Stockton explained he'd flagged the path just before each wire so they could find them again easily. As they waited, the reporter asked how long they'd been working on this, what with all the precautions they'd needed.

"Found the patch two days ago after a flyover in our fixed-wing plane. Haven't got our helicopter turn yet. And we worked most of the day yesterday down here, searching around and removing evidence," Stockton said. Reynolds interjected about the widespread violence in the drug trade, both in the U.S. and especially in other countries. He then drew the parallel between drug violence and political terrorism spreading around the world.

"Once these tactics come into vogue, there's only one way to handle the situation, and that's with maximum law enforcement countermeasures. Similar to the spread of a cancer where the only hope is the most extreme treatment...I know some people might think all this is an over-reaction to one incident, but one instance just proves that it's only a matter of time before the situation gets out of hand and these radicals begin to control territory, and prevent access by anyone else. It's happening over and over again these days."

"What do you think can be done to prevent these tactics?" asked the newsman.

"Have enough funding and resources to wipe out every single marijuana plant and you remove the economic incentive for these criminals to remain in the area."

One of the bomb experts came back up the trail carrying a roll of wire and two grenades. "We disarmed these two, working on the third." His voice was muffled behind the face-shield. "Want us to leave the third one live for a demonstration?"

"Up to you, but that would be good."

"Move these folks further up the slope then, up by the snag."

They moved uphill, and Marty paused to pick up one of the disarmed devices. He turned it over in his hand, feeling its weight and wondering how it would throw. Heavier than a softball, but smaller.

The two cops reappeared. One carried a smaller version of the blanket, holding it away from himself. He set it down and motioned for them to step away. Unwrapping the bundle, he glanced at the sheriff, and then at Stockton, who asked the cameraman if he was ready.

"Rolling," he replied.

The bomb squad cop nodded, picked up the grenade, pulled the pin, waited a moment, then heaved it downhill into the brush. A couple of seconds went by, and then there was a small explosion. Branches and smoke filled the air above the blast.

The bomb-cop said, "They're not all that powerful. More like a glorified smoke bomb."

Stockton looked around at the rest of the group. There was silence as each one of them considered what he'd just seen. The cameraman shut off his camera, and the bomb squad men began packing up their things. The cloud of smoke drifted away above them. Reynolds asked Marty how he felt.

"Sick," he answered. "I'm going to look around a little more. You all don't have to wait."

"We're done here. Not much else to see," Stockton said.

"Good, then it won't take long." Marty walked slowly and carefully down the narrow path into the brush. He looked back, "Been a while since I've been on one of these. Just need a refresher."

The rest of them turned and started slowly up the steep side of the ridge. Stockton looked once more where Marty had disappeared into the brush, then picked up his bundle of plants and started up the hill behind the rest.

When they all got to the top, they decided to head straight back to town and film some wrap-up material there. Stockton and Henderson threw the bundles of plants into the back of the pickup, and everyone else packed their stuff into their rigs and climbed in just as Marty appeared at the back of the landing.

Reynolds yelled to him "We'll debrief back at the county building."

"All right, see you there." Marty wiped the sweat off his face and sat down on an old log to catch his breath. Some climb, he thought, might have to pass up the laps with the team at afternoon practice. He remembered the true story of the state police officer who had a heart attack climbing up one of these ridges from a pot patch. Quieter than a hand grenade but just as effective.

That evening, Jerry pulled into Peter's driveway and jumped out of his truck in a hurry. Dusk was lingering and he could see Peter sitting on the steps of his trailer. Music played through a speaker on the ground near him. It was loud and Peter got up and turned it off.

"What's up?"

"Shit hit the fan." They both sat, Jerry on a nearby round of wood. "On TV tonight. They found a patch with three grenades rigged to tripwires. Showed the whole thing. They even blew off one of the grenades. Scary."

"This all today?"

"Yeah. The DA was saying this proves that the growers have declared war on our law-abiding citizens and he warned people to stay out of unfamiliar areas of the forest. He said this event will only cause the authorities to intensify their crackdown on all pot operations in the county, and that there would be no let-up in the prosecution of all drug-related offenses."

"Did he mention the election campaign?"

"Only that he hopes law-abiding citizens would now realize the size of the problem, especially those who think they can legalize the problem away."

"Heavy. Anyone say where the patch was?"

"Just some BLM land this side of the county. They had film of the plants they took out, and one of the bomb squad cops, and wires and stuff."

Peter took out his pouch and said, "We better smoke for all the plants that are going to die behind this."

Stars were emerging from the darkening sky. Moths flapped their little wings against the light from a small bulb hanging above the door of the trailer. Peter rolled a joint in silence, wondering for the thousandth time what made this substance so heavy that people on both sides of the issue were ready to kill for the pot itself, and the outrageous sums of money in sales and enforcement that went along with it. Wondering also what this would do to Sonya and her campaign. It was a drag. Whoever set that stuff out there was out of their mind. No matter what happened, it wasn't worth blowing someone up for.

Jerry interrupted his thoughts, "You hear they're going to use helicopters this year?"

"Yeah." He lit the joint and waited for the smoke of the match to clear before inhaling deeply. He blew the smoke skyward, took another hit and then passed it to Jerry. "The whole game's changing," he said. "On both sides."

"What do you think's going to happen now?"

"Hard to say. There's so much energy focused on it. People working really hard to get it legal. Government trying to wipe it all out. It's like what we used to call non-combat zones, with armed patrols and booby-traps. Most of the ordinary people caught in the middle. And any moment, any place could turn into a free-fire zone."

"Yeah." Jerry passed the joint back. "I saw pictures from California last year. Guys riding in helicopters, feet hanging out the doorways, wearing camo, M-16s, the whole thing. At first, I thought it was El Salvador, then the news guy started talking, said it was Humboldt County. I used to work down there. Redwoods. It's weird, logging those old trees. Mostly they're just taking second growth, but a couple times a day a big one drops. Half the time they just bust up. Bummer."

A high fog began rolling in from the coast, darkening the sky and easing in below the stars. There was a changed feeling in the air, a cooling that could either bring a little rain, or just go away by morning. "Getting cooler at night," Peter said as he pulled on the sweatshirt that was lying at his side. "How your plants coming?"

"Good. Really good. Pulled some more males, two more might turn male. But that's pretty good, I guess. Only eight out of twenty."

"Yeah, that's good. Females showing hairs?"

"Just a few." Jerry smiled, "Beautiful. Should I prune them back one more time, or just let them go?"

"Doesn't matter a lot right now. Probably let them grow now. Still pretty well hidden?"

"Good enough, I hope. I tied a couple of them back into the berries a little. Know what? I flushed a couple of young guys down near there. Fishing."

"When was that?"

"Last weekend. I was on my way to water and I heard them talking. At first, I thought they were right near the patch, but the sound was just carrying funny. They were a couple hundred yards away and coming toward it. I worked around to come up behind them. Asked them who's land they thought they were on. Said they thought it was public. I told them only the water belongs to the public, but I own the land."

"How'd they act?"

"Kind of jumpy, said they always fished here and nobody ever bothered them before. I said that must have been because no one ever saw them. I told them I pay taxes on that land and want the fish for myself. They laughed a little and sort of apologized. Said they hadn't caught anything worth it anyway. Then they left, back the way they came. Probably nothing'll come of it, but it freaked me out for a couple of days."

"I bet. But they probably been there before, like they said. Other years. You don't go down there very often, do you?"

"No, hardly ever. Now I'm down there for the plants, but I never used to have any reason."

"Sorry I got you into this."

"Hey, Peter, you didn't get me into it. Remember, I came and asked you for seeds. And I'm glad you gave me those plants. They're beautiful. And starting to smell really good. I love 'em. Just wish Carla could enjoy them too."

"She still doesn't know?"

"No, that's why I couldn't let those guys keep my fish. Long as I come back with something to eat from down there, she doesn't ask what I've been doing."

"Well, on another subject, how's the baby?"

"She's great, growing fast. Gives me the feeling she knows who I am now. I mean she likes being with me. Been carrying her around the place some and she seems to like that."

"Good. I want to see her again soon."

"Come for dinner. I'll set it up with Carla and let you know."

"That would be nice. Hey, I'm almost ready to light a fire if it gets any cooler."

"Coolest one so far. Anyway, I've got to go. Stop by if you get the chance."

"I will. Seeya. Watch out for my boobytraps on your way out."

Jerry laughed as he tiptoed out to his truck, got in and drove off. The sound of his engine faded slowly and was gone. The stars were being covered up by a blanket of clouds and the air felt damp. Peter went inside and started up the orchestra again. He came out wearing a jacket, carrying a beer, and unfolded a chair to sit in. He wondered what this latest development would do to Sonya's campaign. Too bad. She probably didn't stand a chance anyway, but she had gone out on a good limb and it looked like somebody had cut it off behind her. If he went to that party, he could see her. But what if she was blaming him for some of that position she'd taken on pot? It might have been partly his idea, but she didn't have to use it. There were lots of ideas any candidate could choose from. Besides, she might still do better than if she'd just played it safe in the middle and not stirred things up a little.

The orchestra reached a quieter part of the piece. He stopped thinking about all that campaign business but couldn't shake off why she had such an effect on him. It wasn't the first time since the war he'd been around an attractive and available woman, and he hadn't gotten involved those times. It was more than that or he probably would have let himself get entangled before now. No, he thought, it was a quality she had that could hardly be described. Trying to think of the words to say it with, words like open, friendly, special, but none of them fit the feeling he had when her name or her face came into his mind. It was more like, for the first time, he felt like this might be someone who could know him and not hurt him for who he was. Trust. That was the only word that fit into the blank space in his thoughts. But what did he have to go on for that feeling? Maybe she was someone he could trust, but with what, with how much? With the holes inside him? There were those wounds that don't heal, that left holes in the heart, that left feelings of fear and fear of feeling. There were things in the memory that you could only avoid some of the time, that you couldn't share, but that you'd never get past unless you could unload some of it sometime, and maybe even to someone.

Beethoven's only violin concerto filled the air around him, filled his hearing; as he listened, he could hear the isolated individual calling out to the crowd, and the crowd urging one another that no one should get any closer. He could hear himself crying with tearless eyes, and he could almost see Sonya standing at the edge of the half-circle of light from the bare bulb on the trailer. He sipped the beer and slumped further into the folding garden chair. Now he became the orchestra booming back at the silence of his life, the years of unsaid thought and unspoken needs. Then he was the violin again, alone and singing softly the theme of what could be, if what was hadn't been. Maybe when he got the harvest in, he'd take a break, head back east. They do something at that new Vietnam Memorial on Veteran's Day, sometime in November. After harvest, and after the election. After now. A memorial to the dead. It might even be for those of us still living who can't ever feel completely alive again, when the dead we killed and saw die still live in our memories, still refuse to go away and be dead once and for all.

He tried to concentrate on the violin, on the passion that couldn't quite break loose enough to disrupt the melody, its theme of loneliness, the infinite longing of the one voice calling, hearing the answer, but fearing the feeling of attachment that comes with such closeness. Knowing that the bond itself is a source of vulnerability, that need fulfilled is the ultimate risk.

He drank the rest of the beer as the music built to its own version of successful reconciliation, as the song of the lonely and the chorus of the many converged and braided together into a final but incomplete resolution. He was tired, and the night was chill, but this was his reality, and if he couldn't change it, at least it was what he as used to. He stood and stretched his fingertips to the sky, then stepped outside the circle of light. He pissed on the ground by the bushes, covered the speaker with its blanket, and went inside to try for some sleep, thinking if this explosion story is true, it's getting too much like the war I tried to leave behind by being here.

Stockton hurried into Marty's office, carrying an armful of maps and papers. He was late, and they needed all the time they could get now. Reynolds had called him just as he was leaving to come over. There was a message from the Bay Area reporter, who was on his way. Now, on top of everything else, that had to be set up. You have all year to get ready for something, and it still turns into a crisis of never enough time for it when the deadline comes around.

"Hi, Marty. Sorry I'm late. Phone wouldn't leave me alone."

"It's okay, but I still have to leave by four. Game's at five o'clock."

"We'll just have to cram it all in. If we get an overall plan worked out, we can still do day-to-day stuff the night before. Want to start with the coast? We'll have to be ready with that one based on the weather. The long-range says it should be okay all next week, but late morning fog out there every day. Who knows after that? Remember last year?"

"Yeah, I do. Things were a lot simpler last year, weren't they? Spread it out on the table and tell me what you're thinking."

Stockton explained the basic division of land areas based on the available hours of helicopter time allotted to them. They would utilize two ground crews, trying to keep them close together. They leaned over the maps, and began making estimates based on previous years and on the information they'd gotten so far. The strategy was to handle each section of the county on one of the four days they were allocated. Their fifth day was optional and could be used to mop up anything they weren't able to get to by then. They didn't want to hit the same area parts of two days in a row, because that gave the growers all night in between to move plants. That had happened to them more than once when they first began using aircraft.

"The problem here is," the detective said and pointed to an area on the map midway between Dixon and the coast, "this is where we know is the heaviest concentration, but if we leave it until Friday, that gives those guys all that lead time from when we get started on Tuesday. They'll hear about it for sure."

"What do you think they could do about it?"

"I still don't think most of them are expecting the chopper for sure. But when they hear about it they could make some adjustments. Besides moving their stuff, they can lean it over and tie it down, cover it with fresh brush, and who knows, maybe more boobytrap action. We have to be really careful as it is, and that's going to slow us down as well."

Marty covered that section of the map with his hand. "What about hitting that section first and just leave whatever doesn't get done until the end? That way, if a couple of days go by after the first raids, maybe they'll think it's over, and then when you hit them again, they might have untied or uncovered."

"Might work as well as anything. Let's see how that fits in with everywhere else when we're done here."

By 3:39, they were organized in terms of the order of flights and searches, and raiding focus for each day. Not having to worry about warrants made a big difference in allowing them to plot the movements of the group patrols and transportation. These would be led by their own deputies, with state police and forest service personnel deputized for the duration of the raid season. The Chinook County Roads Department would provide a dump truck for hauling the confiscated plants to the power company furnace. The thing lacking was a vehicle and escort for the press, including the Bay Area folks and the local TV crew. Stockton said he was pretty sure he could use the DA office's prisoner transport van, and that maybe Henderson was the one to shepherd them around, although he was awfully good in the field.

"Maybe you'd like to babysit that bunch yourself," Stockton said, half-joking.

"No way, buddy. I'll need to be right here to handle all the unexpected fall-out and crap that could turn this into a fiasco. I'm what you call an armchair general."

"You miss out on all the excitement that way."

"Don't worry about me. I'll be following up leads we get from the air for the rest of the season. Are we done with all this map stuff now?"

"I think so. Let's roll it up."

They straightened up the mess they'd made, and as Marty sat down in the chair he motioned Stockton to take a seat as well. "Good," he said. "We've still got a few minutes. Anything else?"

"Just details. Nothing we can't handle as we go along. The only thing that was worrying me was the second metal detector, but it's coming with the chopper."

"Well, then," Marty said, "nothing left to do but go out there and get it done, right? And Tony, watch you step. I understand it's dangerous out there. But you should know all about that, don't you?"

"What do you mean?"

"I can't prove a thing yet, maybe won't ever be able to, but you and I both know that little show you put on last week was a hoax, a good one, but still as phony as shit that floats. Now, I don't know for sure why or how or even who put you up to it, but you listen to me for a minute and see if what I say doesn't make sense."

He picked the softball up from the floor beside his chair and started flipping it from hand to hand. Tony started to say something, but the Sheriff waved it off and watched the younger man across the desk for a long moment. Then he slammed the ball down on his desk.

"Number one, that patch was raided and cleaned out last year. August twenty-first and fifty-two marijuana plants confiscated. Only a fool would plant there again. Number two, you left some leaves along the way when you were carrying those plants down, yes down, that hillside. I don't know where you got them, but I'll bet your next month's pay there's an empty patch somewhere with no record of its eradication in our files or your duty journal. Number three, there was nothing else planted there this year, just your bundles of plants. No roots, no cut-off stalks in any of those hand-dug holes. You tried to make it look like you pulled those plants out of there. Either you ate the roots or those plants were never grown in the ground there. Lot of hard work, though. Number four, the path your tripwires were set on didn't go anywhere or come from anywhere. Dead-ended against a wall of brush nothing could go through, less than fifty feet past where the devices were laid out. And now for number five. Those devices were exact copies of the ones you studied at that training session a couple weeks ago. I checked. But of course, it's all circumstantial isn't it, Tony?

"So, I want to congratulate you on all your hard work, and a job almost well done. And I want to inform you that you and Reynolds, because that's got to be who put you up to this, that you two aren't worth the paper you wipe your butts with. You're supposed to be public servants, and you're worse than most of the scum that's out there. I said I can't prove it now, and it probably wouldn't be worth it anyway because you bastards wouldn't ever admit you did anything wrong. You got anything to say?"

"No, but this is all crazy, absurd, Marty. You've got to get ahold of yourself. Take some time to think it over, because you're making a huge mistake."

"Listen to me, Deputy, I said all along I didn't think we'd gotten to this level of violence in this county. I was wrong. I was right about the other side. They haven't. But I was mistaken about 'our side.' I don't know what I'm going to do about it yet, but I will say this: If I were you, I'd start looking for another job. Sooner the better. If you try to stay around, I'm going to make the next two years the most miserable two years of your life. And don't come to me for any recommendations. Now get the hell out of here. You're a good cop, but you're one sick person."

Stockton got up and gathered the maps and papers. He looked as if he wanted to say something, but Marty waved him out. As soon as he was gone, the sheriff threw the ball against the door as hard as he could and then picked up the telephone. He opened a small book in his top drawer and dialed.

"Ms. Lehman please…Sheriff Johnson…"

"Hello sheriff?"

"Yeah, it's me. How's it going?"

"Well enough, I guess. Why do you ask?"

"Because I think we may have caused you a small setback over here and I wanted to apologize. You, of course, know about the so-called grenades we found wired into boobytraps this past week.?"

"Yes, I do. It's just a terrible thing."

"It may be worse than you think. I never thought I'd be trying to help someone like you, and, don't get me wrong, I'm not endorsing any of your positions on the issues. All I can say at this time is that it looks like the whole incident could have been a hoax. There's no way I can prove it, at least not yet, but the circumstances point to what I'm saying, and I wanted you to know."

"A hoax. I don't think I understand."

"I don't have time to talk right now. I'm just trying to ease your mind a little, and my own. I'm a bit upset myself and haven't yet got a clear idea for how to proceed, but I will want to get together with you and discuss just how we can deal with this thing."

"Well, you've certainly got my interest."

"Let it go at this much for now, I have reason to be certain that your opponent and one or two of my men conspired to fabricate the whole incident in order to discredit you and to justify increased federal eradication funding. Unfortunately, like I say, I can't prove it right now. But I think there must be a way we can use this information to strengthen your position or at least undo any damage it might have caused as far as your election chances go. Maybe."

"Well, Mr. Johnson, this is a complete surprise and I'm still not sure I understand it yet, but I appreciate you're letting me know, and what you're trying to do. You'll just have to let me know what you think I should do about it, and when. Please."

"In the meantime," he said, "don't let it get out at all. I'll deny it if I think you're spreading it around before it's time for that. There may still be some time to set a few traps or something, and I don't want to spoil chances for more evidence. But don't mistake me. I haven't joined up with you or forgot about that lawsuit. It's just that I'd rather have to work with a fox than a snake. And I've got two more years in this goddam job."

"Well, I'm not sure I like being the fox, sheriff, but I appreciate what you're trying to do. I think it's something I can respect, and I'd be willing to meet with you anytime, if that will help."

"All right, you hang on to your respect until we see what comes of all this. I'll let you know what's next as soon as I know myself. Goodbye."

"Goodbye sheriff. Have a nice evening,"

He hung up. Now he'd have to hurry. He grabbed the duffle bag containing his uniform and softball clipboard. On his way out, he stopped to pick up the ball from where it lay on the cheap carpet. He felt a sharp twinge at the base of his spine. Damn! Tension again. It wasn't enough that his boys were tied for first and had a playoff for the league's spot in the tournament, but the goddam department had to fall apart on him at the same time. As he walked past the dispatcher and into the elevator down to the parking garage, he yelled back, "Play ball!"

Tom and Leslie pulled into Peter's driveway at about three o'clock on the Saturday afternoon of the housewarming shindig. Leslie commented that she'd never been to his place, and that she really liked the lay of the land. Tom wandered around a little while Peter moved the sprinkler in the garden. It had been a long while since the last rain and everybody's water pressure was going down all the time. Peter knew he still had enough in the spring, but if it didn't rain soon, he'd have to dig out his uphill catch-basin and make a larger pond for storage of any increased flow. He'd done it all before. Then he changed his mind about leaving the sprinkler on during the heat of the afternoon and shut it off at the faucet. That part of the garden could wait until he got back later that night.

The drive to Ron and Theresa's took about forty minutes, and on the way there they discussed the story about the cops finding the patch with grenades, and the helicopter that would be coming around soon. Leslie said she was really relieved they weren't dependent on their crop anymore, so Peter said he was glad he was retired as well.

"That so?" Leslie said with a smile.

Cars were parked at the end of the paved road when they arrived. The house was quite new and set back from the end of the road with a long lawn and some fruit trees in front of it. It was a smaller ranch-style house with a wide porch and rose bushes planted around both sides. Leslie carried a big cake she'd made, and Tom and Peter unloaded the chicken and bottles of sauce from the back end of the suburban. They could hear people and music coming from behind the house. Peter felt the familiar hesitation and thoughts of running away he usually experienced before entering a social situation. Only this time, it was somewhat different due to the unusual anticipation of seeing Sonya again. Leslie had made a joke about it on the drive over, but he hadn't responded so she dropped it. Now, at least it would be crowded enough that he wouldn't get left alone with her, especially as she was supposed to start off the show. Leslie smiled at him when he entered the kitchen, and he had a clear sense that she knew what he was thinking as he set down the box of pink, pimpled chicken parts.

"Glad to be here?" she asked.

"Yeah, me and the rest of these chickens," he said, affecting a southern drawl. "We can't tell you how happy we are to be here with you today." He knew it wasn't very funny, but she laughed anyway, and told him just to relax and be himself.

"If I was going to be myself, I wouldn't be here," he replied with a smile.

Tom came in from the yard and asked for help carrying the chicken and other things out. The fire was already going in the barbeque. Peter looked around as he went carefully down the back steps. There were already about fifteen people, maybe more, some of whom he knew. But none of them were Sonya. Ron came right over to him and thanked him for coming as he helped set down the box and started laying out chicken parts on the paper-covered picnic table.

"Nice place," Peter said to him. "Looks like a great garden."

"You don't know how long we've been waiting for that garden. It really is a wonderful experience. As a city boy, I don't think I ever thought about how much satisfaction there is in growing your own food. Sounds a little weird to you probably, but we both knew we had to have a garden."

"Yeah, it's worth it that way. Sometimes it doesn't add up if you figure the dollars and hours versus shopping at the store, but that feeling of doing it on your own makes up for it for me."

Ron nodded agreement and excused himself to welcome some other arrivals. Tom added more briquets and said it would probably be half an hour before the coals were ready. Peter pointed out beyond the garden and asked what was back there.

"I don't know, but it's probably all right to have a look around," Tom said, laughing. "I don't think they've got anything to hide."

Peter wandered out into the nearby woods and found a small creek. He smoked part of a joint, skipped a few rocks lengthwise down the water, and whistled a theme from the Brahms thing he'd been working on with his horn. He wanted to stay there longer. It was peaceful, but that wasn't what he was there for. What am I here for? he thought as he walked back toward the laughter and the smell of charcoal smoke.

When Sonya, Janet, and Kristi arrived, he was helping Tom flour and baste the chickens. He heard her before he saw her, as several people started clapping in mock political rally fashion. As she came into the back yard, they began chanting, "Speech, speech."

She smiled and waved, and said, "Sorry, but it's my day off."

Kristi came over to Tom and Peter and asked what they were doing. They showed her and offered her a brush to try it for herself.

Sonya looked around the yard and saw she knew most of these people, some from the law profession in town, and some from the campaign and the party. She suddenly recognized the back of Peter's head with a feeling that combined relief and apprehension. Just then Theresa approached and asked if she wanted to see the garden. She said of course she did, and they walked out that way and slowly toured the thriving rows of plants. Theresa was proud of it, although she gave Leslie credit for the starts and the advice she'd provided. Just then, Leslie joined with them and they all sampled some barely ripe cherry tomatoes. Theresa began gathering greens for the salad. As they started walking back, she asked Sonya if Janet had ever met Ray Matson, a lawyer from one of the insurance companies in town. Sonya said she was slightly acquainted with him. Theresa suggested she introduce the two of them since he was the only other single man in the group so far, other than Peter.

As the food got pulled together, Peter and Sonya found ways to stay busy and out of each other's way. There were now about twenty-five people at the gathering. Someone popped a cork on a champagne bottle, and Leslie gave a little rap about it being a housewarming, commenting that it wasn't cold yet, so there was time to warm the house, or at least the yard, with their festivities. A couple more bottles popped open, glasses filled, and toasts of welcome were given. A while later, Tom announced that the chicken had nearly achieved perfection, and they better get it fast before it disappeared. Folks lined up and began filling their plates. Sonya maneuvered Janet and Ray Matson together in the food line and it turned out they had briefly met once before. Kristi was sitting off to one side with Peter, who was apparently waiting for the line to shorten before getting in. Other than Corinne, no one else had brought children, so Kristi was staying close to the few adults she knew.

The meal was all good and the mood of the event eased into a kind of limbo as the sun dropped closer to the nearby ridges, and the food and the people settled. There was still more champagne and the promise of dessert later. Sonya had just taken an armload of dirty plates and utensils into the kitchen, when Peter, carrying the leftover barbeque sauce and the cooking implements, spoke to her from the doorway.

"So, hello. How's it going?"

"Oh," she turned to face the sound of his voice, found a place to set down her stack of dishes and then looked back at him. "Fine, um, how about you?"

"Doing all right. Good food, huh?"

"Here, let me take that." She took a loaded tray from him and shoved it into a place on the counter. "I see you and Kristi remember each other."

"Yeah, she didn't forget the tractor ride."

"And I didn't forget the one I didn't get."

They stood there for what turned into a long moment as neither could think of what to say next. It was as if they were waiting for someone else to come in and break the silence, but for some reason no one did. They looked into one another's eyes and looked quickly away. Finally, Sonya spoke, "So, what are you up to?"

"You mean right now?"

"Yes," she said and moved toward the door.

"Thought I might take a little walk to settle my meal. Don't usually eat this early. Heard a little creek running out back."

"You and your little creeks. I need a walk, too. Can I come along?"

"You don't have to make a speech or something?"

"No, Leslie's in charge of all that, and Dan might show up a little later."

"Okay." He moved to hold the door open and they went outside. Janet was involved in a small group that included that Ray fellow. She gave Sonya a nod and a smile as she and Peter meandered across the yard, with her stopping a couple of times to greet folks she hadn't talked to yet. Peter could feel Leslie's eyes on them. Why was it everybody had to make a big deal out of obviously nothing? And even if it was something, it was still nothing.

They walked in silence as he pointed out a trail through the berry vines. It was cool in the shade of the alders lining the sides of the creek, and there was a hint of soft breeze in the shifting motions of the leaves above them. They stopped at a small cascade where the water bubbled over smooth black stones, and he motioned to a large rock she could sit on. As he settled himself on the ground near her, he pulled out his pouch and smiled as he got ready to roll.

"Is that your little creek?" she asked, pointing to the pouch.

"Sort of. They go good together. So, tell me how it's going for you? It's been awhile."

"It has." She thought back though the weeks since the Jamboree and couldn't organize an answer for him. "I've been busy. Still having to work for a living, along with all the campaign pressures."

"Saw you on TV with that Mrs. Mondale. You looked good."

"Just looked good?"

"Well, they didn't exactly play very much of your speech, but you sounded good, too."

"Thanks. The other thing that's happened is we ran out of money, campaign funding."

"I heard. Leslie told me. Still a problem?"

Sonya pulled at a stalk of grass until the inside shaft came out, and she twined it through her fingers. "Well, it wasn't going to be, but now, I don't know. You got me in a lot of trouble, you know."

"Yeah, I thought about that. Sorry, but you didn't have to listen to me."

"I knew that. It turned out okay, and what I put out there with makes sense. It's just now with this bomb-trap thing, things have changed. I'm sure you've heard all about that."

"Yeah. I did." He looked straight at her, "It was my patch." He almost lit up the joint, but decided to wait.

"What?" She stared at him.

He had never seen that kind of look in her eyes, and it was tempting to keep her off guard and study more of her reaction. She just kept looking straight at him, waiting until he spoke again.

"No. Don't worry. I don't know why I said that, and I don't have any idea who did it. The stupidest thing I've heard of so far. Nothing's worth starting a war that's for keeps."

She relaxed a bit, but said, "I never know about you. I could believe you either way."

"Which way do you want to believe?" he said seriously.

"What I want and whatever is could be two different things."

"Sorry if I played a little rough with you. I guess I couldn't help it and hoped you wouldn't take it seriously. And I really am upset by the whole thing." He looked down at the joint in his hand, rolling it back and forth between his fingers. "It scares me, if you want to know the truth. It raises the ante for everybody." He smiled weakly and said softly, "Takes the fun out of it, if you know what I mean."

"Okay, that's better," she said. She reached toward his shoulder but didn't touch him. "You almost had me there for a minute. I really don't know anything about you, you know. But I think I know more about what happened than you do. Can I trust you not to mention a word of what I tell you?"

"I'd be a fool to lose your trust at this point. Accept my promise."

"This isn't supposed to go anywhere, and I probably shouldn't even tell you, but there's something that lets me have some trust in you… The Sheriff actually called me and said that he can't prove it yet, but he's pretty sure the whole incident was a hoax cooked up by someone in his department, someone probably working with Reynolds to bring me down, to discredit my position. As well as to get more funding for this crazy 'Pot War' thing."

"For real?"

"It's so real that he called me and said all that. If he's playing some game, I can't see any reason for it."

"That's pretty incredible, but I guess it fits." He put the unsmoked joint back into his shirt pocket. "By the way, thanks for trusting me. What are you going to do about it?"

"Nothing. Yet. He said something about using it later when and if he gets better proof. Whatever. The damage has been done as far as some of my supporters are concerned. Most likely the ones who were looking for an excuse anyway."

"I would say I can't wait to tell everybody I know, but I don't think you're ready to handle any more of my lame humor."

"Thanks for sparing me." Now she was smiling.

He went on, "But it really is too soon to tell how it's going to change things. Maybe it will backfire on the cops and Reynolds. On the other hand, it really pisses me off if we can't prove it wasn't growers. And if it was growers I'd be just as pissed off. I think I should retire anyway."

"That's the first time you've admitted that." She slipped off her still-new running shoes and her socks and pulled her jeans above her knees so she could dangle her feet in the cool, flowing water. They were quiet together for a while until she said, "You can smoke if you want to." Smiling. "Just don't blow that smoke on me."

"It's okay, I can wait."

"So then, tell me something about yourself. If you want to."

"Maybe I will. Like what?"

"I don't know. Like, have you always been alone, or are you divorced, or what?"

"Oh, I've always been alone. When I was born, I was alone. You've heard of the virgin birth? Well, I was the orphan birth. Nobody claimed me and I've been alone ever since." He paused and then changed his tone. "Truth is, never been married, or even real steady with anyone. My turn. How long you been split up?"

"About ten months, maybe a little more. We were married for almost ten years."

"Where's he now?"

"Bay Area. Trying to make it in the Big Time, I guess."

"Miss him?"

She glanced at Peter and then looked away to answer, "Sometimes. Mostly not. It's more that sometimes I miss having someone around in the evenings."

"Yeah, that's the hard time, for sure. Want to get back to the party?

"No, not yet. I like it here. You don't really want to talk about yourself, though, do you?"

He stretched his fingertips out to their fullest extension, shook them, and let his breath out slowly. "I'm afraid if I ever got started, I couldn't stop."

"What's wrong with that?"

"You go first. Have you always been curious? I mean, were you curious as a little girl?"

"I guess I was, but, hey, I'm not trying to pry into you. You just interest me on a lot of different levels and I'm sorry if you don't like it. Maybe we should go back now."

"Wait a minute, Sonya. Sonya. I like your name, and it really fits you. Let me just say that it's awkward for me to be interesting to somebody. I've protected myself for a long time, from everyone, and I might even want to loosen up with you. I might be able to, but it isn't easy for me, see?. Maybe I'm afraid of turning you off. I kind of like hanging out with you, and don't want that to go away." He turned away and flipped a stick into the moving water.

"Really? That's certainly the nicest thing you've ever said to me."

"I know. See how I'm not good at this? Maybe you can teach me how to be nicer." He stared into the water and wondered if she had any idea what she was doing to him, how the shell he had so carefully created all these years was beginning to show cracks, how much he wanted and didn't want to burden her with his struggle to forget some things and recall others. Wondering too if even getting this close was dangerous for her too. Where could it go? It must seem so simple to her, a friendship, and then whatever, an experiment, maybe, but he would be knowing all along that his real truth was that he didn't know how or where to stop if he started sharing himself, if he opened up...No one deserved to have his inner mess dumped on them, especially someone who seemed so genuinely good.

She quietly watched him watching the water, and right then, it was almost as if he, too, were flowing away, some part of him connected to the creek, being pulled away, carried off to join with all the other water. For the first time she sensed the depth of the vulnerability he was covering up, his need to open up, and the strength it took to stay closed off and alone like this. She was almost afraid of him for a moment. Thinking she might be wrong, might have pulled herself too close to his intensity without knowing its source, like a moth that was blind to the candle's flame. But she had always trusted her instincts with people, and there was enough honesty in his sarcasm to help her shake off whatever doubts she might have, at least until he proved her wrong.

Faster than she could see it, his hand darted out and caught her foot. She looked from his hand to his eyes and glimpsed the fun waiting there, waiting for her reaction. "That's my foot," she said, not pulling it back.

"I know that," he said, raising it slowly to the point that she was almost falling backwards off her seat on the rock.

"I'd like it back now, sir" she said, as politely as she could.

"Trade you."

"For what?" She tried to pull free, but his hold was really strong and she was off balance.

A strange look passed over his face and was just as quickly gone. "Nothing." He turned to face her, gently holding her foot in both hands now. "Sorry," he said, letting go, "I don't want to play rough with you, but it keeps happening. So sorry."

"It's okay," she said. "What's wrong?" She leaned forward and placed her hands lightly on his shoulders, looking for his eyes, which were almost closed.

"Nothing, nothing's wrong. This is just too good, that's all. Sorry."

"Nothing's too good, Peter." She touched his chin with one finger and tipped his head up. Leaning forward she grazed each of his closed eyes with her lips and said, "Wake up, the spell is gone, and when you open your eyes, you will see me as I really am."

He smiled and shut his eyes more tightly. “Not sure I can take that.”

“Try it.”

He opened his eyes slowly, finding her face almost touching his, her eyes a pair of mirrors in which his were staring back at him. He whispered, “Is that the real you?”

She nodded yes and her lips brushed his. He let go of her foot and pulled up on his knees beside the rock she was sitting on. They were still looking into one another’s eyes, trying to see beyond the reflections, beyond the past or the future, to see into the now. They kissed and their eyes closed.

Peter was the first to pull away a little bit. He was laughing.

“Now what?” she said, also pulling back.

He said, softly, “I don’t know, I just started laughing.” He reached and stroked her cheek with one hand and took one of her hands in his other. “I couldn’t help it. It felt so good, and then I couldn’t help thinking of a great movie…see there’s this lady DA, and this outlaw…”

“Shut up.” She kissed him again. This time it was her that pulled back.

“Now what?” he asked.

“I don’t know. I just had a flash that we were still sixteen, instead of, however old we are.”

Now he said, “Shut up,” and kissed her again.

Finally, he leaned away and stood up, took her hands in his and pulled her up against him. “We should go back up there, you know.”

She smiled, “I know, they’ll think this is happening down here, if we don’t.”

They made this a quick kiss as he gently eased her back down onto the rock and knelt to start pulling on her socks.

“I can do that,” She said, straightening his hair, and then mussing it again.

“I know, but you get to do it all the time.” He carefully pushed a shoe onto her foot. “Are you a jogger?”

“Just started.”

He put the other shoe on and tied it. He looked up at her and said, “Now run away from me as fast as you can.”

"That's what you think I should do?"

"Yeah." He stood up and looked down at her. "Go on, I mean it."

"What if I can't?" She stood and stepped up onto the rock, her hands on his shoulders. "What if I don't want to?"

He swung her down, took her by the hand, and they started back toward the party. "I gave you your chance. Sweet Sixteen."

"Surprised?" she asked softly and took hold of his arm.

"Yeah," he answered just as softly. "I really am."

"Me too." They walked the rest of the way in silence, automatically disentangling their arms as they came within sight of the yard. Music was playing and dusk was coming fast. They exchanged one more smile, and then he hung back and watched her stroll nonchalantly into the yard. As she joined the people, he moved back in among the trees until it felt like he was in a secluded enough spot to take a couple of hits

Sonya was glad to see that Janet was still there. They had driven separately because Janet planned to leave soon after the meal, but it looked like she was enjoying herself and staying. Kristi was probably inside watching a video. Janet and Theresa were shuffling through a batch of albums near the stereo on the patio table. The Rolling Stones were snarling and twanging from the speakers, and many of the folks were drinking beer from a pony keg Ron had just tapped. Sonya went over to Janet and joined in the record browsing.

Peter wandered back into the yard from a slightly different direction and hung back, debating with himself whether he wanted to dull the sharpness of the sensations he was grappling with by drinking some beer, or whether he wanted everything to stay just like it was, keen and in the forefront of his thoughts. This was new territory for these feelings and he was hardly comfortable. He had many good reasons to split and send her a "thanks-but-no-thanks" card in the morning. The only reason to stick it out and see what happened next was the slim chance that this might be his first chance to move past the place where he'd been stuck for so long. There was risk either way. And that was why he probably knew what he was going to do anyway. He hadn't come this far in his life by avoiding risks.

Ron called him over to the keg and offered a tall, foaming cup of the beer. He took it, blew off some of the foam, and drank deeply. The chill tingling of the beer soothed his throat, but made him want to smoke more. He glanced back over at Sonya, caught her eye for a second, and watched as she went on talking and laughing with her friends. Maybe, he thought, only that one word, *maybe* and then no thoughts followed it. He found a place to sit and settled back to watch the party wander loosely across the threshold between day and dark.

Soon there were a few folks dancing, and then a break for dessert. He got up and went to help Leslie bring out her cake. He held it up under some hanging lights so folks could see what it said. "Welcome Home Theresa and Ron" was written in purple frosting. Leslie made a short speech and then Theresa cut the cake. Tom appeared from around the front of the house carrying a canister of fresh-cranked banana-nut vanilla ice cream. Peter was sitting again and waiting for the crowd around the table to thin out. Then he was surprised when Leslie appeared next to him with a heaping full plate.

"Here," she said, "something for your munchies."

"Thanks. Looks great, but maybe too much."

"How's it going?" She sat next to him, on the ground, and watched while he dug into the dessert.

"Good. How about you? Great party."

"Fine, do you have any extra buds? I don't think anyone here brought any."

"I do, but I didn't think it was the kind of thing you could smoke at. I mean that kind of people."

"It's okay, we'll go a little ways away. Besides, she's not elected yet."

"Want me to roll?"

"No, I want to. Don't hardly get a chance anymore. I've gone so straight." She cleaned the bud from the stem, expertly filled the paper he handed her, rolled, licked and set it aside while she made a second one. "There's someone here I'd like you to meet."

"Who's that?"

"It's like this…We might have changed our plans a little. Tom and I want to stay over since we don't have to worry about the kids until tomorrow night. We could go sail-boating with a friend of ours up at the lake." She finished rolling the second joint and handed him back his pouch.

"So, I thought maybe she could give you a ride."

"Who could?"

"That woman over there. Her name's Sonya."

He looked at Leslie with squinted eyes. "Sneaky. What if she's not going my way?"

"Maybe you should go hers. Thanks for the smoke. You could join us," she said as she walked away.

She's really into this, he thought. What do you do when someone you're afraid of falls in your lap? You jump up and try to get away. But what if only part of you is afraid and the rest is fascinated? He realized he was probably the semi-unwilling victim in a thinlyveiled conspiracy. Maybe, maybe not. Maybe Leslie was trying to pull the same thing on Sonya and neither one of them had much choice. He wouldn't put it past her. At the same time, if something was or wasn't going to happen between him and this person, they might as well find out what it was going to be, or not be.

He finished his dessert and took the plate over to the stack of used dishes on the table. It looked like most people were finished, so he gathered up the pile and carried it into the house. As he went in, he looked over his shoulder toward the garden and saw Leslie lighting up a joint. Several people were standing around her in what looked like a kind of eager anticipation. Since he started growing he'd forgotten how scarce the stuff got in some circles. He went in and unloaded the plates at the sink.

When he got back outside, the dancing had started again, so he looked around for a good wall to be a flower to. He ended up sitting on the steps, watching as more of the group joined in. There didn't seem to be very definable couples so much as individuals swaying and stepping to Ray Charles "What I Say." Now, there were some memories for him. One more beer and he'd probably join the dancers. He wasn't sure which was worse, to stay thirsty or to feel like dancing. He got up and drew another half cupful. Sonya waved to him from within the movement of the dancers. He waved back, remembering the fun they'd had at the Jamboree. But watching her now he realized she'd probably just been being kind when she told him how awkward she felt dancing. She motioned for him to come over and join in. He shook his head, "no," so she came over and took the beer from his hand, took a swallow, set it down, then pulled him out to dance. He tried to make himself want to follow, and it sort of worked if he just watched their feet and no one else.

During a break between records he went back for his beer and she followed. "I hear you're stranded. Need a ride?"

"Maybe, maybe not."

"Well, I came by myself and I've got a car." She slipped her hand under his arm and smiled up at him, saying, "If you're not afraid to accept rides with strangers."

They had fun dancing once Peter got used to it, losing themselves in the party's energy. Several women cut in on Sonya and he had to dance with them, which was an unusual experience for him. But then the whole day was turning out to be unusual. As people began drifting away, they found themselves separating into various goodbyes. Sonya was shaking hands and giving hugs like a good candidate and he was looking around and wondering if he had any choice other than going with her. He could overhear people promising to see each other again at the big event over at Tom and Leslie's. It seemed that everyone wanted a last word with Sonya, and he realized that earlier the two of them had been away from the party for quite a bit of time.

There came a moment when they were both standing alone, looking around, then looking at one another, realizing they were also about to leave, together. Sonya said goodbye and thank you to Ron and Theresa and went inside to get her things. He waited, thanked them himself and said good-bye, and see you again. Then he walked around to the front of the house. Sonya came out the front, still chatting with Leslie through the screen door, and then she came down the front steps. He stepped out of the shadow of the house and said, "Boo." Instead of jumping away, she moved right to him, and once outside the circle of the porch's light they hugged lightly and walked toward her car.

"Where do you want to go?" she asked.

"Up to you. I don't much care." They got in and he commented, "Nice car."

"I'd invite you to my place, but there's nobody there."

"Ha. So, I should get back home anyway, but it's not fair to make you go clear out there. Maybe I could stay here, on their porch or something. It's warm enough."

She turned the key, switched on the headlights, and backed out to the road. "I want to spend some more time with you. If you don't like it, you can take the car home, and I'll come out with Janet or someone tomorrow and get it."

"Sounds possible." He knew he wanted to be with her too, but still wasn't sure what for. His fear of hurting her, of using her for what he needed, and not being able to be whatever she needed, that was the hesitation that suddenly overwhelmed him. That, and not knowing what she thought about him and whatever he could be for her. It was moving too fast. As they drove toward town in silence, he realized he was already closer to her than he'd been to anyone for a lot more than a long time, and he still knew almost nothing about her.

They exchanged occasional smiles by the dim light of the dashboard. From her side, she was no longer concerned about the facts of his life, only more and more curious. What kind of feelings was he dealing with, allowing himself to be this close to someone, given what she'd been told about him? Everything she knew told her this probably couldn't be happening, but here it was, happening now. Her doubts were struggling to win out, along with the big question of what she wanted from him. Was he just a challenge because everyone said he was such a loner, or was he really an echo of where her heart was at these days?

"Should we stop for any snacks, or beer, or anything?"

"Not for me." He was looking out the side window at the glow of Dixon's lights. Probably wouldn't be able to see the stars for all the street lighting.

It hadn't taken very long, and they were already parked in the driveway of a small house on a quiet tree-lined block. She got out of the car first. He followed her up the walk to the porch, and waited for her to invite him in. She didn't say anything, but took his hand and led him inside. She flicked a switch and some lamps came on.

"Nice place," he mumbled.

"Fifteen more years and I'll own it. Have a seat, walk around, whatever you want. I'll heat some water for tea. You'd like some, wouldn't you?"

He nodded yes as she started for the kitchen but then came back to him. "Hey, relax, you're among friends." She touched his shoulders lightly, looking up into his eyes. He managed a smile and she lightly touched his lips. "Look around. You'll see what a dull person I am." She smiled and backed away, turning to the small kitchen.

He wandered over to the stereo and record and tape collection. It was mostly popular music from the last fifteen or so years, some jazz and a couple of collections of well-known classical pieces. He pulled out the Sibelius "Violin Concerto," which seemed a little out of place, read though the liner notes about Heifetz the soloist, and then the notes about the composer. He tried to recall the theme for the orchestra part but couldn't quite get it. He called to her, "Mind if I put on a record?"

"Go ahead. I'm almost there."

He turned on the machine and placed the disc on the turntable. The opening chord sent a tingle down the back of his neck and he wondered if it wasn't out of place for the oddness of this situation. He turned down the volume when Sonya came back with two cups of tea and a honeypot on a tray. "You take honey?"

"Sure. What kind of tea?"

"Peppermint and red clover. Do you have a reason for this piece of music?"

"No, I don't have it at home, and haven't heard it for a long time, can't hardly remember it. Is it all right, or you want something else?"

"No, I'm glad. It was my father's favorite classical piece. In fact, he gave me that record."

"Did he play violin?"

"No, cello, but he always said he wished he could play the violin."

She put honey in both cups of tea and pushed his toward him. The violin seemed to be climbing a mountain in the background as they both blew on their tea. She kicked off her shoes and curled up in a corner of the couch.

"You can smoke if you want to? Maybe on the back porch."

"Not now, maybe later. Have you been in this house long?"

"About five years. We bought it when we both went into private practice. It seemed like a good idea for both of us to risk everything at the same time."

The music filled the space between them, between their words as each of them felt the memories in the room in different ways, felt the music in its different tones, and felt each other's nearness and distance at the same time.

"Peter, there's so much I want to know about you. At the same time, maybe I want you to remain a mystery, or tell me lies. I guess what I mean is that every time I think about you it's different. I'll just say, I don't want to pry, but I want you to feel open with me if you want that. Does any of this make any sense?"

"Yeah, it all does. I guess I owe you something just for you being so patient. Sort of patient." He smiled. "I think about you too, a lot." He looked closely at her and a sudden feeling of distrust filled him unexpectedly. Not the paranoia about her legal life, and not his own apprehension about being a kind of conquest for whatever woman finally got to him. No, he'd already worked through those levels and found them irrelevant. This was, rather, a feeling that maybe she would think she was better than him, that she would be shocked by his life and feel betrayed by her attraction to someone like him.

She pushed one of her feet up against his leg. "What do you think about me?"

That feeling he was having passed through him as quickly as it had come. He was almost positive that she really was interested in him, for himself, whoever that was. Maybe for no other reason, not for any gossip or power trip. He was shaken by how fast he could go through changes in her presence. It had been that way since their beginning. Feelings long unused flowed in and out and through him, bringing the threat of tears to his eyes just as the violin's solo softened and slowed. What could he say to her about the ways he'd tried so hard not to think about her? Tried not to be distracted by what couldn't be, and yet what wouldn't leave him alone.

"I think of you as someone I might hope I can trust," he said, looking down at his hands.

"And you need that?"

"I don't know. I think so. Ask me something."

She set her cup down and turned to face him, her knees pulled up under her chin. "Has it been a long time since you've been with a woman?"

Now the orchestra reached a crescendo in the pause that followed her question. It broke off and then came back with a whispering of the violin, which was now singing alone in the forest.

"Yeah, a long time."

She reached out and took the cup from his hands, and set it on the table, then took one of his hands. He let her take it, instantly noticing the softness of hers and wondering if his hand was too rough for her. She squeezed his palm and said, "I like you very much. Don't know why yet, but I'm glad you want to trust me. And I love looking at you, do you know that?"

"No." He wanted to turn away, but her eyes pulled him back. "Sonya," he said her name softly, "it feels like maybe I'm using you."

"You sure it's not me using you?"

"I don't mean it in the usual way. I mean, I might seem to be someone I'm not."

She pulled him closer until their faces nearly met. She put her finger to her lips, "Shhh."

They kissed, lightly at first, then a real kiss. It was uncomfortable the way they were leaning into each other on the couch, but it didn't matter. Their lips were adjusting to each other's, quivering in a tense blend of nervousness and fulfillment. Her hand slipped through his long hair and she swung her legs off the couch, leaning back against him. He leaned forward, away.

"I can't. Sorry. That's what I mean. It's not fair to you because I can't." He stood up, turning away so she wouldn't see his face working to control itself.

"Peter, what is it?" She stood up too. "Did something bad happen to you? It's okay. Tell me, it's okay, but only if you want to." She held back from reaching out to touch him.

"I'm all right. I didn't get wounded or anything. I just can't be what you need." He turned away from her. She was standing behind him and reached up and slowly began massaging his neck. "How do you know what I need?"

"You need someone who can touch you and it won't...you know...."

"Is there something wrong with me?"

"No, not at all. You're all good." He twisted away from her hands. "What if I tell you some things and you hate me for it?"

"I won't hate you. Believe me. Remember, you said you thought you could trust me. Try it. Try me. I promise, no matter what it is. Please sit back down. Peter, I said I want to know you. Whatever it is, it's okay." She sat back down on the couch, and motioned to him, sensing his tension, begging him with her eyes to be with her, knowing now that this was the key to the magnet that pulled so forcefully on her feelings for him.

"Can I walk around here?"

"Of course, just don't leave," she said and smiled, trying to show what she was feeling, knowing that here was someone, a man, who wouldn't, couldn't, treat her with the arrogance she'd always accepted, a man whose need for her seemed to be for every bit of compassion she could manage, and she knew a sudden depth of loving that had never, ever come inside her before. "Peter, was it the war?"

He was looking at her now, looking down at her, trying to see into her, still wondering if it was right to do this to her. He wasn't wondering if he could trust her, but rather if she would ever trust him again. "Yeah, just something that happened over there." He felt his knees giving way as he sank slowly to sit cross-legged on the rug. He pulled the pouch out of his pocket and set it on the end table. "I don't know how I can even do this to you. I don't hardly know you, but it feels like I do, like I really do. I don't know what it is."

"I'll stop you if it's too much for me, I promise, but now I need to know, or I'll be left thinking it's something wrong with me, either because you can't be with me, or because you can't tell me why. Either way would be worse for me than whatever it is. Can you understand that?"

He was holding his face in his hands while she talked and when she paused for a moment, he looked up, straight into her eyes. Again he felt the flood of the unfamiliar feeling that made him want to share with her, even this, knowing that this moment was as close as he'd ever been to that sharing, and to that risk of trusting that can come from hurting and being hurt. Maybe there would never be another time like this. He knew this was most likely true, and that whatever came of it couldn't be any worse than all the years of secrecy and brooding that was at the core of his relationship with himself.

"I don't know how to start, but I think I want to. I want to smoke something, but I don't." His hands reached for the pouch and papers. "I'll roll it, but I'll wait to smoke it." He was speaking as if to himself, and as the fingers of one hand crumbled the buds into the other, he looked up to the ceiling and tried to think how to begin.

"Whatever you need right now. I'm here for you," she said.

"Okay, thanks. It started when I got drafted, and when I got sent over. It started when I first went into combat. I really don't know when it started, but it did. I don't know when I stopped being the kid I used to be, the one I grew up being. He just wasn't there anymore, and the person who took his place was a stranger to me and a stranger in that land, and to those people he was fighting for or against. It almost didn't seem to matter over there. I never knew who I was fighting for, besides for myself and whatever Americans I was around, and most of them wouldn't have been my friends back here. When you're here you can't really describe it, and when you're there, you can't remember here. There's so much more than an ocean between here and there." He set the perfectly rolled joint on the table next to the pouch and folded his hands together. "I guess that's why it was possible to do things there that can't even be talked about here, how it was possible to become someone you can't even remember once you're back. For a while when I got there I didn't know how much I'd changed. I'd listen to stories and rumors… God, there were rumors, always, about anything, everything. If you wore a certain colored scarf on your neck their snipers weren't supposed to fire at you because it meant you weren't going to fire at them. But the scarf was a different color every time you heard the rumor. Stuff like that all the time. We're going in. We're not going in. They're up ahead. No, behind us. They're under the ground. We're going to get bombed by our own planes. All of it, whatever. And all of it happened, and none of it happened. And what really happened won't ever go away…

"There was terror and torture on both sides. One time we went back to a village that was friendly to our side. Lieutenant wanted to meet with the headman, a Mayor kind of. When we got there, it was abandoned. Nothing but bodies, mostly men, but a few young women. That Mayor was hanging from a tree, and it was horrible what they'd done to him. I overheard the lieutenant and the sergeant talking about how we'd get even.

"A few days later, we got set down about half a mile from another village. It was in VC controlled territory. We never knew when we raced out from under the chopper's blades whether we'd be shot or not. This time it was quiet, and we moved through the jungle between us and the village with no problem. For sure, when you land with a couple helicopters, everyone within two miles knows you're there so they can choose whether to make a stand or just vanish. This village was supposed to be a VC recruiting center. Our orders were standard issue: Wipe it out. I guess what the media back home called 'search and destroy.' It was more like destroy and then search. You really can't have any idea what it was like, and what's so heavy is that it became routine, just routine. Sure, you could get killed, any minute, but even that chance seemed routine after a while."

Pictures of that day flashed through his head and what he remembered most was the insane noise of the operations. Could that amount of sound really exist, the automatic fire, artillery rounds pounding the nearby jungle, fire burning the fields and outbuildings of the village, shouts and screams? Right now, he wanted to whisper *No*, he wanted to be silent, to forget all of it, but one look at Sonya's steady, staring eyes pushed him on. "I never knew the name of that village, or if it even had a name. It was just something to get rid of, or it would kill us."

He tipped his head back to look up at the ceiling. "We move in slow, but there isn't any resistance. We break into teams of two for house to house. I'm paired with this lifer, a sergeant. He'd never hassled me, but I didn't like him much anyway. I don't think he liked me either, but those things don't matter when there's an enemy out there after us, all of us. We start moving into these huts, you can't believe how little these people live on. Like they had nothing but these huts and some mats and we burned them down." He stopped talking and just looked down at his hands at the rubbed the rug. "So, we don't find anyone in the first one, and we torch it, no one in the second one, still coals in the firepit, you can tell they got out just ahead of us, but they're gone now. The sergeant kicks the coals and I light the roof with one of the gas-soaked rags we bring with us just for that.

"In the next place there's two old people, women I think, but you never know. They're dressed all in black like they do. That was one of those myths about over there, that only the VC wore black pajamas. Some places half the people or more were wearing them. It's like all they've got. And anyway, these two old ladies just sit there in the shadows staring out at us. When I think about it now, they're like two vultures, their eyes burning, waiting, and I'm thinking they're waiting for me to die and start to rot and then they'll laugh and feast. Sergeant tells me to cover them, even they could have guns, and he goes through to the animal shed attached to the back of the hut. These people almost never leave their old people alone like this. He's looking for whoever's with them. I look around and see this hut's a little better off than most. It has a makeshift fuel lantern, and a little bit of furniture. Maybe it's the mayor's, that's what I'm thinking when he comes back in dragging a girl, a woman, can't tell. She's struggling, fighting him. He says 'catch' and throws his rifle to me. He pulls out a piece of nylon tie-line. The old women don't move. They don't move when he throws her down on her face. She turns her head toward me and I can see it's a young woman. I keep my gun on the old women, but it isn't necessary, they don't move, they're like statues. I look down at her face next to the dirt floor of the place. She's beautiful. I can't tell you how I know, but her eyes, they're screaming. She's probably the most beautiful Vietnamese girl I saw over there..." He pauses and rubs his eyes, roughly with both hands. "She's biting her lip, not making a sound, but her eyes are screaming at me.

"Sarge rolls her over on her back and grabs her feet, looks at me, laughing. 'Fuck her,' he says. 'I'll hold her feet and you fuck her first.' I say, 'No thanks.' I'm looking at her eyes, they're right by my feet. She must know what he's saying. Her eyes roll back. She spits at him and tries to turn over to kick between his legs. He looks at me and there's a strange look now in his eyes now and he says, 'That's an order, kid!' And I don't move, I can't move. 'If you don't, I'm going to slice her from the bottom up. Now fuck her!' He pulls out his knife.

"Her eyes fix on mine and I swear she knows what he's saying, and it doesn't matter because now maybe I know I have to do it. I can't even remember my thoughts..." He looked through his tears at Sonya. "I just hoped I was trying to save her from him. But I don't know that..." His legs were cramped from sitting on the floor, sitting for so long and he shifted his position, coming up on one knee first, and then the other. He reached for the joint and took it in his fingers, rolling it back and forth between them. He'd come this far on the story and he couldn't stop now. He couldn't look at this woman on the couch, so close to him. But he couldn't stop now. He'd said this much now, and he had to go on, but her hands were in her lap and when he glanced at her eyes, he was suddenly wondering if he'd ever be able to look into them again. He settled back on his heels and rubbed the cramp in one of his legs. "So, I try to do it. I drop both guns, drop my pants. I duck under his arm and come up between her legs. I'm standing there in front of him and he pulls her up against me, face up. I'm looking at the old ladies. They're still not moving, no expression on their faces. What happens next isn't in here anymore," he said, and placed his hands on either side of his head. "I don't have anything left in my head from that moment. I swear. I can see her eyes, and she doesn't hate me. I can't take that. I bang into her and I want her to scream, to hate me so I can hurt her, but she just twists her head so I can see her opening her mouth and screaming with no sound. I fight my way away from this monster holding onto her, and back away from her. I don't even know if I came or not. I don't know how I could have." He gave Sonya a quick look, but she had her face in her hands. "I pull my pants up and I'm crying. I hate it, I hate crying and don't want him to see it.

"He says, 'Now watch this.' And he grabs both of her feet with one huge hand and drops his pants. He twists her legs so she rolls over, her face to the ground. He looks at me and says, 'Boy, you watch. You never got nothing like this,' and he grabbed her around the waist and pulled her butt into his crotch and started humping." Peter looked at Sonya again, but her eyes were closed, and now her hands were in her lap. "So, he's humping and laughing and the gunfire outside is moving further away from us. We need to get out of there. Then he reaches down for his pants and gear around his feet, still holding onto her. He pulls out a small pistol. Lot of guys carry them for protection in town, on leave, stuff like that. He's humping and he's laughing and he puts the gun low on the back of her head and he looks at me and then back down at her. Now she finally screams, shrieking, and he fires one shot...Why did I have to be there? Why? She starts jerking and he's humping and yelling, and the two old women cover their faces and she won't stop her spasms and jerking and he's kind of jumping up and down and the blood's coming out of her head and out of her mouth. I puke and pick up his rifle and I look at his naked ass just banging away at her thrashing body and I open fire and I cut him in half..."

"Peter," Sonya is holding her hands in front of her face as if she's praying, and she whispers, "Peter, you don't have to go on."

"I have to, I have to go on because that's when I stopped myself, and then I put a couple of rounds into his head and now he's jerking and his body twists and he's falling to the ground in a spasm that won't seem to quit...I bend down to the girl's head and pull her away from him and I turn her face up and I see the light is gone from her eyes and I set her head back down. She's face up now and I stand up, pick up both guns and I motion the two old women out of the hut and when they don't move I sling the guns over my shoulders and drag them outside and push them as far away as I can, go back in and grab the lamp and smash it to spill the fuel and I drop a lit book of matches onto the spilled fuel and it flares up and I want to stay there, right there, and I do until it gets too hot and the smoke is choking me and I bend down and kiss her bloody forehead and say how sorry I am and I crawl out of there as far from the fire as I can and maybe I faint, I don't know...Someone grabs me and drags me away from the fire...and I finally come home a couple months later."

His hands trembled as he lit the joint and sucked deeply. The smoke rushed into his lungs and he held it there, long as he could. He glanced up and looked at Sonya and saw the tears streaming down her cheeks, thinking if only I could cry now, cry with her. But strangely he couldn't. She raised her head and opened her eyes and they found his.

"Oh, my God, Peter, that happened to you? You're all right. You're still alive, and it wasn't your fault. Oh, Peter." She came down on her knees to him and took his face in her hands and he looked into her wet eyes and she pulled his head to her heart and she held him there, rocking slowly back and forth. And then deep inside of him, it broke. It broke loose and his grief burst from his guts like a damn bursting and he gave in to it and he wept for himself, and for Sonya, for the girl, and for a world that had to be like this.

The sobbing still shook both of their bodies a long while after the tears stopped coming. He noticed the joint had gone out between his fingers. He could feel her breathing, her face buried in his hair, and he could hear and feel her heart beating next to his ear. He circled his arm around her and held her tightly, knowing that she was a part of him now, that he'd made it so she carried some of his pain now, and in that moment of knowing this he gave himself over completely to her, to her kindness, and to her touch.

She might have thought before this that sometime he was going to come to her and give something of himself to her, and explain himself, but never could she have known he would give her so much, any more than he could have known he would do this to her. She was swept along by the sadness and relief that flowed from him. She was able to feel that maybe some of what he needed was here within her. She was able to feel herself filling up with the sense of good that comes from giving.

Together they suspended time and filled the moment's emptiness with a sharing that was unexpected but would never be forgotten.

Then slowly they returned to themselves, to the urgency of cramped muscles and itching eyes. Slowly they eased apart, enough to use their fingers to explore the space between them, lightly touching one another's hands, unable to separate completely.

It was Sonya who spoke first, "I want to thank you."

"I'm sorry." Now that he'd passed some of it on, now that it was shared, it scared him to think he couldn't ever be a stranger to her again, no matter whatever else did or didn't happen between them. He lifted his eyes to look in hers, found them and hesitated, ready to flee their look if they threatened him. He couldn't believe she wasn't horrified, but she wasn't. She wasn't showing anything like that, she seemed almost totally calm. He was prepared for sympathy, pity, but not for the gentle waves of compassion that were absorbing him softly in her presence.

"Maybe you need to go on and finish." And she asked, "When you think about it now, not like this, but when you're just all alone and it comes back, what do you think about it?"

"When I got back home and there was nobody I knew who could ever understand any of it, nobody could've…I realized that what happened in that hut, what they call a hooch, what happened in there was the same as what we were doing to their whole country, the exact same thing as happened to that girl was being done to her whole country, and I was the one doing it."

He pulled away a little, fumbled for his match book, relit the joint and toked deeply once, twice. "Got any air freshener?" he said trying to smile.

"You don't have to answer, and maybe I shouldn't ask. But is that the last time you were with a woman an any way?"

"It's okay. You might as well know everything now. So, no, I got way drunk one night and tried with a bar girl in Saigon, just before I came back. No go. Then there was this girlfriend I'd had before I went over and when I got back I guess I tried to pretend everything was the same with us, and I guess she was trying to pretend she still cared, but nothing came of it. We didn't even get undressed before we gave up."

Sonya moved to be on her knees behind him, gently kneading his shoulders.

"Can you tell me how you feel now?" he asked.

"I feel like you gave me something really big, and you're still not sure you wanted to."

"I wanted to, but I'm not sure I should have. Now you have to live with it, too."

"But I was living with it. We all are. I just didn't know what IT was before. Now I know this much, and I know more about myself because I know more about you."

"Maybe you didn't hear everything right. Maybe you didn't hear how bad it really was."

"Peter, I did. I heard it all."

"Maybe you didn't hear me say, when I said… maybe I was into it."

"I heard that, but it doesn't make any difference in how I feel about you. You weren't in your right mind. I just feel so bad for you and what you had to go through." She had moved around and was lying down on the floor, her head on his leg. She reached up behind his head and pulled it down to her, kissing him lightly and turning herself up into a hugging position. "You know," she said, "there's really nothing wrong with you. You're just so afraid there is. You were caught in a trap." She pushed herself up and stood slowly. "More tea?"

"No thanks. I need to use your bathroom."

She pointed down a hallway. When he came back she was waiting. "Come on, I'll show you the rest of the house before you go." She took his hand and led him past a study, and then opened a door into a garage that looked kind of full of stuff. He followed her without wanting to say anything, without wanting to ask any questions or to give any answers, wanting only to stay close to the safety he felt in her touch.

"This is the bedroom," she said, leading him into a darkened room barely visible in the glow from a streetlight outside the house. She pulled him gently to the side of the bed and sat him down. "And now it's bedtime." She knelt and began taking off his shoes. When he pulled his feet away from her, she said softly, "You get to do this to mine all the time," and she slipped the shoes from his feet. She sat beside him and they were both silent, waiting for something else, something besides the two of them to make something happen. After a few long moments she whispered, "I'd like you to stay with me, not as lovers," she paused, "more like friends who haven't seen each other for a long, long time…"

He lay back into the softness of the bed. "I guess I'm here anyway." Suddenly, he was very tired, and it felt good to stretch and then just give in to the moment. She pulled a blanket from somewhere and settled it around them. "Thanks," he said, "thanks for being my new friend."

As they slightly pressed into each other's warmth, the feeling of closeness was a fulfillment of a new and different kind for each of them, and sleep slowly filled the room. Outside a light rain began to fall, and Peter's last thought was that he wouldn't have to water his plants the next day.

Sonya lay awake longer, listening to his breathing. Every so often there was a catch in its rhythm likely left over from his crying. She still hadn't fully absorbed the energy and intensity of his openness to her. It was like she'd heard it all, and been there, but almost not as herself. The emotions he'd called up in her were so mixed and unclear that she wondered if she would even remember all of it in the morning. Lying there with her arms around him was so completely peaceful that she wondered if she would even remember this part in the morning. Now it hardly seemed like earlier, driving home from the party wondering if it would be all right to have more of a complete physical connection with him. That was somehow transcended by the outpouring of feelings so total that it almost felt like they had made love. Knowing that was probably out of the question, at least for a while, wasn't a disappointment. Rather, she now had a sense of existing togetherness she'd never known was possible with anyone. Perhaps now it could grow into a true love, and maybe it was up to her to find the lover he lost inside himself. Whatever it was, wherever it went, this night was a undeniably special, a once in a lifetime experience.

They slept for a few hours, moving occasionally as their bodies reacted to the stranger in one another. As the first hint of daylight filtered into the room, Peter stirred first. His eyes opened and his mind awoke, and there was a moment of puzzling to fit together her face so close to his own, the room, and the softness of the bed. He noticed they were both still fully dressed, and he was suddenly roused by the memory of the night before and all that had happened and changed for him. Now, in this first light of dawn he realized he was no longer alone with his story, and no longer alone in his own bed. Lying next to Sonya, he perceived her as someone completely new, someone different than he had known before. It seemed too fast, that he could lose his loneliness all at once and he wondered if there wasn't something left behind as he reached out for this new reality taking the place of his usual longing. As he awakened into this new morning, he knew he could no longer feel sorry for himself, and hopefully he would never want to again. He had confessed, and unloaded the deepest sources of his long-term solitude, and if he chose to continue it, he could never again blame anyone else, it would be his responsibility, his own failure, rather than that of a world that wouldn't let him be himself. He wanted to wake her up and see if she could help him make sense of these thoughts, but he told himself he had taken more than enough from her for now, probably forever. He needed to wake up and see how it really felt to be so different.

He eased his arm from under her head and moved carefully to the edge of the bed. He had to find the bathroom before anything else, no matter who he was or wasn't this morning. There was a door adjoining the bedroom. He went in, closed it and emptied his stressed-out bladder with great relief, splashed cold water on his face, and studied the mirror for the reflection of his eyes. He looked the same as he did at home except this mirror didn't have a scratch in its silver backing. He wiped his hands and face and turned back into the bedroom.

As he carefully slid onto her bed he saw her smile, with her eyes remaining closed. Her hands came up and felt for his head. Pulling him close and kissing him softly. He rolled himself tightly against her, repaying the kiss with interest, and with a surprising birth of desire. Sonya's eyes opened and twinkled in the dim dawn's light. In this new morning there was no longer anything holding them back, they were free and each of them knew without words that the other was ready.

They knew too that they'd never been here before. Without a past to guide them or to decide for them, they were like children again and they played like children do. He let her fingers explore his face, lay back as she pinched open the button of his shirt and tapped on the skin of his neck with her nails. She watched his face with a questioning look as he rolled his eyes in pretend confusion. His hand found her backbone and his fingers counted vertebrae as she kissed him, his mouth, his throat, his chest. He reached lower down her back, massaging and pulling her closer and sliding down until his face was buried in her breasts.

A shaft of the sun's light filtered its way through the space between curtain and wall, hit the mirror above the dresser and reflected onto the bed. It caught her auburn hair as she raised her head and arched her back, accepting his face. He slipped her shirt over her head, paused in admiration of her evenly tanned torso, and again buried his face in her breasts, now pulling down on the bra with his teeth. Her hand unbuckled and slid beneath his belt and found his eagerness hard and perfect for her grip. They rolled across the bed, first one way and then the other, him on top and then her, hands everywhere at once, mouths seeking, finding, losing track, and coming back home. He helped her undo the buttons of his jeans and then slipped hers down her legs.

As her pants fell away, she stopped for a moment, pushed him away on the bed and left for the bathroom. As he lay there alone, he heard her moving about in that next room, and had the special and unique thought that if this never happened again it would always be happening. From now on, this was his reality. He slid out of his jeans and under the sheet and thin cover. He propped himself up with pillows and locked his hands behind his head in the most casual pose he could assume. The only thing that wasn't casual was the major lump in the bedding halfway down the length of his body, and he smiled to think he was being just like thousands of other guys on a sunny summer Sunday morning.

Sony reappeared at the bathroom door and her beauty almost took his breath away. He tried to speak, paused, and then asked, "Did you bring in the Sunday paper?"

"No," she said, "I must have forgot what day it is." She took two quick steps and jumped onto the bed. He grabbed her and they wrestled together until the covers became a tangled, knotted mess between them and they slowly undid the mess and tried to catch their breaths. They were sitting up, staring into one another's eyes, looking as serious as they could. Finally, she asked, "Are you ticklish?"

"No, are you?"

"No, sorry."

At that, they each began madly trying to tickle the other, giggling and slapping hands away. "Liar," she said, "you are too.'

"So are you."

"Truce?"

"Okay."

They sat facing each other, cross-legged, gently holding hands with the sublime smile of the recently enlightened. Peter said, "I've heard there are those whose bodies leave their minds at a time like this."

"That's right, but yours better not because I want all of you here, now."

"Ah so, here and now," he said slowly, as they leaned across the space between them and kissed silently, not moving, and that moment stretched out to include everything they could possibly feel about each other, possibly forever.

They lay down slowly, still holding on to the kiss, their hands seeking each other's pleasure. Touching and rubbing, stroking and arousing, they explored and exposed all that was most personal and most to be shared. These were their last moments of separation as their mouths gave and saved sensations, lost to thought and found in ecstasy. An urgency came on Peter as the long waiting and abstinence of his life built up inside and demanded release. She felt this in him and helped him to find his way within where the warmth and softness exceeded all description, and the body knows what the mind can only guess at.

Inside, he was inside, and her heart and body surrounded and absorbed his energy. Holding, she was holding all of him, pulling him deeper, deeper to where the beginning is, and an ending will always be.

He climbed higher and went deeper. She thrust higher and held tighter. He peaked, paused, and simply exploded as the years fell away and she took into herself all of the aching need he had to give up. As he collapsed into her, surrendering, giving in, giving out, she took him and felt her own self go rigid as he relaxed, feeling a tremor that was not yet orgasm but was not any less than that either. What she felt was complete by itself and new to herself, and maybe she would never feel it again. Tears burst into her eyes, a moan escaped her throat, and the weight of a lifetime of pleasing others lifted away from her as she took what she needed for herself, from him.

Slowly, slowly the tensions of satisfaction slipped away from their bodies and they were left with the delicious fatigue that follows such a fantasy made real. In a state of near dozing, they lay silently within that in-between world of timelessness, sharing for an interval the same feeling, the same fulfillment, and the same sweat. Consciousness darted in and out, playing hide and seek among the concerns of daily life and the escape to once in a lifetime. Fingers caressing as thought massaged their minds, neither requiring attention, neither noticing as the sounds of the world outside slowly began to take up their positions on the edges of awareness. It was over because it had begun, because it had never happened before, and was happening once and for always.

"Thank you," Peter whispered, and that sound licked into her ear.

"Thank you," she said, and he swallowed her words with a kiss.

"Got any coffee?" he asked.

"It isn't made."

"That's all right. I'm not ready yet."

"Good, because I'm not here yet." She pushed up on one elbow and looked down into his eyes. "Was that good for you?"

He smiled, wondering how to answer such a question. For a moment the silence was good enough. The he said, "Was being born good for me?"

"I have to be careful here. I could love you." She smiled and pushed his hair back.

"Yeah, I know what you mean. Me too. But we're more mature than that, right?"

"Right." They smiled, kissed smiling and smiled kissing, and then laid back to rest a bit more.

It was a Tuesday morning and the fog hung late in the valleys between the ridges. Two convoys of official vehicles carried officers of the state police, sheriff's deputies, U.S. Forest Service, and DEA personnel. As the sun slowly burned through the fog, the sound of an approaching helicopter vibrated through the hills.

The day's first raid began in a series of small patches strung along a creek only a couple of miles from the South Fork store. While the men on the ground worked their way through the dense underbrush, the chopper made large circles above them, searching for more locations and keeping a lookout on the roads in the vicinity. The men of the first convoy settled into cleaning out the patches and the second group moved along the logging roads beneath the copter, waiting for another location to be pinpointed and communicated.

By noon over two hundred plants had been chopped down and loaded into a sling hanging down in the draft from the rotors above, as the aircraft kept returning to assist the work on the ground. A television crew arrived and filmed an actual raid adjacent to a piece of private land where the owners were briefly held for questioning, and then released when they were able to produce a tax map of their land showing where the survey markers defined their property.

The heat of the day increased as the raiding parties moved further onto national forest land. It was getting harder to access the patches spotted by the overhead scouts. At one patch they found a trip wire attached to a bright battery-powered light. One of the detectives held things up while he and two others searched for a camera that could have been used in tandem with the light, finding none. Elsewhere they destroyed elaborate irrigation systems and punched holes in 55-gallon water drums. In almost all cases, they were dealing with twenty or more plants in a single area, interspersed with brush. Some of it was so far down the sides of the ridges that it required great effort to move the contraband to a safe place for the chopper and sling to gather it up. The task force had discussed burning the plants on nearby landings, but it was clear that the forest was too dry to risk it.

By midafternoon, each man on the ground was exhausted, scraped and scratched from the brush, tingling with nettle stings, and soaking in his own sweat. For those with military experience it was comparable to boot camp and reminded some of them of combat—except this time their enemy was plants instead of people.

The helicopter had passed over Jerry and Carla's place in the middle of the morning, circled twice and moved on toward Peter's. Carla commented to Jerry how glad she was that they had nothing to hide but wondered why the helicopter was spending so much time in their area. Jerry said he didn't have any idea, and a little later on found an excuse to go down to the store, to get oil for his chainsaw mix.

First, he went by to see if Peter was home. He was. They were discussing the copter's flight pattern when a convoy roared by them on the road. They watched as four pickups and two vans slowed briefly and then sped off again toward the nearby logging road.

"There's your answer. They'd have been at your place already if they saw anything."

"You think they'll be back?" Jerry said, worried.

"No telling. Never seen it done this way before."

"Hate to be coming the other way on the road when they're on it."

"No shit. Hey, this should be on the news tonight. Maybe I could come by?"

"Sure." Jerry was still scanning the sky. "You know when it came over our place, I've never been so close under one. Leaves being blasted out of our apple trees from the down draft."

"Were your plants tied down?"

"No, but I let berry vines grow all through them."

"Good thinking. You're probably safe. I don't think they want to get too low yet."

Jerry wiped his face and said, "I sure hope mine are okay. Carla would kill me if they got found and we had any hassle. What about your stuff?"

Peter didn't answer for a moment as he imagined troopers thrashing through his patches. "I won't know until I get up there. I did all I could. If they got them, they got them."

"Yeah, well I've got to get to the store and back. Need anything?"

"Don't think so. Might pick up a six-pack." Peter reached in his pocket and handed over a ten-dollar bill. "Your TV, my treat. See ya later."

As he turned to leave, Jerry stopped and said, "Kind of weird, isn't it? How much do you think those guys get paid, just wages, right? And they're wiping out who knows how many thousands of dollars' worth of stuff. Seems like they ought to be happy with just taking a share. There'd be enough for everybody."

"Not here. Guess that's the way it is in some other countries, but not here. I bet some of 'em stash some pretty nice stuff in their lunch boxes, though."

"Yeah I sure would. Okay, later."

As Jerry drove off, Peter went out to his garden and tried to get back to weeding. He was behind, and it really needed it, but he couldn't concentrate. He had a strong urge to get on his motorcycle and head up into the forest and spy on the raiders. He'd like to check them out, see what they were doing, up close, talk to some of them. But there was no way to do that and not draw suspicion to himself. Couldn't afford that. Every so often, he thought he could still hear the throbbing of the helicopter and it only increased his restlessness. He wondered if he knew any of the day's big losers, wondering also if they'd be back the next day, and should he sneak out in the dark to move some of his stuff as a little insurance. If it was still there at all.

To keep from thinking about the pot, he tried to focus on wondering what Sonya was doing, and feeling, and if she'd made it to work on time after staying at his place Sunday night after she brought him home. That had been kind of ridiculous, the two of them trying to fit together and sleep in his small bed. They'd finally moved outside into the warmth of the night, made love and slept beneath a sky that looked like rain, but hadn't.

In the end, as his reverie faded, he got back to work and got some weeding done, then cut up firewood from an area he was trying to clear to use as pasture for he didn't know what. Late in the afternoon, a chopper flew across the valley. It was quite high up. A few minutes later, trucks and vans raced down the road in front of his place. He caught a glimpse of some plants in the back of one of the rigs, but not a lot. Hopefully they were done for the day. They probably wanted to get back to town to see themselves on the news.

He cleaned himself up with a dip in the nearby creek, got a snack, and jumped in his pick-up to head over to Jerry and Carla's. He got there a few minutes before news time, and Carla said Jerry was still out somewhere. She seemed glad to see him and wanted to know what he thought about the helicopter and the cops. She was more upset than he thought she'd be, almost as if she knew something about Jerry's secret. He held Maya on his lap while Carla busied herself with supper.

"Can you stay to eat? We're just having some refries, rice, avocado salad, and berry pie."

"I'm not super hungry, but it sounds so good. Berries are great this year."

"Sure are. And so many. Did they fly right over your place?"

"Pretty close."

"I think it should be invasion of privacy or something. They shouldn't be allowed to come so close to peoples' homes. I mean unless they already know something's there. What if they crash or something?"

The baby was amazing him with the curiosity of her hands as she explored his face, his shirt, and anything else she could get hold of. "Technically, you're probably right," he said. "They're searching without a warrant, but no one I've heard of has been able to stop it. Maybe if we get this new DA she can do something about it, at least over private land."

"But how can they do it if it's illegal?"

"Here's what I've heard happens in California…When they bust somebody with an aerial search, they go through all the steps until the last minute, until it gets all the way through the courts to where the law will be tested, then they drop the case or scare somebody into making a deal. Besides, it can cost a person a lot of money to put together a case against the government."

"Well, I think somebody should do that. Maybe all the people who want to sunbathe nude in their own yards." She laughed. "What do they call it? Class action. It could be sunbathers anonymous. It's not just the pot, it's everybody's privacy that's gone, plus it's really nerve-racking, even when you don't have anything to hide."

Jerry came up onto the back porch, kicking dirt from his boots. When he got inside, Maya reached for him. He took her from Peter and swung her up in the air. "What do you think of her?"

Peter smiled, "What can I say? If I say she's anything less than perfect, I'll lose my dinner invitation. Really, she's great. I mean it. I think she even likes me."

Jerry grabbed the six pack from the porch and set it down by the refrigerator. With his one free hand he picked up two beers and handed one to Peter. He went into the other room and turned on the TV. "News is on," he called.

They watched through stories about terrorists, hostages, trade deficits, and the drought in central Africa. Then there was an ad for Tylenol and another for life insurance. These were followed by national news about the presidential campaign and the squabble over the format for the debates, then some unemployment figures, tornadoes in the South, and unusually high record temperatures in the Southwest. Then the announcer said there would be coverage of the first pot raids of the season coming up right after the next commercial messages. Ironically, the next ad was for small four-wheel drive pickups at a local dealership.

Peter wondered out loud, "Do you think they plan to advertise the grower's favorite kind of truck right when they've got every one of them in the county watching this?"

"Somebody probably thinks about that stuff," Jerry said.

The second ad of the break was for a local discount store, and then the screen was filled with the unmistakable green of fresh marijuana being loaded into a dump truck by sweating, jump-suited cops. The announcer started up with, "State police, Sheriff's deputies, United States Forest Service personnel and even federal DEA agents, aided by helicopter reconnaissance, today combed the coastal mountain areas for illegally cultivated marijuana plantations. This was a first for local authorities as they were aided by a law enforcement helicopter in their efforts to eradicate the crop from public and private lands. Our reporter, Tom Jepson, covered the story and reports on the success of the new techniques. Tom…"

The reporter stood on a landing above a clear cut with a series of ridgetops as a backdrop, saying, "There were times today when District Attorney Bill Reynolds's declaration of war against marijuana producers was becoming a reality. As spotters in a low-flying helicopter located isolated patches in the forested landscape, crews of men on the ground chopped their way through brush and logging waste to reach the illegal operations in what authorities are calling the most comprehensive and successful raid in Chinook County history. Inaccessible isn't the word for some of the locations these men had to get to today." The screen showed several of the raiders struggling up a clear cut, dragging plants to the landing where a large truck was parked and waiting. "When asked at midafternoon if he thought the effort was going well, deputy sheriff Tony Stockton, coordinator of the multi-agency task force, spoke with us for an exclusive interview."

Stockton appeared on the screen, sweating and smiling, "This is the most successful single day we've ever had out here, and much of the credit has to go to our 'eyes in the sky.' The men in that helicopter have just been fantastic in what they've accomplished so far. I think you could say this is the beginning of the end of the pot business in Chinook County."

The reporter reappeared in front of the pile of plants being transferred to the dump truck. "As you can see," he said loudly over the engine noises, "Detective Stockton wasn't exaggerating. Police estimate they have killed and confiscated over three-quarters of a ton of this 'green gold,' with plants ranging from four to ten feet in height and an estimated street value of close to a million dollars. The fresh cut plants will be transported to the public utility steam generating facility, where they will be burned for energy. Those of you who live downwind of there may be in for some high times. This is Tom Jepson with the Anti-marijuana Task Force in western Chinook County."

The studio announcer came back on to say, "Now we go to the press room of the county Courthouse, where DA William Reynolds is about to make a statement."

Reynolds appeared on camera, and read from a sheet of paper, "Ladies and gentlemen, I have a brief statement for you at this time. While it is too soon to evaluate completely the impact of today's enormously successful operation against this county's marijuana industry, it is certainly not too soon to congratulate and praise the dedicated men of the combined police and government agencies who took on great risks to themselves and performed so well under the most difficult conditions imaginable. If nothing else, we have shown the criminal growers, their supporters and clients, and the apathetic sectors of the public, that we mean business when we say, 'no more marijuana business as usual in our county.' For as long as there are laws against this weed, we will make relentless enforcement of these laws one of our highest priorities. I would like to quote from one of my colleagues in a neighboring county when he was asked to comment on this situation in his area: 'We have a law which is strangely unpopular with some segments of our society, and the rest of society seems apathetic to the dangers it seeks to prohibit from taking place.' He goes on, 'The war against marijuana will end the same way the War in Vietnam ended, in inglorious defeat, unless much more is done and done quickly.' Those are the words of someone who has fought well and still not yet succeeded, and I wish them the best. But I am proud to say that we are fighting well, and we are succeeding. Here in Chinook County we will not be satisfied with only winning battles, we will win this war. Thank you."

A Diet Pepsi commercial replaced his face on the screen and Jerry turned the sound down.

"Wow, what do you think of that?" he asked.

Peter watched the happy beautiful people dancing across the TV picture and shook his head slowly. "He means business, his business. There's a lot of money in this thing, on both sides. More than I thought. How much would you think today cost them?"

"No idea, but it was full on."

Carla was nursing Maya and asked, "Do you think he's really serious about this being a like a war?"

Jerry answered her, "For them it is, and the best kind of war. They're not getting shot at."

"That's all we need now," Peter said. "Some crazy getting so pissed off about losing his crop he starts shooting at them or at the chopper."

"Could happen, huh?" Jerry turned the sound back up, but left it low as weather predictions filled the screen.

"Guess it could." Peter sat forward in his chair and added, "Their figures bum me out. What did he say? Figures out to three-quarters of a ton, worth a million dollars. But that's green, wet and with leaves and stalks and branches. Nobody gets more than 10 to 20 percent of that fresh weight in dried and cleaned buds. Maybe less on small plants. But they use those absurd numbers so it sounds like everybody's getting super rich out here. That's probably how they get so much money for eradication."

"I wonder how they do figure it?"

Peter answered him, "At $100 an ounce, it would take 10,000 ounces of dry pot to make a million. So, at five times that for fresh harvested weight, it's 50,000 ounces." He looked at his fingers and said, "You got something to write on?"

Jerry reached for a notepad and pencil on the desk behind him. Carla returned to the kitchen with Maya as Peter wrote down some numbers.

"That would be 4,125 pounds of plants to make a million bucks, and they said they got 1500 pounds and it was worth a million. So, maybe it means they only raid the very best and heaviest, at least three pounds a plant. Never seen one like that." He laughed and added, "Guess they'll leave mine alone."

Jerry laughed with him and then said, "You need to write this all into a letter to the editor or the TV news program."

"Yeah, ask them to show us how to grow stuff that good."

Carla called from the kitchen to say that dinner was ready and to bring in another chair. They went in. Maya was happily jumping up and down in her Jolly Jumper, which hung in the doorway. Jerry eased the chair past her and sat down at the table. The TV was left on and alone.

"What were you guys talking about?" Carla asked when they were all seated.

"Oh, just the amount of money they bragged they harvested today. Peter figured out they're claiming it's worth three times or more the usual price."

"And that figuring was really loose. Their numbers are probably more like five times what it's actually worth. Carla, this is good." Peter was trying to eat slowly, but every bite made him realize how hungry he really was.

"Thanks. It sure isn't much. But we're lucky, as long as food stamps keep coming. Hey, are you going to that party over at Tom and Leslie's?"

"Should be quite a party, I guess. I heard there's probably going to be a lot of folks."

"It's to raise money for that woman candidate Leslie's working for."

"Seems strange, doesn't it?" Jerry commented. "All these people out here trying to get somebody elected for top cop."

"It could make a difference," Peter said quietly. "Sounds like she's serious about not busting people for their private stuff. I mean, she's not saying she'll let people grow it by the acre, but maybe she could shut down these aerial searches over private land. I still think they're illegal."

"Do you really think she has a chance?" Jerry asked him.

"Depends on what happens between now and then. A lot could change before the election, so I have no idea."

"Yeah, well, I never figured it made any difference who gets in. The system's rigged on automatic pilot and nobody can really change what's going down, except maybe make it worse." Jerry got up and went over to the refrigerator. "Another beer?"

"No thanks. I've still got work to do before dark and beer makes me lazy. Carla, can I help clean up?"

"Sure. Not much to it. Just rinse off the plates and stack them by the sink. I'll wash them after the baby gets to sleep."

Jerry took Maya and his beer out to the porch while Peter straightened up and Carla put away the leftovers.

"That pie was great," he said.

"Thanks. Last of last year's berries."

"It's pretty tough isn't it, not having that paycheck?"

"I don't know what's going to happen to us. I almost wish we were growing that stuff. It's a risk, but at least it's a possibility. There really isn't anything else out here these days, and I sure don't want to move to town."

"Don't blame you. Tell you what, you know I grow a little, and if it gets through all this scare business, I'll need some help cleaning and trimming it. It's good pay if you want it. And you can even do it right here at home."

"Thanks. I'm sure it would help out, but I've never done it before."

"That's okay. It isn't hard to learn." He glanced out the window. "Hey, getting late. I've got to get going. Thanks again for the dinner. Don't worry too much. Something's going to work out."

"Thanks for wanting to help us, and I hope they don't get your stuff."

"Me too. Have a good evening."

Jerry was helping Maya stand up on the porch stairs. He asked, "Got to get going?"

"Yeah, I want to go check on some of my stuff. But might not be enough light left. No moon until late. Just can't help wondering."

"I know the feeling. I wonder who they did get."

"Got a lot. Course there's a lot out there, and they won't get it all."

"They're sure trying."

"Yeah, they are, but they're not offering us any better way to make it out here. Guess I'm not going to make it up there tonight." He sat and pulled out his pouch. "Want to smoke one?"

Jerry nodded. "Sure. Hey, you know, it's all such a gamble."

"Yeah but look at you. You didn't know you were gambling when you had the mill job. Looked like it could be go on forever."

"No shit. Now what's left? My unemployment's going to run out, can't get any more extensions, unless they pass another one."

Peter was rolling the joint. "Well, if I do get my crop through, I'll need help manicuring. And you should be able to sell all the firewood you can cut."

"Sure, but where can you cut these days? No more permits in this district 'for the foreseeable future.' More bullshit."

"Why?"

"I don't know. Maybe they're trying to freeze everyone out of this area. Turn it all into one giant tree farm, or subdivision."

They smoked in silence. Suddenly the dog shot out from under the porch and ran barking almost to the road. They heard a vehicle moving slowly along the gravel. It was a state police rig with two troopers. It sped up as it passed the driveway and then they could hear the sound fading away.

"Still around," said Peter.

"You think they're checking us out?"

"No. Last year I heard they leave a patrol in the area after their raids. Looking for signs of people harvesting or moving their plants at night. Guess I was right not to go anywhere tonight. Wonder if they stopped when they went by my place?"

"Probably did the same thing. Cruised it slow."

Peter held the remainder of the joint into the air and made a circle with the burning tip, then blew smoke skyward. "Can't figure it. I really can't figure what freaks them out so much about this stuff."

"Look what it does to you."

"Hey, what's that supposed to mean?" Peter laughed.

Inside, Maya started crying, and Carla brought her out, and sat in the porch swing to nurse.

"Carla, look at Peter. Wouldn't you say there's something wrong with him? I mean, his whole attitude. He won't work for a living, drives an old wreck, and his idea of success is a bag of smoke and a place where he can be alone. Like, where's the profit in that?"

Peter smiled and said, "Guess you're right. Once people get independent, get to work for themselves, no bosses, they either turn into cutthroat capitalists or laidback dregs like me."

"Dig it. Drugs for dregs program," said Jerry.

"But what if everybody just wanted enough income to get by on, comfortably?"

Jerry looked over at Carla, "Seriously, can you imagine our society if nobody cared about having to make a profit? Even the growers want to make money, but the way some of them act, the way they talk, you'd think life was all communism and free love, all rolled up together." He swatted at Peter's shoulder.

Carla said quietly, "All the same, I'll bet there's plenty of growers who are pretty capitalistic."

"Better believe it," said Peter. "You can grow it to live outside the system or you can use it to play the game to the max. That's part of what's screwing it up for everybody. Too many people getting into it just for big bucks."

Carla moved Maya from one side to the other and asked, "What are you in it for, if you don't mind my asking?"

Peter thought for a minute before trying to answer. The dog came back and crawled part way into Jerry's lap. The sunset was clearing away the overcast and painting some of the cloud cover red and yellow. "I'm partly in it for some bucks to live on. And I guess I'm mainly in it for my head. It helps me make a living to get by on, and I don't want to work for someone else. Besides, I don't want to contribute to making this country any stronger, I've seen how bad it can be." He paused and then went on, "And also I like making something that gives people some pleasure in their lives. Sometimes I try to imagine who's getting high on my stuff, where they are, what they're into...I feel good about it because maybe I'm helping somebody get through their day or night. But I guess the main thing is, it lets me be this free, and that's something I can't give up."

"But you always run the risk of losing it all and getting busted," she said.

"Yeah, I know. Maybe that's what freedom's all about, surviving the risks."

Jerry put in, "Maybe that's why it's against the law."

"How so?"

"It makes me feel free," said Jerry, "when I smoke it. Because it tells me I can't change anything by worrying about it. If I can do something about it that's one thing, do it, but worrying, like about what I have or don't have or losing what I do have...that doesn't make any sense to me when I'm stoned. But that's where a lot of people are at. They act like worrying is going to fix something."

Carla stood to take the sleeping baby inside. "Mosquitos," she said. Then she looked back at Jerry. "You just leave the worrying to me." She went in.

"She does worry a lot." He pushed the dog off his lap and walked over to some bushes to take a leak.

"Yeah," said Peter getting up, "it's hard not to sometimes. Hey, I'm going to head out."

"Think they'll be back tomorrow?"

"Who knows?"

"Yeah, who knows. Well, see ya soon. Let me know if everything's all right."

"Yeah," Peter said and smiled. "Just don't worry." He walked slowly to his truck. The dog escorted him and then turned back. He remembered something Sonya said about jogging, and thought about how he could have jogged over here and back. He'd been tempted to try and call her from Jerry and Carla's, but then he remembered it was Tuesday, her campaign meeting night.

He backed out of the driveway and drove slowly along the familiar roadway, trying not to think about his plants. Like Jerry said, it doesn't do any good to worry. But that's easier said than done, yeah, a lot easier said than done.

The first day of the raids was the most successful, as far as the authorities were concerned. After that, no other part of the county yielded as much pot, although they had to work just as hard for it. This was especially true in the foothills of the Cascades where the growers seemed to have made use of rock-climbing techniques to place and tend their widespread plants. By Friday evening, the men were exhausted, badly scratched-up, scraped and strained, but mildly euphoric from the results from the previous four days. They were having a minor celebration with a couple of cases of beer and ten buckets of fried chicken while they waited for the honchos to decide if they were going out again the next day.

Stockton, Sheriff Johnson, and Lieutenant Brenner of the State Police sat discussing results and strategy in an office just off the parking garage. Stockton and Brenner were beat, and their green jumpsuits were ripped and dirty.

"Had enough?" asked Johnson.

Brenner replied, "I have, but the question is, did we make our quota?"

"For what?"

Stockton answered, "I'd say for two things. One, to cripple the business enough to make a lot of folks out there want to give it up, and two, to justify our costs to the feds."

"What are your thoughts?" Johnson lit a cigarette, smiling to himself at the idea of lighting up a pot joint in front of the other two.

"I think we justified our expenses, but I'm not sure we could ever destroy enough of it to stop them all."

"Brenner?"

"No question, we've had the most successful effort yet, in this county and pretty much anywhere I've heard of in this state. Whether we could get enough tomorrow to justify the overtime cost of the men and the helicopter, et cetera, I don't know. Nobody really knows what's still out there, and by now they've had time to hide it better if they wanted to. I do know my men are really bushed, no pun intended, and they're for sure not wanting to go another day if it doesn't get great results."

Johnson looked them both over carefully, watching them chowing down on the chicken, and was glad was he wouldn't have to get his old self out there no matter what they decided. "Well, you're right, nobody knows what else is out there. So how do we decide? How much area is left that hasn't been covered at all?"

Stockton answered, "Not much, but we can go back where we started out and hit it again. We can look closer than we have. We couldn't have gotten it all."

"I know we didn't get it all. Never will," Brenner cut in. "But if we didn't see it the first time what's making the difference this time?"

"Fly lower and slower," Stockton said.

"Increase the risk?" said Brenner. "We don't have the advantage of surprise and there's guys out there that are probably madder than hell."

"What's the forecast? I see clouds coming in out there," the sheriff said.

Stockton answered, "We'll get clouds, but too high for rain. Clearing by afternoon."

Johnson got up and walked to the window. He stood there for a moment, looking west where the clouds were gathering in the dusky light of the fading day. "Seems to me we should cut Brenner here and his boys loose. And Tony, you and everyone else head out at noon and see what you can do. That cuts the manpower expenses by about half, gives everyone a bit of a rest and avoids the morning weather. I'd say spend more time flying over private land, but still grab what you can on the public side. Might not get much contraband, but it'll stick in people's minds over the winter and maybe slow them down some next spring. But for God's sake don't let that chopper get low enough we get airspace violations to hassle with. Probably be folks with cameras out there this time. That sound all right?"

"Okay by me," said Brenner.

"Yessir, it's okay," agreed Stockton.

"Good, let's send everybody home. You've done a great job," Johnson said as he gave Stockton a hard look. "Tony, stick around another minute, there's one more thing. Brenner, it was good having you on board. Hope we can have you back next year."

"Sure thing. Hope I see you before that." The lieutenant left the room and Stockton stood up, waiting for the Sheriff to say something.

"Find any more bombs out there, Tony?"

"No sir. Not yet."

"Well, you keep looking. That reporter was disappointed when he had to go back to the Bay Area with no stories of maimed cops or dead backpackers. You keep looking, because maybe there's still something out there for you. A chance for more headlines. That'll be all."

"Yes, sir."

"And don't sir me. Just nod your head yes or no. Understand?"

Stockton nodded his head up and down.

"Good work today. Now get yourself some rest."

Stockton turned on his heel and left the room. Johnson went back to studying the slow changes in the western sky. He was thinking about how everyone in this whole business has to be scared at least part of the time. Paranoid growers, nervous cops, worried hikers, all chasing around and around like two dogs after each other's tails. Why? Why, because there's a law and any time there's a law there's got to be two sides to it. But this law is getting to be a gigantic pain in the ass.

Before dawn on Saturday morning, Peter had taken off for a lightning inspection of his patches. So far, so good was all he kept thinking as he sped home with his bike in the back of the pickup. Too noisy up there so he hadn't used it, just tried to hide the truck, hoping those guys would all be too tired to get going this early on their supposed day off. There was no sign of heavy traffic anywhere near his spots. Of course, they could still be coming back for what they knew they must have missed. The morning clouds started out looking like it might shower some, but by the time he was pulling into his driveway, they were breaking up as the sun burned its way through to heat the ground.

He unloaded the bike and went in to make coffee. It felt good to have the suspense and worry of the last few days done with, but there was nothing for sure in any of this. All the way up there he'd dreaded what he might find, or more to the point, not find. And all the while his mind was conjuring up images of getting down there and being trapped and surrounded by cops. If he could have stayed calm about it, he would have waited a little longer before checking it out, but there are some things you just can't put off. Now, as he made coffee, he was wondering who had been hit. He especially wondered about the ridge across from his spot. As far as he knew, no one was tending a patch there, unless they were coming to it from the other side.

He was just finishing his first cup of coffee and considering whether he should go out and call Sonya, when she came driving in. She pulled to a stop and jumped out, smiling and calling to him, "Surprise you?"

He set down his cup and hurried to meet her. "Yeah, I was just thinking about calling you." They embraced and kissed. "So how come? What's happening? Want coffee?"

"Well, I was scheduled to speak at some reception today, but they called and cancelled for some reason, so I just had to get away. It's been such a heavy week. Are you, all right? What's happened out here? Did they come here?"

"Slow down. Everything's okay so far." He kissed her again. "Good to see you. Do you want coffee? You didn't say. Here, sit down." He opened a folding lawn chair for her.

"No thanks on the coffee. I've had plenty already. But tell me if everything's all right?"

He took his cup and reached inside to the pot on the counter. Then he sat on the ground beside her and looked up at her face framed by a background of blue sky and puffy white clouds.

"Everything's okay so far. You're beautiful. What's been so heavy about your week?"

"Oh, too much of everything else and not enough of you." She reached to muss his hair. "More disagreement on the campaign committee because of the police raids. We might lose a couple of people, volunteers. I hope not, but what can you do? And the judge accepted the overcrowding lawsuit, as submitted and presented, but he gave the county ninety days to comply, which means it won't come to a head until after the election. Then there was all the media attention on the raids. You're sure you're okay? It sounded like a lot going on."

"Sure," he said and placed his hand on her leg. "Besides, what's any of that got to do with me?"

"Right, I don't know anything, but for some reason I couldn't wait to see you and I really was afraid something might have happened to you. I don't know what, and I'm sure it was silly, but I was worried."

"You were probably picking up on my vibes, but you're not supposed to know anything. I'll just say it was a little scary. The helicopter came right over a couple of time, and the convoy was on the road. But I'm innocent." He winked at her. "At least anywhere around here. How long can you stay?"

"How long can I stay?" She kept messing with his hair. "This needs a good brushing."

He set the coffee cup down and caught her hand. "I'll give you fifteen minutes of my valuable time, maybe a little more. There's not much to do around here, so you probably won't want to stay any longer than that anyway."

"Well if it rains there's no room for me anyway."

"We could probably arrange something." He was trying to tickle her feet through her jogging shoes. "Go running this morning?"

"No, I was in too much of a hurry. I am so glad to be away from my phone. All week I had to keep saying, 'No comment. I'll have a statement when it's over and the reports are in.' Or, 'I can't really say anything at this point. I'll get back to you. We'll try to have something to say after the weekend,' et cetera! Everybody wanted to know how I was going to handle it, what did I think, what would I do if I was DA. I still don't know what to say next week. For sure, I'll have to face the press, no matter how it turns out. Want to take my place?"

"No way." He smiled and said, "you made that bed for yourself."

"At least I have a bed."

"Oh my, you don't approve of these accommodations, huh? Let me tell you this, there's always a waiting list at this here Paradise Inn. You're lucky you even got a parking place."

"And who's on this waiting list?"

"Wouldn't you like to know."

She leaned over him and he pulled her out of the chair, onto the ground. They wrestled a bit, then settled into a long embrace. Finally, they both rolled onto their backs and stared up at the sky with its puffy white clouds.

"Did you ever see things in the shapes of the clouds?" he asked.

"Sure." She pointed up at a large cloud and asked, "What does that one look like to you?"

"A donkey," he said. "A Democratic donkey and he's wearing your picture on his back. Can you see it?"

She reached out and pulled a tuft of grass and tried to stuff it in his mouth. "That's strange, he's got my picture, but he looks like you."

They tangled again and started laughing hard enough that it was difficult to sit up. As they settled down again, looking into each other's eyes, they shared a kiss that fit the peacefulness of the day.

"Want to take a walk around?" he asked.

"If you're sure there's no boobytraps."

"Hey, did the Sheriff ever get back to you on that?"

"Not yet. I wish he would though. I'm in bad need of something good to come along."

"Hope you get it. Come on." He jumped up and gave her a pull, then led her toward his garden. They walked around for a while and he showed her his land, talked about some of his plans for it, and then ended up at an old growth stump near the creek. They sat on a log and he pointed out a small fir tree growing out of the top of the stump. "That's my image of the best that could happen around here, new growth coming out of the wipe-out of this whole area."

"Tell me what you mean."

"Well, see, in my way of looking at it…For a long, long time that big old tree and all the rest of the trees lived pretty much the way they always had. Then all at once, they found themselves on our frontier. They didn't change their way of growing and where they grew, they couldn't do anything different, but everything changed for them pretty quickly. So many of them got cut down and hauled off and turned into somebody's house somewhere." He pulled out his pouch and started making up a joint. "Get what I mean?"

"Yes, but there's more, isn't there?"

"So, the stump stays where is always grew and waits, and it rots some and then one day a cone falls on it from another nearby tree. Maybe that one." He pointed. "Or a chipmunk carries it up there and cracks open the cone's seeds. One of them falls out into a crack in the top of the stump. Then the rains come and the sun and before too long it sprouts and there's this new little tree growing up, reaching for the sun and it all starts over again."

They sat quietly. He lit up and offered it to her. "No thanks, not yet. They'll probably be drug-testing the candidates." She laughed. "You know something? I never really notice anything different about you after you smoke."

"Good, because I don't think it makes me any different."

"Then why do you do it?"

"Because it makes me feel different, inside."

"Well, some people act a lot different when they smoke it. I probably would."

"They're just not used to it."

She stood and walked over to the stump and reached up to touch the baby fir. "Do you think it will make it?"

"I hope so."

She leaned back against the crumbly surface of the huge stump and asked, "So, what do you think it means, that all this might start over again?"

He didn't answer right away, and then said, "I don't know exactly. I just know that the way it was here lasted a long time until us Americans came along. And what was here was working good for here, probably ever since the ocean pulled back and the trees got started. And now all of it is getting used up, and the mills are shutting down, everything that was easy to get is got and just a lot of small stuff planted to take its place, and how long is that going to take? Won't be anything besides smaller trees and pot, and I don't see how you can build a way of life on just that. At least not one that can last until the trees are ready to be cut again. Maybe everybody will leave. Maybe this little tree will get a chance to get big, and maybe whoever lives here then will be living a lot like those people who were living here when this big old grandfather was young. Maybe I'm crazy, but I like to think like that."

"Sounds nice, but what happens to all the people?"

"I don't know. There really aren't that many of us out here. Maybe they adapt to the way things were or go back where they came from. Or maybe people start going into space, the next frontier." He snuffed out the roach, stood, and stretched. "See, the stuff really does change me."

"Not really."

He smiled, "Want to get something to eat yet?"

"Not me, but I'll take that cup of coffee now."

She was still leaning against the stump and he stepped over to take her in his arms. "Thanks for coming out. I missed you this week. I admit it was pretty hard." They kissed and held tight.

"Missed you too. What do you think that means?"

He just looked into her eyes and didn't answer. Instead, he gently pulled her away from the stump and started walking her back to his trailer.

"How long have you been here?" she asked.

"Six years almost. On this place. I started out renting a smaller place and had a tipi on it the year before I got this. That was over near the store."

She stopped and reached out to pick some blackberries, saying, "Why do you think we finally met, now?"

"Who knows? Maybe just to complicate things. Good berries, huh?" They both filled their hands and mouths with the sticky sweetness. "Free food."

"Really. Do you make anything with them?"

"I made wine one year. Didn't turn out too good. It was all right, but not great." He stopped picking and looked off toward the far ridge.

She followed his look with her own and asked, "What's that?"

"Helicopter."

"Is it police?"

"Can't tell, but it's circling."

"It's getting closer. Would they come here?"

"There's nothing here. Couple of small plants for seed. They can't see them."

The throbbing sound of the copter came closer. They had both stopped picking and were watching in the direction of the sound.

"There it is." He pointed to a small speck above the trees far away. The sound was changing and growing louder.

"It's coming this way," she said.

"Yeah, looks that way. Come on." He took her hand and they quickly walked back to the trailer. They stopped under the porch roof.

"I can see the papers now," she said. "DA candidate picked up in local pot raid."

"Get you elected for sure." The copter made a long circle toward the headwaters of the valley and then headed back toward the ridge it had come from. "Might go away. But now we know they're working on Saturday."

"Must not be finished." She bent over to pull stickers from her socks.

"Better move your car just in case. If they do cruise by here, they might take down license plate numbers."

She glanced at him, as if to ask a question, then went over to her car. "Where?"

"Over there." He pointed to an old cat road that led off into the woods. "Just drive in far enough to hide it from the driveway and road."

As she eased the car through ruts and low branches, he ducked into the trailer to grab a plastic bag and a small garbage can. Hurrying into the woods, he stashed his load under a big log and returned to her. She was looking up through the trees trying to see if she could see the copter. Then they could see it, hovering about a half mile up the road from his driveway. It was still quite high above them.

"What do you think they're doing?"

"Waiting for the ground patrol to catch up. They got something on the backside of that ridge last Tuesday. Maybe there's more."

"Do you think they'll come here?"

"No reason to. If they do, just stay here unless they get out and start looking around. Then play hide-and-seek."

"But I haven't done anything."

"Yeah, but you don't want to have to prove that."

The aircraft began moving again, slowly coming toward them, its sound thumping and then becoming a roar that could be felt in the body. It circled slowly above the trailer and garden at about 300 feet. Sonya stared up through the trees as the helicopter stopped over them. Leaves fluttered to the ground, shaken loose by the downdraft. Sonya gripped Peter's arm, and there was a look on her face he hadn't seen before. He was scared too. Even though he was ninety percent sure that nothing was going to happen.

Then a sheriff's pickup pulled into his driveway. Two officers sat in front and one in the back. Peter put his finger to his lips and motioned for her to go deeper into the woods while he himself crept through the underbrush to where he could see them better and intercept if they came toward her car. The driver and the one in the back were discussing something, but there was no way to hear them. The one in back waved out the back window to the helicopter and it slowly moved away over the road. The pickup rolled back out the driveway, and then both the truck and the copter took off in the direction of Jerry and Carla's. More trucks shot by on the road following the first one. The copter dipped once over Jerry and Carla's place, but then kept going. Peter waited until the sound became a soft thumping again and then turned back to look for Sonya.

He reached her car and called that it was safe to come out now. There was no answer. "It's okay," he shouted again. "Come on out."

He heard her answer from over by his property line, "Are you sure?"

"Yeah, come on."

She came out from behind a stump, pulling moss from her hair and brushing off her pants. "What was that all about?"

"They're still looking, but mostly trying to scare us, I'd guess. You all right?"

"I'm all right now," she said relaxing into his arms. "But I really got scared."

"It's pretty scary."

"Has this ever happened to you before?"

"Not here. This is the first year they've had a helicopter."

"You seem pretty calm," she said with a nervous laugh. "Unlike me."

"Come on. You still want that coffee?

"I sure do. If it's safe now."

"It's safe. We'll hear them if they're coming back. I liked your hiding place."

They walked to the trailer. The air was silent again. He wondered how Jerry had taken it. Did he freak and harvest, or did he just freak?"

"That was awful," she said as she sank into a lawn chair in the shade of the canopy. He nodded and went inside to start the water heating, then came back out and sat on the ground in front of her.

"Feel better now?" he asked, reaching for her hand.

"I'm all right, but I didn't know what I was going to do if they got out of their truck."

"I'm sorry you had to go through it. I had no idea they'd be back today."

"No, it's good in a way. I guess I needed to feel what it's like. I bet Reynolds never had to hide from one of his raids."

He looked at her and asked, "What's that got to do with it?"

"Oh nothing. Just that now I have a lot better idea what it feels like out here than I did before. What would you have done if you did have plants here?"

"Grab you and split. Wait and see what kind of bust it was going to be."

"What kind?"

"Sometimes they just cut 'em down, load up and take off. Other times they might have a warrant they try and serve."

They were silent for a while, each reflecting on the separateness of the life paths they were on. Her seeing his life as very portable, feeling in him the acceptance of insecurity and the readiness to drop everything he was doing in order to continue living as he chose to. And him seeing her reaction to the threat of hassle with the authorities as an ironic counterpoint to her profession and involvement with the law as a valid institution. Then there was her candidacy for a position enforcing those laws.

Sitting there in the now relative quiet of a beautiful afternoon with the first hints of fall in the air and the rustle of falling leaves, they were both face to face with the question of why and what they were together, perhaps a unique question for every pair of lovers, yet common to almost all who truly love.

Just then the whistle of the boiling water cut through the silence of the now incredibly clear air. Peter jumped up to tend it, and Sonya let her head fall back and her eyes drift upward toward the bluest of blues, the clean sky scrubbed to a shine by the faint cool breeze coming from the ocean. There were only a few puffs of white cloud still wandering the sky like little lost sheep as the sun began its downward slant toward evening. She felt as if she were sleeping with her eyes open, and the peacefulness of the moment made it nearly impossible for her to recall the tension that had so recently shaken her to the depth of her insides.

Peter returned with coffee and waved a steaming cup beneath her nose. She shook herself out of the trance, sat up and smiled. He said, "I offer you alertness in a bitter brew, sweetness if you so desire, and above all, half-and-half to remind you of the true nature of reality."

"Why thank you, kind sir. Can I have everything?"

He came back with honey and cream. They blew on the full cups and sipped the coffee slowly. When they were done with it, she asked him if he wanted to go for a short run.

"Tell you what, you do the running for both of us. I already used up my legs early this morning. I'll stay here and start fixing a late lunch, early supper. You'll eat venison burgers with me, won't you?"

"Never had them, but I'm game."

"No, the deer was the game. Sorry for trying to be punny. When you get out on the road, you can turn right and go to the turn-off." He laughed. "Sorry again, I just thought how you're not the 'turn-off,' the road is. Anyway, that's about a mile. How far do you want to go?"

"That's enough. You sure it's safe?"

"Yeah. If you run into any cops, tell them you know me. That'll scare them off."

"Gee, I didn't know you had them all afraid of you. I have to get some shorts out of my car. Think it's all right to leave it there?"

"It's good there. I'll take your cup."

They embraced and stared deeply into each other's eyes, eyes that were slowly becoming familiar, turning their heads slowly, bumping noses, brushing lips, and tasting mouths. It was a long kiss that put all the questions aside, for a while.

After a barbecue supper of venison burgers with homegrown tomatoes and lettuce, potatoes cooked in tinfoil on a small open fire, and big bowls of berries Sonya collected after her run, after all of that, they had more coffee and drifted through some stories from their childhoods as the dusk filled the sky with turquoise, and then quickly deepened into that blue-black of night coming on, and on. Their moods shared in the changes of the first stars as the mystery of their encounter and their feelings now hovered just above the fact of their togetherness.

They held back, kept conversation going, postponing the pleasures and satisfaction they both hungered for, but somehow intuiting that each fragment of knowledge about the other person they could share was one more space between them filled in and filling up. Peter got to his feet and added branches to the fire, stirring it and sending a shower of sparks skyward. Sonya lay on a blanket, her chin in her hands, her eyes staring into the embers.

She said, "You know, sometimes I can't help looking at people as if their personality can be described in political terms. Like, I guess, Mike and I were never quite on the same page about anything. That's not bad, but it's not easy either. When we had a decision to make, he was the most careful, even though he liked to think he was pretty daring. We invested when we hardly had enough to pay for office rent and the house, but we were extra careful to invest 'wisely.' I think I had more of a 'let's see what happens' attitude, know what I mean?"

He sat next to her, rearranging her hair with his fingertips, and said, "Tell me what you mean."

"Compared to you, my new friend, I'm probably pretty conservative. And I don't just mean about the laws, but about feelings too. I need to know what I'm feeling. I don't know if you do."

"Sure, I do. I have feelings. Some I don't want, some I do, but they're all there."

She took his hand, tracing the fine lines of his palm with her fingertips. "That's what I mean. You have the feelings, but they don't control you because you don't seem to analyze them so much. Like today, what were you feeling when the helicopter was right over us?"

"I don't know. A lot, I guess. I was afraid some. It made me remember all the times we were up in a chopper near a village, freaking out all the people hiding out down below. Maybe I felt like I had this coming, my turn to be the one being hunted. I don't really know what I was feeling, except I hoped they'd go away, at the same time trying to be ready for whatever happened."

She looked sideways at him, at the firelight glimmering around his eyes as he looked down at the coals. She realized how many fires there must have been in his past and now felt bad if she was bringing him down tonight with all this. "I'm sorry, I didn't mean to bring all that up."

"You didn't, they did. But it's okay. Like I say, we all pay our dues in our own way. How did you feel this afternoon?"

"It was very weird. I was scared, but I couldn't say of what. I didn't really know if I could believe there was nothing on this place to worry about. And I was angry, angry at them, at whoever could make me feel so petrified. I couldn't believe how it made me feel, even though I hadn't done anything wrong." She wiped her eyes. "Here I was hiding, and who knows what could have happened. I was so worried about you, afraid you might do something crazy if they came any closer, not because you're crazy, I don't mean that. I just mean the situation was so crazy, and they had guns and if we'd tried to run they might have shot at us, and if we came out and gave up...What might it have turned into? I don't really know, do I? I just don't think I ever felt so vulnerable in my whole life."

"Seems like you got way into it. You were thinking all those things?"

She smiled a little and said, "And more, much more. Maybe I was thinking that you're becoming really important to me." She turned up on her elbow and looked into his eyes. "Maybe I was thinking that if this is what I have to go through to be with you, it's still worth it."

"No way."

"Yes, way."

He was lying beside her now, very still. She eased over on her back and slipped her hand under his chest. He stiffened for a moment, holding himself back out of a mixture of habit, doubt, even shyness, holding back just long enough to feel overcome by remembering this was the person who made him feel safe. He slid as close to her as he could get, pressing the length of his body against hers, feeling the trembling that passed between them, feeling both the softness and the tension of their touching. There was no moon yet and the stars were shining with extraordinary brightness. Sparks from the fire climbed up there as well, winking out as they reached the darkness above. The two of them lay together, motionless, the warmth of their bodies building between them. Them warming, the night cooling.

Peter reached for the sleeping bag behind them and spread it over them like a quilt. He settled back down next to Sonya, next to the firelight dancing on her hair, stars reflecting in her eyes, the gleam of her teeth between moist and slightly parted lips. All so close to him, and him now not thinking about all that, thinking of what it was like when she wasn't here, trying not to think of when she hadn't been anything to him, and trying not to think of what this was becoming, seeking thoughts only of this moment and its beauty and hoping it could last forever and knowing it could never come again. His hand slipped around her waist, and slid up under the sweatshirt, lightly tracing the taut lines of her arching belly. She raised her head toward his, and they kissed, holding breath, holding tight, not even moving now. Then breaking the spell, him stroking her breast, her bending her neck to the gentle nibbles of his teeth, now with their bodies beginning to thrust with urgency, legs interlocking as their hips twisted, rubbing together, the sensations of friction and pressure. It was a wrestling and a waiting, a closeness and an opening. They played and it was serious, they worked, and it was pleasure, slipping from their clothing in stages, interrupting the dance of their desire with the clumsiness of buckles, buttons, snaps and laces. They were silent and beyond words, dipping and diving deeper into one another's passion, losing time and individuality, leaving behind the fears caused by that which is outside of us as well as that within. They coupled with a kind of abandon new to both, her mind full of thoughts and questions falling by the wayside, his heart still thawing and forgetting what it had been to be frozen. Together they reached for a freedom that hangs suspended from heaven. And they made love happen, collapsed into it, and fell to earth again. She slept almost immediately, He lay there beside her, listening to the steady sighing of her breath, watching the rhythmic rise and fall of her breasts, him now half-dreaming of a night without end.

CHAPTER SEVEN

September

This month bringing with it the most change sneaks in on the tail of summer, looking for all the world like more of the same. Days shorten bit by bit, one by one, and the effects are mostly unnoticeable at first, a few leaves here, a few leaves there losing their green, a few new shoots of grassy green easing up through the dried-out brown of the old summer grass, baked ground and all the drab colors of summer's heat. Showers of big raindrops come now and again with a sudden darkening of the day, followed by brilliant rainbows spanning the ridges. The creeks cool quickly as the nights take on a fresh chill and sometimes bring a light frost. Seeds have formed in the lush carpets of the world's vegetation and from the fallen fruits of orchards and bushes. Gardens and woodlands come full term and harvests begin. As the moon of the celestial Virgin proceeds, her potential is gathered from the last of the hot days to be held in trust through the coming winter until spring brings birth from earth's womb again. Smells change as the rains increase and the fallen leaves begin to decay, releasing the sun's shine they have collected, into the ground at the feet of their own trees. The cash crops, too, stop growing like weeds and turn their energy to flower, bract, and resin, their big leaves turning yellow and dropping or being picked off, their essence transformed into consciousness-changes and money. Rip-offs polish their skills and increase their range as they seek what the authorities have missed in their raids. The deer fatten in preparation for the next month's rut and the annual slaughter by hunters. Each night jockeys for equality with the day, and all forms of weather are permitted in this month if only they come and go quickly. Stinging insects grow frantic with the approach of their annual famine, and the earth shrugs her shoulders nonchalantly as she selects her new wardrobe for autumn.

On the first Saturday in September, Sonya, Dan, Terry, and Janet attended a wine-tasting reception held in the candidate's honor by the Media and Advertising Council of Chinook County. This was a loose-knit group of journalists, educators, broadcasters, and public relations personnel who got together for specific functions, but did not constitute a formal organization. The event that day was arranged at Dan's request by several local media people sympathetic to Sonya's campaign, or at least opposed to the treatment they'd received from Reynolds over the years.

The gathering was held at a large motel complex outside of town. The banquet room had a classy yet informal atmosphere. When Sonya and staff arrived, several small groups of people were clustered around the tables of wine and hors d'oeuvres. Some of these folks were known to Sonya through her years in the law profession, and some more recently from her press conferences. Terry immediately joined with some of the local TV people in a conversation about the role of local media in a national election. Dan went to check in with the people who organized the affair, while Sonya and Janet drifted toward a group of women that included one of the local news anchors. All the wine was from Oregon and represented a good cross-section of this thriving new regional business.

By five, the room was quite full, the guests' voices blending into a general hum as the wine bottles were emptied and replaced at a steady pace. Sonya renewed some acquaintances she'd know during her days with Mike and was especially glad to run into one couple who had started their own agency since she last encountered them. They were enthusiastic about her candidacy and offered to help in any way they could. Sonya promised to introduce them to her campaign manager before the event was over and said she hoped they meant what they said because her campaign needed all the help it could get.

For about an hour she circulated as much as she could among the crowd. Conversations ranged from challenges to her positions on particular issues, aspects of her personal history, and the always present question of whether she really thought she had a chance to win the election. Her answers were short, her smile bright and sincere, and her ability to remember names surprised her and many of the people she talked with.

At a certain point, Dan took her aside to discuss her presentation to this group. They were interrupted when one of the hosts called for quiet and asked Sonya to join him at the podium. The guests moved to the rows of chairs arranged in a semi-circle, settling into place for the program. Sonya took a seat facing the audience and looked over the crowd. She couldn't help but notice that they were mostly her age or younger. Obviously, this was a pretty good reflection on her constituency in the larger population—she really needed to concentrate on broadening her appeal if there was a way to do that without losing these folks and their peers.

The MC was introduced and opened his remarks with a couple of lame jokes about the difficulty of covering a national campaign when one candidate was too old to remember the answers to questions prepared for him by his staff, and the other one kept getting tangled in all the strings that tied him to the special interests behind the scenes. He then introduced the "guest of honor" and presented her with a corsage and a scroll that declared her the most interesting candidate of the election. She accepted with a smile, and said, "I wonder what your criteria for 'interesting' is."

"Quite simple actually," the MC responded. "All the other candidates are extraordinarily dull, but you were chosen on the basis of your fresh approach to the problems faced by law enforcement in our county." He pantomimed smoking a joint and got a good laugh for that. He then bowed to Sonya and sat down. She reached over to him and continued the pantomime by plucking the imaginary joint from his fingers and taking a hit off it.

"Don't Bogart that joint now," she said as she handed 'it' back. This got a bigger laugh. When things quieted she went on, "Seriously, it's an honor to be here and to accept this recognition for whatever reason it's being given. This is a wonderful opportunity, being in the same room with so many of you at the same time. I keep feeling a little like an amoeba that gets to look backwards up the microscope at all the scientists who've been studying her. I appreciate all your coverage of our efforts and hope you are able to share more good news about our campaign. I don't have a prepared speech to give, the wine is too good to spoil with something like that, and I certainly don't want to turn this fun time into another press conference, so how would you all feel if we use this occasion to pick your brains and ask you some questions that relate to our issues and the campaign? Terry Lindsay, standing right over there, has paper and pencils for those of you who don't have your own. I'm sure some of you already know my media coordinator through his great work on the campus radio station...Well, Terry has prepared a short set of questions that we hope you will answer.

"If this seems like an odd process, just look at it as part of our attempt to remain the 'most interesting' in this campaign. So please help us out. You don't need to sign your name or even answer all the questions. We just thought this was a great opportunity to get some good free advice from the experts on how we approach the public in these last months before the election." There was a quiet pause while Janet and Terry dispensed paper and pencils to the outstretched hands reaching for them.

"Okay class, number one," she said, enjoying the change that had come over the group. They were quite serious now and she got the feeling this idea of Terry's might turn out all right. "What do you think is the most important issue in this election for County DA?" She waited for folks to write an answer and looked over at the MC to see how he was responding. He was busy writing, so she though that must be a good sign.

"Number two: What is the biggest difference between me and Bill Reynolds? Wait, I already know that he's a man and I'm a woman, but what is the big difference between us as we come across to the media?"

She gave time for them to write short answers, and then went on, "Number three, and this has two parts, the first being: Should we seek a debate with the other candidate or not? If yes, what format would be best for you folks in the press and media? For example: One or two debates, questions submitted beforehand or by a panel during the event? Just tell us what you'd like to see and cover. And we'll do our best."

As they were writing their answers, Terry came up and quietly told her an idea he'd just thought of.

"OK," she said to him, and then turned to her audience. "This is the next-to-last question: What kind of advertising will be most effective for us to concentrate on and how can we raise money to pay for it?"

Someone called out, "Sell some pot." There was an immediate round of laughter.

Sonya joined in the laughing and shot back with, "How much do you want to buy?" Dan gave her a signal and she also sensed that it was time to wind up this part of the event. "The last question is simply this: Write down what question would you most like to ask me if you could, within reason, of course." She smiled over to Terry.

She gave them enough time to answer, and then asked them to sign their names if they wanted to, and to fold their papers and pass them to Janet and Terry. "Thank you very much for your help, you'll all receive your grades in the mail. I'm eager to find out your answers. Just a few more minutes of your time if you don't mind. The reason we were so pleased to have this affair and this minisurvey is because we truly recognize the power and the responsibility of the media and how much this power has grown in every election for the past couple of decades. We want to be responsive to you and include your concerns and ideas in our strategy, and I want you to know that I'm not simply running for this office to further my own political career. What I hope for is to see that certain crucial issues get raised and addressed at the local level, issues I see threatening the very traditions and fabric of our national identity. One of these issues is the freedom of the press in this society, and the future of this freedom in light of current conditions and direction.

"Since even before Watergate, throughout the Vietnam War, there has existed an antagonistic relationship between whichever administration was in power, and with the entire range of media. Under President Reagan, this has increased greatly, by virtue of his isolation from interviews and press conferences to the degree that he and his people are governing more by decree than by disclosure and discussion. I feel that this same symptom exists here on our county level as well when our DA declares 'war' on certain segments of our population, grabs headlines for his own programs, and refuses to discuss charges brought against his office in the courts, such as the inmate overcrowding issue. By the way, as that progresses, the court has found the county guilty of violating the civil rights of many of its prisoners but has also given 90 days for something to be done about it. I brought that up because this just happened yesterday, and I don't want it to escape your notice. I believe that so far this issue has been downplayed by both the courts and the media. I invite you to call our Sheriff and ask for a tour of the jail facility. It truly is a disgrace to the county to be operating even a prison in such a medieval manner.

"Before I digress too much and exceed my allotted time here, I want to bring up one matter that I hope will clarify for you my position on the issue which has gotten the most exposure in the press. That is the issue of marijuana production or growing in our county. My position is not an endorsement of violence as has been suggested by my opponent, nor is it support for the commercial aspects of an illegal business. What I do stand for is an individual's right to determine how they use their own body when that use doesn't harm anyone else, and they remain capable of carrying out their responsibilities to society. The logical extension of this is that a person can produce on their own private property, a substance for personal use, and, I repeat, while growing and using it does no harm to others. This, in my mind, is analogous to the making of one's own wine or beer, neither of which require government permission or intervention, and both of which are capable of causing great harm if, for example, they are used in conjunction with driving or operating machinery. But the role of society is not to prevent the activity of making or using those products, rather it is one of enforcing laws against their misuse when such misuse constitutes a threat against others. Am I sounding too much like a lawyer here? Well, I guess that's what I am, so I'll say that I submit to you that I believe marijuana should be treated no differently. Its personal and non-threatening use is not an arena for legitimate government intervention, and the freedom a person has in this society must not be limited by the moral attitudes of one or more segments of the whole of our society.

"Again, let me emphasize what is at stake, both in our freedom to seek out and report the news, and with our freedom to decide for ourselves how we will use our bodies and our property. These rights are fundamental to the future of a free people at every level, from the most local to the broadest impacts of national issues. Thank you for inviting me here this evening, and I hope I can continue to be 'interesting' at least. Be sure to let my staff know if you have any suggestions or questions for us. We would certainly prefer to take the time to be clear with you than to have to deal with misinformation. Thank you so much and all of you have a nice evening."

She sat down to a solid round of applause. The MC thanked her and said he hoped for the best results in the election, and the program came to a close. People dispersed quickly, many of them pouring and drinking a last cup of the free wine on their way out. Sonya was corralled by several people who wanted to argue with her position on pot, which she politely declined to do. Dan rescued her and took her aside to compare notes on some members of the audience who'd volunteered different kinds of help for the remainder of the campaign. Terry was busy scanning the results of the survey questions.

Janet had waited patiently for Sonya to be finished so they could go out for dinner together. They hadn't had any time for such since the housewarming party and benefit, and they were each curious about what was going on with the other. They drove separately and met up at a quiet steakhouse near downtown. They were shown to a small booth within minutes of their arrival. They passed on cocktails or wine, still feeling the glow from a small amount wine at the reception.

"How do you think it went?" Janet asked after they ordered.

"OK, I was pleased with the turnout. I'm curious to see what they had to say to those questions we asked."

"They were pretty surprised when you started doing that. Maybe because most of them are the one who ask the questions, as reporters I mean. I don't think I've ever heard of a candidate interviewing the media before."

"Terry's idea. He can't pass up the opportunity for a poll, no matter how farfetched it is," Sonya continued, looking closely at her friend. "So, how are you these days?"

Janet swirled an ice cube in her glass of water. "Oh, everything's fine. Kristi starts school next week, so that's a big change for us. Mom's doing as well as can be expected, but she is slowing down. And me, I'm okay. Mr. Reynolds doesn't bother me anymore. I think he's thinking he has it in the bag."

"You or the election?" Sonya said, and had to laugh at Janet's disgusted expression.

"He thinks he's got you in the bag," she replied.

"We'll see. But what's wrong? You say you're okay, but you don't sound okay."

"It's nothing. I'm just not cut out to know how to have a good time."

The waitress brought their salads and a tray full of dressings. Sonya helped herself to something called Herb Delight Dressing, and said, "What's that supposed to mean? I've seen you having a good time."

"I don't know. The party was nice, and I did have fun, and then he called and invited me out and it didn't work the first time. We were both busy when the other was free, and then last weekend we finally got to go to a concert, and it was nice. Nothing special, I guess." She stopped talking and poured dressing on her salad, spinning the lettuce around in it.

"We are talking about Ray Matson, aren't we?"

"Yes."

"Well, what happened?"

"Nothing. Not a word since that night. I don't know what went wrong. Maybe I had expectations, I don't know. It's stupid, isn't it? I just didn't know how to be with him. Maybe he wanted to spend the night with me, maybe he couldn't wait to get away. I just don't have any experience with this sort of thing anymore."

"Don't blame yourself. After all, it's early and you just met."

"Maybe when he found out that not only do I have a daughter, but there's my mother in the household too, maybe that was too much for him."

"And if that was the reason, it's a lot better for you to find out now instead of later. But most likely he's waiting just like you are, waiting to see if you want to see him again. Things have changed in the last twenty years, you know. Now men play hard to get, too. At least that's what I hear." Sonya smiled at the thought of what that had just meant to her, with Peter. Then she went on, "Call him tonight, get him to come out tomorrow for Leslie's own party. Maybe he's even already coming."

"Should I really call him tonight?"

"For sure, and if he's not there I'm sure he's got a message machine, so just make it clear you'd like to see him again. He's probably just as insecure as you."

"I'll think about it."

"You know what they say, you snooze, you lose."

Their dinners arrived at that moment and they both realized how hungry they were as they dug into the fried rice, mixed vegetables, and steak.

"Good," Janet said holding up her second bite of steak. "Speaking of snoozing and losing, or is it winning? What's going on with you and Peter?"

"You think I'm going to tell you. Snoozing or losing, indeed. Aren't you the one assigned to find out who I'm snoozing with?"

"Well, I guess what I don't know can't hurt you," Janet said with a teasing smile.

"Really. Well, suffice it to say, I'm very happy for the moment, and I'm trying not to think about the future."

"Good for you. From what I've heard about him, you must be pretty special."

"Whatever it is, it's all special and kind of scary."

Janet looked up from her plate and asked, "Why scary? Could he get caught for something?" Real concern showed in her look as various possibilities raced through her mind.

"I don't think so. That part's scary, too, but it's okay. I think he's cautious, and I guess it was good for me to see that side of the issue. No, what I mean by scary is how perfect it seems to be between us. But how impossible at the same time. Know what I mean?"

"Sure. Most true love is like that, at least in all the stories I read."

"I know, and that's what's scary. It's too much like a fantasy, but at the same time it's happening, and it's happening to me. Feels like it's turning me inside out. When I started this election thing, I was alone, lonely, and it seemed like an important thing to be doing. Now there's something else that's important to me, but it doesn't at all fit in with any of the rest of my busy, legalistic life."

"You'll just have to wait and see what happens."

"I know, but there's no way I could choose between them now."

"You don't have to. The election is also a kind of fantasy, let's face it. So, if you're caught between two fantasies it's unlikely you'll have to choose, unless they both become realities."

"You're so wise, so logical. I suppose you're right."

"I'm too logical," Janet said. "That's what's wrong with me."

"First of all, there's nothing wrong with you, except you didn't finish your dinner. Are you done, or just distracted?

"I guess I'm done."

"Then let's get the check and go. I have a bath to take, and you have a phone call to make."

Later, stretched out in the tub she barely fit into lengthwise, Sonya felt the tension of the afternoon ease out of her muscles and mind. Every time she got up in front of people these days, she had to get past the fact they were checking her out physically before they were going to listen to what she was going to say. She could see the women looking her over and thinking, 'What's so special about her?' or 'Who did she sleep with to get to be the candidate?' or things about her hair or her clothes. If she thought about it afterward, she knew that wasn't really the reaction she got from most women, many were probably grateful to see another woman taking it on. It was probably her paranoia and questioning of herself that gave her these feelings. As for the men, it was much more common. Many gave her a good once-over, and sometimes she just wanted to stop with the politics and ask them point-blank what they were thinking, would they like to undress her right then and there, or what?

She splashed around a little and began soaping herself. She knew the strain was getting to her because of those kinds of thoughts and the insecurity they were based on, but she could still tell herself that it couldn't be helped. After all, it was better to be looked at than to be looked through or away from. She turned on the hot water and took deep breaths, the steam soothing her lungs and condensing on her face. It would be nice to have a sauna, she thought, a two-person sauna, just for her and Peter. It was funny...She knew he found her attractive, and she wasn't bothered by the way he looked her over. Either she liked it or just didn't mind because it was him and he wasn't obvious about it. In any case, he never made her feel like a package on a shelf, and she could hardly wait to see him at the party the next day.

Peter got up and out into the forest early. There was one last patch that needed checking, and then he had to get back to cook something for the potluck and party. The sky was holding motionless its pattern of gray clouds, the kind of a day that could go either way, rain or shine. He hoped the sun would break through for the sake of the party as well as for the sake of his plants, which were just beginning to flower. It had been cloudy most of the past week with on and off drizzle, and a good dose of hot days and cool nights would be most welcome.

He stashed the dirt bike in the usual place and walked toward the landing less than a mile away. As soon as he got there, he could see someone had been through recently. Small piles of sawdust littered the area in a broken line, along with the branches from a large fir that had been dropped. Most likely no problem, just a firewood project, another kind of lawbreaker. Chances were a thousand-to-one they wouldn't have gotten thirsty enough to climb all the way down to the creek at the bottom of the clear-cut and stumble onto his patch. Their work looked finished, so they probably wouldn't be back either.

He slipped over the side and worked his way down as fast as he could go without falling. Every so often his feet would send a shower of rocks and gravel cascading down the bare spots below him. He passed through a freshly dug colony of mountain boomer dens, damp dirt piled outside the entrances. He remembered an old timer telling him that people coming into this area were like those boomers, "Here one year, gone the next." To some extent it was true. It seemed like a lot of people tried it out and then moved on. It was hard to find many folks who were still on family land for the second or third generation. Once you logged the timber off, it was hard to make a living with it by doing anything else.

He reached the first set of plants and quickly checked through them. One of the holes had two females and the other four held one of each sex. Two of the males had already opened their first flowers. He was a little late, but a few seeds wouldn't change much. Buyers still wanted it totally clean, but they weren't as picky now as when growers first started producing seedless stuff.

He never liked killing the males at this point, but the market dictated and there wasn't much else he could do. You either force them to reveal their gender in the spring by depriving their light, or letting them grow until they reveal themselves naturally and then cut them out. They were now between six and nine feet tall and have more sparse branches than their sisters, but they look strong and healthy, at the peak of their cycle, and he felt it as he chopped through the stalks and dragged them into the brush. Insects might still find some pollen and transfer it to his females, but not so likely if he covered them with brushy debris. Moving through the undergrowth to the next plants, he wondered how the beaver were doing, as there was still no sign of them around the plants. Maybe they were also waiting for the ripening before they did their harvesting. He hoped not.

This second set of plants had one double-male hole and a double female set. It was a toss-up whether he would gain anything from transplanting one of those females to the empty spot once he dropped the males. The transplant shock to the nearly full-grown females would probably outweigh any advantage. They were both about seven feet tall and he decided to leave them as they were and tie them both over in opposite directions so as not to be so conspicuous.

He kept working through the plants which were more widely separated now at this location, offing the males and transplanting a few of the undersized females. Again, he felt bad for the males he took out and stuffed into the brush. They had given their all and for what? It came to nothing, and he could never escape the comparison between this step in the growing process and the war and what it did to so many of his buddies, thinking how there's something strange about a world where the males of so many species grow to their full potential, and then are eliminated in the competition for breeding rights, or in wars for ideology or territory, or even market conditions like these plants. How many young men were killed or maimed in Vietnam, how many deserted or jumped the border before they got drafted? How many extra women were there now in this generation? He looked back at the patch, thinking again how ironic it was that the most desirable high came from the female plants, and how his single gender patch now resembled a nunnery. It had to have something to do with frustration of this enforced celibacy that increased the potency of the superior resin of the females. Sinsemilla in Spanish, without seed, also must mean sin hombres, without men.

He climbed slowly back up the long, steep flank of the ridge, hoping that it was better for the plants to have at least had the companionship of each gender while they were growing up together. The next step in these developments would be the use of clones. He'd heard it was already starting down in California. There, you just plant the tips of female branches which have been chemically treated to grow roots and develop into full-grown plants during the winter off-season. That was the wave of the future, and once the bugs got worked out, Peter could see himself taking advantage of that method. It sure would reduce the gene pool and diversity, though.

It was easier climbing out than usual, since he hadn't worn himself out carrying buckets of water, counting on the forecast of rain over the next two days. From here on, there shouldn't be any need for watering unless the weather hit an unusual dry spell. There wouldn't be much else the plants needed from him until harvest. So, now it was just a case of waiting and hoping they didn't get stumbled across by any of the various predators that roam the forest in the fall.

Back at his place, he threw together a venison stew from meat he'd thawed overnight, set it to cook, and got himself ready for this party. The sun finally made up its mind to sweep the clouds from the sky and it quickly turned into a warm day. When the time came, he wedged the stewpot into a space on the floor of his pick-up, threw in some heavier clothes for the cooling of the evening, and checked around for anything else he might need. Since the next day was a holiday, there was a pretty good chance Sonya would stay over with him, but they hadn't made any arrangements. By driving himself to the party instead of catching a ride, he was leaving open the option that he could drive to town if they decided on that. He took note of the way he was assuming he and Sonya would be together for the night. Why not? As far as he was concerned, it was good for him, and it was up to her to let him know if she had another preference or maybe a complication in her schedule.

When he arrived, the long driveway was already filling up with parked vehicles and the band was unloading their equipment onto the makeshift stage. Leslie greeted him at the table for admissions, donations, and campaign literature.

"Well, look who it is," she said with a big smile.

"Hi, how's it going?"

"No trouble yet. But have you heard about our candidate for DA? We're raising money for her campaign and she's promised to do everything she can to, um, make things safe for some guy she's seeing lately. Heard anything about that?"

"Can't say as I have." He looked around, "How much do you want?"

She stepped around from behind the table and gave him a big hug. "From you, nothing. You're contributing just fine. She seems happy. Keep it up. I'll sell you a bumper sticker, though."

"Thanks, I'll get it later. Where do I put food?"

"Down by the creek, you know, where we had that picnic. Isn't it turning into a beautiful day for this?"

"Yeah, best kind of day. I'll take this down there. Later."

As he walked across the small field toward the creek, he wondered how many other people besides Leslie knew about him and Sonya. Didn't really matter, but it might change the way some of them related to him, given who she was. He kept his eye out for her, but didn't see her, now remembering he hadn't seen her car either. There were quite a few people scattered around the immediate area. Most of them he'd seen before, but nobody he knew very well. It was cooler under the trees by the creek, and an occasional gust of wind knocked a few leaves from the branches above. A fire pit near the picnicking area was sending out quite a bit of smoke. This was going to be one of Tom's well-known chicken frys, and he wondered where the host was.

Looking around, he thought back on this being the first place he ever saw Sonya, trying to recall if there'd been anything to tip him off, any indication of what lay ahead of them. He knew he'd certainly noticed her then but didn't remember any bolts of lightning or bells sounding in his ears. He decided to go over and have a look at the garden and see how it was doing. Oh yeah, he recalled he never gave Sonya the promised tractor ride, that must have been the beginning. As he walked across the field to the garden, he also realized they'd never been together in public, as a couple or even as good friends. Maybe they would be better off spending this time as individuals, since after all it was a party for her, and she probably wouldn't want their private thing to be obvious. Need to play it by ear, wait and see.

There were horseshoes, volleyball, and a couple of kegs at fifty cents a glass. Quite a few people were with their kids down at the deepest pool in the creek. The afternoon moved along with the crowd growing, and small groups within it constantly shifting and reforming in different spots. Tom was starting to fry his chicken, and another table was being thrown together to accommodate the food. Most of it was freshly harvested from gardens and orchards and it looked like it had been a great year for leafy greens and broccoli, as well as wild blackberries.

Peter got involved in a couple of hard-fought games of volleyball, something he hadn't done for years, then finally caught a glimpse of Sonya standing over near the stage. She was surrounded by a group and probably answering political questions. He couldn't tell if she'd seen him or not. During a break between games, he joined a circle of growers off near the woods. Most of them he'd know over the past few years. They smoked, joked, and tried to make light of the raids. It was beginning to seem to Peter that he was one of the lucky ones. A lot of these folks had lost some or even all their crops to the cops. It was clear that most of the losers had hoped for at least another year of winged aircraft search-flights and had been unprepared for the intensity of the new helicopter strategy. There was some loose talk of revenge, but most of the conversation focused on next year, whether it would still be worth it or not, what could be done, and questions about how to successfully avoid the searches.

Al joined in the circle and offered a joint he said was the first of this year's stash. It tasted a little green and quick-dry harsh, but strong. Someone asked how he got buds so early. He shrugged and said something about lights in the early spring and kelp juice feed. He also admitted that the high didn't last very long yet, but it was a fun rush for a change from the stale remains of the previous season. When that joint was gone, he eased Peter off to the side, saying he needed to talk to him for a minute.

"Want a beer?" He gestured toward the keg.

"Sure." Peter was thirsty from the combined effects of the volleyball and the smoking. They passed several people who greeted one or the other of them on the way to the keg, where Al poured a couple of tall cups from a pitcher. He threw a few bucks into the gallon jar on the bench.

"Need to talk to you alone." They strolled over to a fallen tree and sat down on it. The sun was still warm, and Al pulled off his outer shirt. "Good sun for the buds," he said, and then went on, "Listen, I've got some crazy information I don't know what to do with. Probably nothing, but I wanted to talk to someone who could either keep it quiet or do something with it."

Peter leaned back and said, "I'll try."

"Good. What it is…is that last week I ran out of water for one patch. Spring went dry on me. That's okay, probably don't need it much from now on, anyway, but just in case we don't get any rain I wanted to tap into another source about 300 yards up and across the ridge. I knew it was there because that's where I had a patch last year. Anyway, I went back over there. When I got part way down, I came across a pretty good trail, been cut through recently. It was cut messy, so I figured it was a Forest Service survey of something, and I was relieved I hadn't tried to use that area again. It was close enough as it was. So, I got down near my old patch and was about to head into the brush where I'd stashed my hose after I got ripped off last year, and I found a loose garbage bag. Didn't think much about it, probably just some litter. Didn't feel like much was in the bag, but I looked anyway. Guess what was in it?"

"Can't." He was listening, but it was hard with so much going on all around them. Plus, Sonya had finally spotted him and given a wave.

"Inside the bag were some McDonald's wrappers and the packages from two rolls of videotape. Right away I knew why I got such a funny feeling when my TV friend showed me the tape he worked on when the cops found those boobytraps out on the brush. Didn't tell you about that, did I? They must have used my old patch. Shit, at first I was totally paranoid, wondering if I left any fingerprints out there. I thrashed over to where the hose was. Still there. All overgrown, so they hadn't found it. I was pretty freaked out though, so I scrambled down into the actual patch and there were signs of somebody being there, all right." He waved to a couple of women walking by. "The dirt in the old holes was turned up, but it didn't look right. I mean, no one could have grown there because the brush wasn't even cleared back. I grabbed up the rolls of hose and followed their trail out. Man, it was like a highway, even some branches of pot along it. Anyway, that's about all there is to it. I can't prove anything, and I don't want anyone to know it had anything to do with me. All I can figure is they must have brought in some plants, put them in my old holes, then filmed it like a bust. I guess I'm telling you, because I heard you know this lady that's running for DA, and maybe the information could help someone like her. I'd be willing to show you where it is, but I don't want to get any more involved than that, know what I mean? Tell you what it makes me want to do..." He paused and drank the rest of his beer.

"What's that?" Peter was paying much closer attention than he had been at first.

"Makes me want to set some traps for those bastards. Because if they're out their setting up false shit to get more bucks and come down heavier, let's give them what they want. They're asking for the real thing...Let's give it to them since we're getting blamed for it anyway."

"I know how you feel, Al. But that might really be just what they want. If they can provoke us into hurting somebody, they can do anything they want to when they come out here. Like martial law or worse."

"I know you're right, but they're going to keep on coming on heavier no matter what we do, unless we all give it up, roll over and quit."

"And you're sure you don't want to talk to anyone about this yourself? I mean, I could introduce you to this Sonya lady. She's over there right now, and we could set something up for another time. Or maybe we could talk to a lawyer."

Al looked down into his empty beer cup and shook his head. "No, no way. I can't prove anything and I don't want more heat on me. Shit, I could probably get popped for that patch from last year if I admitted I was hanging around down there. Nope, if anything comes of it, good, but keep me out of it. I think I can trust you better than anyone with this, or I wouldn't have told you. Let's get some more beer." He stood up. "I'll tell you one more thing, it put me through some crazy changes. I went from being totally paranoid to being totally pissed off. If your friend can't do anything about this shit, then one of these days somebody's got to."

Peter agreed and said, "Somebody, somewhere is probably going to do something. It's just a question of when and what. People need to be able to get by around here, and there isn't much else. Thanks for telling me. I'll keep it quiet and won't say where I heard it if I do tell someone."

"Good, let's get those refills."

"I'll be along later," Peter said. He stayed on the log, watching Al walk away. So, he thought, it really was a phony. Now what? Thinking, If Sonya knew for sure maybe she could use it, but it was just like the Sheriff told her, it still couldn't be proven. He thought he better wait until later, after the party, to talk about it with her. Maybe after a while he could think about it more clearly. The clearest thing right now was that the level of violence had the potential to get out of hand, and the level of talk was escalating right along with the reality of what both sides were thinking. Since what was ahead was anyone's guess, he decided, might as well party.

That weed of Al's had a nice buzz, but it wasn't quite mature enough to keep him high for very long, so he pulled out his own pouch while he scanned the party with his eyes half-closed. Still folks arriving, and there was already quite a crowd. Some of the local musicians were warming up on the stage and looked like they were about to jam. He cleaned a bud and rolled it carefully, thinking how little was left of last year's stash. One of these years he was going to have to put enough away to take off during the growing season. Head for Alaska, maybe the Yukon. That part of the world intrigued him and, while he didn't want to be just a fair weather visitor, he figured it was best to go there in the summer, meet some folks, find somewhere to hang out for a while and get to know the seasons.

He was scanning the crowd for a group he might feel comfortable sharing the joint with when someone grabbed him from behind, saying, "So you're such a good soldier and guerilla in the woods, huh?"

It was Sonya. He stuck the joint in his mouth, took hold of both her arms and twisted her around and pulled her over his shoulder until she was sprawled in his lap.

"Yeah, and you fell right into my trap." He gave her a quick kiss.

"Not here, silly." She got to her knees quickly.

"I know that," he said. "But you started it."

"I just don't know that we're ready for our debut."

"I know, I wondered how we would handle it."

She stood up, reaching her right hand out for a shake. "Hello, I'm Sonya, I'm running for office, and I wondered if you had any small creeks in the area, because I might be interested."

"Sure, over there." He stood up and they walked slowly through the alders to the bank of the creek. Neither spoke until they were out of sight of the party and then they had a real kiss.

"Well, by now people who know anything probably think I'm an undercover for sure."

"Good," she said. "Because they already think I'm a front for the growers."

He smiled and asked, "How you been?"

"Fine. Nice party, huh?"

"Yeah, you should do all right."

"I know, and even if we don't make much money, people seem to be having a good time. What about you?"

"Yeah, it's great. But I might have played a little too much volleyball."

She watched him light the joint and take it in. "Yeah, a person your age should begin to be more careful."

"At whose age?" he coughed. "Bet you're older than me."

"Depends on what we're doing."

He reached down into the creek, cupped a handful of water and splashed up at her. "See, I'm still a kid."

"Do it again. Felt good."

He did and then they were quiet for a while, him smoking and looking at her profile, and her staring down into the moving water.

"Will you be making a speech?"

"Not really. Leslie's going to say a few things and introduce me, and I'll talk a little, but nothing big. Maybe answer a few questions."

"And after?"

"I don't work tomorrow so I thought I might stay out here somewhere. Maybe even go over to the coast."

"Sounds good. Wonder how late this will get over?"

"I don't know. But, hey, are you feeling all right?" She looked over as she said this, but he couldn't tell if she was serious or not.

"Yeah, I'm fine. You?"

"Fine. Just checking. I was worrying about you." She reached out and stroked his cheek. "I better get back. It's a party for everyone else, but I'm supposed to be campaigning."

"Sure. Catch you later?"

"Peter, you're sure nothing's changed? I guess I mean...Do you think we should hang out together at this thing or not?"

"Maybe not, up to you. But nothing's wrong with me. I'm just kind of speechless in your presence, and besides, once you get to know me, you'll find out I'm always fine."

"I hope so. Coming back with me?"

He stood up, looked around, and took her in his arms. Their eyes laced them together and they were both truly fine. They knew it as they kissed, and he said, "I'll be along."

She smiled and turned away, walking back toward the party. She looked back several times and each time he was still watching her. He really seemed fine, it was just that every once in a while their whole thing seemed so unlikely and so delicately balanced it was hard to hope it could succeed. She deserved to win, impossible as that was, she deserved it and the people deserved her energy and ideas, but what would her winning do to the two of them, how could they continue if she were in the public eye even more than she was now? He didn't see anything he could do about it one way or another, but it still complicated his thoughts sometimes, and it wasn't something he wanted to bring up to her, at least not yet. Anyway, they were still just getting to know who they were together, but it was likely that after this first rush and excitement there would prove to be too many differences for it to work out. So, he figured, it was better to take it as it was for now and not let speculation get in the way...

Once the food was eaten, the chicken bones all picked clean and the ice cream makers cranked to exhaustion, the band tuned up and started jamming some quiet sounds for after dinner and calming things down. As usual, the adults kicked back to let the food settle and the kids got wilder, racing through the area in many-levelled games of pursuit and escape. Long shadows from the trees by the creek crept out across the open space and the bugs began showing up for their own feast. Shorts and shirt sleeves were traded for jackets and jeans, and the coolness of the incoming coastal air signaled the opportunity for a fire. A new keg was tapped, and the people collecting money for the campaign totaled up the afternoon's take and said the event was a financial success with time still left to contribute more. Leslie made her way to the stage to make the announcement and went on to introduce Sonya.

She made a few comments, mostly thanking everyone for their support and saying she hoped they would do what they could to persuade their friends and coworkers of the need for change in this county's law enforcement establishment. This got plenty of applause and then someone shouted, "Let's hear it for Tom and Leslie for having us!" That comment was greeted with a great roar of approval for the party. Sonya came back onto the stage, clapping along with the crowd.

"Where's Tom?" she called out over the microphone. "Leslie, please stay up here, and Tom, come on up." She stood between them and went on speaking, "These two people are so wonderful that I want us to all let them know how much we appreciate what they've done and are doing for the cause. Let's really give them, a big thank you."

Someone at the back of the crowd set off a string of firecrackers as the band turned up its speakers to the max and cut loose with a crescendo of sound. When it had all quieted down a little, Tom eased over to the mike and said over the diminishing noise, "Thank you all for coming out here today. I guess the chicken was okay, because it's all gone, and it's been a great afternoon. Thank you all for being here." There was more cheering as Leslie and Tom left the stage. When it all quieted down a bit, Sonya stepped to the mike and looked out over the crowd for a moment.

Then she spoke, "I know a lot of you just came to party, so I'm not going to make a long speech or anything. I do want to say one or two more things, and then we'll dance to the light of that beautiful half-moon. First, though, I want to mention what's happened with the Oregon Marijuana Initiative. I'm sure most of you have heard by now, but if you haven't, I'll run it down for you. Over 85,000 signatures were collected, but the secretary of state determined that the law requires 62,500 valid signatures to get the measure on the ballot. By only sampling a few thousand names, and applying so-called statistical methods to the rest, it was declared an invalid petition, by somewhere around one thousand signatures or less. The courts have ordered a reverification and those results should be out next week. In any case, I think the important thing to realize is that this initiative was subjected to unusual scrutiny, far more than, say, a property tax hike or a school bond levy, and that it still came up only a few hundred less than needed by the statistical method. If the reverification process fails to allow it, then the issue will be dead for this coming election. What is important here, I think, is that everyone on either side of this ballot measure be aware that, 'Yes, the times they are a changin' and it won't be long now until the voters have a real opportunity to voice their opinions on this measure that the legislature is afraid to touch."

She paused and then went on, "In the meantime, I'm asking you to register to vote if you aren't already, and to vote if you want to, for me, for the office of district attorney in this county. In return for your vote, if I succeed with your help, I have promised to deemphasize prosecution of victimless crimes, including the possession and use of personal amounts of marijuana, and to try to eliminate the climate of violence and the illegal intrusion into people's lives that currently exists. Please, please, let's not give them any chance to crack down any heavier. Don't let this thing get anyone frustrated enough that they jeopardize lives in order to protect their income or their crop. It just wouldn't be worth it, it won't help anyone in the long run, and it will hurt everyone in the short run if these authorities can justify an ever-widening war on marijuana and marijuana people.

"Enough of the heavy words from me. If you want to know more about what I stand for on the other issues facing this county, please pick up some of the brochures at the table right over there. Now, does anyone have a quick question you think I should answer in front of everybody? Also, I'll be over there by the table for a while, and will be glad to talk with anyone."

Form the back of the crowd someone yelled, "Yeah, what makes you think you can do anything if you do get in?"

"Good question. I believe that the best approach to changing things like this situation is through the budget. There's not enough funding for everything that's supposed to be done by the DA's office, so the DA has the power to prioritize the expenditures of the office."

"And you think you can make a difference? You're just like all the rest of the politicians these days, you take sides just to get votes, and then you forget all you ever said once you get in. It's all bullshit."

Sonya looked out toward the voice. The dusk and its shadows were deepening, and she couldn't see the source of the questions. "I hope you're wrong," she said. "I really hope you're wrong. I also hope I would quit rather than betray the people who voted for me. If we don't start changing things, they will always be the way you say they are, but give this system another chance, at least on the local level. Nothing else is going to make a difference either, so that's why I'm trying to make it happen this way."

Another voice shouted from the same area as the first questioner, "Blow 'em away. You want justice, blow 'em away."

Sonya didn't know quite what to do next. It was turning into an absurd hassle and she only wanted things to get back to the fun and good vibes of the party. She glanced back at the band and caught the eye of the guitar-player. He gave a quick 'V' with his fingers and jumped forward, aiming his guitar at the crowd and banging out an incredibly accurate imitation of a machine gun.

Sonya moved out of his way and he shouted into the mike, "Blow 'em away, if you want war. Blow 'em away!" He fired off another burst with his guitar, and then played softer, saying, "But if you want justice, if you want justice, then you've just got to be just." With that the whole band joined him with the opening chords of a reggae-style song called "Peace in Our Time." There was a nearly tangible change of mood, and a feeling of relief spreading throughout the gathering, as a majority of the crowd moved into dancing mode.

Sonya slipped away behind the band and off the stage. She was feeling numb from the encounter and lost for an explanation. The last thing she'd expected, especially at this gathering, was heckling. These were supposed to be the people she'd risked losing the Democratic

Party's support for, risked her own professional reputation for, this was supposedly her constituency, and here was the first taunting of the campaign, the first actual ugly moments. She felt limp and too confused to be angry, thinking, what next? At the same time, she knew that none of it was anywhere near the sentiments of most of these people, just a few weirdos...

Tom came up and put his arm around her shoulders. He eased her over near the campaign table and sat her down. "Can I get you anything?" he asked, "A beer, ice cream?"

"Sure, a beer would be nice now, thanks."

Leslie took Tom's place by her side and told her not to worry, she'd been terrific, and those guys who hassled her were just some migrant growers nobody paid any attention to anyway.

"What's a migrant grower?" Sonya asked.

"Oh, I'm not sure how to explain it. There're some people who just stay here, rent or camp out, just for the growing season. As soon as they get their crop harvested they split for the tropics or the cities. They're mostly a pretty rowdy bunch with no attachments here, so they can afford to talk big and act bad. It probably actually helps to have them hassling you."

"That would be nice. I didn't know what to do up there."

"You did fine. Feel like dancing yet?"

Tom came back with a beer for her. She thanked him and told Leslie she'd join her in a few minutes. She drank some of the beer and it felt really good going down. There were lights on the stage and the moon above, but it was fairly dark where the dancing was going on. There was no definable style to it, not really any pairing up, and the music was great with a good strong beat. People were rocking and turning, shaking their thoughts into oblivion. She set the half-finished cup down behind the table and moved in among the people, looking for Leslie.

Peter spotted Sonya in the crowd and worked his way toward her. He wanted to see her, to be with her, but not to talk about what had just happened, not now. He tapped her on the shoulder and when she turned, he bowed slightly and mimicked an invitation in formal style.

She accepted and they danced somewhat together, trying to keep track of one another in the surging mass of happy bodies.

Marty didn't mind that Henderson was late. If anything, it showed that the man was dragging his feet and a little reluctant to face the Sheriff in a private conference. Marty often used a person's arrival timing to get a handle on their state of mind. Even when they tried to be on time and something beyond their control held them up, they would still be on the defensive for being late. He flipped the league championship game ball from one hand to the other. At least one part of his life had gone right. The boys had pulled it out, extra innings no less. Maybe a bit more stressful than his doctor would like to see his old heart go through, but if you win, extra innings is a great way to do it. Now the problem was going to be fitting practices for the state championship tournament around school days, weather, and the fact that it was getting dark earlier and earlier.

All along he'd planned to have Henderson on the carpet, at some point, about the booby-trap crap. It was the obvious way to pursue it, but he hadn't felt quite sure of himself, of pursuing it, until Sonya Lehman had called him a couple of days back. She'd asked if he was doing all right at reducing the jail population, and he'd quipped that reservations were falling off as they usually did toward the end of the summer season. She then went on to inform him she had received independent confirmation that the bomb scare had been a hoax. She was unwilling to reveal her source but said that someone who knew the area was certain no marijuana was grown there this season since that location had been busted the year before. He told her that made sense, and that he was still working on the case from his end. She asked if he had any idea of what she could expect in terms of public exposure, and he told her he was sorry, but he couldn't promise anything.

The buzzer sliced through his thoughts. He flipped the intercom switch, "Send him in," he said as he hung up the phone.

Henderson closed the door quietly behind him and stood at semi-attention.

"Sit down, sit down." Marty gestured to the chair across from the desk, and asked, "How's it going?"

"All right, can't complain."

"Good. Well, no sense batting around the bush. I've been wanting to have a talk with you for a while, just couldn't find the time. It's about Stockton." He watched as a slight expression of surprise flitted across the Deputy's face. Good, keep him guessing. "I don't know if you've heard or not, but it seems like he's moving up in the world, might even leave us behind here. Rumor has it the DEA is interested in his work. He's always been a little too gung-ho for my taste, for us small-timers, and there is a slight problem. Say, you want coffee or a soda? I'll have someone bring it in."

"No thanks. You said there's a problem?"

"Yeah, it's like this. They want a recommendation from me. Now I don't mind that, but the problem is, there are a few unanswered questions. Obviously, the thing that really caught their attention was the discovery of the boobytraps. They like that sort of thing. On the lookout for it. And I don't mind him getting all he deserves, but…" The ball started going back and forth between his hands again. "But if he's taking credit for this whole thing and he doesn't deserve all of it, we've got a problem." Henderson raised his hand as if to speak, and Marty went on, "Now, just hold on a minute, hear me out. Firstly, I don't want to give a total endorsement to someone who hogs the credit if it's not all his, and second, if you're just as responsible as he is, then you should get some of the credit."

He paused and took note of Henderson's poker face shielding the mental process he had to be going through. The sheriff went on, "Now, there's going to be a grand jury looking into all of this whole mess around the pot, the raids, feds, bombs, helicopters, what-have-you, but this part of it can't really wait for that process to sort itself out. Number one, if he does move on I'll have to replace him and you're the obvious choice. I happen to think you're the most qualified man in the department to take over his spot, but I need a reason to reward you and leapfrog you over a couple of other guys with more seniority." Now Henderson was at least looking interested.

"So, there you have it. If you can tell me that you discovered this thing, or at least had as much to do with it as Stockton, and I happen to think you did, if you can tell me that, then I can still recommend him for that job and I can justify moving you up as well. If we wait until it all comes out later on, then, who knows?" He leaned back and kicked one foot up on his desk. He was very curious to see which way this fish would jump, and he felt an old angler's patience settling on himself. Sheriff, he told himself, you're wasting your talent, you should have been a fishing guide all along.

Henderson seemed to be sorting through the information, considering the possibility that everything the sheriff said was true, and trying to figure out his best option. He couldn't quite come up with the right thing to say. Why had he helped Stockton anyway? It was looking stupider and stupider every time he thought about it. He took the plunge. "Sheriff, I appreciate your confidence in me, but I have to tell you Stockton really did most of it himself."

"Most of what?"

"Uh, finding it, and organizing the whole thing, the press, all that."

"Sorry to hear that Henderson. It's pretty hard to believe one man could do all that heavy work by himself."

"Excuse me, what heavy work?"

"Well, for one thing carrying all those heavy plants down that steep hillside must have been a bitch. Take one man most of a night." At least Henderson wasn't a weakling. He returned Marty's gaze without wavering, although the corners of his mouth showed his mind was working through some quickening changes.

"Carry them down, sir?"

"That's what I said. Probably too tired to clean up the trail down the ridge on his way out. I found several leaves and even a branch on the way down that day."

"That's impossible." Henderson looked like he'd made his decision, but Marty couldn't quite tell what it was yet.

"Why? Because you had them all wrapped up so that wouldn't happen? Or do you expect me to believe that you found those plants growing down there? Man, there wasn't a single stump or root wad in the whole patch. They'd just had their stalks shoved into the ground. Now, you want to tell me what really happened? Or do you want to wait and tell it to the grand jury?" This was the part that Marty never liked, he just didn't have a cold enough heart to enjoy watching someone break down under interrogation, no matter who it was, and Henderson was really an all right guy. What this would do to him wasn't clear yet, but the Sheriff was feeling deep down that this man had the potential to be a good public servant, and in this case was just a dupe. He'd probably come out of it all in okay shape and be a better cop than before. But now he knew he had to play it careful and not humiliate the man, or he could lose the line of questioning and go anywhere with this.

"I guess I really didn't think about those things, sir. He told me this kind of thing was going on all up and down the coast, the booby-traps, I mean. He'd just got back from that training where they showed him how dangerous this stuff is, and he told me that if we didn't scare the public enough, there could be some serious accidents in the woods this summer. He told me what we were going to do would be okay because the people in charge of things around here were in on it. I thought that included you, sir."

"Me? Me and who else?"

"I don't know, sir. Maybe the DEA, maybe the DA. He didn't say, but he said there'd be nothing to worry about. It was a mission and we'd been chosen to carry it out. We had our orders."

"What do you think now, Deputy?"

"I don't know, sir. I just don't know."

"All right, Henderson. That's all for now. I'll get back to you if I need to. In the meantime, don't, for God's sake, don't talk about this to anyone, especially not Stockton. I'm pretty sure I believe you and I'm going to try my best to keep this thing from going any further. I'd hate to see this department run through the mill because of one sonofabitch's warped ambition. So, listen, if he does try to talk to you about any of this, just tell him you don't want anything to do with any of it, ever again. Matter of fact, if he hassles you about it in any way, just tell him to come and talk to me about it. Got that?"

"Yessir."

"Good, now get back to work. You're a good cop, but you made a stupid move. I'll try to save your ass if I can. I don't want a grand jury in on this any more than you do. After all, in the end, it's my department, my responsibility. And, one more thing, Henderson, don't worry about this going on your record. If we can squeeze out of this okay, I'll make sure it stays between you and me. Now, get going, you still have to work your way up around here."

"Thank you, sir."

"Don't thank me," Marty said loudly. "Here, catch!" He flipped the ball to Henderson just as he reached for the door handle. The man made the catch. "Now throw it back." He did. "Thank you," Marty said and smiled.

Henderson stepped out and closed the door. *Good*, thought Marty, damn good, now what do I do with it? He really didn't want to see the department torn apart by scandal. And he sure didn't want to face any of that kind of music himself. At the same time, he had less and less reason to like Reynolds, and more reason to help defeat him if he could. He'd just have to think it out, and the best place to do that was alongside the Sachute River with his own handmade spot-wing #3 fly waiting for the bite of an early-run blueback.

All day long Sonya had been acting as if she were an actress. Makeup, lights, memorizing her lines, all of it. So far, they'd filmed four TV spots to be used during the next and last month-and-a-half of the campaign. She was happy with the ideas used in these short clips, most of which came from Dan and Terry working together with her. Once those two finally got over their differences, they turned into a very good team, the Pro and the Kid, as she referred to them in her own mind.

The ads were designed to follow each other at one-week intervals, with each treating a separate issue and aspect of her platform. She had to ask the guys to tone the anti-Reynolds pitch a little in some of it because she never did approve of mudslinging politics, but where there was a clear contrast between the two of them, she'd let those references stay in.

On this day, they were scheduled to finish by midafternoon, but it ran on until nearly six. Janet came by after she got off work and invited

Sonya to dinner and a movie. She seemed a little let down when Sonya told her she was on her way out to see Peter. Janet handled it, though, and made a little joke saying, "Wait until I tell Reynolds." It was too bad, because Sonya really did want to spend more time with her and several other people, but the campaign was taking up more and more of her time and energy, and now she felt stretched thin by this thing with Peter, even though they weren't going back and forth to each other's places all that much. How could they work it out? He obviously wasn't about to give up his ways and move into her world. And vice-versa.

As she left the outskirts of Dixon behind, she glanced again at herself in the rear-view mirror, seeing traces of the excessive makeup they'd used because of the lights. At moments like this it was beginning to feel like it was someone else running for office, and the person who used to be Sonya was standing outside and watching it happen. At any other time in her life, she could see herself going full steam ahead with either the campaign or the romance, but both at once? Both at once was an overload that she couldn't really handle and yet couldn't say no to. And that didn't account for what would happen if she did happen to win, unlikely as that seemed at this point. Still, it could happen, and then what?

The sun was now low enough to shine directly into her eyes whenever the road turned west. She fumbled for her sunglasses and glanced in the mirror again. Ah, the actress. Also now, as if she wasn't already overwhelmed, who should call the night before but Mike, dear old Mike, just checking in, had to be in Seattle next week, thought it would be nice to stop in and see her next weekend, old times sake, how about it? Now, how do you say no to somebody you have that kind of history with? Besides, she was curious about him, about what he was doing, and enough time had elapsed that old stuff shouldn't come up and tear at them again. In a way, she wanted to see him if only to try and figure out what there had been about the two of them that made it possible and good, and then what had made it impossible. Her memories were clouded by the intense hurt and hassles of the past, but now that she was somewhat distanced from all that, she really was curious about the connection that once existed. She was surprised that these days she no longer missed him at all, although that was probably true only because of Peter, and on this call she'd detected a kind of probing in Mike's questions. Over the phone, it's hard to tell for sure, of course, but something in his voice said that he really did want to see her again. Well, in any case, when you're already over-stressed, what's a little more? If nothing else, she'd find her limits before collapsing.

In the meantime, there was this thing with Peter and all the confusing and wonderful feelings he brought tumbling into her life. "Don't analyze," she said out loud. This had become her motto when thinking about him, him and her, and her and herself in the light of it all. Why do these things happen when they do? What if he'd come along before she became a candidate? Would she have been as drawn to him then as now? Or was part of their connection based on the pot issue drawing them together? God, the questions she could ask herself, just like a trial lawyer, but knowing that one of the worst things you can do to yourself is asking 'what if?' about anything. Still, what if they'd never met? Would they have just stumbled along in their old routines of lonely waiting, and were they so ready for something new they'd jumped at the first excitement that came along? That really didn't seem like the case for him, though, or he'd have gone for something else a long time ago. And, as far as she was concerned, when he showed up, she wasn't anywhere near ready yet. "Don't analyze," she said again into the mirror as she reminded herself she wanted to stop at that little store and pick up some wine. She hoped he wasn't expecting her much earlier, not that he was the type to follow schedules, or even get impatient. Dinner would be whenever it happened, but maybe, just maybe, he was wondering where she was, and feeling the same anticipation that she was as the miles and minutes that separated them passed by. If anything confirmed for her what she was doing, it was this eagerness that came on her before seeing him, and the impatience and good feeling that made her smile at herself for being so childlike. She told herself she was doing something so good for her that it was a crime to question it so much. She laughed. Misdemeanor or felony?

She stopped at the store, bought some Oregon loganberry wine, and hurried on to his place. No one in the store seemed to recognize her, which was probably a good thing. The sun was now down beyond the ridges and the sky was turning turquoise. Flashes of yellowing maple leaves caught the corners of her eyes as she drove the twisting road that followed the low, slow, rock-filled creek. She turned onto Peter's road and passed the house of his friends. He'd mentioned introducing her to them, but it hadn't happened yet. Their dog barked at her car from beside the mailbox as she drove by. Funny how this backwoods countryside fit her image of country. Except for some recreation breaks in the back country, she'd spent all her life in Dixon or bigger cities. Until this summer she'd never spent any time in a rural setting where people were scattered about. She was finding it interesting and soothing in ways she couldn't really explain, and she envied people who could be satisfied with it. She also knew that she required a more social and human-oriented environment, and she thought she understood Leslie's dilemmas. Catching herself in that train of thought, she had to ask herself who she was having this internal discussion with. Was she actually considering some kind of compromise living situation with Peter? Was her mind exploring possibilities without consulting her conscious self? She was glad when she reached his drive for more than one reason now, and once again, she repeated her mantra, "don't analyze," checked her reflection in the mirror, and gathered her overnight bag, the wine, and her jacket from the seat. She climbed out of the car, ready for his greeting.

A fire was burning low in the pit by the trailer, but no sign of Peter. She knocked on the open door, then stuck her head in and looked around. Nobody there. She slipped the wine into the refrigerator, set her stuff on a chair, and moved back out to the fire.

"Where you been?"

She spun around to his voice and he put his arms around her. When they finished their first kiss, she pushed away from him and said, "Don't do that to me."

"Why not?" He mussed her hair, touched her dangling earrings, and framed her face with his fingertips, saying, "Quiet on the set, Take One, Take Two. So, how did it go?"

"It went all right. Glad I don't have to do it for a living, but it was all right."

"Good, I was worried you'd be discovered and whisked off to Hollywood. Maybe I'd never see you again unless I paid admission." He kissed her again. "Hungry?"

"Yes, it was a low-budget film. No lunch."

"Good for you," he said, pinching her waist and turning to put more wood on the fire. "Roasted marshmallows for dinner. All I've got, but there's lots of them."

"I need to wash some more of this gunk off my face."

"You know where the creek is."

"Yes, I know where the creek is. Where's a towel?" She went inside and washed her face in the sink. A couple of steaks were marinating on the counter. They smelled great. She also saw potatoes wrapped in tinfoil. "You want me to bring anything out?" she called.

It was dark by the time the potatoes and steak were ready. They ate with their plates on their laps, knees touching, talking little, and smiling often. There were stars above them by the time they finished the ice cream Peter brought out from his little freezer. The bottle of wine had evaporated, and a chill was beginning to creep into the air, one more foretaste of fall. He stoked the fire and they pulled together for warmth and affection. Peter asked if she would like some music and she replied, "Maybe later." Then she asked him if he ever played the horn she saw hanging in the trailer and he told her about his howling at the moon with it on occasion. She asked if he would play it for her sometime. He told her he'd try to practice something for her.

The fire died away as they lay back quietly in each other's arms. Once Peter pointed out a satellite passing high overhead. When it came time to make a bed, they roused themselves and spread a tarp and mattress between the firepit and the trailer. It was an unspoken realization for them both that they would have to move inside soon if they kept seeing each other at his place. They were lucky it hadn't rained on them already. Neither one mentioned it, though, because it would only bring up the whole tangle of questions about who they were, who they were becoming, and what they were going to do about it. It was easier to thank the stars for shining and put off the real problems until they could no longer be put off. They got ready for bed and crawled into the snug little cave of their two sleeping bags zipped together. In their mutual tiredness, they made love slowly, gently, and silently. It was good for them to be combining passion and patience as they grew more aware of one another's physical mysteries and desires. The moon, some four or five nights past full, rose among the trees on the eastern ridgetop as they finished and the aftershocks of their pleasure faded and finally ended with sleep.

By morning clouds hinted at the possibility of drizzle. They made coffee and did some stretching exercises together. They were just having a second cup when Sonya mentioned that she'd never seen a real marijuana patch.

"Do you want to?"

"Sort of. Would you show me?"

"Yeah, but only if I could blindfold you on the way there and take all your jewelry as collateral."

"Okay. I really would like to see it. It would be like research for my professional development. In case I win, I mean. Besides, it would help me know more about you and what you do more than anything else I would care about."

"You'll have to ride on the back of my little dirt bike once we get close," he warned.

"Sounds like fun."

He had her dress in an old pair of camo pants and a green sweatshirt with a hood. The problem was boots since she only had her running shoes and street sandals, and she didn't want to ruin either. First, he tried stuffing newspaper into the toes of his own rubber boots, but they were so big on her that she could hardly move in them and had to grab on to him to keep from falling over. Next, they tried on a pair of his old sneakers, this time with socks pushed into their toes and it worked a little better. It was hard for him to keep from laughing at her, and he said he wished he had a photo of her in over-sized pants, droopy sweatshirt and absurd shoes on her feet. She said she was glad he didn't have a camera.

"It would make a great contrast to a picture of you the way you arrived last night, all dolled up from your film debut."

She laughed again and struck a pose like a runway model.

"You have to admit it would make a really original campaign poster, or even better, a huge billboard," he laughed.

"If you say so. Guerilla clown runs for DA," she said, bowing somewhat gracefully.

"All right, you finally found a way to get my vote," he said, bowing back. "You want to eat now or when we get back?"

"I'm not hungry yet. How long will it be?"

"Two hours, more or less."

"Let's just go. It might rain later, and I'd much rather wear these than those rubber boots."

"Okay, I'll get the bike in the back of the truck, and grab the machine guns, and we're ready."

They loaded up and drove off. Within minutes they were off the pavement and into the forestland. The gravel road climbed quickly until they were almost up into the cloud cover.

"It's beautiful up here," she said, but a couple of minutes later after a few more turns in the road, she asked, "Is it logged like this everywhere?"

"A lot of it is. They started out with an alternating pattern, like a checkerboard. Then they took every other unit of the ones that were left. Now, probably 70% of this area's been logged in the last ten to fifty years."

"And it's still going on?"

"There's still some left, but a lot of that is harder to get out. But the thing that's really got it slowed down is the economy. Nobody can afford a new house anymore. So most of what's left is safe for now. Hey, we're almost to where we get out."

The bike was nearly too small to carry both of them, but they managed with her hanging on tight. It was rough going until they could pull off the road and stash it. After hiding the bike, they walked toward the landing, and he pointed out big deer tracks on the left shoulder of the road.

"Only about two weeks until deer season. That buck better start staying off the road." When they reached the flat area, he pointed down the steep slope, and asked if she still wanted to try.

"You might have to carry me back up, but I'm pretty sure I can make it down."

"If you can't make it back up, you just stay there until you can. I'll come back in a day or so. Come on, it's almost fun."

He took her hand and led her over the side and down the long switchbacks toward the bottom. He was making it as easy as he could on her, and they rested several times, talking little, absorbing the silence and remoteness of the place. When they finally reached the salmonberry growth near the bottom, he pointed out a sort of tunnel through the brush and told her to pull her hood tight around her face so her hair wouldn't get caught and she wouldn't be scratched. He led the way, crouching and sometimes crawling. Struggling a little to keep up with him, she wondered if this was his usual way to go, or if he was making it harder just for her.

"Do you always go this way?" she whispered to him.

"Yeah," he whispered back. "Why are you whispering?

"I don't know. I guess I always whisper when I'm sneaking around."

"Good idea." Suddenly he was out of the thicket and standing up. He reached back for her hand and helped her up to stand beside him. She looked around, and then at him. She hadn't seen them yet. He pointed to something several feet away, a ten-footer growing up through the surrounding brush. Then she saw it and stared at it. She had never expected anything so big, so green, so lovely. She looked around again and could pick out two more of them, not quite as tall.

"They're beautiful," she said.

"Yeah, they are." He walked over to the biggest one and ran his fingers through its leaves, picking off the large ones and letting them fall to the ground.

"How much is that one worth?"

"I don't know yet. Anywhere from four hundred to a thousand. Hard to say at this stage. If it finishes out good it can go between a quarter and half a pound. It's really a pretty good one, Bushy, even though I cut back a lot of it, so it's harder to see from up there." He pointed above them.

"Incredible." She reached out and stroked the plant. "I'm beginning to see why you do it."

"The money?"

"That, too, I guess, but I mean just how beautiful they are. I've never seen a plant so big and so beautifully shaped."

"Yeah, that's what makes them so hard to hide. That and their color isn't like anything else out here."

She went to each one of these three plants, touching them gently. It was nice for him to see her reaction. He'd wondered about bringing her down to see them, but now that he could watch her response to their sheer beauty, he was glad he had. He'd never shown his plants to anyone before, not while they were still in the ground, and a rush of pride filled him as the plants swayed to her touch as if it were a whispering breeze. Both she and the plants were so beautiful.

"Here," he said as he stepped over to her. He pulled a branch down near their faces and pinched the bud at the end of it. "Smell."

She sniffed and then sniffed again. "Wow, I never smelled anything like that. It's so strong." She sniffed again. "Is it always like that?"

"It varies some. There are some strains that even smell like skunk, but most smell like this."

"Now I know what pungent means. You should make perfume."

He smiled and said, "I wonder if smells can be illegal? Possession of a controlled scent." A low croaking sound came from above them. She clutched his arm. "What's that?"

"Raven," he answered. "There's one I know of lives around here."

"Just one?"

"Probably a pair, but they can be pretty solitary. I usually only see one at a time. They nest in pairs away from other birds, though, and they get old too. Forty, fifty, maybe even seventy years old. This one might have been here longer than we've been alive. They get to see a lot of changes in their forest."

The rasping sound came again, repeated three times. "They're loners too, huh?" She placed her hands on his shoulders and looked into his eyes. "Do you think they want it that way, or does it just work out that way?"

"I don't know. Some Indian tribe has a story that the world was an egg sitting in the dark for a long, long time. Finally Raven came along and sat on the egg. It hatched and that's how the world began. Probably always been single ravens as well as pairs."

"And you're like the raven?"

"I don't know," he said, pulling away a little. "Do you want to see any more plants? They're not too far, but hard to get to."

"No, that's okay. I loved seeing these, but it's enough."

The drizzle was starting, a fine mist with droplets falling and rising at the same time, a hesitancy when the rain is just beginning, and promising the rainy season on its way. They could no longer see the trees on the ridge across from them and a slight wind was moving through the brush. Peter gave one of the plants a shake and small drops flew off it.

"Now the danger is mold."

"What molds?" she asked.

"The whole plant eventually. If it's left out to die. The bad part is what happens to the flowers, the buds. That's the part for smoking. If it rains and the water gets trapped in the buds, and then it stops raining and warms up again, the mold starts in the moisture. It spoils the part of the plant it gets to."

"Does that always happen?"

"Depends on the weather. You could stop a lot of it if you just shake off the plants every time it stops raining, but I can't come out here every time it's like that."

"What if it just keeps raining and raining, like from now on?"

He was picking the larger leaves off the branches and dropping them on the ground as he answered her. "That would be a little better than if it rained on and off. See, as long as it's raining the water keeps moving through the plant, and the mold will mostly only grows in pockets of water that stays in the same places. Problem then is, you have wet plants to harvest, and they haven't finished up as good without sun. Terrible business to be in, farming."

"What would you do if it were legalized? Either where people can grow their own for personal use, or even where farmers could grow it for sales by permit, like some other drugs."

"Are you getting wet? I think it's going to keep raining."

She brushed away some drops collected on her eyebrows, and smiled, "I kind of like it. At least so far."

"Good, I do too. You can help me by picking off any leaves as big as your hand or bigger. It'll save time later. Don't pull them off, though, pinch through the stem with your thumbnail, like this. If you tear them off the branch, it makes a little wound the mold can start in. The mold is like any predator, and it takes advantage of weaknesses. It only happens because the plant is at its end and dying anyway, and it takes the dying, the weak, and the sickly."

"Is this right?" She plucked a couple of leaves while he watched.

"Yeah, that's good."

"You didn't answer my question."

"Just postponed it, because I don't know," he said, moving to another plant. "I don't know how to do much else and if it were legal, prices would probably be too low to make a good living off the black market. And I wouldn't want to have a job growing it for some big company. A straight job growing pot, I can't imagine it. So weird. I guess I like things the way they are."

"Risk and all?"

"Yeah, risk and all. Like you. You're taking a risk on maybe wasting your time running for that office. Taking a risk hanging out with me. Some people can't live without risk."

"I know, and some people can't handle it at all." She was getting faster as her hands became accustomed to the work.

"I guess one of the things I learned in the war was about me and risk, taking chances. I hated the war, but I admit I loved the feeling I got from making it through each day alive. There's something about putting your life on the line that can be addictive. Lot of guys talked about it over there. Not so much after getting back. People think you're crazy if you say you like war, or anything about it. So, you try to find something that takes your mind off how dull your life is now, or you find something to keep yourself on the edge. I saw guys turn into insane gamblers when they got back. Some drank and picked fights, maybe get thrown in jail for stuff. Some smoke pot and grow."

Peter glanced over at her to see what her reaction was. She just looked back at him with that expression that was coming to have a lot of meaning for him, the look that says, "I don't really know what you're saying, but I'm glad you're telling me."

He turned his eyes back to what his fingers were doing. "Does that answer your question?"

"Sort of. How am I doing?"

"Fine. I think we should go soon, though. It's going to be slippery climbing back up with this rain."

"Whatever you say."

He picked off a few more leaves and then a couple of buds which he stashed in one of his inside pockets. It was always nice to dry and taste the fresh stuff, even if it was still a bit immature. He stepped over behind her and put one hand onto her shoulder, turning her into a hug. "You know," he said, "in the olden days, the peasants made love in their fields at planting time, to make them more fertile, and just before harvest they would do it again to inspire the crops."

"Is that what you want, Mr. Peasant?"

"Maybe when we get back. I was just telling you that as part of your education." He stroked her body through the over-sized clothes and laughed. "Besides, I don't think it's the right ceremony for outlaw clowns. Let's go."

The trip back to his place was a sad-sack cartoon of clumsiness and discomfort. They crawled and stumbled their way to the top, up and over slick, wet rocks, and fresh mud, grabbing at roots and ferns to help themselves along. The bike was soaked and so were they, and by the time they reached the truck it didn't matter that one of the windows was left partly open. It was raining harder on top of the ridge than at the bottom, but once you're wet, there's not much to do about it until you can get dry again. On the drive, they laughed and joked about Abbott and Costello growing pot in the rain forest, and by the time they got back to the little trailer they were more than happy to strip and splash around in Peter's outdoor shower.

After the shower and putting on dry clothes, they fixed a huge breakfast and decided to go on into town and spend the rest of the weekend at her place. Without actually mentioning it, they were already beginning to deal with the situation of his space in the rain and the logistical problem of them being together. Also, during breakfast, she told him she might not be able to see him the next weekend because of the unexpected visit from her ex-husband, Mike. She brought it up as casually as she could, but his reaction still took her off guard. He simply didn't respond at all.

"It's just something I have to go through," she said, watching him go on eating and wondering what he was thinking. "In a way," she went on, "I'm glad he's coming because it gives me a chance to tell him face to face that I'm happier than I've been in a long, long time. I think he still thinks I can't get along without him.

Peter continued to eat silently until his food was gone. It was hard to move around each other very well in the tiny kitchen, but he stood up and poured himself a cup of coffee, offering her one at the same time.

She accepted and asked, "Are you all right?"

"Sure."

"You seem strange."

"I am strange," he said, smiling. "Always have been."

"But what's wrong? Do you think I shouldn't see him?"

"How can you not see him? It's okay, it's just something I never thought about."

"Well, don't worry, it doesn't change what we have. I hate to think what it would be like these days without you. I'm sure I wouldn't want to be with him again."

"You never know."

"Probably not. You don't know what it was like and, besides, even if I was crazy enough to want to get back together, he's the one who left, and he's the one who's doing what he wanted to be doing."

"We'll see."

"Peter, look at me. I want to say something I haven't really said yet, and I want you to look at me when I'm saying it."

He blew on his coffee, took a sip and looked into her eyes, "What?"

She smiled softly and leaned forward until their coffee cups were touching. "I love you," she said, clicking her cup on his, "I really do."

They were silent for a long moment. Her words hung between them as the sound of the rain on the metal roof intensified and the steam from their coffees mingled and vanished in the warm damp air of the small space.

"I guess I know that," he finally said. "And it's a little depressing." He glanced up at her and took as big a sip as he could without burning his tongue.

"Depressing?" She pulled away.

"Yeah, because I love you too. I know that now. Have for a while. And it's really going to make it hard on both of us. What can we do about it? With it?"

She reached forward and traced her finger across the back of his hand. "I don't know. I don't know either, but I know it's good and it's worth it and somehow we'll work it out."

"Yeah, I hope so."

"Hey," she said, "don't analyze."

The next week turned out to be a frantic time for the campaign. Dan had decided to press for a face-to-face debate with Reynolds sometime in October, and of course the offer was turned down. This meant they had to go to the media for support and enough publicity to pressure him into accepting. The basis for even having such an event was that this was the only local race where there were clear-cut differences between the candidates, and Sonya's people felt she really needed the exposure. There was no doubt in anyone's mind that she would come across well, and even hold her own with her opponent, although there was some hesitation among the party leadership about her representing the Democrats in such a visible way. Some of that had been alleviated, however, by the evident failure of the marijuana initiative to make it onto the state ballot. The court case had gone in favor of the secretary of state, allowing him to turn it down, and there was only one more level of appeal available to the sponsors of the measure. In any case, it was looking almost certain that she could not be held to her promise to follow the county's vote on the initiative, since it most likely wouldn't be voted on at all.

On Thursday evening, the local TV station interviewed Sonya and she publicly demanded a debate. The media folks were encouraging in every way because they needed something to liven up their coverage. By week's end, the consensus was that Reynolds was likely to lose more support by avoiding the debate than he would by debating, even if he didn't do well. Terry was all over it with his own polling and said that the issue of whether to have the debate was quite possibly the turning point they had been waiting for. According to one newscaster, the ball was clearly in the DA's court and he owed it to the public to come through. By Friday evening, Dan informed Sonya that he was hearing the event was virtually assured.

Combined with her normal workload, the campaign drama had served to distract her from Mike's imminent visit and all the complications associated with Peter. But on Friday evening she finally had some personal time. Peter called from the South Fork store and they had a good conversation, and she began cleaning the house for Mike's visit, even though he'd be staying elsewhere. Distraction arrived again in the form of an unexpected visit from Janet, who apologized for coming by without giving any warning, but said there was something urgent she needed to talk about, and she was willing to help with the cleaning while they talked.

"You know what?" Sonya said as she took Janet's coat and hung it up for her. "I'm glad you came by. I need to get centered on something and housework just won't do it. Glass of wine? I need one."

"Sure. I hope I don't keep you from anything though, but I wanted to tell you right away. I got laid off today."

"You what? Oh, Janet."

"No, it's okay. Now I can work fulltime for you on the campaign, collect unemployment until you take office, and then you can rehire me at the same job. It's perfect."

"Long odds on that." They went into the kitchen and sat at the table. Sonya got the wine and poured out two glasses.

"When's Mike coming?"

"Tomorrow sometime. He's in Seattle now and stopping by on his way back south. I don't know what his trip is about, but everything seems to be happening at once. Almost way too much, but tell me what happened."

"I'm not quite sure. At the beginning of the month, Mr. Reynolds called me in and said he needed a list of the contributors to your campaign, along with the amounts they donated. I said I didn't have that kind of access but would try. He said it was getting more and more clear that a lot of your backing was coming from the criminal element in the county, and maybe even from outside interests. I said I couldn't believe that. Although, to tell the truth, he did convince me that could be at least somewhat true, but I still didn't think there was anything illegal going on."

She paused, waiting for Sonya to comment.

"I don't know. I guess it depends on how you define 'criminal element.' I'm sure that people growing pot have given me money." She smiled and added, "and I doubt very much that they're giving any to him."

"That's what I decided too. Anybody who donates to a political cause has to have some interest in the outcome. Besides, I don't care where it comes from if it gives us a chance to beat him." She held her glass up to Sonya and then took a sip. "Anyway, he asked me again last Monday if I had gotten anywhere. I said not really, and he said he didn't think I knew just how important it was, both to the public and to my own future. So, this morning when he called me into his office, I had a feeling something like this would happen. I was a little scared until he said he was letting me go for budgetary reasons. There wasn't enough money to pay my salary under a staff re-organization plan. I'll bet he finds some way to use that 'plan' to show voters how careful he's being with their money. Anyway, I said I understood, but I didn't think that was the only reason. He gave me a strange look and said, 'You can probably get a job with your friend when she wins my job.' I told him I'd think about that. And that was all there was to it, except he said I had a two- week notice. One of those week was unused vacation time and he didn't care if I came in or not for the other week. I just said goodbye and walked out. Once I got out and away from him, I realized how happy I was. I was free from that job, and from worrying about losing it. I haven't felt so good about something like this for years."

"And I was about to feel sorry for you." They both raised and emptied their glasses. Sonya asked, "Are you hungry?"

"No, just ate with my Mom and Kristi. What can I do to get started? Place actually looks good? And maybe I'll tell you what's happening between Ray and me. If you tell me about you and Peter." She smiled and wet a sponge to start wiping down the counters.

It was Autumn Equinox, Saturday night, and a few clouds were picking their way across the starry sky. All day it had looked like rain, but as the evening faded into dusk, the cover had broken into pieces of cloud that all seemed to be hurrying somewhere else. Peter got back from plucking leaves at just about dark, and he was hungry enough he didn't even stop to change out of his damp, sweaty clothes before starting up the stove under the beans and rice he was having for supper. As he was changing out of his dirty fatigues and washing up, he couldn't help wondering where Sonya and Mike were having their evening meal. All day he'd been shoving that kind of thinking under the carpet edges of his mind, trying not to be distracted by something that shouldn't matter anyway.

He was tired, legs sore from long climbs up the ridges. As he hung the dirty clothing on hooks outside the door, he thought how appropriate it was that they should be called fatigues. And then he wondered why he'd never thought about that before. Maybe he had and just forgotten. He took tortillas out of the fridge and heated another pan. Might as well pretend he was at a restaurant, a Mexican restaurant with cheap wine and a beautiful cantina dancer who looked like Sonya and kept looking at him from behind the fan she held so casually between her many-ringed fingers as she danced. Oh yeah, and the owner of the restaurant was her husband, a big fat bully who kept looking at Peter between the fingers of the huge hand supporting his chin as he leaned on the bar. Rumor had it they had broken up and she was supposed to be free to flirt and even go out with anyone she wanted to, but somehow the expression of hatred on the heavy man's face warned Peter that this might be one of those situations when survival and seduction were hardly compatible and caution was the best move...He grabbed the beans from the stove just as they started to burn.

He finished off three of the burritos, drained a mostly empty bottle of wine, and sat back to roll a joint that he hoped would keep him pleasant company for the rest of the evening. He wondered if Mike smoked, probably not, probably into coke, big city strokes and lines, a lawyer from the skyscraper world of SF. How could this trailer compare to a Playboy Penthouse, how could this grubby grower begin to match the bucks and style of someone who not only had a career, but was moving up in it, leaving behind anything or anyone that might hold him back? Only Sonya was in any position to compare them. If he was going to trust her, she'd already made her choice, and if he couldn't trust her, then he was better off if she did go back to her ex. She had assured him she didn't want that, but she hadn't seen the guy for almost a year so how did she know?

He sat in the silence of his trailer for a long time after he carefully picked the burning coal from the end of the half-smoked joint. He tried to remember what he'd done with all his time, what he'd thought about, before he met her. He was trying not to name his feelings for what they were, but it was useless. He was jealous, and he knew it, and if being alone all those years had any advantage at all, not having had to experience jealousy was at the top of the list. What the hell, he'd asked for it, comes with the relationship turf, you let someone get inside you and the fear starts. How long can this last? Why should she care about me? Why me? All that.

It was dark outside when he stepped out into the late evening, dark with a hint of wind coming up from somewhere. He pulled on a jacket and walked to the truck to make sure both windows were rolled up. He remembered leaving them open when she was with him and it looked like rain. All it took was the distraction of one Sonya to throw him off enough to leave them down even when he was sure it would rain. It had been a fun day otherwise, and if she could easily give him the feelings he'd been having since they got together, then he had no right to blame her for these circumstances left over from her earlier life. As he stared up into the sky a simple little refrain whistled itself from his lips, and he smiled when he remembered where it came from. He needed to play some music, and he needed to play that particularly special music. He turned back to the trailer to set it up, and since there were more stars showing up in the sky, he felt safe to bring the speakers outside. He needed to get into himself, into some great music, and then he wouldn't care what she was doing, or maybe he'd still care, but it wouldn't bother him nearly as much.

He hadn't realized how late it was, almost too late, but he went ahead, knowing sleep wouldn't come easy to him anyway. This was a night when the light and dark were held in balance by the earth and the sun, yet he felt way out of balance himself. Maybe that was the lesson he was supposed to be learning, how the happiness of the past month had to be balanced somehow, and if this one night of worry about where she was and what she was doing was all he had to go through, it would be a pretty good deal. He couldn't help thinking, though, that the real test of their balance lay somewhere up ahead. That you don't get anything for nothing was a pretty accurate description of his life this far, no reason for it to change now.

The recording had all four of Mozart's horn concertos on it, and even though it was the fourth he wanted, he went ahead and put on the first side, thinking no harm in hearing them all. He adjusted the volume and sat on his chopping block as the sounds began filling the night. He was just cold enough to find himself thinking about a fire, so he started one in the pit while the orchestra played its games with the horn in the first part of the initial piece. As he added more branches to the fire, he couldn't help wondering how many other people were at that moment listening to Mozart beside a campfire. Maybe quite a few considering how popular backpacking was becoming and how small the new tape players were now. Mozart probably wrote much of his music while sitting in front of some fireplace or other. Again, he found himself trying not to think about Sonya and what kind of music the two of them might be listening to. Were they dancing, or hassling, were they driving around or were they already in bed together? So what? And where did this come from, this actual cramping in the belly, like fear before combat or the stomach flu, a real sickness inside when he pictured them in his mind? You got it bad, he told himself, and then answered himself: Well, it'll go away. When? When he's gone and she's still here?

As the music wove its figures into the night air and he let the fire absorb his eyesight, he found some relaxation, acceptance, and a slow turning over of the whole situation inside himself. If he truly cared for her, then he should probably feel more concerned for her than for himself. After all, it might be a pretty terrible thing to go through after she'd gotten the guy out of her life and maybe even out of her thoughts, and now to have him pop back in with no chance to turn him away, another kind of balancing, a debt being taken care of a little at a time. It just couldn't be very easy for her.

He relit the half-smoked joint, finished it, and went inside for a drink of water and his horn. As he waited for Violin Concerto No. 4 in D Major, the one he'd been working on lately, he sat with the horn on his lap, wondering how it was that one man, a man so young, could have contained so much of the world's most beautiful music. Mozart, the genius, was also the guy who'd had all of that trapped inside and had to get it out, who died trying to empty himself of it all. What an incredible life to find yourself in the middle of, constantly writing down sounds from beyond hearing, from beyond the brain, sounds that couldn't even be heard until after they were written…

Peter let the second concerto pour over him. As it came to its exquisite resolution, he hung suspended in the silence that followed it. His thinking stopped and his body was lulled into near sleeping. He skipped ahead, past the third. Grateful that he didn't have close neighbors, he turned the volume up even more as the first strains of the fourth announced themselves to his part of the valley. He listened for a while before succumbing to the invitation to join in the orchestra's quest for the essence of the music, waiting until he felt the calling to place horn to lips, and began breathing in and out his own sounds of enchantment.

He played as well as he could, still having trouble keeping up with some of the cascading runs of notes difficult enough to challenge any virtuoso, even ones secluded in the backwoods, but he kept at it, caught up when he was left behind, or stopped if he couldn't and waited for the next opportunity to hop back on board. Almost halfway through the piece, he began to feel a new sense of familiarity, the sense that always let him know when he'd turned the corner on a piece of music, and he was closing in on making it his own, it becoming something he could do, and even do well. It was a great feeling and he stood up in his excitement for the music, the flickering light of the fire, and the vastness of the night. He played louder and louder as his confidence with the piece grew and his satisfaction filled the empty spaces within himself. He knew that he wouldn't have worked his way through this piece six months before, it was too ecstatic, too cheerful. Until recently, he'd stuck with mostly the somber compositions of the ages, indulging in his feelings of loneliness and isolation. Now, almost without intention, he was taking himself a little off-guard with how exactly the music and his playing were reflecting the changes inhabiting him and his psyche. Now when he was alone, it wasn't the same kind of solitude, it wasn't the absence of anything, but rather the expansion of who he could see himself becoming. The horn on the recording was still playing different music, in contrast with the orchestra, but they were still together, instruments making a unity out of separation and enjoying themselves. The horn ran faster and the orchestra, led by its woodwinds, raced to catch up, swirling and blustering like the first winds of spring. He was different now, and even if everything in his life changed again, he would never be the same as who he'd been and now no longer needed to be.

Early in the evening, Sonya and Mike went to dinner on Mike's expense account, at the best Italian restaurant in town. He said he'd file it under "old business." It had been one of their favorite places, and it seemed to help them settle into each other in a somewhat calm way. He had arrived late in the afternoon, rented a car and picked Sonya up at the house. The first few minutes were awful, at about the same level of communication as a difficult blind date, but as they got used to being together again, their mistrust gave way to a kind of a class reunion ritual. Where's so-and-so, who's doing what, have you seen or heard from? They even managed to laugh together at the memory of another dinner at the same restaurant with some friends who had also been visiting each other again after their divorce.

It seemed to take a long time to be served, and several times they settled into silence and drink-stirring. They avoided asking each other about one another's personal or professional lives until after the food arrived. Then, as they were eating their favorite dishes, Mike began describing his current activities.

"Told you, didn't I, when I first went to work with this firm, that we mostly handle big-name sports contracts and spin-off endorsements? Well, the best way to move up in this game, no pun intended, is to get your own star, someone, say, in the half million-dollar bracket. That way, besides his actual contract with a team, you're hustling his name, investments, media spots, taxes, the whole bag for a healthy percentage. Some of these guys are turning more than a million a year from all their spin-offs, and besides their agent, they need a nearly full-time lawyer and that guy's salary is just one more necessary deduction. I couldn't have fallen into a better setup if I'd looked for years."

"How did you get it?" Sonya asked.

"I'm still not sure. My dad went to school with one of the partners, but I didn't even know that when I first went in to see them. I think the first time I heard about them was at a party Teddy Campbell, remember him, was throwing for one of the Giants' pitchers. Crazy world."

"Sure is. He still with his wife, the one with the show horses?"

"If he is, I sure couldn't tell. He's a mover and I never thought to ask about her."

"Lots of parties?"

"Partying all the time. Too much, but it's where a lot of the business happens. See, last month I had to handle one of our accounts in a beer commercial with him and several other players. Just so happened I got some one-on-one time at a party by the indoor pool with one of those guys. He's from the Seattle Seahawks, football, right?"

"Right." Sonya was enjoying his enthusiasm and wondering if he could keep it this high all the time these days. The last time she'd seen him for any length of time that intensity had been turned against her, in particular and Dixon in general, as the key obstacles that were dominating his life and undermining his future. He was certainly doing something completely different now, and it seemed to suit him.

"Well, he invited me up there for some time this week. Seems he was getting screwed by his legal help and wanted to ask my opinion on a couple of things. One thing led to another, and now I might be on my way to Seattle. Not the greatest town for parties maybe, but a couple of teams and not so many guys like me."

The waiter came by and asked if they cared for dessert. Sonya declined, and Mike ordered cheesecake for himself and coffee for them both. He rambled on about meeting this superstar and that one, and how much rumors had to do with the constant personnel shifting that went on in pro sports. He was the same Mike, with the same steady rap about himself and what he was up to, but he seemed a lot more into it than he'd ever been about their law practice or liberal politics in Dixon. Finally, just as the check arrived, he asked her to tell him about her campaign. She said she would, but first they needed to decide what they were doing about the rest of the evening.

They ended up driving around the area, letting him see some of the changes and some of the old familiar spots that had been important to them. As they settled into the situation, they both realized they couldn't just drive around all night and would have to go somewhere. When she asked him where he was staying that night, he just shrugged and said, "We'll see."

She said, "I guess we can go to the house for a while." They bought a bottle of wine, and when they got to the front door, he asked, "Did I ever carry you over this threshold?"

"I don't think so," she said as she fumbled with the key and unlocked the door.

"Maybe that's what went wrong," he said and made a gesture offering to make up for it. She slipped through the doorway and held the door open for him.

The house was cleaner than it had been in months, but she was pretty sure he wouldn't notice. He went straight to a table full of campaign literature and began leafing through it piece by piece. At one point he called to her in the kitchen, where she was getting snacks and wine glasses. "This is all for real, isn't it? Guess I had trouble believing it until I saw all this stuff. You look good in these pictures."

"You always thought that," she called back.

"Yeah, but I never saw so many of you at one time. Hundreds of you here."

She came back into the room, "I know. It took a while to get used to. I'm still pretty freaked out when I see myself on TV."

"Well, congratulations, you really did it, big time."

"Haven't done anything yet," she said, sitting down in the easy chair across from the couch. "Still a long, long-shot, at best."

He sat on the couch across from her and picked up his glass, holding it up, "To your victory."

"To your superstars."

They drank and smiled across the familiar space of the room between them.

"The place looks nice. Comfortable."

"Not like a bay-view condo, I'll bet, but it's okay."

"Any house is better than an apartment, let me tell you."

"Okay, so tell me. About yourself, not your work. You party and you meet lots of people. Lots of women?"

He smiled and took another sip of wine. "My dear, that is an interesting area of conversation. I should probably say, No Comment, and leave it at that. But since you ask, I'll tell you. It's a weird trip. A real ego twister. The women are all after the jocks, but there's more women than there are jocks. The players call them 'cheerleaders' and they're like groupies, only instead of teenagers, these are definitely women, like models, actresses, socialites, reporters, what-have-you. I don't think any politicians. If I even get noticed, it's because all the big guys are taken, and that's kind of a kick in the face for me. But I shouldn't complain. I don't have to be alone unless I want it that way."

"Sounds like you're doing pretty well for yourself," she said, kicking off her shoes and pulling her legs up under herself on the chair.

"Sort of. Sometimes I question it, but we all do, don't we?" He reached into his coat pocket. "Want to do a couple of lines?"

"Cocaine?"

"Yeah. Some righteous pure stuff. Just a little goes a long way."

"No thanks."

"Hey, I thought you were the pro-drug candidate." He waved one of her pamphlets in the air. "This is really good stuff."

"No, I said no. And I'm pro-freedom of choice, not pro-drug. You make the same mistake the media and the Democratic Party people do."

"Guess so. Just thought you'd like to try it. Something we never did together."

She watched him closely as he poured some of the powder onto the glass top of the coffee table. "Are you involved in it very much?"

"No, just when it comes my way. Sometimes you do somebody a favor in my business, and they don't really pay. But this stuff comes under the table. You don't mind if I do a little?"

"Could I stop you? No, it's okay. Just don't get yourself caught in a DA candidate's house."

She excused herself and went into the bathroom. She looked at herself in the mirror. She realized she didn't look quite like all the photos and billboards anymore. Maybe she was just tired, or tiring from it all, but she thought she looked older than the woman running for office a couple of months ago. It was getting hard to imagine herself as the person in the posters, and the person involved with Peter, and the person who had lived those years with Mike. How was that possible? Those two were so different, and she was the only common denominator. So, what did that say about her? She held the washrag under hot running water, then placed it over her face, breathing in the welcome steaminess. Mike had changed, that was part of it, and this made her think about how much she must have changed or she couldn't have handled the last couple of months. Now she was her own person, but part of her wanted to belong to Peter. Not that there was any way for that to happen. Before, she had been Mike's person and wanted to be her own. She remembered someone telling her a long time ago, "Always be careful what you pray for." Had she learned what that meant yet? And should she pray to win the election, pray to lose, or just leave it up to the Great Whoever? She dried her face, slipped out of the skirt, and pulled on a pair of jeans. A robe would have been more comfortable, but she didn't want Mike getting any ideas about where she was at. As she left the bathroom with one more quick glance in the mirror, she had a sudden flash of Mike and Peter meeting. What would that be like?

Mike was reading the pamphlet titled, "The Priorities of Law Enforcement," the one that contained her main arguments concerning personal use of marijuana in Chinook County.

"You actually put this up front?" he asked.

"Yes, I did. Things have changed fast around here. Both for the economy, and for the sheriff's and DA budgets. So, there was no way to avoid it. Besides, there was a statewide initiative movement for it as well. I talked to some people, and decided to treat it as a victimless crime, and a civil liberties issue. At first there was some pretty strong negativity. I got misquoted a lot, and I already told you the party wanted to cut off their support. But I think it's settled down now. The state court kept the legalization issue off the ballot unless there's a miracle reversal in the appeals court, and my polls show the issue did a lot of good in getting me known among voters. Whether they vote for me or not remains to be seen, but at least most of them know who I am."

Mike looked over at her thoughtfully, and then said, "Well, tell you what, when I left, I was afraid you might just crumple up and break down. I really did feel guilty. I guess it was an ego thing that made me think you couldn't get along without me. Was I wrong? You know, when I got my first apartment down there, I made sure it was big enough for both of us, and that it was one I thought you would like. I think I really thought you would follow me down there." He paused, emptied his glass of wine and went on, "I never wanted us to end, I just wanted it to change. Even now, sometimes I wake up in the night and think you're there. Or I tell myself we'll get it back together."

"That's nice," she said filling both their glasses again.

"No, I mean it. Especially now, seeing you again. If you lose the election, think about it, think hard about it. Seattle's not such a bad place, sort of a compromise between here and San Fran, wouldn't you say? Sort of an average of the two. In a way, I'd like that. I still need you in funny ways, no, not funny, but unexpectedly, know what I mean? And I still haven't met a woman I'd want to know me like you do."

"You will, I'm sure. You'll find somebody much better for you than I ever was. Sounds like you just haven't stop partying long enough to really look."

"How would you know? But that's partially true. And if you ever want to give us a rematch, I'd be into it. We had a lot of happiness, Sonya, remember?"

"Yes, I remember. But you seem pretty happy now, too."

"Most of the time, but not like deep inside, know what I mean? I'm happy ha-ha, but not happy contented. I still miss you a lot. Have you got someone else yet?"

"Maybe." She didn't really want to go into it with him, but it had never been possible to lie to him either.

"Don't tell me about it. I like you better alone, waiting here for me to come back, or packing your bags to join me, seats for two, fifty-yard line. Super Bowl, Miami or wherever." He looked at her. "Can't see it can you? You want to stay here, be the big fish in the Dixon City pond. Go ahead. Best wishes. Is he in politics?"

"It doesn't matter. It's just casual. And besides, I'm sure you're doing much better without me than you ever could have with me. I can tell you're more excited by your work than you ever were before." She paused. "Mike, I'm glad for you."

"Thanks, but it doesn't appeal to you, does it? Nothing. Zip. Small-town girl all the way. It's okay. I wouldn't want you to be as unhappy there as I was here. But you could give it a chance, maybe not with me, but give yourself a chance. Someday you might surprise yourself with how different you could be."

"I kind of have. I certainly never thought I'd see my face on a billboard."

"Okay. You'll do what you need to do. And it really is good to see you. It really is." He stood up and crossed over to some large photos on the wall. One was of a dog they once had. The other was of her parents. "I don't see any pictures of the two of us. Where are they?"

"Put away," she answered. "I put all of that away."

"Good, no sense dwelling on the past. Well..." He came over to kneel by the side of her chair. "How about one night for old times?"

She looked into his eyes, seeing the humor, and also the pleading that was behind much of what he'd been saying. She knew it might be easier to give in to him than not to, but how would that make her feel? "No, I don't think that's a good idea."

He stood up, looking down at her, "Are you sure? I won't tell anyone."

She stood up and eased away from him. "Yes, I'm sure. It wouldn't be good or right for either one of us."

"You're probably right. But it always was the best part."

"Maybe that's why all the rest of it didn't last."

"God you're serious." He didn't move away, or even move at all. He looked honestly sad. Sonya stepped closer to him and put her hands on his shoulders. "Mike, what happened between us will never be over. We'll always carry it with us. But it really is also over."

"Yeah, I know," he said, wrapping his arms around her. "I really am sorry, Sonya. It could have been better. I could have been better, maybe I still could, but we'll never know."

"Oh, Mike, don't go there, it's going to be all right. See, we're almost friends."

They pulled away from each other, hugged again and then separated from one another's touch.

"Guess you'll want me to leave, so I'll be going. Might as well stay out by the airport. Got a six-thirty plane. Can you imagine, six-thirty on a Sunday morning? Pilot's probably sleep-walking that early."

"Thanks for coming. I'm glad you did. I was curious about how you're doing, and you seem fine, a little burnt-out maybe, but you're doing what you need to do for yourself, and I'm sure that's what's important for now."

"Thanks, Mom. I'll try and write home sometimes."

"I'd like that, and I'll let you know how it goes with the election."

"Yeah, let me know how much you win by." He picked up his jacket, drained his wine glass and started for the door. "You're sure now?"

"Yes, I'm sure now. And thank you for understanding."

"Understanding what? I'm just not about raping the next DA."

They lightly hugged again and almost kissed, hesitated and then pulled apart.

"Good luck," he said.

"You too."

The door closed behind him and she pulled aside the curtain on the living room window to watch him leave. He turned once to look back, and she realized how easy it had been. She wondered what it would have been like if she were still on her own, if there was no Peter to help her ignore the parts of her heart that were still attached to Mike, or more precisely, the part of her life that had been Mike. All of that was mostly gone now. Really, the house was the main thing left over from the whole period with its ups and downs, that and all the leftover memories and photographs put away now for good reasons. And right now, she felt more convinced than ever it was good this way for them both. As he drove away, she had the strong feeling he would keep coming back, at least as long as she was living alone. And who knew how long that would be?

She went into the bathroom and started the water running in the tub. It was still early enough in the evening and a bath would make it easier to fall asleep. She was half-tempted to head out to Peter's, but it didn't make any sense at this hour. She had a brunch in the morning for the District's congressman, and besides, Peter might not even be there. Of course, that was unlikely, but it did make her question what she would be feeling if he were with any other women. It was all so confusing to be happening at this stage of life. When you start out, she was thinking as she undressed and climbed into the hot water, when you're young it's all tied together, the romance, sex, marriage, relationship, but now, as the middle of a lifetime approached, and with no one else to answer to, how do you know what the level of commitment is supposed to be? It was clearer to her all the time that she and Peter were definitely avoiding the issues of long-term and one-to-one. But what choice did they have? And now, was tonight and her resistance to Mike, in its own weird way, an example of her already being "faithful" to him?

When Peter first woke up, he heard rain on the roof, and his foggy mind thanked itself for being careful enough to put the speakers back inside. The rain wasn't coming hard yet, but the cloud cover looked like the kind that stayed around a while, a real Fall rain. After all, it was technically the second day of the new season. He drifted back toward sleep, alternately thinking about mold on the plants, and Sonya and her ex. One part of him wanted to ride into town, surprise them, and call the guy out, do the tough guy trip, but that was so absurd he let it go as soon as it came up. The Mozart was still there as well, swirling its notes in and out of his thoughts. It really was a satisfying piece of music. He rolled over and pulled the cover up around his eyes. He wanted to sleep longer, and did.

He was awakened by a car horn, a long loud blast, a pause, and then another. He threw off the cover, stumbled into his pants and boots and inched the curtain on the front window aside just enough to see out. Cops, shit! A sheriff's patrol car and two men, one in uniform, the other in an open raincoat and suit. They were standing beside the open doors of their vehicle, in his driveway. What first? He pulled on a shirt and jacket. They honked again. If he didn't show himself, they'd come right to the door. He grabbed a bag of buds and his bong and shoved them into the garbage bucket under the sink. Line of a damn song came into his head: 'Nowhere to run, nowhere to hide.' Okay, so maybe this was it. Okay. He knew he had to open the door now, show himself and find out what they wanted. Nothing to it, he had a right to be in his own home, and they obviously thought they had a right to be in his driveway. Okay, time to face it.

He opened the trailer door just as the one in uniform was starting his way. Peter took a few steps out from under the covered porch into the rain, realized he'd forgotten a hat, and had a flash of what they'd do if he suddenly ducked back inside for one. He stopped and stood still, looking at them, knowing he should say something before they did.

"What can I do for you?"

"You mind stepping over this way? Just want to ask you a few questions."

He walked toward them, hands out in front of himself. The twenty or so steps seemed like walking through mud, as he tried to read them. They didn't look either angry or smiling. They were just there, in his driveway.

"What's it about?" knowing that the answer to that question could have everything to do with his future, or, if he was lucky, maybe nothing to do with him.

"It's raining," the one in the suit said. "Mind if we talk in the car?"

Peter weighed the question in his mind, and decided there wasn't really a choice here, and he moved toward the back door of their car. He probably could have kept all three of them out in the rain until he found out what it was all about, but even as he climbed into the backseat and heard the door close behind him, he knew there was no sense resisting anything now. He settled into the center of the seat as they took their places in the front and turned to face him. Okay, he thought, here it comes, you wait and wait for it and it never comes and then when you think maybe it won't ever come, here it is.

"I'm Detective Stockton, sheriff's department, this is Deputy McCullough. You live here? Alone?" He removed his dripping hat.

"Yes."

"You know these people on down this road? Specifically, do you know Gerald Edward Bates?"

"You mean Jerry? Some. What's it about?"

"We'll get to that. Sorry to bother you this way," he smiled to show he didn't really care who he bothered, and Peter tried to smile back, to show he didn't mind being bothered. "What's your name?" he asked.

"Peter."

"Peter what?"

"Peter Barrett. Why?"

The Detective wrote it down. "Two r's, two t's?" Peter nodded yes.

"Where were you last night, say between 11 PM and 1 AM?"

"I was here."

"Happen to hear any gunshots?"

"No. What do you mean, what kind of shots?"

"I'll ask the question," the detective snapped. "The kind of shots I'm talking about, you would have to have heard if you were here. So, tell me again, if you were here."

"I was. But I couldn't have heard anything."

"Why not?"

"I just couldn't have. Not at that time." Peter could see that he better be explaining what he meant, or he'd be in conflict with this guy, but how do you explain playing along with "Mozart's Violin Concerto No.4" in the middle of the night, out here?

"We'd like some answers here, now, or we can get them later downtown at headquarters, if maybe you prefer that."

"All right. I couldn't hear anything because my sound system was outside here and it was playing loud, really loud."

"You had a sound system out here in the rain."

"It wasn't raining then, it's covered over there, and it was just the speakers. Now, could you please tell me what this is all about?"

"All right. Your buddy down the road here shot somebody last night. Seems some kids were stealing his marijuana, and he jumped them and says it was an accident, but he shot one of them. Claims they fired first, hit him in the leg and he fired back. Self-defense. We can't say what really happened because we only found the one kid who was wounded, and he hasn't regained consciousness. Maybe never will. Your friend's in deep trouble and I don't think you can help him since you didn't hear anything. We've got both guns and they're different enough a witness could have heard that, but apparently the only one who did is his own wife."

Peter was stunned with this news. It was too heavy. Jerry. He tried to think clearly, tried to think at all. "Where is he now?"

"Who?"

"Jerry."

"If he's out of the hospital, he's in custody. County lock-up."

"Bail?"

"Probably won't be any until the other guy dies or pulls through."

There was silence in the car. The deputy lit a cigarette and asked, "Do you have a phone?"

"No, sir."

"You sure you don't know anything about all this?" The smoke from his cigarette was filling the car. Peter reached to roll down the handle. No handle. The Deputy rolled down his own window and blew smoke out of it. He turned back to look at Peter.

"You think I'd be hanging out here waiting for you guys if I knew what was going on?"

"All right," Stockton said, "we'd like you to be available in case we have to talk to you about anything more. You work somewhere, or what?"

There was silence except for the rain on the car roof.

"Sure, you do." The detective gave him a long stare and Peter looked away out the window. It was raining harder now. "How's your crop this year?"

Peter looked back at him, saying nothing.

"All right, that's all. We'll be in touch." The deputy climbed out and opened the back door so Peter could also climb out. Stockton handed a card across to Peter. "Give me a call if you remember anything that might help us out."

Peter took the card and waited while the car backed out of the driveway and spun around and headed out. He listened until he couldn't hear it anymore. It didn't sound like it stopped anywhere, but it was hard to tell. He turned and walked slowly back to his trailer. Rain was dripping from his hair, running down his face and the back of his neck. He was shaking, but not from the cold. Inside, he grabbed a towel and turned on the fire under the coffeepot. There were a hundred thoughts crashing through his mind. He couldn't stop them long enough to deal with any single one. Carla and the baby? He'd have to check on them. Jerry had to get a lawyer. Sonya? She'd help, she'd have to. This wouldn't make the newspaper until tomorrow. It's Sunday morning. Have to get to town to see if Jerry's okay. The cops would come back at any time.

Suspected him of growing, but who wasn't a suspect around here? Cops coming around now, right at harvest. How could he get harvest and dry his stuff if cops might come to his door at any time? Shit!

He poured fresh grounds into the top part of the pot and waited for it to start bubbling. What if he hadn't been playing Mozart, what if he'd heard the shots? Probably couldn't have done anything to make a difference. The only thing he could maybe have done was to refuse Jerry the plants back in the spring. Carla must be absolutely freaked. This was so much worse than a simple cultivation bust, and even that had been enough to make her threaten to split if Jerry ever got involved. He didn't wait long enough and poured out a first weak cupful and tasted it. Terrible. He poured it back in the gurgling pot, took the thermos down and rinsed it, then changed into dry pants. He had a stash of about $2000, and he thought maybe he should take it along. The cops didn't seem to think there would be bail any time soon, but you couldn't tell for sure. Take the money along just in case. He poured the nearly done coffee into the thermos and turned off the burner. He grabbed the stuff he'd stashed in the garbage and locked the trailer. Hadn't done that in a while, probably since last year's harvest. Where the hell would he be able to do his processing? He had to be a lot more careful because they seemed to be taking an unusually special interest in him. What a mess.

He drove quickly over to Jerry and Carla's. It was quiet. No one around. He got out and looked everywhere he could see from the driveway, then went up to the porch. There was a bloody sheet on the floor and a towel on the awning support. Had to have been terrible to go through. If only he hadn't had the music on so loud. He wondered what happened to the other guy. Had Jerry carried him from where he was shot? Who had helped? What really happened? There were plenty of fresh tire tracks now being washed out by rain that was getting heavier. He went inside, but there wasn't anything out of place in there. If an ambulance came, maybe Carla had taken the truck. Why hadn't she come and gotten him? Possibly couldn't leave the two of them wounded. The cops mentioned more than one thief, maybe the other was still hiding out here somewhere close. Unlikely thought, probably still running.

He got a plastic bag from under the sink and carefully used a stick to push the bloody sheet and towel into it. He started to get rid of it, but had the thought it might be evidence, and he'd better leave it there. He got back in the truck and headed home to his place. He had no idea where to start to look for Carla, and he didn't want to go asking questions at the jail himself. Sonya was supposedly at some brunch deal but might have heard about all this. He didn't know what to do next. Drive into town and maybe figure out something on the way. Seemed like the only choice now. Maybe get ahold of Leslie's brother Ron? Might be a good thing to do or should he wait until he talked to Sonya before getting involved? He flashed that this would obviously have some kind of impact on her campaign.

All the way into town, he kept having the urge to refuse to believe it. Then in the next instant he would feel that not only had it happened, but that it was his fault. All over a plant. Thieves, cops, growers, all crashing around because of a plant. Like moths around a candle. And now it was his friend, maybe his best friend, although Peter had never thought of themselves in that way, more just like buddies. You don't have best friends again after you lose a few to enemy fire. And now Jerry was shot up, caught in this place's crossfire, hurt, how bad, it's always a buddy, the names and faces of some of them came back to him, some he'd carried bleeding to the medivac choppers, some there was nothing to do but hold their head in your arms while you waited for help. You don't get used to it, and right now it was coming back to him, and he was trying to reject it, keep it away. Would it ever leave him alone? Some of the guys he knew best over there had been hit when he wasn't around. You get word the next day, you can't deal with it, but you go on, and on. The ones that died quick were bagged up and shipped off like their unit's stateside mailbag. The ones that can't die, but want to, screaming through the drugs that can maybe stop some of the pain, but can't do anything about the anguish. Bobby from Indiana blinded. Andy, begging somebody, anybody to please find his arm, just look for it one more time. He shook his head to try to clear the faces from his mind, some faces he never had names for. And all that time, him wondering, Why not me? Or worse, when will I get it? Who's next? Jerry got it last night, who's next? It was starting to rain again after a short pause and he flipped on the wipers. Their thwack-thwack reminded him of distant choppers as he fought against the memories threatening to overwhelm him.

It seemed to take a lot longer than usual to get there. He was worn out and edgy from the morning's strain and the detective's talk of his crop, from trying not to think of the war, and from not knowing what to do about any of this now. If he went to either the hospital or the jail he could get drawn into other things and be of no help to his friends. Best to get someone else in there. He turned off on the road to Ron and Theresa's. He hoped they could help. Maybe they wouldn't want to get pulled into anything like this, them being so new in town. If Ron took a case like this it could affect his whole future, but everyone has to take a risk sometimes, and no one seemed safe on a morning like this.

Ron was instantly concerned and ready to get involved. Peter was grateful he didn't have to justify anything or make any excuses. A couple of phone calls and they'd traced Jerry to the hospital where he was doing well after some minor surgery on his wounded leg. The other victim was still unconscious and likely to remain that way for a while, although his condition was listed as stable. He'd been hit in the head by a glancing shot that left a small crack in his skull but didn't penetrate. The best estimate they could give about Jerry was that he would probably be ready for transfer to the jail in two days. His wife was with him but didn't want to talk to anyone.

Peter relaxed a little, enough to accept some late breakfast from Theresa and to go along with Ron's suggestion that they go to the hospital. Ron would go in alone and attempt to see Jerry or Carla. He could possibly arrange for Peter to see one or both later in the day, if that seemed wise. Peter left a message on Sonya's answering machine, saying only that he was in town and would call or drop by later. Then he and Ron left for the hospital. Theresa wanted them to make sure to let Carla know she was welcome to stay with them if needed.

Peter spent a tense forty-five minutes in Ron's car waiting while the lawyer was inside the hospital. When he came out, his first words were reassuring, that Jerry's wound was not going to cause any lasting damage. The bone was chipped, but not broken, and the muscle was torn, but not completely. Jerry was quite conscious and said he was glad that Peter knew what happened but was terribly concerned and apologetic about bringing this down on all of them.

Peter shook his head as Ron was describing Jerry's state of mind, and said, "I'm the one should be apologizing. I'm the one that got him involved."

"How's that?"

"Nothing." He realized that how it all got started didn't matter now and asked, "How's Carla, and the baby?"

"She's the more upset of the two of them and wouldn't really talk to me. When I invited her to stay with us at our place, she said she had somewhere else."

"Did you talk about what happened?"

Ron answered yes and started the car. "Sonya might be home by now…Let's swing by. She should know about this if we can find her. Jerry says the dog woke him up barking like crazy in the direction of the old orchard. Do you know where he means?"

"Yeah, I know."

"It was dark, and he thought it was probably a raccoon in the fruit trees. The dog kept racing down into the brush and then back to him. He turned on the porch light and got his .22 out of the truck. He also had a flashlight and went toward where the dog was running back and forth, barking all the time. Jerry says he followed the dog down to the creek and heard some splashing, as if something large was in the water. He said he thought it might have been a deer."

"Too bad it wasn't."

"Yeah," Ron went on, "anyway, the first thing that let him know something weird was going on was when the dog gave a sign. I guess he'd got it trained. Anyway, it gave a sign that there was something just ahead. Jerry said he gave the dog the word to attack and it lunged into the brush where he couldn't see it and there was a shot. The dog gave a shriek, he said it was a shriek, and crashed off into the brush. Jerry fired a shot into the air, and according to him that was when he was instantly shot in the leg. He instinctively fired back at the flash from the other gun, heard a scream and then some splashing off through the creek. At first, he couldn't move because of the pain in his leg, and he was afraid to use his light to see what was happening. After a few seconds, he heard something moaning not far away. He turned on the light and crawled to the sound. By that time, he could hear Carla yelling to him from the house. She'd heard the shots."

Ron turned the car down Sonya's street, and drove slowly up the block to her house. Her car wasn't there, so he parked in front and went on with the story. "He yelled back to Carla, flashing his light around, and she got to him about the time he found the kid with the head wound. What happened after that isn't exactly clear to either of them. I'm sure they were in a panic. Carla went back to the house, called an ambulance, and came back with a bunch of diapers to use as blood-stoppers. Apparently, the kid was bleeding pretty bad from the head wound. Jerry said it seemed like a long time before anyone showed up and it was a sheriff's deputy who arrived first. About five minutes later the paramedics arrived, and Jerry and the wounded guy came in here together in the ambulance. Carla and the baby followed in their truck. I guess that Sheriff called his office and there were more deputies waiting when they arrived at the emergency room."

"What about the dog?"

"They said they didn't see or hear it again after it took off."

"What I have trouble believing is that this was all going on less than a mile from my place, and I didn't know a thing about it."

"Yeah," Ron said, "Jerry even said you must not have been home, or you would have come over to help. Obviously, neither one of them could leave to go get you."

"What can we do now?" Peter asked.

"Legally, we wait until there's an arraignment, charges filed, and bail set. That isn't likely until they can move him down to the jail, although we might be able to pressure for it to be sooner. I personally don't think it makes much of a difference right now. They're probably not going to set bail, or they'll make it high, while the other person is still unconscious. He said that for obvious reasons you should stay away. He'll talk to you as soon as he can. In the meantime, he wants you to look for the dog. He's upset that he doesn't know whether it's alive or dead out there in the brush somewhere, and he said it would be a help if you could clean up whatever you can if you don't mind. His wife mumbled something to him, and he told her not to take it out on you. I didn't understand that part of it, but maybe you do. She'll probably stay in town, but who knows, she might head back out there this evening."

"So, that's pretty much all of it, isn't it?"

"Sounds like it, except there's marijuana involved, isn't there?"

"Yeah, I guess so."

"Sometimes that makes a difference in how the charges come down. That's up to the DA."

"Well, it was trespassing, and they shot his dog."

"That's what he says," Ron replied after a moment. "but it might take a jury to decide who and what to believe. What I mean, Jerry can't really prove what happened or didn't"

"That's why the cops told me this morning, that if I heard the shots, I could be important to the case."

"They said that?"

"Yeah, probably wanted to know how many shots I heard."

"And probably what order they were fired in if they were different-sized guns, and you could tell them that, but you didn't hear anything?"

"No, I had my stereo turned up all the way, and after that I went to sleep."

Just then Sonya drove up the street and pulled into her driveway. As she got out of the car she waved to them. They got out and joined her near the front steps.

"What are you two doing here?" She reached out and took Peter's hand. He looked at her and didn't know how to answer.

Ron suggested they get out of the rain, which they did. As soon as they were inside, she said, "Something's wrong, isn't it?"

"Yeah. My neighbor got in a shootout down at his place. He's in the hospital and so's one of the other guys." He briefly explained how he found out from the cops, and then he turned to Ron, who told her about the hospital visit.

"And you didn't hear a thing?"

"No, I was playing along with a Mozart piece. Must have played right through it all. Had my speakers up loud. I was probably asleep by the time the ambulance arrived. Guess it didn't need a siren out our way. It's still really hard for me to believe any of it."

"The police say what is was about?"

"Said it was about pot. Jerry had a little patch down across the creek below his place. These guys must have found it and were probably ripping it off."

"I need a cup of coffee," she said. "Anyone else?" They both nodded yes, and she went into the kitchen. "Ron? How did you get in to see him?"

"I sent a message in to his wife, saying I was a friend of the family. She came out and I told her I was a lawyer and Peter had sent me to see if I could help. She told the guard I was their lawyer and he let me in."

She came back into the front room. "Couple of minutes for the coffee. Any idea what the charges will be?"

"No, they can't have figured that out yet," Ron said. "Waiting to see how the other guy comes out of it. Said Jerry should be able to be moved to the jail or get bail in a couple of days."

"How is the other one?"

"No idea. Young, maybe sixteen or seventeen. Still unconscious."

"Jerry said there were two of them?"

"Yes. No sign of the other one, I guess," Peter said. "I looked but didn't find anything."

There was a long silence, as they each thought over the implications. The water boiled in the kitchen and announced itself with a piercing whistle. Sonya moved to get it and came back in a couple of minutes with three cups of coffee.

"I just wonder what Reynolds is thinking right now," she said. "He's got to be overjoyed."

"Yeah, and it's pretty much up to him right now. The charges, at least."

"Peter, what are you going to do?" Sonya asked, placing a hand on his arm.

"Guess I'll head back out. He wants me to look for his dog. Maybe I'll find something else that might help. I want to help Carla, but she probably doesn't want me around."

"Why?"

"I gave him the plants to start with. He didn't tell her because she was always paranoid. Never wanted him to get involved in it. Looks like she was right, but he was out of work and said they needed it."

The phone rang and Sonya answered it. She listened for a long time and then shook her head and said, "I'm sorry. I have no comment on that. I can't say anything at this time...What's that...Yes, I'll try to have a statement for you sometime tomorrow...Before noon? I don't know, I'll try... Thank you. Goodbye." She hung up. "Howard Tate, from the newspaper," she said. "Wanted to know how I'd prosecute a hypothetical case. Someone shoots a trespasser who discovers an illegal activity on someone's property."

"Why hypothetical?" Peter asked.

She looked over and replied, "Because he knows I can't comment on an actual case that I might have to prosecute later. He's probably asking Reynolds the same question."

Ron said, "Guess you'll have to come up with an answer."

"I know," she said sitting down. "But what? It could get to be a very important question."

Ron looked over at her, "What if I take Jerry's case? Will that screw you up, technically?"

"No, I don't think so. Let me think about it today, and I'll have to talk it over with Dan and a couple of others on the committee. I don't know. This thing could go either way. It could ruin me, or it could help. I think it depends a lot on how Reynolds uses it.'

Peter finished his coffee and set the cup down. "I guess it's important for your campaign and everything, but Jerry's a friend of mine and he needs help. I'd like Ron to take the case if he can. I'll cover as much of the expenses as I can."

"It's not the money, or even the campaign exactly," Ron said. "I want to help, but legally I'm connected with Sonya in both the ACLU work and in her private practice and I'm worried about the conflict of interest if she got elected. I suppose I'd just be disqualified, but then whoever took the case would have to start over."

Sonya shook her head no and spoke directly to Peter. "We'll take care of it, don't worry. It's not a problem of legal assistance at this point, and if that turns out to be a problem, we can get someone else."

"He'll need it. If nothing else, he's got a cultivation bust."

"We can hope it's no more than that," Ron put in. "Listen, Theresa and I have people coming over to the house this afternoon, so I need to get back. Want me to give you a ride so you can get back to your truck?"

Peter glanced over at Sonya and she said, "I'll take him later. I'd like to see him a little bit. If you can wait, Peter."

"Yeah, I can. Thanks Ron, you're a big help. Sorry, I'm so uptight."

"It's okay, you're doing all right. We'll get through this. Sonya, get in touch with me as soon as you know how you're going to handle your response. I'll let you know if anything changes, Carla has my number as his lawyer, and they'll have to let me know if they press charges or anything else changes."

Sonya walked him to the door, saw him out, and then came back and sat next to Peter. She put her arms around him and held his tense shoulders tightly until he began to relax and soften to her touch.

"Hey, I missed you," she said.

"Yeah? How was it with Mike?"

"It was okay. We had dinner, compared notes. Mostly he told me about what he's busy with and I showed him campaign stuff. He's changed. Seems happier, but sort of lonely." She turned his face toward her and kissed him. "I couldn't believe I related to him for so long, especially now that I know you. You two are so different."

"I'll bet we are." He kissed her lightly and was quiet for a long moment while she rubbed his neck. If only he could forget it all, Mike, Jerry and Carla, the cops, the campaign, all of it. If he could just rest his head in her lap and take a little nap, wake up and have everything be all right.

"You hungry?" she asked softly.

"Yeah, I guess so. Haven't eaten today."

"I'm still stuffed from that brunch. What a scene. Totally boring, then I came home to all of this. What a contrast. I'm so sorry for you having all this fall on you. I want to help…starting with eggs and muffins, smoked salmon, what else?"

"More coffee. I'm sorry for you. I don't know why it's all coming down at once."

She stood and pulled him up, taking him in her arms and holding him close. "Come with me. It's okay. It's going to be all right. And we have each other."

"We'll have to hope things get better, huh?"

On Monday afternoon the *Dixon Press-Herald* carried the following front-page news, accompanied by a photo of DA Reynolds at a news conference earlier in the day.

SHOOT-OUT LEAVES TWO WOUNDED
DA says South Fork Incident Pot-Related!

> Late Saturday night, a double shooting occurred in the South Fork area of western Chinook County. Sheriff's deputies who responded to the emergency reported that they found two wounded men and a number of marijuana plants at the scene. The incident took place on or near the property of Gerald Bates, 34, one of those wounded. "As far as we can tell at this time," stated DA Bill Reynolds at a news conference this morning, "the two men exchanged gunfire in a dispute over the illegally-grown marijuana."
>
> Hospital authorities listed Bates in satisfactory condition following surgery for a gunshot wound in the left leg. The other victim, still unidentified, sustained a head wound and remained unconscious as of press time. His condition is listed as serious but stable. The sheriff's office indicated that a third person was involved, but their whereabouts is unknown. According to DA Reynolds, the marijuana was being grown near a creek in a brushy part of the secluded property, and apparently discovered by the unidentified

individuals. They were removing it when they were accosted by Bates. An unknown number of shots were fired, the two men were wounded, and the third apparently ran off.
It is not known if the third party is injured.

Reynolds announced that the investigation will continue and charges will be filed, including illegal cultivation of a controlled substance, and attempted murder for Bates, and trespass against the other party. The DA went on to say, "This is one more proof that violence and bloodshed are part and parcel of this out-of-control marijuana business, and that the continued efforts of all law enforcement agencies and law-abiding citizens must be constantly maintained and increased until this intolerable threat to life and public safety has been completely eliminated."

Related story from Northern California, see page 3.

CHAPTER EIGHT

October

Clear nights bring frost, cloudy nights bring rain. Gone are the day-after-day heat spells of summer, gone too are the days of gray when the clouds sail by overhead on their way to somewhere else. Winds of greater and greater force accompany the changeovers between these days and nights of cold or wet. The creeks cool and rise and the salmon leap and twist their way to the places of their birth. Nights are now noticeably longer than days, and the waxing moon brings harvest energy to a peak. Brown leaves pile up everywhere there are trees, from the back roads to the city streets. The Saturday feeling of perfect football weather pervades the crisp clean air as children run and play in new and bulky winter coats. Everywhere the world is storing up; animals layering on the fat that will see them through the coming hard times, sap flowing back under the ground to the refuge of their root systems, and the people in the countryside gathering in the produce for canning, freezing, and drying. Time seems to run out more often as more must get done while it's still possible: firewood, roof-patching, butchering, mulching, and covering anything that won't make it through the rainy season exposed. The growers are gathering in too, armloads of fragrant branches that must be dried quickly and completely, buds to manicure and package, all with the haste of a nervous energy that comes from having a bird in the hand and the bush in the drying room.

A whole year's expectation and concentration now vulnerable to all the demons of mold, rip-offs, and snitches. Those who lost their crops to the various predators of summer can now find work helping those who didn't, and buyers begin making inquiries as early price estimates zing through the rumor mill. October, when the trees drop their cover and reveal their skeletons, the geese beat their way to a warmer world, the growing season tips the scales, and all while the northern hemisphere finds itself searching for and arranging satisfactory shelter.

"You can't charge a guy with attempted murder when he's defending himself and his own property," Marty said again as he paced back and forth in Reynolds's rather spacious private office.

"You can if what he's defending is illegal. Sit down, Marty, and take it easy. It's not your problem anyway."

"That might make sense to you, but in a country where half the people are armed mainly so they can protect themselves and their property, it's going to be hard to find a jury to convict on this kind of thing. Do you know if the pot was even on this guy's own land?"

"And if that kid dies?"

"Depends. It's still likely the case of an armed intruder shot trespassing on someone else's place in the middle of the night." Marty finally sat down, and then got up again. "And the guy you're charging also got shot, so maybe we've got self-defense on top of private property here."

"I know all of that," said Reynolds, twirling a pen between his fingers. "Just don't worry about it. Besides, there's nothing says the charges we start out with are the ones that we take into court. You know that."

"Bill, tell me what charges you would put on him if this wasn't an election year, if you didn't want to grab every headline you can get and your pictures on the front page every week?"

"Marty, I don't need all that or any other kind of publicity for this election, and you know it. This woman couldn't win a catfight. Now settle down and tell me what's on your mind, what's got you so worked up. It's not every day you drop in, so I know something else is on your mind. I'm ready to hear it, whatever it is."

The Sheriff leaned on the back of a chair. "You know something, Bill? I can't even begin to tell you what's on my mind. Start with the fact that I care about this county or I wouldn't be doing this job. That might seem strange to you, but it's true. I also care about the role and image of law enforcement in this county, and I think it's got to a piss-poor level when we spend more time and money chasing around these hills looking for a bunch of plants than we do on patrolling people's neighborhoods and maintaining highway safety. We haven't got enough facilities to avoid a lawsuit that's going to end up forcing us to cut loose real criminals, and now we're holding somebody, without bail, who's most likely only guilty of self-defense...just because he had a couple of these goddam plants growing on his place."

"Whoa," Reynolds interrupted. "Slow down and we'll take these one at a time. First, you know all that time and money we spend in 'these hills' comes from the federal side and we couldn't use it on anything else. Maybe you forget that both of our departments depend on matching grants for damn near everything we do."

"That's part of what's so screwed up. If we don't hunt pot, we can't afford to try and stop theft, arson, rape, whatever. And I think it's the guys like you who've turned it into all this."

Marty sat down and folded his hands across his stomach. He was beginning to relax because he really didn't care anymore, didn't give a damn what Reynolds thought of him, and he realized he'd spent too much time in this job worrying what Reynolds or the county commissioners, or anyone else was thinking about Marty Johnson.

"What I mean is this: I look around and I ask myself who profits from this pot business and who loses because of it. It's damn obvious who gains: the growers, truck dealers, gardening suppliers, irrigation sales, anybody who can stay in business because there's still money coming into this county from the outside. And we profit from trying to stop it, as long as it keeps going and growing. What if we did wipe it out? Then where would we get the bucks to make ends meet?"

"Maybe there'd be less crime to worry about if we got that element out of here."

"Maybe, but I don't think so. I think most of them only break this one set of laws and are downright careful and law-abiding about everything else. And that's not really the point, the point is who loses because of the pot trade? I think I finally know. And I think you already know, and I think they're all friends of yours."

Reynolds continued to be surprised by this unfamiliar intensity in Marty, a characteristic he'd never thought of in connection with the Sheriff, but which must have been there all along if only the right buttons got pushed. "Marty, I don't know what you're driving at, but you've got my interest. Go on."

"All right here goes. I never could figure out why you made such a crusade out of this part of your job, almost like you had a personal stake in it or something, but then I started thinking about who your backers are, who the Republican big boys are in this area and what they want to see happen in this county now that the timber business will never be what is once was again. And you want to know who I come up with? Real estate, land sales, escrow companies, speculation and tourism, et cetera. See, the pot growers are trying to settle down, right? They buy land and try to live on it, use it, raise food and families, like homesteaders back in the day. I'm talking about most of them, right? And if one of them can down-pay a piece of land and can support himself and pay for the land by growing a little pot, then he's not going to sell that land very soon. You guys want faster property turnover, big recreational developments, and runaway speculation. Marijuana is almost shutting down the sales of rural property for two reasons. One, folks who aren't willing to grow it are afraid to move out there because you've got them scared off with your phony war, and, second, all the ones who are growing already have a foothold on the land and aren't into the selling market. Real estate used to be much bigger round here, didn't it? Now, the best way to free up a piece of land is to either bust the owner or destroy his crop, not to mention forfeiture of that land. Am I right? Seems crazy and if I went public with this I'd be shot down.

But am I right? Yeah, it seems crazy, but there's always a money reason behind everything in this country. Money and greed, right?"

"Marty, I must say this is a fairly brilliant analysis you've come up with. But so what if it's true? What's wrong with it? Not that I'm agreeing with you on all this…But what if you are right? What's wrong with our way of life defending itself against intruders who bring with them a criminal economy and dangerous behavior? Surely you don't expect the people who settled and built up this area to just walk away and leave it in the hands of a bunch of riff-raff and newcomers. You've been on these places, these cute little homesteads of yours, and what do you see when you look around? You see a lot of stoned-out people whose idea of progress is to give the land back to the savages, and whose solutions to our problems is to go communist. Now Marty, listen, I don't begrudge someone working hard and owning a piece of property for the rest of their life, but when that property is taken out of circulation for criminal purposes, then I say society has an obligation to regain control of that land and the good institutions that ought to be maintained by it, and the taxes and profits it generates."

Marty stood up again and even started for the door, then turned back and said, "I'm glad you get my point. It helps me understand a lot of stuff going on around here. It helps me understand why you keep the bails so high that the jail can't hold anybody else no matter what crime they commit. It helps me understand why you and your backers will do anything to scare the public so that when you find some goddam bombs somewhere you get all the credit for making life safe again. I'll tell you one more thing, Reynolds, and it might be the last thing I ever bother to tell you. This is still the frontier out here. It's still a place where a person gets respect if he can take care of himself, raise a family, and use the land for something besides a quick sale to a California gold-digger. There's enough of that old pioneer spirit left that some people still go by the motto, 'you leave me alone and I'll leave you alone.' And, in spite of that, they'll still go out of their way to help someone who's really in trouble. I told you I liked it here, and I'd like it to stay the way it's been as much as possible, and your progress and development don't mean shit to me." He put his hand on the door handle and then turned back to face Reynolds. "And the last thing is, if you or your buddies ever come on my land, armed or not, I'll probably shoot you first and ask questions later. And that's self-defense." He flung opened the door, and slammed it shut behind.

Reynolds sat thoughtfully for a long moment, waiting for the first wave of reaction to pass through him and for calm to return to the atmosphere of his office. Poor Marty, he mused, must think he's Wyatt Earp or somebody like that, way he's carrying on. Too bad he can't just be ignored, but there seems to be a real possibility he's got an even worse breakdown coming. Reynolds wasn't sure what he should do about it, but one thing was clear: the Sheriff was beginning to sound more and more like someone speaking out on the side of the lawbreakers. Next thing you know, he'd be endorsing that Sonya Lehman candidacy. He thought on this a little longer and then decided not to let it worry him, unless it really started to get out of hand. He was glad Marty had shown his hand as much as he did. It never hurt to know what a man really felt when he was upset about something. What was truly surprising was that this one incident, the attempted murder charge against a trigger-happy grower, was turning out to be the final straw for the Sheriff.

For his part, Marty left the DA's office with a genuine feeling of relief. Never again would he kowtow to Reynolds on anything. He knew the man didn't think much of him, but now he also knew that his thoughts about the DA were right on target. The man was in this for the power and influence he could gain with the money people in the area, and to hell with the spirit of the law or the customs of the people. Marty himself was still not about to endorse marijuana, but he sure was going to try and minimize its negative impacts on his life and job for his final two years.

As Peter worked his way down the slippery side of the rain-soaked ridge, he was thinking mostly about the things that hadn't gone wrong with his crop. He had worried about thieves, cops, beavers, and mold, and so far, nothing had really gotten to the plants. He reached out and tapped his knuckles on an old stump. Now it was time and nearly past time to harvest and he could no longer put it off. That detective and his partner had been back twice, fishing for more information about Jerry, and about pot in the area. Each time they'd given Peter the kind of probing scrutiny that suggested they were looking for the right handle by which to get to Peter himself. The guy also mentioned that they expected Peter to make himself available for testifying when the case went to trial. No idea when that would be, but they'd asked him not to leave the county without letting the DA's office know about it.

For the past several years, he'd been able to spread his harvest out over most of the month of October, gathering, drying, and processing it in manageable amounts. In that way most of it was able to fit inside his trailer and although it made living there somewhat absurd, and he slept outside under the awning as much as he could, it worked out. Now, with the threat of unannounced visits, he'd had to come up with something else. It wasn't a very good solution, but the biggest trailer he could get from the U-Haul place was parked about 100 feet from his live-in trailer and covered with green canvas and brush. The only way he figured it could be discovered would be if someone tripped over the extension cord that ran under the leaves from his home place to the small electric fan-heater in the U-Haul. At first, he'd thought it was a good solution, but the more time he had to work with it and think about it, the more he realized that anything on his land was subject to discovery, accidental or with a warrant, and there was nothing more he could do about it except leave it all behind, or live with the risk. Since he couldn't afford to leave without the crop, and he'd been living with plenty of risk for a long time, he knew he'd stick it out, come what may. Up to the point that detective or some other gung-ho cop got carried away trying to find out more about him, he thought he'd be all right. But he wanted to be sure and ask Sonya about search and seizure laws next time he could, just as a kind of preparedness.

The rain stopped during the night, and that morning brought with it perfect mold conditions. He reached the patch on his hands and knees and felt the usual sense of relaxed tension to see that it was all still there. He heard the low boom of a hunting rifle repeated twice, far away. He'd hoped by coming this late in the morning he could avoid both hunters and Forest Service workers. Sounded like somebody was still on the chase out there a couple of ridges away. He took his garden clippers out of his jacket pocket and stood up beside the first plant that had gone in the ground what seemed a long ago, in the springtime. In his mind and with his lips moving, he told the tall female how much he appreciated what she and her sisters had done with their lives here, with the nutrients and the sun, with the water and the care he brought to them. He asked her to understand that she was beginning to die anyway, but that he had to take her now so she would be able to repay him for his efforts in giving her this life. He reached as high as he could and bent the top of the plant toward his face, inspecting it carefully. Barely any mold yet, but plenty of the tiny red hairs that signaled ripeness. He inhaled her perfume, and even rubbed the top flowers across his face. He held the foot-long sticky top of the plant with its solid thick cluster of flowers, held it in one hand and inhaled once again. Then he clipped the top from the rest of the stalk, and this year's harvest began in earnest.

He went on clipping branches from the six plants in this patch, all of them in primo maturity. He stuffed them in a plastic garbage bag and sat on a stump to rest up for the climb out. It seemed to him that he was getting tired easier these days, and he hoped it was just the change in the seasons and not some sickness. He couldn't afford any of that. Not yet. He took out his pouch and rolled a joint. As he smoked, he looked around with the familiar sadness of this time of year. He always felt the loss of the plants that were his living companions for a good part of the year, and even though he was impatient for the product of his work to be bagged up and sold as soon as possible, he knew he would miss the challenges of the growing season. The way things were going he didn't even know if he'd still be around for the next year, or if this would even be possible anymore. Then he thought about how much work there was before this harvest was over. One thing at a time, he reminded himself, it must get done, and it will be done.

He pinched off the tip of the joint and put the unsmoked remainder in his shirt pocket for the ride home. He'd really been counting on Jerry and Carla to help him with cleaning and manicuring the buds. Carla was civil toward him, but since that night when they got Jerry out on with his bail money, she hadn't allowed him to relax around her in any way. Of course, she blamed him, even though Jerry had told her that Peter only gave him the plants because he'd asked for them. And that had been because he was out of work. In any case there was no way she would or should take any pot into her house now, no matter what they owed Peter for putting up most of the collateral for the bail bond. Once the thief regained had consciousness after a week and a half, the bail came down to $50,000 with $3,000 in cash deposited with the bondsman. It looked like the young guy would recover, but he hadn't regained his full memory yet, and there was still no trace of the other thief or Jerry's dog.

He stood up and shouldered the bag of green branches. Maybe, he thought to himself, laughing, maybe he could get Sonya to help trim the buds. He started up the ridge thinking about her campaigning with telltale black resin stains on her fingertips. She was going to be completely swamped the next few weeks anyway. The election was less than a month away, and she had to prepare for the debate and appear at so many events. It was getting to be a hassle trying to be a somewhat secret visitor to her house in town, but that was the only way he could get to see her.

He pulled on vine maple branches to help him climb, admiring the flaming colors of the leaves, the brilliant reds and yellows that meant each leaf had done its job and was now about to drop. Again, he heard a faraway shot, and wondered what might have died, a deer, or just a beer can on a stump. Never know this time of year. He looked back down the way he'd climbed this far and wondered if his tracks could be noticed by anyone happening along here. Pretty unlikely anyone would be here anyway, still he didn't want anything to go wrong now. He scrambled over rocks and then walked the length of an old charred tree trunk lying crossways on the slope. A raven croaked from the opposite ridge, and he could see it flying away toward the coast, almost losing it in the gathering darkness. He hurried up the rest of the climb and reached the landing. He figured it would only take coming back for two more trips down in this area, two more trips here and then the two other patches.

He was hungry and trotted down the road to where the pickup was hidden. He wanted to stop by Tom and Leslie's to ask if they or someone they trusted might want trimming work, but there was still too much to do with this batch tonight. He'd have to talk to them the in next day or two. He also needed to get hold of Ron and find out what was happening with Jerry's preliminary hearing, but what he really wanted to do was drive to Sonya's so they could try to enjoy themselves. It was over a week now since they'd had any quiet time together, and he was truly missing her. He tried to imagine her house filled up with drying bundles of fragrant branches and wondered why he hadn't thought of her place before. After all, it would be a great way to end a campaign, a bust of the candidate in her own house, especially if she wasn't going to win anyway. No, be serious, he thought, he was already jeopardizing her enough in several ways, no sense making it worse. On the other hand, who would suspect her? When he got to the truck, he arranged the bag behind the seat and headed for home. He'd make some phone calls at the store, see if he could line up some other help, and then it would be home to eat and start the drying work.

Sonya felt like a leaf in a whirlwind. It wasn't so much that she had more to keep up with than anyone could possibly do alone, it was that everything seemed so equal in importance, and nothing seemed optional anymore. There was either some personal appearance or interview scheduled almost every day until the election, as well as the debate to prepare for. Meanwhile, she knew Peter wondered if there was any time for them to be together, and she still needed to put time in at her own law office or run out of money for paying the bills of her regular life.

All along she'd been afraid of a letdown at the end of the campaign. She just never figured on being a contender and had often thought how unfair it was to the staff that they were putting in all this energy and heart with no real chance of success. However, somehow the opposite was now going on. Terry's latest polling showed that about half the voters considered the shooting incident a case of self-defense rather than the DA's charge of attempted murder. Of course, they had to know the poll wasn't totally reliable because of the haste with which it was put together, but it did confirm her original intuition about the incident. She had come out with a statement before that young man regained consciousness and had tried to frame the issue by dividing it into two distinct legal frameworks. The first was the matter of the shooting, trespass, and the right of self-defense. In her interpretation, the issue of the marijuana cultivation was totally separate. In response to follow-up questions from the media, she said that although in this case the two issues were certainly linked, legally they had to be separated and handled that way. Of course, all the public discussion was being carried on in the abstract so that no one involved in the prosecution or defense would be commenting on the actual case to prejudice the proceedings when the trial came to pass.

The biggest surprise among all the unpredictable aspects of the event was the Sheriff's call the day before she was to address the countywide Neighborhood Watch meeting. He'd offered her his support for her stand on the issue of self-defense and assured her that he hadn't forgotten his pledge to do something with the information he had concerning the boobytrap incident. He confided that he still wasn't sure how to go about it, but that some time before the election he was planning to go to the public with that information regarding the operation of his department, as well as about the rest of the law enforcement effort in the county.

Sonya had thanked him and asked what she could do for him in return. He replied that since he wasn't doing it specifically for her, she didn't owe him anything, but if she really wanted to help him, she should win the election so he didn't have to deal with Reynolds and his wealthy backers anymore. When she asked what he meant by that, he said it wasn't important, just one of his pet peeves. He also asked her not to discuss their conversations with anyone, and she'd agreed.

At the Tuesday campaign committee meeting the week before the debate, Dan announced they now had enough money in the media account to run two more TV spots during the final week before the voting. Sonya immediately thought of the Sheriff and wondered if he'd be willing to go so far as to give his support, either on film or just in a quotation. Although she couldn't speak directly about it to Dan, she did let him know she might have something for the final TV blitz and she would let him know as soon as possible if it worked out. The meeting showed that morale was high, and the group was getting caught up in an emerging sense of a possible victory. There was still nothing tangible to support that feeling, but the enthusiasm of those who worked the telephones with Terry was hard to disregard. Janet was now working fulltime, coordinating a mobile leaflet and information booth, hitting the circuit of shopping areas and entertainment events. Her report indicated a lot of interest in Sonya's candidacy from people who probably never before cared one way or another who was in the DA's office.

After the meeting, Corinne privately told Sonya that her partner was going to be released from prison within the next week, and that he wanted to do anything he could to help out with the campaign. One thing he'd mentioned was that Sonya was getting known inside the jails for her work on the overcrowding issues, as well as her other positions. Even though they couldn't vote, the inmates were passing the word to their families and friends to support her. He said he'd like to organize a "Convicts for Sonya" group, but he knew it wouldn't be too good for her if she was known as the candidate of choice among the criminals.

It was still mid-evening when the meeting ended and she turned down a couple of invites to go out, making the excuse that she was just too tired. In fact, just the opposite was true, she was restless and lonesome, getting to the point where it seemed everything was dropping out from her and it didn't feel like anything was coming back in. Sure, now there was some optimism and hope that maybe all their hard work would at least allow for a decent showing in the election, and there were plenty of people who stopped her on the street just to say they recognized her and wanted to wish her well. Of course, she was happy the Sheriff was promising to try and help her, but for Sonya herself, not Sonya the candidate, but herself, there was a kind of background unhappiness that was getting harder to ignore. As close as she could come to identifying it was to pin it on the unresolved nature of the relationship with Peter.

She looked at the clock as she came in the front door of her house. It said 10:10. If she hurried, she could be out at his place by 11 or so.

It didn't make any sense though. She told herself she wouldn't think about it anymore and went ahead trying to finish off her evening, alone. Suddenly, she changed into some jeans and a sweatshirt, grabbed some things from the bathroom and stuffed them into an overnight bag. She was still arguing with herself about how much she had to do the next day, both at the office and at campaign headquarters. It wasn't until she locked the door behind her that she admitted she really was on her way, running away. What the hell, she thought, everybody deserves some personal life, even when they're running for office. As she drove down the street and turned west, she had a mental picture of Joan Mondale, wondering how she was holding up in the final weeks of the campaign. She must realize it was looking bad for her husband, but they couldn't afford to admit it or act like that. As she left the bright night lights of town behind, she was still wondering about the other women on the campaign trails. How did Mrs. Mondale and Mrs. Ferraro get along on the personal level? Sonya thought she herself was probably being helped in small ways by Ferraro's nomination to run for vice-president, if only because it helped to legitimize the role of women in politics. All in all, she realized this whole campaign was a mind-opener for her. Even though she was feeling on the verge of burning out, she knew she wouldn't want to change much of it if she could have. It was the most exciting thing she had done with her life up to this point, and she was satisfied she was giving it her best effort.

See, just break loose, jump in the car and head for the hills, and you'll feel better, guaranteed. She was thinking too about the irony in her life now, how the more she gained in stature as a woman and as a political player, the more she would have to sacrifice some of the attachment she felt for this man. Suppose she did get elected, then what? An ongoing part-time, see-you-when-I-can relationship that would require each of them to make sacrifices that neither of them would be comfortable with? Or would her success put an end to it for them? Why did she think that way? Because they'd have to hide it? And what if she lost and was her own person again? Could they ever find some way to harmonize their lifestyles and come up with a living arrangement satisfactory for them both? What, like marriage? Why not? Well, lots of good reasons why not. So, Miss Sonya, why even think about it? Except that you grow up assuming love and marriage go together like an old song and you feel somehow incomplete without the legal license to love. Besides, if you're not married, what are you? Of course, these days it isn't supposed to be all that important; individuals have their own identity, even within marriage, and theoretically if you don't have children no one should care one way or another. But that's the subject that will have to be confronted someday, or just forgotten about all together. How many times during the years with Mike had she told herself, Later, we'll get to it later when things will be better anyway, we'll be more secure, more mature, and with more time for having a child or two? Now it was later, much later, and too late for her and Mike, that was for sure. Objectively you could say it was best this way because it's better not to have divorce complicated by children. On the other hand, children might have made it different.

She was already halfway to Peter's when she happened to check the gas gauge and notice how low it was. There would be enough to get to his place but getting back to town before the country store opened might be a problem. So, one more thing to worry about. She put it out of her mind and let the subject of children take over her thoughts again, this time thinking she really didn't know where he was at about children. Not that it mattered yet, but when do you get around to discussing that kind of thing in a new relationship? She could wait for him to bring it up, but he probably wouldn't. And if either of them wanted children they probably ought to get started on it soon. There was a kind or urgency in it all that didn't just come from her age but had its roots in some intangible feelings of responsibility to her family, bloodlines and all of that. Curious how long she'd been able to put off the whole issue, only to have it come up now when it wasn't even clear it would make any difference anyway. Again, the election exerted its unknown and significant power over her future. The term of office was four years and it would be hard to have a baby while on that job. So, here she was, stuck between the possibility of professional fulfillment, or personal satisfaction with a man, and the chance for a family. Was it truly possible that losing the vote was her best chance for happiness? She resisted it turning out this way and tried not to believe it was so difficult. It wasn't fair. From the beginning it had always looked like she didn't have a chance, and now she was catching up to where it at least looked like a contest. She could always quit. Wouldn't that look great. How? Screw up on the debate and make stupid comments over the next few weeks? That would be a great way to repay all the people who helped her, no she couldn't, it was a matter of conscience now, she had to go on giving it her best, even if it jeopardized some of the things she might want most in her life. God, why did it all have to be so complicated?

It was 11:10 when she turned onto Peter's road and drove past Jerry and Carla's house. That was one of the biggest chunks of irony right there, she thought, nothing like having your lover's neighbor turn into a key factor on the whole election thing. Sometimes it seemed like the world was just toying with people when coincidence rules so much of everything. Maybe it was just that the older you get the more things there are in your life that can overlap, but this one was almost too much for her, and she had a hard time believing it was really happening.

The light was on in Peter's trailer and his truck was parked in the drive. At least he was home, she thought, relieved. Would have been a great ride out for nothing if he wasn't. She got out of her car and walked across to the trailer. She looked in a small window and didn't see him inside. Then she looked around the yard. Seeing nothing in the darkness, she let herself into the unlocked trailer. The place held an overpowering aroma of fresh pot, but she didn't see any of it around inside. She heard a sound behind her and turned to see Peter smiling in the doorway.

"What the hell?"

"Hi," she said. "I needed to see you."

"Anything happen?"

"No, not yet." She stepped toward him and placed her hands on his shoulders. He was standing on the ground just outside the doorway, giving her the height advantage. "How's it going?" she asked, "Smells great."

"It's okay. You're all right?" He pulled her face close and they spent a long, steadfast moment staring into one another's eyes. Then they kissed. When they finally took a break to breathe, she answered, "Yeah, now I'm all right," and stepped back so he could come in.

He pushed stuff around until there was room for them to sit and then he started water heating for tea. "I was just about to crash. Been trimming buds since this afternoon."

"How's that going?"

"Pretty good. Still not much mold, and I got help from some of your people."

"What do you mean?"

"Leslie's doing a little work for me when she's out here and that woman Corinne and her old man that just got out of jail. They're staying with Leslie until they can get settled somewhere. So, it's a relief it's getting done."

While they waited for the tea, she filled him in on what was happening with her, the places she'd spoken, the Sheriff's call, preparations for the debate and the recent polling that showed her chances still improving. Peter poured the hot water over the herb bags, stirred in honey and asked if she'd like a shot of brandy in hers.

"Sure," she said, and he poured a little in each cup.

"So, you might win?"

"Still doubtful, but now they say it's a remote possibility. A lot of it seems to have to do with your neighbor. How is he, by the way?"

"Jerry's okay. Leg healing pretty good. Still pretty freaked out by being in such a jam, but he's trying to stay on top of it. He and Ron think that if her can get a fair trial, he'll be all right."

"What does he mean by fair?"

"I guess if you win. And if the pot can be kept separate from the shooting part of it. He's scared of what Reynolds might do to him."

"A lot will depend on the judge, on what gets admitted as evidence."

"Yeah," he said, "and the actual charges once it goes to trial."

"Of course. Good tea. Let's just enjoy it and be together." She was glad she'd come out and so was he. The space between them was filled with unanswered questions and assumptions about what they'd have to work out at some point, but for now it was good just to touch and to be together for however briefly.

"When do you have to get back?"

"Early in the morning. What time does the store open? I need gas."

"Seven-thirty. I have some, but you need unleaded."

"That's early enough." She lay back against a pillow, feeling suddenly very tired. "So where are you going to sleep?"

He lifted her legs onto the narrow bed and crawled on top of her. "It's a bunk bed, see?"

"You know, some day we really have to have a long talk."

"About what?"

"Oh, just little things, like a bed, like the future. Stuff like that."

"I know, and like how are we both going to fit here tonight?"

She smiled, but neither of them laughed. It was too much a part of the whole and too much a very real problem to be funny. Where could they fit, as a couple? And when would they start dealing with the realities of their entanglement?

"Don't worry, we'll make it work. I've got to go out and check my dryer one more time. You could get ready for bed. You can push anything out of the way. I'll be right back."

She tried to arrange things better, went into the cubbyhole bathroom and changed into a long T-shirt. There was hardly enough room for her to bend over and put in her birth control and she pushed away the half-formed thought to just forget it and see what happened. Wouldn't that be total irresponsibility after so many years of caution and planned un-parenthood?

She straightened the bed and lay down, thinking how absurd that her heart had the power to overcome every mental obstacle she threw in its way. She almost wanted to cry, out of self-pity, but she knew she didn't deserve it and how would she explain that to Peter? Anyway, best to be happy for the moment and not think about anything else.

Peter tiptoed in and pretended he was trying not to wake her. She watched as he brushed his teeth and undressed. He really had become a very special person for her, and if she could only have faith this was all supposed to happen, maybe that would be enough to carry them through. He eased into the bed beside her and turned off the lamp.

"I know you're tired," he said. "Thought you might already be asleep."

She didn't answer and they lay together, breathing softly, each waiting for the other, waiting for their bodies to ignore their thoughts and either fall asleep or begin the touching. If only there was something that could take them away from the concerns of having to name and define what was happening to them, coming both from the outside world and from within.

They made love slowly, patiently, silently, sharing the awkwardness of the cramped bed as they shared the tastes and touches of one another. Over their time together they'd become lovers in spirit as well as in body, and their need for one another had been growing even as it was being satisfied. Even though they were still new to each other, their easy compatibility made it seem as though they'd been together much longer. By contrast, with the empty years for him and the Mike years for her as the backdrop, there was just a natural comfort in their intimacy that gave this closeness a feeling of history, as if they'd been together somewhere else, before, if not in this lifetime, certainly in some other.

Then they fell asleep, both very tired, tangled and crowded in the cramped space of the bed. They slept restlessly in these unfamiliar confines, and when daylight came, they were both already awake, and nowhere near fully rested, but it was impossible to sleep any longer and Peter crawled out first with a semi-fall to the floor. He put water on to boil for coffee, and came back to the bed and knelt beside it, kissing Sonya and brushing her hair away from her face.

"I love you," he said, "but I guess you know that."

"Mmmm. Do I?"

He pulled the sheet and blanket up to her chin. "Try and sleep a little longer. I'm going out for a couple minutes."

"I can't sleep. Besides, I should get going." She pulled him close to her face and looked into his eyes. "What would happen to us if I won?"

She felt him stiffen slightly, but it passed, and he smiled. "I'd apply for a job, as your secretary."

"I doubt you have the qualifications, but seriously, don't you think about it?"

"Yeah, but I try not to."

"Okay, then how about, what do we do when I lose?"

He got up to make the coffee with the almost boiling water. "I don't know. Maybe I could get a bigger trailer and a good bed. I don't know."

She sat up and wrapped the blanket around her shoulders. "I'm not trying to pressure you. I just don't have any answers myself and I need help, because whenever I think about it I don't get anywhere."

"So maybe I'll leave and make it easy for both of us." He was pouring the water through the grounds. The smell of the fresh brew filled the small space, and the morning seemed a little more friendly.

"Okay, I'm sorry," she said, swinging her legs out from under the covers. "I just feel like it's all so out of our control. I mean, the voters have more to say about our lives than we do. And I don't like to think about it anymore than you do, but it's there and it won't go away."

"That's all true, but we don't have to decide anything right now, do we?" He sat beside her and handed her a cup of coffee. "We just have to let go and see what happens."

"Yes, I know. Wait and see. Here and now. But when I got into running I didn't have much else. Now I do. And if that office is going to get between you and me then maybe I don't want it anymore. Don't you feel how different it is now? In the beginning, I didn't stand a chance. Now, thanks to a lot of weird circumstances, they say I'm going to make a pretty good showing. I mean, if much else happens to help me out, I might really win."

"Are you sure this isn't something you really want?"

"It is if it doesn't cost me too much. But if I can't do it and have you and maybe a chance for a family or something, then what good is it?"

"Hey..." He put his arm around her and drew her close. "You're backing yourself into a corner. I think there's certain things we can count on, but a whole lot more that's outside our control. So, I'd say we have to take what we can get and let the rest of it take care of itself."

"I know. I know." There was more she wanted to say, but she held it back, knowing how different they were when it came to what to worry about. Here she was, all worked up about the personal aspects of their future, and she could tell he was just being patient with her and was a lot more concerned about the day-to-day problems like his harvest, the investigation of Jerry, and even the election, but not in the same direct way she was.

"Look," she went on, "it's just my basic insecurity. Don't let it bring you down."

"I won't, but don't let it bring you down, either."

"No, that's right. I'm not allowed to have normal feelings right now. I especially have to be sharp and on target in this debate or kiss the whole thing goodbye. And I have to put on an act that being the Chinook County DA is the only thing on my mind. But listen, if you happen to get some glimpse of the future, I sure wouldn't mind being let in on it." She pulled herself up off the bed, picked up her clothes and shut herself into the cupboard-sized bathroom.

"I'll be right back. Have to turn on the dryer out there." He grabbed a jacket and let himself out the door.

It was already past seven o'clock when she came out dressed and ready to leave. She made the bed as best she could, pulled on her coat, stepped outside and waited a minute or two. When he didn't return, she got in her car and started warming it up. She couldn't help thinking that he was like somebody holding himself back or holding something back. Why couldn't he just make a commitment that was based on making the best of whatever happened instead of putting it off and leaving it up to the unknown? More to the point, what was there in her own self that was behind this sudden urgency? She could see the logic in where he was at but couldn't just accept it. She saw him coming back toward the trailer from the woods, waving to her. She didn't want to leave this way, but there was no way she could cover up her thoughts completely either. She got back out of the car.

"I've really got to get going."

He came to her side. "Sure, but when do I see you again?"

"I don't know. Call me every chance you get. I wish you had a phone."

"Never needed one before, but I'll get one, one of these days. But listen," he said slowly, "I was just thinking about you. Your life is full right now, probably too full, but there's more than enough to keep you busy and satisfy you if you let it. And I'm here for you. Really. It doesn't seem easy for you to accept that, but I am. So, worry about Reynolds, not me. I want you to win. For you, for Jerry, for the good of the people around here. Now, get yourself some rest and get back there and give'em hell."

"Thanks, Peter. I know I don't give you enough credit for helping me, but you do. You really do. After all, I need someone around to take it all out on."

"Good, whatever you need. And I'm really glad you came out."

"Even if I was on a bummer?"

"I can take the bad with the good. And last night was really good."

He took her in his arms and held her close for a long time, breathing deeply. Then he let go and opened the door for her, helped her in, and leaned down for one more kiss when she rolled down the window.

"Are you going to be able to watch the debate?"

"Wouldn't miss it."

"Okay, I'll wave at you. And thanks again."

"For what? Bye."

He stepped out of the way as she turned around and pulled out. He waved and turned back to the trailer. A strong wave-like feeling came over him, the kind of nameless feeling he wasn't used to. He missed her not being able to stay, not being around more. It was getting harder to think about not being with her in the future, and no matter how much he tried to reassure her, that same sense of impossibility continued to take up a lot of his own thinking. He poured another cup of coffee and tried to focus and the day's work ahead. He had to start with packaging the stuff he'd picked up from his helpers the day before. Then head up to harvest the rest of that patch. The forecast was for rain and he wanted that batch while it was still mostly dry.

A few hours later, when he was fixing some lunch, he heard a rig coming up the driveway. He checked out the window and was relieved to see it was Jerry. He was always so jumpy this time of year, but now there was more reason than ever to be paranoid. He waved out the door to show Jerry he was home and went back to the sandwich. His friend stopped in the doorway, and asked, "How's it going?"

"So-so. Want a grilled cheese?"

"No thanks, just ate. And I found my dog."

"Where?"

"Down past the patch. I kept looking every couple of days. Finally, yesterday, it was the smell took me to it."

"Could you tell anything?"

"Too far gone. Pissed me off again. I was getting over that part, still hoping he might come back. Me and that dog been through a lot. I buried him in the patch where the stuff was dug up."

"Sorry that happened. The whole thing is a bummer."

"Yeah. Got any coffee?"

Peter got a cupful for him when he sat on some firewood just outside the doorway.

"Saw somebody headed out this morning. Your girlfriend?"

"Yeah. You sure got involved in trouble at the right time for her."

"What do you mean?"

"Reynolds is so gung-ho to get you that she's looking good to some people for standing up for your right to protect yourself."

"Yeah. That lawyer, Ron, says the publicity is great. Says it's great to have the candidates debating my case even if they can't mention it directly. He also said the more time we have before the trial, the more it's going to cost, but it's still to our advantage. Not sure I understand that."

"Don't worry about the cost," Peter said. "You've got enough else to deal with."

"I can worry about it. I just can't do much about it."

"I'm willing to put in as much as I can. It's like insurance to me. I haven't been busted all these years, so I kind of owe it." He knocked on a piece of wood.

"Yeah, but that's not fair. I appreciate it and I'd like to do something for you. If I can. I know I can't trim your pot at my place because of Carla and everything, but if you need firewood or whatever, let me know. I already owe you for the bail."

"I'll get that back, if you don't split on me."

"Sometimes I think about that," Jerry said. "I get pretty depressed thinking about how I really could get convicted and do a lot of time.

And the way things are with Carla, she's still so pissed off maybe I should leave for a while."

"Let me just say, it wouldn't do any good. You start hiding, it'll never stop, especially when you've got a chance to beat this thing. And if Sonya does win, she'll for sure lower the charges."

"I know. Sometimes, it just seems like running away is the easiest way. I'll probably never get a job around here now, even if things do open up again."

"Don't be too sure. You might end up some kind of local hero. There's still a lot of people more scared of rip-offs than pot growers. A lot of people who are tired of watching the cops chasing after plants when they don't even patrol the neighborhoods."

"Yeah, I hope so."

"So, Carla's still pissed," he said as he went back inside to make another sandwich. "But how's the baby?"

"She's fine. Except when she's getting a new tooth. That's pretty hard on her."

"Must be. I've never lived around a baby. It must be amazing."

"It is. She's so anxious to do everything. She's funny too. Hey, there's something else I need to tell you. That detective was back out here. Asked me more questions about you than about me. Didn't say what he wanted, but asked how long you lived here, what you do for a living, did you have a wife. That was about it."

"Shit," Peter said as he came back out with his second sandwich. "Did he say when he's coming back?"

"No, but I don't think he will. Just wanted to measure everything one more time. I think they might have found out who the other guy is, the one that got away."

"The wounded guy probably told them."

"Yeah," he stood and set his empty cup on the chopping block. "Well, I actually have a possible fencing job at the Petersons. Have to go see if they've decided. At least people still talk to me around here."

"Hope you get it. And let me know right away if the cops come back, or if you hear they're asking about me anymore."

"I will." Jerry turned to look at him. "Again, I'm really sorry about the heat on you. Couldn't have come at a worse time."

"Yeah...They don't have any right to hassle me, but who knows what they do these days."

Jerry stopped again, on his way back to the truck. "Hey, be sure to let me know if I can help in any way. Like if you need to use this truck or anything."

"I might. I might do that. Good luck on that job."

"Yeah, see ya."

Peter went back inside the trailer. He probably should be using that truck for its looks, but if he did get stopped in a truck registered in Jerry's name, it would make it worse on them both. Just what he needed...A cop curious about him in the middle of harvest. It never let up. If you make it past the beaver, mold, road crews, thieves and helicopters, you still need to deal with what happens to your neighbor. Jerry wasn't the only one who sometimes considering splitting from the area. If the heat got any more intense there might not be much chance or choice.

The debate was on a Wednesday night, three weeks before the election. The newspaper that morning ran a story in which the DA was quoted as saying they were able to find a witness in the pot shoot-out case, but that the testimony of the witness couldn't be revealed pending the preliminary hearing. While the witness's name and connection to the case was kept secret, the article surmised that it had to be the other thief, and that the wounded man had supplied the investigating officers with the information. The article also reported the shooting victim was about to leave the convalescent home on his way to what looked like a complete recovery.

Sonya and Dan were going over the list of already determined debate questions when Terry rushed in with a copy of the newspaper. He thrust it in front of them, saying, "He's sure got great timing." They scanned the article and Sonya asked, "Do you think this will make any difference?"

Dan finished reading the conclusion on the second page and replied. "No, not at least tonight. He can get away with saying this kind of stuff, but he can't comment directly on the case if it involved either his opinion or information that isn't already in the public record. But Terry's right. He's using everything he's got and using it all pretty well."

"So, help me out here. What should I say when I'm asked about the way he's handling it?"

"Same as we've said all along. He's using the pot to make the shooting look worse than it is, and he's giving prejudicial advantage to the thieves by not charging them the same as the property owner. By the way, the pot wasn't on that man's property either, but we should hold on to that until the right time."

Terry nodded and said, "Shouldn't both of those guys be charged now?"

"I don't think this new witness makes any difference except that it reemphasizes that nothing is being done to prosecute what we're pretty sure was trespassing. This second guy should be charged now that he's been found, along with the first guy. And Reynolds knows it." He handed the newspaper back to Terry. "But he's banking on the anti-pot sentiment to isolate you. Who knows what he'd do with the case if he won the election?"

Sonya turned to Terry and asked, "Have you got any more results on your new poll?"

"Not really. The urban-rural breakdown is holding steady. Much higher percent of the rural agree with your position, either because of the gun angle or the pot. The people here in town react to how the question is being phrased. If we mention guns, they back away, but if we just ask about the right to defend property they're into it."

"I'll try and remember that. What else?"

"The other split is between senior citizens and the rest. The older folks are funny about this because they all want to talk to someone, and we're who they're talking to. What they want is more patrols, especially in rural areas. When we redirect the question to self-protection, they are very much in favor of people being able to protect themselves. The ones living out outside town really feel vulnerable. A lot of them mention

Neighborhood Watch and how they want more programs like that. Younger people, heads of families, seem to feel they can't do much about crime, that's it's random, and that they pay for insurance because there's not much alternative. That's an overview, a generalization for sure, and I won't defend any of this as perfect polling, but's we're finding it's a lot of gut-level stuff."

Dan asked, "What have you got ready to follow up with tonight?"

"We'll place between 300 and 500 calls between the end of the debate and tomorrow night. Here are the questions we've settled on. And I left room for about two more to be decided on after we see how it goes. Sonya, the more you concentrate on prevention rather than prosecution, the better off we'll be. People really understand the difference and Reynolds is pretty shaky on his crime-prevention programs. I think they're less than five per cent of his budget right now, but don't use that figure"

"Okay, thanks Terry, good work. I hope I can remember everything,"

"You will. Good luck." He raised his fist to her.

Dan and Sonya returned to their prepared list of questions. When they'd covered as much as they could, they arranged to meet at the studio by seven that night. Sonya gathered her coat and briefcase and said goodbye to several people working on campaign projects, and waved across the room to Janet, who was on the phone. She accepted the good wishes of everyone as she left. She wanted to be at home, spending a couple of quiet hours alone before this thing happened.

When she reached her home there was a letter from Mike among the junk mail and bills, He was doing fine, still waiting for the situation in Seattle to be resolved, missing her and wishing her the best of luck in the election. As she read it over a second time, she ran water for a bath and started a new pot of coffee. It was hard to decide whether to eat before the debate or not. She settled on a salad and added tuna for protein. Janet had invited her over for dinner if she wanted it, but she'd declined, knowing that the best preparation for her was this quiet time alone. She placed the salad in the refrigerator for a little later and went into the steaming bathroom.

It still took her by surprise sometimes, when she looked in the mirror and saw the face from the posters and billboards staring back at her. She wiped the fog from the mirror, thinking, yes that's me and I'm really doing this whole thing and I still don't know why except that it happened to me and it seemed like a good idea at first. Besides, it's too late to back out now. She stepped into the tub and slowly lowered herself into the hot water. It felt good, so good, and as she lay there soaking away the tension in her muscles, she let the rest of the world float away for many minutes. It was ironic that Mike was coming back around, and even seemed interested again. She supposed that should make her feel good, kind of like a backup in case everything else fell through, but going back to him, to them together, would be like more of a defeat than losing the election.

She wondered about herself and the way things happened to her. Was she lacking in some drive or attitude so that the most important things in her life, like Mike breaking up with her or the nomination, the most important things in her life happened to her rather than being caused by her own initiative? She soaped one leg and drew the razor smoothly across her skin. Was she just the passive type who was somehow miscast in a competitive role? Or was she really a competitor who didn't recognize it in herself and didn't express it very much? Here she was, only hours away from a verbal duel with a heavy-duty opponent, and she still didn't really feel like competing with him. As she shaved the other leg, turning it carefully to meet the blade, she told herself she'd better start her mental countdown soon. Look at her and Peter...Who was the aggressor in their situation? Certainly not him, but she didn't feel like she'd chased him either. Maybe things just happen to some people while other people make things happen. In any case, a whole lot about her own future would be decided by how she acted and what she said in this debate. If for no other reasons besides her personal feelings, she'd better be ready to do her best at something she'd never done before. She wondered where Peter would be watching. He's said he would be. Probably at his neighbor's place or with Tom. Leslie would be with her. She hoped she didn't think about him once it got started, it could really throw her off if she started worrying about losing him by winning the debate and the election. But really, she wouldn't be losing him no matter what. Their thing, whatever it was, wasn't something that could be possessed or lost, it was just a feeling that felt good, and it was her insecurity that wanted it labelled, wrapped and set outside of time and process.

She could have stayed in the tub for hours, but she knew it was time to get a move on, time to get ready, to go through the last-minute clothes frenzy, the final review of the note cards, and the nerve-wracking steps that still had to be taken, like the makeup session at the studio. The next few hours were going to be awful, so might as well get them over with. She stood up, brushed the water from her skin, toweled and stepped out to give herself one last bit of advice in the mirror: "Sonya, you can do it. Give him hell!" She shook her fist at her foggy reflection and pulled on a robe. Time to get serious.

Once she arrived at the studio, there was no turning back. She said a polite "Hello" to Mrs. Reynolds, whom she met on her way to the women's dressing rooms, waved at some of the production staff she was acquainted with from campaign functions, and was relieved to find Janet waiting for her in a dressing room with SONYA taped to the door.

At five minutes to eight there was a knock on the door and the words, "Places, please," from a voice on the other side. She patted her hair and straightened her clothing one more time, took a kiss on the cheek from Janet, and stepped out into the passageway to the stage. In the wing, she spoke softly with Dan about his advice to play down any connection with the national party. They had agreed to avoid linking her with Mondale as much as possible without denying she was a Democratic candidate. The larger polls showed that Chinook County, like the rest of the country, was leaning toward what could turn into a Reagan landslide. Although she was running against some of the Reagan-style policies, even the local party people acknowledged that identifying with Mondale-Ferraro would gain little or nothing on the local and state levels.

The moderator for the debate was the public speaking instructor and debate team coach at the local community college, and the panel who would be putting the questions to Sonya and Reynolds was made up of three representatives from the local newspaper and radio stations. They were already seated in place when Sonya took her seat on one side of the stage and Reynolds took a chair on the other side. At precisely eight o'clock on the stage set timer, a red light flashed on above one of the TV cameras and the program began. The moderator introduced them and explained the format, and then the first series of questions, concerning fiscal and staffing matters, began.

Both candidates agreed that available funding from the usual sources of county revenue was shrinking and all departments of local government had to find ways to adjust to this reality. Reynolds emphasized the mandated responsibilities of his office and pointed out there might be grants and other sources available for discretionary programs such as Neighborhood Watch and others involving citizen participation. Sonya spoke of the need to prioritize the law enforcement functions of the office, and said she felt that prevention programs such as Neighborhood Watch, and the Rape Crisis Center should have dependable funding rather than the erratic nature of gifts and donations. These programs, she said, could do so much to eliminate costs by significantly reducing the number of incidents that need to reach the stage of court proceedings. On the question of staffing, both candidates pledged to operate the office with as few employees as possible. Reynolds claimed it was already that way under his management, especially in the light of recent layoffs. Sonya said that if elected she would have to evaluate the personnel situation once she was in office. She mentioned the need to make sure that the number of deputy prosecutors wasn't higher than it needed to be since law clerks and others could do so much of the pre-trial work and were certainly more economical as the Deputy Prosecutors. She also went on to say that, as DA, she would try to prosecute more cases herself than her opponent seemed to be willing to take on. Reynolds replied that he thought it was nice of her to promise to give the county so much overtime since he was already working as much as possible and it wasn't enough to keep up with the duties he couldn't neglect. She said maybe she would work at her own desk and eat lunch at the same time rather than spend as much time and money on high-class luncheon appointments. The moderator interrupted the exchange and moved the debate to the overcrowded jail issue.

Reynolds went first and portrayed that issue as simply one of economic recession and higher unemployment, and the resultant increased crime. He said that one of the main projects of his next term would be to get a measure on the ballot, and get it passed, one that would lead to the construction of new facilities without adding to the burden of the taxpayer. Sonya responded by questioning whether that was either possible or necessary. She said that her research showed a much higher percentage of pre-trial inmates could be released on affordable bond or their own recognizance with almost no change in the trial appearance ratio. She said that if new accommodations were really needed, it would be more affordable to create more halfway housing and to improve the existing jail and associated facilities so they could more readily meet the standards outlined in the current court action concerning this problem. Reynolds replied somewhat heatedly that if the county could hold all the offenders deemed a flight risk or danger, then it was up to the sheriff to push for more facilities rather than leave it up to the DA to set more criminals free to roam the streets. Sonya then produced a graph and read from it. It explained that over thirty percent of the inmates currently in the county jail were being held for victimless crimes and their average bail was being set at the same or more as the twenty-five per cent being held for assault with and without weapons. The remaining forty-five percent were being held for crimes involving property or failure to pay fines, child support, or other court-ordered penalties. She asked whether it was reasonable to assume that county government needed to spend more money on facilities that would be used essentially to keep harmless individuals off the street. Or was it perhaps, she suggested, that this was another great construction project designed to line the pockets of people who had already grown wealthy from civic improvements such as the still unfinished sewage treatment plant that wouldn't be needed for at least another ten years. Reynolds countered her argument with an emotional declaration that those who were considered harmless by his opponent were exactly that element who refused to pay the bills of living in this society and lived by ripping off decent people's property, and by living off the fruits of illegally gotten and untaxed income.

The moderator announced a time out for a station break, and the moment the red light went off the whole stage relaxed into a school recess atmosphere as technicians rearranged their cameras and panelists got up and moved around. An assistant wiped Sonya and Reynolds's faces free of sweat from the lights and their make-up was redone. Dan came over to Sonya and told her she was doing well, but to be very careful in the next segment not to be drawn into an emotional reaction no matter what came down. He reminded her that her image was best expressed as one of concern and practicality, and she needed to maintain that stance through the hot issues still to come. She thanked him and took her place behind her podium as the warning buzzer sounded.

The first question was from the editor of the newspaper, and he asked if each of them would comment on their approach to the problem of illegal drug trafficking and marijuana cultivation in the county, for the time being leaving aside any violence often associated with this activity. Sonya was called on first and stated her position as clearly as she could, saying that there were already more laws on the books than could be adequately enforced and it was therefore the obligation of the DA's office to prioritize crimes and the resources available to handle them in the correct manner. In the current situation of reduced people power and resources being stretched thin, they needed to concentrate on those classes of criminal activity which result in injury or loss to the county's citizens. Secondly, she said, those offenders who avoid paying court-ordered fines should be the object of detection and rigid enforcement since their apprehension contributed to the overall expenses of law enforcement. If, and she emphasized if, there was still money and personnel available, then they could address those laws which covered personal behavior, as well as the laws which were viewed as outdated or unnecessary by the majority of the population. As examples she mentioned the laws against plowing and harvesting on Sundays, which were still on the books, as well as the laws against non-addictive drugs. The bottom line for her was that she would continue to work against laws that attempted to police victimless personal behavior, since the abolition of a bad law was as important to a functioning democracy as the enforcement of good ones.

Reynolds was called on and took a long pause before launching into his description of a county held hostage by the illicit entrepreneurs of illegal and dangerous drugs. He pointed out that the definition of a victimless crime had to be broad enough to include the health hazards of marijuana as well as the decline in learning and productivity that accompanies its use by school-age youth and by workers. He said it was very difficult to separate the issue because he knew of no place where drugs and violence did not go hand in hand. He said that he remained committed to supporting the President's efforts to wipe out the trafficking and manufacture of all illegal drugs. Only when the people of Chinook County stood up for their rights and made it too hot for criminal activity to flourish, only then would the decent people of this county be safe from the side-effects of drugs, such as terror and degeneracy. As his final note, he added that if his opponent weren't so personally involved with elements of the growers' underground, she would be able to think more clearly about the danger this element posed to the public in general. Sonya shot a quick look at him and wondered exactly what he was referring to, but the moderator called for another question before she could ask.

That next question was posed by the local TV news anchorman, and it was a thinly disguised account of the shooting which had occurred over an alleged marijuana theft. The candidates were asked to comment on how they would handle a hypothetical case of trespass, theft, and shooting if the possession of the good being stolen was in itself an illegal act. It was Reynolds's turn to answer first, and he said if it was the mafia getting ripped off, or a drug dealer or grower, that this made the situation different than if it were a law-abiding citizen defending their own legal property. He said he recognized the apparent legal double standard, but that was no excuse for protecting one criminal from another. He went on to cite two instances of court proceedings in other jurisdictions where stolen property and drugs were taken from the original criminals by others and all parties were given heavier sentences than they would have had the objects or substances had been legal property. He emphasized again that decent citizens have the right to defend their property against criminals, but that criminals have no rights to defend the spoils of their criminal actions.

When it was her turn for rebuttal, Sonya let a long moment of silence pass by as she looked out at the panel and over the studio audience. She wanted to remain calm, and she wanted to make sure she covered everything. She also felt that the atmosphere of the debate was on the verge of becoming hostile and that she would either have to play along with that or find a way to return the whole thing to a tone of reasonable disagreement. She took a deep breath and began talking about how it felt to live in this county and travel through all parts of it during her campaigning. She said she had heard almost nothing about this "state of siege" the DA portrayed, and that with the exception of military-style raids by the summer Marijuana Eradication Task Force, there were only two examples of violence associated with the crop and its growers in this county. Those two examples were very interesting she said, and that the one incident of boobytraps on federal land had apparently been a completely isolated incident rather than the trend that her opponent was trying to make it out to be. The second case of violence involved self-defense rather than defense of illegal property, and for his misuse and misunderstanding of the facts, Mr. Reynolds should perhaps return to law school for a brush-up course on the definitions of assault, attempted manslaughter, self-defense and attempted murder. The very fact that the property owner, in any hypothetical case of this sort, had not even known that the thieves were stealing from him, but had defended himself from being shot at made this kind of incident clearly one of self-defense and not simply the armed defense of stolen property. The moderator flashed her the sign to wrap up her answer in thirty seconds. She finished up by saying that on her watch if a citizen shot back after being shot at then they would not be prosecuted for a crime, certainly not attempted murder. She quickly pledged to uphold the rights of all property owners to protect themselves and their property, and that if possession of that property was illegal, then that must be treated as a distinctly separate matter.

As she finished her sentence, the moderator announced a second and final station break and said that the candidates would return to answer a few questions to clarify their previous comments and then would finish up with final statements. Again, Dan was beside her for a hurried but encouraging conference as someone gently wiped her face so as not to smear the make-up, and she was handed a glass of ice water.

When the red light went on and the moderator started things up again, he attempted to return the line of questioning to the more routine aspects of the DA's functions in county government. Then, the last question came from the newspaper editor who asked each candidate to offer their position regarding media access to the DA's office. As an example, he mentioned the press conference format that Reynolds had been using on occasion and wondered if Sonya would continue to use that or whether there were other types of relationships she or Reynolds could see developing with the media. They both stated their willingness to hold press conferences concerning major issues or breakthroughs in special cases, and they both pledged to maintain an open dialogue with the press. Reynolds stressed the fine line between damaging publicity and accurate information in some controversial criminal cases. Sonya said she was willing to work for the presence of cameras filming in the courtroom if it served the public's interest and didn't jeopardize chances for a fair trial.

For their final statements, each was given five minutes. Sonya was to go first, and as she looked at the panelists and glanced over at Reynolds she felt a wave of weakness pass through her. As the moderator summed up the issues that had been covered, she was thinking that this was getting to be so hard. She let her mind go blank for a moment. Precious time, she told herself, get to it. But there was something holding her back. The whole tone of the proceeding had reached a kind of ultra-seriousness that seemed alienating to what she really wanted to say. In a flash, she realized that it was the format, that of a prize fight, that was wearing her down, and she fumbled with her notes as she tried to think of a way to alter the context of the situation. She almost felt like telling a joke. Had she had known a good one that fit the occasion, she would have. It felt to her like she was taking too long a time, but actually very little time had passed before the moderator asked her again if she were ready with her final statement.

"Yes," she said calmly, "I am. However, I would like the television audience, my opponent, and those here in the studio to imagine with me that we are in a courtroom and I am presenting my final argument in a case, and all of you are the jury." She smiled and added, "Just a little make-believe to lighten things up here a little. Okay?"

The moderator and the panelists nodded agreement and she stepped into the open space between the two podiums and the panel.

"Ladies and gentlemen of the jury, you have before you two defendants. Your duty is to choose which one you will set free, and which shall be sentenced to four years of hard labor in the office of the Chinook County District Attorney. So, me and him." She gestured toward Reynolds. "This choice is of great importance because it has a lot to do with how your money will be spent and what the quality of your lives will be during that time. On the one hand, you have Big Bill Reynolds, known far and wide as a no-holds-barred, nitty-gritty proponent of strict and tough law enforcement, high bails, and no-nonsense treatment of criminal tendencies. He will promise to give you the kind of law enforcement that fills the jails to overcrowding, builds new ones, and prosecutes marijuana growers and self-defenders to the maximum extent of the law. Ask yourselves: Will it be better for you and your families to have this man out on the streets looking for ways to make a living, possibly running for other, higher public offices, or do you want him where you can keep an eye on him, right there in the DA's office he has held onto for the past long years? Think carefully. Do you want this man for your DA?" She paused, knowing she was on thin ice between being silly and being entertaining. Some people might even say she was carelessly throwing away her chances of winning, but her instinct told her it was worth the risk, so she smiled and took two steps closer to the panelists.

"On the other hand, dear jury, you have Miss Softie Sonya Lehman, a woman, yes, a woman who, as we heard tonight, is secretly involved with elements of the shadowy, evil 'Grower's Underground,' a woman who has been on the record as favoring crime prevention over prosecution as a strategy for public safety and saving the people's money. Unlike General Reynolds here, she will not wage war against the producers of smoking substances no more dangerous than the ever-present tobacco because she believes there are better things to do than charge around the countryside spending hundreds of thousands to burn up to a million dollars of the local economy simply because this weed makes people giggle and stay home at night…She thinks it's a better plan to let the people who buy the stuff burn it up themselves and save the taxpayer's money for preventing and dealing with crimes against people, property, and corrupt institutions that do cause widespread harm to the public good and really do threaten the individual citizen's rights to life, liberty, and yes, the pursuit of happiness. Think carefully, given the state of the world, of the country, and of Chinook County, can we afford a woman, this sickeningly sweet woman in a position of responsibility and influence over our lives? This choice is up to you!"

She turned and went back to her podium, then spun around and faced the cameras again, saying, "Seriously," and then continued by describing her very real concern for protecting the freedom of individuals to live without the fears of bodily or material harm, and her determination to make every dollar spent on legal services in the county do more. She closed by once again addressing the audience: "Dear Jury, you don't have to decide tonight, but you do have to decide. No matter who you vote for in this race or even if you don't vote, you are making your decision. Please think carefully about how you would deal with the issues that have been raised in this campaign and in tonight's debate. Vote for the one of us who is most like yourself, and you will be helping to set the direction of the county for years to come. Thank you for your attention."

Reynolds let a few moments go by before he began his summation. When he did start, he said he really didn't think he needed to say very much at all, because it should be clear enough who was the serious candidate and who wasn't in this fight. He went on to paint a verbal picture of a county overwhelmed by the drug trade, and overseen by "Softie Sonya, the Grower's DA." He mentioned Sonya's background in attempting to overturn laws that were passed by the legislature during her years as an ACLU representative and lobbyist. He described the chaos that would follow the election of a person whose attitude toward such important issues was downright frivolous. Once again, he mentioned booby-trap explosives, gun-toting outlaws and the atmosphere of violence that was spreading like a disease wherever illegal dope trafficking was tolerated by the authorities. He then talked about his record of bringing criminals to justice and he promised to continue to protect the law-abiding citizens of the county from the undesirable, unwelcome so-called growers who were seeking to open a bastion of lawlessness and contraband with a lifestyle based on fear and intimidation.

When the moderator motioned that his time was almost up, he closed by saying, "I am not afraid of these outsiders and outlaws, and they know it. If you value your comfort and safety, I'm the one who can give you that as we work together to rid our county of this evil plague, and its supporters who would have you believe that some crimes are better and nicer than others." Then he stopped talking and held out his hands in a pleading motion before going on: "There really is a choice before you, but that choice is not between the other candidate and myself, but a choice between law and order and the forces of lawlessness and disorder." He closed by asking the voters to consider not only their own futures but the futures of their children as well.

With that, the time expired and the red light went off. Sonya walked across the stage and offered her hand to Reynolds. He shook with her, gave her a curious look and said, "You're an interesting opponent, to say the least."

"Thank you, and so are you. See you at the polls." She returned to her podium and gathered her notes and accepted congratulations from her own supporters. Dan gave her an especially strange look didn't say anything that wasn't encouraging. She was feeling the exhilaration of getting it over with, along with feeling of letdown that can come from a particularly intense outpouring of energy. The debate was really the final major event until the election, and it was truly a relief to have it over with. Now to deal with the aftermath.

She realized that neither Janet nor Dan had yet to comment on her break with the traditional seriousness of such events, but she couldn't do anything about it now. That all really came about as an instinctive survival impulse as she felt herself getting sucked deeper and deeper into the conflict, and a seriousness that wasn't at all the way she viewed herself as a somewhat well-rounded person. She was glad she had done something about it on the spur of the moment, and if it was a mistake... Well, whatever, it could have been worse.

Janet said she'd like a ride back to her car at campaign headquarters, and offered to drive for Sonya, who said thanks and slumped into the passenger seat, letting a wave of fatigue pass over and through her. It was almost over now, and she was hoping she could look forward to a somewhat "normal" life once again, whatever that might mean. Janet broke in on her tired thoughts and asked if she had a Softie Sonya costume for Halloween.

"When is it? I forgot all about Halloween."

"In a week, next Wednesday. Got any plans?"

"No, not yet. Is anything happening?"

"I don't know. Hope so," Janet said.

Janet parked the car in the lot next to the office and they went inside. Four people were working the phones and Terry was shuttling back and forth between them. He waved to Sonya and nodded his head up and down enthusiastically. She realized that part of her exhaustion came from standing in a tense position for the entire debate. Janet led her to an easy chair near the backroom door and asked if she wanted any coffee or tea. She sank into the chair and kicked off her shoes, "Sure, if it has brandy in it."

"I'll see what I can do."

She closed her eyes and let phrases from the evening drift through her thoughts. Reynolds had been unexpectedly polite, although he hadn't pulled any punches concerning his themes and his judgements about her. She supposed she could have defended herself a little more, but somehow that didn't seem that worth it. Let the voters decide. It was up to them now, because she could hardly remember why she was even doing this.

Two hands closed over her eyes and a squeaky voice said, "Guess who?"

She could imagine who would be playing like this with her now. "I can't."

"It's just me." The hands pulled away. "One of your personal involvements in the Evil Underground," Peter whispered.

She turned her head around. "What are you doing here?"

"Nothing, just checking out your scene."

"Well, you can see we have no security if you got in here." She held his hand tight, suddenly glad he was there.

He retrieved his hand and asked, "How do you feel?"

"Okay. Really tired and glad it's over."

"I bet," he said and pulled up a folding chair. "I probably shouldn't even be here."

Janet arrived with two cups of hot coffee, and smiled at Peter, then walked over to the phones.

"Why not? Can't make any difference now." She sat up straighter and balanced the cup on the arm of the chair. "But really, why are you here?"

"Had some business in town. Had to get to it this week, so I came in today. I went over to that country-western bar to watch your show. Wanted to see how you do with the cowboys."

"Well, how'd I do, pardner?"

"They, uh, like your looks. Lots of comments on that. And I didn't hear anyone get real upset about what you were saying, hard to tell. Lot of those guys are into pot now on some level. I think that Reynolds has got himself stuck in the past."

"And what about what you thought? Really?"

"You did good. So, you're some kind of stand-up comedian, huh? What made you do that?"

"I really don't know. Intuition, instinct. It was all just getting too serious. Was I bad?"

"No, it was fine, just pretty unusual, I'd say."

"I just figured I had nothing to lose, except the election, of course. Not supposed to win anyway. Peter, it's nice to see you. It really is. I have to stay around here another half hour or so, and then we could go out or go home. Are you staying in?"

"Yeah, if it's okay. Do you think Reynolds knows about me?"

She looked at him and saw real concern in his eyes. "If he does, can't do anything about it now, can he?"

He spoke softly, "Can try and bust me."

"God, I hope not!"

Terry was standing several feet away, waiting to talk to her. She introduced him to her friend Peter, and they listened while he ran down some of the early polling results. She was holding her edge in the rural areas and her support cut across multiple generations so it wasn't just the pot issue, more likely the combination of self-defense and pot. It was looking like she picked up a little in town, with most people responding favorably the question about her ability to handle the job. This was an improvement since before the debate when only two-thirds of those polled thought she was qualified for the office.

"If the election were tomorrow," Terry said, "according to these very approximate projections you would only lose by 12 percentage points. You're gaining fast and we still have more than two weeks."

"But there's not much more happening to make a difference in those two weeks."

"Who knows," Terry said, excitedly, "and, like I said, these results are shaky. Give me two days with a lot more calls and I'll bet you're within ten points."

"Well, thanks for the optimism, Terry. How much longer are you going to work?"

"I'm shutting down the phones pretty soon. If we call after about 9:30 we're bound to bum some of our people out and aggravate some we call. I'll stay a while longer, but I want to get started early in the morning. Dan wants something firm as soon as possible, so we can decide how to use those last two TV spots. Have to know by this weekend."

"Great, thanks again. I think I'm going to go. I'm kind of worn out."

She stood up and sat back down to put on her shoes. Peter leaned over and helped her, smiling as he did. She walked over to where Janet was putting away the last of the files she'd been working on and talked with her for a minute, then she came back to Peter and said she was ready to go.

They decided to just go straight to her place and pick up a pizza on the way. She was too tried to go out and didn't really want to see anybody right then. They got to her place in plenty of time for the 11 o'clock news and snuggled on the couch with the pizza while they waited.

The debate was the lead story of the broadcast. The newscaster introduced the story as the "Showdown between General Bill Reynolds and Softie Sonya Lehman down at the Dixon City Corral." Several excerpts were played that emphasized the candidates' differences on various issues. Reynolds gave a few quotes for his conclusion, and Sonya's summation was given a nearly complete replay. The newscaster came back on, chuckling, "Like she said folks, it's up to you out there to decide who gets sentenced to four years at hard labor in the DA's office." There was a commercial and the news came back on with a story about a house fire that was still burning at news time.

"You got their attention, and it was nice of them to give you that much time."

"For better or for worse," she said unthinkingly, and those classic words hung between them for a long moment. "Sorry, I didn't mean to bring up that kind of stuff," she said quietly.

"You're just something else." He gave her a long kiss and started massaging her feet and calves. "To the world you come on awfully strong, like nothing could fluster you. But I see deep inside there's this little worry-girl who never gives it up. You know what I think? You need to think of all the bad things that can happen and then you can forget about them all unless or until they do happen."

"Thanks, I guess I'm happy you're not like me."

"Maybe I am," he said. "Maybe I am."

He helped her up and then went outside for a few minutes. When he came back in, she was undressing and getting into bed. For the first time since they were together, they didn't make love, just lying there quietly, holding one another gently and drifting through the pre-sleep stage with a comfortable feeling that came from her tiredness and his empathy. He lay awake for a while after she'd fallen asleep, thinking about the DA's comments and their possible effects on his plans. If he really was being watched in connection with Sonya, he would have to be even more careful than he had been, for her sake as well as his own. In a way, they were each jeopardized by the other. Nothing like a little equality, he thought and let sleep come the over him the rest of the way.

It had been raining for several days. Peter lucked out before it started in and was caught up on all but the final bit of his harvest when the rain let up and he had to head up for the last of the plants. It was always this way with him, a few left until the very end, not because they were still growing, but because he put it off as long as possible, knowing that when the last plant is brought in, it's a long time until the next harvest. The harvest stage is the most rewarding, not just in terms of bringing in the value of the processed buds, but also in the way the plants look, smell, and how it feels to be at the end of a whole process rather than somewhere along the way.

As he drove up the steep roads he enjoyed the brilliant reds of the few chittum trees. The vine maples, too, still flashed their remaining reds and yellows through the dark greens of the firs and hemlocks. The sun broke through the clouds and cast bright shafts of light in moving patterns on the wet roadway. It was a good day to be up high.

He parked the truck in a turnaround just past the clear-cut and sat looking out over a series of ridges between where he was and the ocean beyond. It was more than peaceful, above all the tensions of the lowlands, the constant insecurity and scramble that made people into awkward and erratic versions of what the rest of nature was trying to do. He could see clouds without end to the west, looking like more rain was on the way. He sipped the last coffee from the thermos cup and climbed out of his truck. It was perfect weather for a jacket and hat, not cold, but brisk and the air was clean, scrubbed that way by a week of rain and the whole area now briefly shimmering in the temporary glow of the sunlight. Peter thought about how used to this weather, this place, this cycle of planting to harvest, how used to it all he'd become.

It had taken a few years to grow into it, but now it was hard to think about any other way, any other place.

He walked to the slope and started down, taking a new route and startling some quail before he'd gone twenty yards. Looked like a mama and this year's brood, now nearly grown. As he worked his way down and across the open, logged-off land, he could easily remember the springtime and the hot months of summer. He was grateful for this patch making it through. If he used it again next year it would be a little easier; it always was the second time around. His pant legs were soaking from the ferns and brush, and every so often his feet would slide out from under him and he'd bounce down part of the way on his muddy butt.

When he reached the plants, he was sweating enough to take off the jacket and stuff the hat in its pocket. There were still three big ones left here now. He thought he remembered there should be four left. He looked around, counted the empty holes and stumps from the ones he'd already taken, and found one of them was ripped out instead of chopped off. A broken branch lay on the ground and a few leaves were scattered along the ground. He followed the trail of leaves into the brush and found a low, tunnel-like opening. More leaves were snagged on the stickered branches of the salmonberry, going deeper into the brush. On hands and knees, he shoved himself through the thick tangle, working his way closer to the creek. When he reached a point where he could see water through the brush ahead, he found another couple of branches and then half the plant. It was lying at the top of a slick mud slide that went down into a pond in the creek collected behind a beaver dam.

So, they couldn't wait any longer, or maybe they thought he wasn't coming back, or they'd already gathered all the usual food they collected at this time of year and this was all that was still available, maybe a beaver dessert. In any case, it looked like he'd arrived back at this patch just in time to save what was left. He shifted the top four-foot section of the damaged plant around so he could drag it back, thinking, close call. So many things can happen to a plant or a patch between the time its seed sprouts and its buds are smoked, but this had never happened to him before. Did they get high from eating it? Could have been a lot worse, they could have taken it all at any time. Instead, just like him, they waited until the last moment, the morning he was also coming for it. Maybe it was just tax collection, their protection fee for not messing with it before. They were welcome to the part they'd got, but if he hadn't come for another couple of days…There was still a lot left on the other three plants. When he got to where he could stand up again, he checked out the part of the plant he'd recovered. It was a little muddy, but that would shake off when it dried, otherwise it was okay. He spread out his jacket, clipped off the branches and laid them on it.

He went to the smallest of the three remaining plants, admiring its perfect structure and the intensity of color and smell. He took those branches as well, shaking them off to remove any leftover moisture. It was both killing the plant and taking the final product of its life that gave him the feelings of a sort of ritual. He left the stalks of this one and the next, just to symbolically mark his space in case he wanted to use it again, if the beaver had moved away.

The last plant stood alone in the now open space created by his taking of her sisters. A gentle breeze set it to swaying, and the leaves vibrated to the touch of the sunshine. It was a moment of glistening resin and delicate motion. Streaks of purple lined the stalk, signaling its approaching death. He felt he wasn't so much killing these plants as just accelerating their deaths, collecting what would be left behind before mold and rot could get to them, salvaging the body and releasing the spirit. As he took them home and dried and packaged them, he was preparing them for a cremation of sorts in the pipes and joints the beneficiaries of his hard work and their great growth would light up and inhale from. He knew his mind was getting carried away, as if he were more stoned than usual, but that was what happened in the patch, in among the fumes of their final glory. He sat down on a rock to roll a joint. Might as well be normally stoned along with the mental tripping he was doing. It was a bit of a holiday, after all, two days past the new moon, and some five months before he'd be soaking the next year's seeds for starts.

He took a final hit from the smoke and pinched off the still-smoldering coal. He looked over the last plant of his crop and the word "sacrifice" appeared in his thoughts. It wasn't a sacrifice to kill it and then gain from it, was it? A sacrifice was the giving up of something you couldn't afford to lose until you gave it up, and then it turned out to be possible to get along without it. The whole idea of sacrifice was maybe as complicated as peoples' ideas could get. Lots of things were sacrificed by folks who didn't think they could do it or didn't really want to. Like a story he remembered from Sunday school where Abraham had his son all tied up and ready to be killed, the knife held above him, then God changed his mind, and he didn't have to do it. He had to prove he would do it without really knowing why God wanted him to. If you're made to give up your son, you should at least get to know why. Strange how, once he proved he would do it, he didn't have to do it. Peter remembered he never did understand that story and nobody seemed to be able to explain it to him. It was just a test, they said. Kind of like when people need to send their sons off to fight for somebody else's country. You didn't hear much about God being the reason guys had to die in Vietnam. They said the enemy didn't believe in God, or didn't believe the way we do, but he didn't think that was why we had to have the War. No way. It was a waste more than a sacrifice. Strange how many people on both sides had to die and then after more than ten years of it, it didn't seem to make any difference in the world, just screwed up a whole lot of people, and didn't make much difference anyway.

The breeze kicked up again and the plant bowed toward him and waved her branches in gentle swaying movements. She was saying she was ready. He stood and stretched his fingers skyward, pausing while the dizziness passed through and his circulation returned to normal in his legs and arms. "All right," he thought out loud, "Enough of this sentimental stuff. The season's over." He stepped across to the last plant, took the lowest branch in his left hand, said "thank you," and started cutting and clipping. When he'd reached the very top, he took all the branches over to the growing pile on his jacket. He pulled a new plastic garbage bag out of the bushes where he'd stashed his fertilizers and supplies and shoved the branches into it. Then he went back to the last plant with its foot-and-a-half top section, the most potent and most delicious part, the grower's choice, if there was a such a thing. He usually saved these tops for his own stash and for birthday gifts. Now as he reached up for it and bent it down to him, inhaling the vapors of its climax stage, he had a sudden feeling that this part of it didn't belong to him. He let go and it sprang away, up, swinging from side to side, almost enough to brush against him on its way back and forth. Leave it to the beaver, he thought, or the mold, or whatever, but leave it because you want it so you leave it and see that you don't need it, you can get along without it. He put the clippers back in his pocket. Leave it, an offering, and you won't need it anyway. He put his clippers in his pocket, wrapped the jacket around his waist, stuffed his hat into the bag with the harvested branches, and turned to take one last look at the scene of so much of his energy and source of so many of his feelings. He remembered Sonya standing here with him, picking leaves, remembered the vulnerable little plants at transplant time, the watering in the hottest day of summer, and now the end of a season. It had been a good one, his life was much different now than when it began, and he had no clear idea of anything that was going to happen next. He said goodbye and turned to push his way through the brush, up the hill, and home again.

"This is Marty Johnson," the voice on Sonya's message recorder said. "Monday morning I'm calling a press conference in the main meeting room of the county building at 10:30 AM. You need to be there, with one or two of your top staff. You won't be wasting your time."

In the morning as Sonya and Dan walked down the hallway, she felt her anxiety and curiosity peaking. She had faith enough in Johnson's fairness to trust that he wasn't going to try and take advantage of her in any way, but she couldn't quite figure out what he could be up to. On the drive over, she and Dan speculated on several possibilities, and she told him a little of what she knew about a possible hoax around the boobytrap incident. Neither of them felt that would be enough to merit a press conference, unless of course, the Sheriff had substantive evidence. In that case, it could only help Sonya's cause and be a friendly gesture for him to have invited her personally. The large clock in the hallway said 10:28.

The room was half-full with members of the media and their assorted equipment, and the rest with people she recognized from the county's bureaucracy and law enforcement. Terry waved his press pass at them when they came in. Several reporters noticed Sonya and she could see them quickly conversing and nodding in her direction. She looked around for Reynolds but didn't see him. At 10:32, Sheriff Johnson, dressed in his full uniform, came out through the small door just behind the desk at the front of the room and stepped to the standing mike beside it. He looked around the room slowly, carefully, setting his papers down and taking a large drink of water from a glass on the desk.

He called for quiet and attention, "Ladies and gentlemen, I have called you here this morning because there are some things I want to bring before you and the citizens of our county. Some of these are things I wish I didn't have to talk about, or even think about, but this can't be avoided unless I resign from my job. I've thought about that, but I know it isn't in the best interest of the county and our citizens for me to do that right now. The first thing I want to announce is that I am using my authority to call for a special grand jury investigation into marijuana-linked violence in Chinook County. I am making this request as an official action because I can no longer function as head law enforcement officer here, as long as certain questions go unanswered and those answers are not made public.

"First of all, there is the matter of the suspected boobytraps and the placement of explosives in connection with a marijuana growing location west of here, discovered during this past summer. Without going into detail and leaving the full examination up to the grand jury, I can say that I have more than enough reasons to believe that this entire incident was a hoax perpetrated by certain members of my department with the direct knowledge and involvement of our present District Attorney. Can I prove this? I'm not saying I can or cannot at this point, but I can say that there is more than sufficient incriminating evidence and testimony to call for this process I have outlined. I am personally angry and ashamed that such a thing could happen, and I know that I must accept full responsibility that some of those involved are my direct subordinates. As far as facts or names of those involved, they have been turned over to the presiding court along with my request for this investigation, and it would not help at this time to go any further into these details. What I will say is that I am staking my job and my reputation on the outcome of this full examination of the facts as we now know them and as more may be revealed as this action proceeds. I am also using this press conference format to protect you of the media from any future charges of false accusation or libel. I am saying all of this, and you have the right to just be reporting it."

Hands raised and the calling out of questions began immediately as soon as he took another drink of water, but he waved them off and went on, "The second thing I have asked to be investigated is the so-called shootout which occurred in the South Fork area last month. I refuse to continue jailing and holding, for excessively high bail, a person who, as far as the case shows at this time, simply exercised his right to self-defense and protection of property, and is now being held to face trial for attempted murder. I find this to be a gross miscarriage of justice and I don't really care if I'm speaking out of order and the trial has to be moved somewhere else due to my comments. But I'll tell you this, if it had been me being waked up by some gun-carrying, trespassing thieves, then you'd have to put your Sheriff behind bars for attempted murder if that's the way things are done around here now. And I mean this, regardless of the nature of the other potential charges and actions involved. Besides, evidence says that the marijuana plants themselves were not on anybody's private property, but the trespassers were at the time the shots were fired. I think the point is that we don't have enough money in this county to protect everything and everybody, and when people have to take these matters into their own hands we should be a little more understanding. Now I recognize that there were marijuana plants involved and that our DA says this is a case of outlaws fighting among themselves, but there's a helluva a lot of difference between the legal penalties for small-scale illegal cultivation and those for attempted murder. And a helluva lot of difference between trespassing and armed robbery. Why, I ask, weren't these other parties involved in the incident also charged with attempted murder the same as the property owner?

As far as I can see, it's because they were stealing pot instead of growing it. Now what kind of sense does that make?

"The third thing I want to bring up is that I don't think it's my job as your Sheriff to figure out how this county can spend more millions on buildings like a new jail when we can't even afford deputies on patrol in many areas, or public defenders for all the cases that need them. It was suggested by Mr. Reynolds the other night on that TV debate that it is my job to push for more facilities if we have overcrowded conditions at the jail. Well, I'm not going to do that. I think we have more people in jail than we need to have, and if there was any attempt at a sensible approach to bail and 'own recognizance' we wouldn't be having some of these problems. So, I'm throwing it back where it came from, and notifying the current DA and the county that we have about one month to straighten out this mess before the lawsuit that's been brought against us takes effect and we'll have to start cutting people loose anyway. Enough said?"

A reporter from the Dixon newspaper, sitting near the front, waved his arm in the air and asked in a loud voice, "Okay Marty, I think we'd all be interested in what you think about all of this, you yourself. It sounds like this has all been pretty hard on you."

"Well, those are most of the details behind what I have to say to you at this time, and I think you can see something in common with each of these examples. That would be the current District Attorney, Mr. Bill Reynolds. Honestly, I don't feel I can work with him any longer and perform the mandated duties I am sworn to carry out. So, I guess you might say I'm feeling somewhat trapped between my responsibilities to this office, and my own conscience. On a personal note, and it's only my opinion, but I believe he and some of his cronies and supporters want to use law enforcement to get rid of a lot of people in this county, so they can buy up their land and turn it into profit-making real estate and developments. In order to accomplish this, he has declared war on some of our struggling population, using the laws against marijuana to instill fear with the near militarization of our county during the summer months. Now, don't get me wrong, I don't smoke the stuff, I don't approve of its use, and I certainly will never advocate breaking the law. However, we live in a county that can't pay for its schools or roads, and we find ourselves spending money and funds from the federal government to wipe out what some say may be hundreds of thousands of dollars in so-called illicit income. So, where's the common sense in that, in chasing people out of here who want to own their own places, raise families, and get by from year to year without having to sell their places to someone from California who's just going to sell it again when it starts to rain? Is that the kind of county we want when we pass our land use laws? Is that the kind of place we want to live in, or is it just a place that makes a lot of money for realtors and developers and drives people out of the rural areas into the cities where we'll end up having to support them on welfare and social services because there's no jobs in here either? And that will certainly increase the crime rate, which nobody wants. So, I'm not saying there's a simple answer to any of this and I hope you understand that. What I am saying is that something's got to change because the climate of fear and over-reaction that exists now is no good for anybody and it's just going to get worse. The capabilities of our law enforcement agencies are stretched all too thin, so somehow we've got to get things back onto a basic common sense basis before it's too late, before we really do have a war going on around here."

The same reporter again waved his arm around as he asked the Sheriff, "So, what do you think about the election, about the candidates?"

"You really want me out on a limb, don't you, Jerry? All right, here goes, the way to do this, or try to do it, seems to me to be to support a change in the way we approach our law enforcement crisis, and it is a crisis, believe me about that. If you had asked me about this a few months ago, how I was feeling about all this mess, my answer would have been a lot different. But you're asking me today, and my answer today is…My answer is I now support Ms. Sonya Lehman for the position of District Attorney. I don't agree with everything she says, and there's no way to predict what she can actually accomplish once she's in office, but I'm willing to ask the people of this county to consider the changes she has proposed and to weigh carefully the things I've talked about today. I guess it comes down to a matter of trust, and I trust this woman to at least try to do her best for the people of this county."

As he stopped talking and turned to leave there was a rush of questions from all parts of the room. He gathered his notes and said loudly, "I'm not prepared to answer any of your questions today. I've said what I came to say, probably a lot more. There's a copy of the main part of my statement for each of you at the back of the room. Thank you again for your attention, and I hope you'll be fair in your reporting." He quickly left the room through the door he'd come in.

As soon as he had gone, the reporters and cameras turned their attention to Sonya. Questions were fired at her all at once, and she was forced to raise her hands and wave back the sudden pandemonium that seemed ready to engulf her.

"One at a time, please."

"Was this a surprise to you, or did you know about it?"

"I had no idea."

"Do you think all this will make a difference in the election, in your chances for winning?"

"I don't know. It certainly should help, I think. If people get a chance to hear all of what was said here today, I think they'll see more clearly what we've been saying all along."

"Ms. Lehman, Do you think it's possible the Sheriff is just playing politics for some reason or another?"

"I don't think so. You can't call for a grand jury just for political reasons."

"How will this change your campaign strategy in the time that's left before the voting?"

She glanced at Dan, who was standing quietly beside her, and said, "I'm sure it will change things in some ways, but we'll have to discuss this among ourselves. We certainly didn't expect this, but we'll cope with it, won't we, Dan?" There was some laughter in the room and Dan nodded his agreement with a smile.

"Have you got any ideas how Mr. Reynolds will react to this development?"

"No, and I wouldn't want to be around him to find that out," she said. "Anything else, before we have to get going to some other appointments?"

"Yes, ma'am. It has been suggested that you're personally involved with some elements of the pot-growing 'underground' and it has also been speculated that a significant portion of the funding for your campaign originated from there as well. Would you please comment on these allegations?"

Sonya looked straight at the TV reporter who asked the question, then at Dan, and then back at the group in front of her. "My personal life is just that. I intend to keep it separate from my public obligations as much as possible. In terms of financing for this campaign, we've been so poor we haven't been able to run background checks on every dollar we've spent. To tell the truth, I really don't know if any of the money was ever connected with marijuana, and I'm not sure what I could do about it if it was."

"One more question, please," a young woman said as she stood up. "Have you and the Sheriff ever discussed the election or matters such as pot-related violence before today?"

"We have spoken on two occasions. The first time he asked me if I was crazy to run for this job, and I said probably. The other time, he let me know he thought there was something strange about the booby-trap incident, but he said at the time he had no proof."

"And he does now?"

"I don't know any more than you do. Thank you all, and I hope you're still interested in me a week from Wednesday. Thank you."

She turned to leave, and Dan took her elbow and ushered her through the crowd to the door. She'd understated the significance. This new development could change their whole strategy for the coming week, including the TV spots that were already filmed and paid for.

"Well, what do you think?" she asked Dan as they left the building and walked to his car.

He looked over at her and said, "I think you're a very lucky woman."

"Maybe I am," she said, walking faster, "and maybe I'm not. We'll see."

CHAPTER NINE

November

When the first major storm of the season hits the Oregon Coast Range, it usually lasts for several days and changes the way this part of the world thinks and feels. The last leaves let go and are blown loose, the creeks rush to new highs, filled with mud, branches, and even whole trees. It becomes clear that most things won't dry out for several months. Once this storm passes, the air is clean and the sky is blue, but the nights are icy cold and now much longer than the days. From the ocean's pounding surf to the heavy snowfall in the Cascade mountains, the world turns its other cheek and shows its inhabitants the hard side of getting though the year. From Halloween to Thanksgiving, the rain and the cold take turns, with the rain getting the greater share. The fish find their way through spawning to death, their eggs deposited beneath the gravel of the creek-beds, waiting for the right time to hatch. The last fresh apples are made into cider, the canned goods sit on the shelves with this year's labels, and hunting and butchering is wrapped up for the winter. Smoke climbs out of the chimneys, as people return to projects left unfinished since the last rainy season. The harvest of the cash crop is in packages and the first pounds reach the markets at quick-sale prices so both buyers and sellers get a good deal. November, spanning the social energy levels from ghosts and pumpkins to Indians and turkeys. The month when death is most evident and rebirth again lies dormant in the roots and seeds of the landscape. High-flying geese can be heard overhead, sounding like a playground full of noisy children as they "V" their way across the lead-gray skies, and the real children, playing below, are bundled up in all manner of down jackets and woolen clothes. Mud takes its place in the habits of the people as porches fill up with boots and raingear. November, the long evening of the year when Nature props its feet up in front of the fire, settles back in the old rocking chair and takes it easy while the taking's good.

Sonya's week was the most frantic yet. The Sheriff's press conference catapulted the local election race into the whirlpool of statewide focus and attention. Reporters from Portland dashed from Reynolds to Sonya to the voter in the street. The Sheriff remained firm in his no further comment posture, but Reynolds took the offensive by declaring that both the Sheriff and his own "ultra-liberal" opponent were paid off by wealthy growers, and he promised to provide proof on the relationship between them and the "underground." Dan was the most excited anyone had seen him since the beginning of the campaign, and they'd revamped the two TV spots for the last days before the election, adding quotations from the Sheriff and hammering home the point that what the people needed was "common sense and not nonsense," honesty and not malicious mischief in the DA's office. And that public safety was everyone's business, not to be controlled by an elite conspiracy of well-to-do land sharks and developers. A grand jury was impaneled and began issuing subpoenas. Terry's polling took on a new dimension as the numbers flipped and flopped their way to a narrow but still indecisive margin in favor of Sonya. By week's end there wasn't much more to do besides gather up the necessary energy for the election itself.

Dan told Sonya to take a day off and rest up during the next week. He said no one would get much sleep or rest on election eve and through those next few days and nights. She then promised to try and meet Peter on Saturday morning for a drive to the coast and a day of doing nothing, but she'd almost given up on it, when somehow it worked out, with others on her staff filling in for her and urging her to take a break while she still could. As she drove out toward his place, she still could hardly believe it was possible to get away, but here she was, out of town and wonderfully out of touch with the rest of the world, not even turning on the radio.

The morning mist was dissolving into a crisp, blue heaven of a day, the kind that made the previous week's long storm vanish from memory, and somehow give one the feeling that spring was six months early. She could hardly believe the free feelings flowing through her mind and heart as she shook off the intensity of the past week's pressure. They had known all along the final week would take maximum effort, but here it was, the whole effort almost over, and she was not only still functioning, she was feeling better than she had for weeks, although it was probably just the pause before the coming storm.

Peter was waiting for her in front of his trailer. He had a small backpack and a Frisbee on the ground beside his chair. She jumped out of the car and ran to him. They hugged, checked into each other's eyes, and burst out laughing together.

"How are you?" they both said at once.

"Fine, fine," they answered.

"Are you ready?" she asked.

"Yeah, let's go."

They listened to music and held hands on the drive to the beach, not talking much, saving their words for later, enjoying the beauty of the day and the sense of holiday catching hold of them. They had no plans and wanted to keep it that way. The question on both of their minds was what would the weather decide to do, would it be the same as inland, or foggy with cold wind? The answer came when they topped the last rise overlooking the coastline and could see nothing but blue sky to the far horizon.

They stopped at a small store featuring seafood and bought snacks and a bottle of wine, filled up with gas and had a mock hassle over which direction to go, up or down the coast. They ended up going north toward a small inlet with a quaint unused lighthouse on the point that jutted out into the breakers. They raced from the car to the sand and fell together, laughing and brushing off the sand as they picked themselves up and looked for shelter from the breeze that carried a hint of a cold night to come in its playful gusts.

Peter jogged back to the car and brought their things down to the beach where they could hunker behind old-growth driftwood logs. They spread out a blanket and Peter poured coffee from a thermos. He offered some to Sonya and they shared the steaming brew while staring out to sea with squinted eyes and soft smiles.

"So how are you really?" she asked.

"Great, I'm more than fifty percent relaxed for the first time since last March. I do enjoy it when that season's over" He refilled the cup. "What about you?"

"Wait a minute, why only fifty percent?"

"Ahh, nothing. Nothing I want to think about on a day like today."

"Tell me, and then it'll be over for the rest of the day. Otherwise, whatever it is will just keep hanging around us."

"Okay, I guess you're right. That detective was back again, the one that keeps coming around Jerry's place. He came out last Thursday, said some things I didn't really like. I said so and he promised to work on my case until something broke."

"What case?" Sonya asked with some alarm in her voice.

"That's what I asked. He said I'd find out when the time came, and then he handed me a subpoena to the grand jury. Said they want me to testify about what I know about Jerry and his pot. Said it would be better for me and everyone concerned if I helped as much as I could. I could tell he was bullshitting, but it was a bringdown."

"I hope he was. You heard Reynolds' threats? I wonder if he knows about us?"

Peter turned to her, took her face in his hands, and looked deep into her green-tinted eyes. "So what? This is legal." They kissed and lay back on the blanket. The sun warmed them as they embraced and snuggled beneath the strengthening breath of the breeze. "Besides, if he hasn't used it yet, it's too late. Congratulations, Ms. DA."

"Not yet, you can't get away that easy. I still might lose, move in with you, and become a happy little housewife."

"Somehow, I can't quite see that. You could lose, I guess, but the rest of that, I doubt. Walk down by the water?"

"Sure." They both kicked off their shoes and rolled up their pantlegs. "Yeah, I might lose, but at least it's a contest now. Can you believe it?"

"Not really," he said. "What'd you have to promise the Sheriff for endorsing you?"

"I told him you'd take his job for the next two years and all he'd have to do is collect his paychecks." She laughed and ran toward the edge of the low tide. He chased her and caught up at the water's edge. They jogged along in the shallow moving water, splashing slightly and jumping out of the way of an occasional higher wave. Far down the beach another walker could be seen, accompanied by a dog. They reached the rocky point that held the old lighthouse and climbed in among some rocks where it was warmer and sheltered from the wind. Peter took out his pouch and started rolling one.

"You know, I can never believe it when the season's finally over. It's like a ten-ton truck just got lifted off my shoulders and I can't even remember hoe it got there."

"I think it must be hard to worry and wonder all those months, and with all that risk. I guess you could do something else if it gets too hard and stressful."

"You mean if you don't get elected and things keep going on the way they are? Yeah, seriously, huh? I guess I could find something else, but then I'd be dependent on that instead."

"Everybody's dependent on something, I mean to make a living."

"Yeah, but this dependency is different. I'm not only the producer; I'm a consumer as well. And I think there's a very fine line between addiction and dependency in this case." He cupped his hands around the match and lit the joint, took a deep hit, and exhaled slowly. "It's so good when it's fresh," he said, half offering it to her.

"Still no thanks." She smiled and waved his hand away. "Just being polite, darling."

"Oh my, first time you ever called me that."

"It's what I call all my potential housekeepers."

"Oh dear. Anyway, back to our conversation. What's the difference between dependency and addiction?"

"It's a fine line, but I think there's a difference. It has to do with choice. I hope it's by choice for me to be dependent, both financially and psychologically, on this weed. And long as I can produce it myself, I'm independently dependent. If I can't get along without it and need to buy it from someone else, I'm addicted. I've seen a lot of addiction, mostly to other stuff, guys all strung out… It was sometimes worse than getting wounded. I don't know what I'd do if I really needed this stuff and couldn't grow it. That would be super hard on me, 'cause I get high on the growing too. Matter of fact, I think sometimes smoking it is almost like a way to keep the growing high going. Sorry to go on like this. Stuff makes me talk."

"You are weird, you know. You really try to think it all out, don't you?"

"Yeah, I know I'm weird, but that's not why."

"Then why?"

He reached out and picked a seagull feather from between the rocks and stuck it in her hair. "I'm weird because I tell you what I think about stuff."

"You think so?" She picked up a length of dry seaweed and reached it around his neck. "Then I hope you keep on being weird, because I like hearing what you think."

They leaned back against the warm rocks and let the sound of the waves roll over them, soothing their minds and massaging their bodies with their regular rumbling roar. The rest of the day was spent looking for pretty rocks, wading in the surf, eating their snacks, and driving along the coast, admiring its seemingly eternal beauty. Toward dusk, they stopped at an Inn, had dinner, and decided not to spend the night there. Peter said he preferred to go back to his place, and he'd cleaned a lot out of the trailer so they'd be more comfortable. That was fine with Sonya and they headed back toward the coastal mountains, tired and refreshed from a day of salt air and seafood

When they got back to the trailer, Peter built a campfire and brought out his speakers. He put something on and they wrapped up in blankets and watched the fog forming in a high bank above the ridge, coming their way and blotting out the first stars.

The music was Mozart, "Horn Concerto No. 2." There was something about this night that seemed perfect for that music, or vice versa. Sonya asked if he was still playing the horn himself. He thought about it and answered that he was still playing, but not as much as he had been. When the piece came to its end, he said there was something he could play for her if she wanted to listen. She said of course. He went in, turned over the tape and got out his horn. He warmed it up a little inside and came back out explaining to her what he was doing.

"It's the fourth horn concerto, by Mozart again. It's what I was working on the night Jerry got shot. Probably why I didn't hear anything. Anyway, I never felt closer to a piece of music than I did that night. It's probably not still there the way it was, but I wanted you to hear it." He went back inside and started the tape, came out, sat on the chopping block, and was staring up at the sky as he waited for the orchestra to begin.

He played, and he played well. When he and the orchestra finished, the silence echoed with the feeling of triumph that ends the piece. Sonya was looking at him in the dim light of the dying fire and he looked transformed to her. She had never seen him appear so free of tension, so simply free as he was looking at that moment. He let the horn sink down onto his lap and closed his eyes. There was something there, something inside that music that could not be used up, that would always be there no matter how many times he played it, no matter how many times it was played. He shook his head and remembered that for the first time since high school he had an audience. He looked her way and was struck by the visual fact that he was looking into a face that gave him the same feeling the music did.

When he finally spoke, it was almost in a whisper. He said, "I wanted you to know that about me. Whatever happens I want you to know that part."

She reached out and scooted over to rest a hand on his knee, one of her fingers brushing the smooth surface of the horn. "Thank you. So very much."

The fire flared up again as they watched, its embers glowing and sparking.

"It's getting cold. Want to go inside?" he asked.

"Soon," she said, "but not yet. It's so beautiful right now."

He reached down and pushed a couple more pieces of wood into the fire.

He got to town after dark on election night, parked his new-to-him truck (five years old), and the U-Haul trailer several blocks from Sonya's house, then let himself in with the key that was behind the mailbox. He had been busy almost every minute since she'd left his place on Sunday. As he flipped on the TV and settled into the couch, he could feel the fatigue flowing through his muscles and mind. It was good now to just sink back into the cushions for a moment and try to sort through all the clamoring emotions fighting for his attention. On the screen Reagan was building the greatest landslide in history and smiling broadly as he prepared for four more years. A station break promised a full update on state and local races in fifteen minutes. He stretched and went to the kitchen, looking for something to eat.

He'd never been in her house when she wasn't there, and it gave him a somewhat different sense of her. She was neat, not so much from fussiness as from not having a lot of stuff that could mess things up. Her little office alcove was a bit ransacked, but this was certainly a result of what must have been a terribly hectic during the past few days. As he opened the refrigerator, he had a slightly guilty feeling, as if he were an intruder, but also knowing that was silly, especially since he'd told her he would try to be there that evening. He made a sandwich from some leftover tuna salad, found a beer and went back to the TV. He knew that he was putting off what he still had to do, but there would still be time for it. He got a writing tablet from her desk and put it down next to the food on the coffee table.

He couldn't decide whether to start writing the note first or finish eating. He went ahead on the sandwich and drank part of the beer, then turned up the volume as the local commentator replaced the network coverage. As they ran through the polling results, it was obvious that the race between Reynolds and Sonya carried the most interest. So far, with half of the urban results counted and a third of the rural precinct reporting partial results, she was a couple of percentage points ahead. The announcer pointed out that this was a strong indicator of an upset, in that pre-election polls gave Sonya the edge in the rural areas, but Reynolds had continued to maintain his lead in town. He went on to say that if Ms. Lehman continued her surprisingly strong showing in Dixon itself, then there was almost no question that Chinook County would have a new DA.

That does it, Peter thought, while still wondering if there were any other choices. No way. There was a lot more than he knew going on behind the scenes, investigations between the cops, the DA and the grand jury, and who knew what else. Even if Sonya were to lose, by him staying around he would still be seriously jeopardizing himself. He'd never thought of himself as attached to anything before. It had been easy to leave home, even for the army, and he never had any regrets about leaving the places he'd lived since the war. But this was different, this wasn't just leaving a place, this was, what? He turned down the sound again and picked up the tablet and pencil.

> Dearest SONYA,
>
> Congratulations! Right now, I'm pretty sure you did it. You had the power to make yourself special enough to beat "Big Bad Bill" and his backers. I'm proud of you and happy to have known you. I'm glad I did help a little bit, if I did. I'm waiting here now to watch you make your victory speech. I hope it's one of the high points of your life.

He took another couple of swallows of the beer and thought about rolling a joint. He decided against it and continued writing.

> I can't really believe all this has happened to you and me since we first met. If you had told me last year at this time we would have been able to have this experience together, I would have said you were crazy. I only hope you can try to understand me now about all this like you have about everything else. Simply said, I can't stay here any longer.

> I am leaving you a copy of a newspaper article that will explain why. Please don't open the envelope and read it until you have finished with this note. I am also leaving you a notarized quit-claim to my property and trailer. Use the place yourself if you want to or give it to Jerry and Carla to help them keep it together by selling or whatever. I will be sending them some money to help cover the costs of the court case as soon as I sell enough produce. I am hoping the legal stuff about my property is enough and you don't have trouble because of it... I know now I should have stopped you from getting involved with me because you could only get hurt. But I couldn't help myself. I needed you too much. I've probably never acted so selfish in my life. It seems like it was good for you too, but now it won't be and I am as sorry as can be.

Reagan still hadn't lost a single state when Peter tuned in again and then shut off the sound. He was losing the clarity he'd had on the drive into town. He was thinking he probably should have written it before he came because her space was starting to distract him. This house and the things that happened to him and for him, right here, the feelings that broke loose and were now turning in on themselves, all it was hard, even though he knew he had no other choice.

> I wouldn't leave if I had any other choice, but you once asked me what was the most important thing in life, in my life. I know my freedom is what I need to have most and that without it nothing else can save me from myself. Right now, my freedom is at stake because the risks have gotten too great and the chances of me losing everything are higher if I stay here than if I give up almost everything including you, and still have only myself.
>
> I don't know why I had to do what I did. I came back to this country and nothing made any sense. I missed war, the high that it gives is unbelievable long as you keep on making it through OK... But I also hated that War because of what

it was doing to the people on both sides. It was a bad War! I looked at the Peace people and I could see they couldn't stop it because they wouldn't make war against the War, and I don't think anything stops a military momentum except another military force. I saw that the Vietnamese couldn't do it themselves either, at least I thought they couldn't. I guess they finally did, but it took a lot of the world supporting them. Anyway, I knew a person can't oppose all war, that won't work because it's always going to be here, it's part of the human race…But you can be against one side in a war, and you can try to stop what's happening to innocent people, and if you risk everything you've got it might be worth it if it stops the killing and stops turning our guys into killers for the wrong side. This might sound all confused because I never wrote anything like this down ever before. But I think about it a lot of the time. About us, what can I say? It was like a chance to get born again, to use a funny church term. I was at a birth in May, Carla's and Jerry's baby, and I never knew the similarity between birth and making love, and even between those and death. It is

The phone rang. He looked over at it, and let it go on ringing until it stopped. Probably someone calling to congratulate or interview Sonya. He tried to think about the letter and how to keep going. His hand was tired and beginning to cramp from never using it for things like this...

hard to believe we all go through these things in life and in love. I love you! I always will. I never knew what it could be like before, and never felt this with another person (except maybe my mother). That another person could care about me so much no matter what. Now you will have to deal with the consequences of all that caring. Please love what you can about me but try not to hold the rest of it against me. I can't help the circumstances that are making it end between us, even though I always knew something like this would happen.

Even without the grand jury and Jerry's case, I would still have to find a way to avoid all the notice and attention you will be getting as a public figure. Maybe it's for the best that this all came down this way since we couldn't seem to come up with a way to live together anyway, especially if you win. I know you will do your job well and that you can help the people around here.

As for me, I can't say what I'll be doing. I hate it, having to leave this way, but I can never prove my innocence even though I never killed anyone since Vietnam. As far as what's going on in this country and in this county, it's not just about pot. It's about what happens to people who can't put up with being stressed-out and bored at the same time and take it out on others, and the people who want their freedom and who are willing to take risks for it. When the frontier is gone, then the outlaws and the free people must make a stand. And they need to make a living. America is running out of its frontier, but it still has the myth of freedom. I don't see much good coming for a while, but I sure hope it doesn't turn into a battleground around here. You and what you're trying to do is maybe the last chance to save people's rights to do what they want when it doesn't hurt other people. I hope you can keep it going even if it looks like it won't succeed. Watch out for Reynolds. He'll want revenge, on you and on that Sheriff.

I never knew I could write so much. I want to touch you, to hold you one last time, or to take you away with me, but none of that can happen now. Please believe that nothing else could take me away from you, but I am now afraid to be here, afraid of what might happen if I lose my freedom for the rest of my life. How long would it be before I did something crazy?

I love you and I'll never forget you. But you should try to forget me. You won't be able to find me, so don't try. Just get back to your life. It's a good one, and you're the best person I ever knew.

Love forever, Peter

There were tears in his eyes when he finished, tears he'd been holding back all through the letter. He wanted to read it over again, but he didn't want to. It didn't matter. It was good enough, and bad enough. He folded it carefully and pulled the sealed envelope out of his shirt pocket. He wondered where to leave them. Probably on the bed since other people might be coming home with her and he wanted to let her celebrate a long as possible before finding all this out. Let her have her high, she deserved it more than anyone he knew, and it would all get harder and harder for her as time went on. He couldn't imagine how difficult this new job would be for her, mainly because she couldn't possibly do all she wanted to do with it. Her ideals would have to crash into reality, and she would have to find someone besides him to help her through it.

He watched the numbers roll by on the screen, and then the local commentator was back on. Peter reached forward and turned up the sound.

"We take you now to the campaign headquarters of Chinook County's new District Attorney. We're calling this race based on 70% of the results and Whitney Connors is there with the victorious candidate, Ms. Sonya Lehman. Whitney?"

"Thanks, Ben. As you can see and hear, I'm standing in the middle of a scene of pandemonium and jubilation. No one ever thought this was possible. Sonya Lehman didn't think it was possible, and yet, here we are. Sonya, our projections give you a clear-cut margin of victory, and while Mr. Reynolds still has not conceded, can you tell us how it feels to have pulled off this really amazing upset?"

"It feels absolutely wonderful. What can I say? Thank you everyone. Thank you voters, and campaign staff, all of you. What an amazing group of people. Nothing could have happened without them. They're wonderful. They never stopped believing in this possibility, no matter how out of the question it seemed. That's really all I have to say right now. Just a great big huge thank you to everyone."

She looked directly at the camera and Peter and he was sure he could feel her thoughts coming through the screen to him. How could he be doing this to her? It was worse that she was so happy, and he was doing this now. Maybe her happiness over winning would help her through it. Hell, he thought, maybe she won't be so hurt by me leaving, how do I know? It solves the problems we were up against. He reached out and snapped off the TV when it cut to a commercial.

It was awful seeing her and knowing that he wouldn't see her again. And even if he stayed and went to prison, she could still come visit. No, that's not the way. He needed to move out now. They could already be coming for him. He went into the bedroom and laid the letter and the sealed envelope on the bedspread. He picked them up again and folded back the covers, kneeling beside the bed. He bent forward and placed a kiss on her pillow. A rough sobbing suddenly shook his shoulders, his throat caught, and the tears came. He shook himself to make them stop. He wiped his face on the pillow and set the letter just sticking out from under the pillow. On the way out of the room, he grabbed a picture of Sonya and a dog from off the wall.

Leaving the house, he locked the door and walked quickly toward the new-used truck. He had used ID he'd saved up, to register it in his new name, and to get a new driver's license as if he'd just moved into town. The trailer was filled with his records and all the other stuff that mattered, along with the packages of crop in insulated sealed foil packages buried deep among his clothing. He didn't have any idea where he was going.

Sonya was alone when she finally made it home after three. As she let herself in, she called Peter's name, but there was no answer. A few lights were left on, and an empty beer and a writing tablet were on the coffee table. Probably went to sleep, she thought, after all it wasn't his victory. She was torn between rushing in to wake him to share the thrill or taking a nice long bath and then slipping in beside him, savoring the whole complicated, unexpected reality that her life had just turned into. Patience might be a virtue, but she couldn't wait. She walked quickly and quietly to the bedroom and looked in. He wasn't there. Hiding? She snapped on the light, opened the closet. No one. The covers were turned back, and she saw something sticking out from under the pillow. She picked up the letter and saw her name at its top. His handwriting was nice; she'd never seen it before. But why a letter? Where was he? She fell back onto the bed as she started reading. She felt herself gasping as she read the words, "I can't stay here anymore." She kept reading as fast as she could, not understanding. What? Why? His property, the trailer? What was this saying? She glanced at the sealed envelope in her other hand, and then kept reading. Tears formed in her eyes as her mind read what her heart couldn't comprehend. By the time she finished reading the whole thing, she was weeping, her whole body consumed by it, her whole self that had only such a short moment before been in an ecstatic, exhausted state of joy with the anticipation of sharing it with him, was now crushed by the terrible realization that none of it mattered now, winning didn't even matter now. The envelope had 'This is why' written on it. She ripped it open, pulling out the well-preserved copy of an old news clipping. She wiped her face with one hand, sniffled deeply, then the words, "Oh no," whispered from her heart.

...Turn page for news clipping...

Suspected Bomb Destroys Munitions Bound for Vietnam

Exploding Train. Thirty Units of Oakland Fire Dept. responded to possible sabotage incident. No estimate of damage available or claim of responsibility found.

OAKLAND (AP) Late last night, a train reported to be carrying napalm, phosphorus bombs, and artillery shells was destroyed at the Oakland Army Terminal rail yards. Military authorities report that they received a warning to clear all personnel from the area prior to the explosion. Military Police (MPs) surprised two intruders in the vicinity of the train, and shooting erupted. One MP was killed and one of the attackers was seriously wounded and taken to an area hospital. Authorities will not reveal his condition, saying only that they hope to obtain both his identity and that of his escaped accomplice, if he survives for interrogation. Authorities stated that this is the worst case of wartime sabotage since World War II. No further details were available as of press time. Name of the deceased MP is being withheld pending notification of kin.

End of Homegrown,
Book I, Land of the Evergreens